FOLLOWERS

CHRISTINA BERGLING

Let the world know:
#IGotMyCLPBook!

Crystal Lake Publishing
www.CrystalLakePub.com

CRYSTAL LAKE PUBLISHING RECOMMENDATIONS

Before He Wakes by Mark Allan Gunnells
Bayou Whispers by R. B. Wood
Midnight Horror Show by Ben Lathrop
Belle Vue by C.S. Alleyne
324 Abercorn by Mark Allan Gunnells
Doll Crimes by Karen Runge
Of Men and Monsters by Tom Deady
The Pale White by Chad Lutzke
A Season in Hell by Kenneth W. Cain
Wind Chill by Patrick Rutigliano
Little Dead Red by Mercedes M. Yardley

WELCOME
TO ANOTHER

CRYSTAL LAKE PUBLISHING
CREATION

Join today at www.crystallakepub.com & www.patreon.com/CLP

WELCOME TO ANOTHER CRYSTAL LAKE PUBLISHING CREATION.

Thank you for supporting independent publishing and small presses. You rock, and hopefully you'll quickly realize why we've become one of the world's leading publishers of Dark Fiction and Horror. We have some of the world's best fans for a reason, and hopefully we'll be able to add you to that list really soon.

To follow us behind the scenes (while supporting independent publishing and our authors), be sure to join our interactive community of authors and readers on Patreon (https://www.patreon.com/CLP) for exclusive content. You can even subscribe to all our future releases. Otherwise drop by our website and online store (www.crystallakepub.com/). We'd love to have you.

Welcome to Crystal Lake Publishing—Tales from the Darkest Depths.

To my online followers

1

"**CAN YOU ARCH** your back a little more, honey?" Brady said, peering around the barrel of his lens. "I'm getting a bulge in that position."

Sidney strategically pinned herself in the base of the large, empty bathtub. She rolled her hips forward to obscure her pubic hair with her thigh and draped her forearm across her nipples. She flinched at the word *bulge*, wanting to contort to smooth her side. Without unraveling the meticulous pose, she strained to turn her gaze toward Brady. She felt the sharp tug as her skin held fast in place.

"Uh, no, I can't," Sidney replied. "I'm stuck."

"Damn it," Brady huffed, placing his camera down on the bathroom counter beside him. "Is that blood dry again?"

Sidney's bare flesh glistened in a liberal coating of fake blood. The thick, red liquid drew patterns over her naked skin in drips and spatters. Stark, crimson smears tainted the garish white tub, evidence of Sidney's every movement.

Brady snatched the small spray bottle from beside his camera and bent over his model.

"This stuff looks so good, so real, but it dries so fast," he said.

The spray bottle honked loudly before the chill of the water droplets bit at Sidney's skin through the blood. She contracted against the cold, flexing her muscles to hold the pose. She did not want to endure Brady's exasperation at having to align her again, and she did not want to tug her skin into bruises as it peeled away from the dried blood, like last time. She hissed through pursed lips and lay frozen until the water began to loosen her syrup bondage.

"At least we learned about the water last time," she laughed.

Brady replaced the water bottle and gathered his camera back into his hands, climbing up on the tile platform encasing the bathtub. He straddled the basin and leaned forward over her.

"Do not fall on me," she said, still giggling.

"Oh honey, I don't know if that would be more traumatic for you or me."

"You. You would be stuck to a naked woman."

"Plus, I would probably break my camera." Brady peered through the view finder. "OK, there. Now, arch. Little more. Little more. Yes, right there. Bulge gone."

Sidney let a subtle, relieved breath escape her lips before going rigid in the awkward position. The blood tightened as it dried on her skin. The unforgiving curve of the tub pressed into her hips, her knees, her elbows. She craned her neck until a light burn stretched along her tendons. Then she stopped breathing as the camera's shutter snapped furiously.

"I think we got that one," Brady said, dismounting the bathtub platform. "It's some creepy shit for sure."

"That's what we're after!" Sidney remained

immobile, splayed on the bottom of the tub. "Can we turn on the water now?"

"You want to go full blood bath?"

"Sure, why not?"

"You just want to wash off the blood," he laughed, placing his camera down again.

"That too."

"We could add some blood to the water. Really make it red. Brace yourself for all the period comments online!"

"We get those every time we do blood. No matter where the blood is. Blood plus woman equals menstruation, apparently." She rolled her eyes without moving her head.

"I blame straight men."

"You blame straight men for everything."

"Am I wrong, honey?" Brady's light laugh danced against the tile. He popped out a hip and raised his eyebrow high at his model. "We can do blood bath, but I want to get some shots of you kind of gripping the edge or climbing out of the tub first. Bloody like you are."

"Um, you're going to have to spray me again."

Brady emptied his lungs dramatically, allowing his hands to fly up then slap onto his pants. He rolled his eyes with his entire face before his smile betrayed him. He snickered to himself as he brandished the spray bottle again.

"You enjoy this too much," she said, slowly unhinging her limbs like the Tin Man.

"Taking bloody pictures? Of course I do. I love our twisted little art."

"No, my suffering while we take bloody pictures."

"Well, that's just a lovely bonus." He smirked.

"Sadist," she returned.

Brady mimed a gasp and pressed his fingertips to his chest. "What has Jordan been telling you?" he laughed.

Brady stopped spraying and pursed his lips sideways at her. Finely misted, Sidney released her pose, peeling her limbs from their suggestive positioning. Slick with the mingling of fake blood and water, she slid and skidded over the porcelain as she struggled to pull herself out. She slipped and groped, wrapping her fingers around the edge of the tub.

"Shit!" Brady exclaimed. "Right there. Don't move!"

"You are just the worst." Sidney shook her head. "That's moving."

Brady hastily tossed the spray bottle and replaced it with his camera once more. He dropped expertly to his knees and leveled the lens with her fingertips.

"Oh, it's dripping perfectly," he mused, clicking away. "Now, move closer. Get your eyes up behind your knuckles."

Sidney submitted to his guidance, as she always did.

"Yes, right there," he continued. "Now, give me creepy eyes. One, two, three!"

Sidney snapped her eyes open to the limit of their lids and tugged her lips tightly across her teeth. Brady gasped quietly before the sound of the ravenous shutter drowned him out.

"Yes!" he laughed, staring at the back of the camera to review the shots. "Shit, you are creepy! I love it."

He turned the screen to her. She barely recognized

her contorted and blood-stained face. Her creased forehead drew up her brows to show the whites of her eyes in full, panicked flare. Her grimace drew awful lines in the blood trailing her chin. She looked maniacal, frantic, possessed.

The image struck her in its entirety, before her brain could pick apart the residual shape left in her consciousness like a sunspot on her eyes. Could she still see that bulge? Would the filters Brady applied deepen the creases in her face? When would she post the image? How many clever blood bath puns could she come up with for captions? When the commenters became vicious, she thought she might say something about bathing in the blood of her enemies.

"It's perfect," she smiled.

Brady snatched the camera to his eye and captured the honest grin on her face before it faded back into the blood on her cheeks.

"Now, you can have the water," he said from behind the lens.

Sidney peeled herself carelessly from the tub and cranked on the faucet. She captured the spray in her hands and smoothed it over her skin. The blood swelled and spread at the contact.

"Don't go washing it all off," Brady scolded. "I don't want to have to completely reapply. It's bad enough I have to pour the blood on you myself. We really need an assistant for this."

"Aw, you poor baby," Sidney mocked. "Yes, please come pour fake chocolate blood on some naked girl while she whines and the photographer yells at her."

Brady gasped again. "I do not yell at you."

Sidney puckered her lips and furrowed her brow.

"OK, I don't yell at you that much," he laughed.

Sidney pressed back from the faucet and lounged in the deepening water. Smooth warmth swelled around her, glorious in comparison to her dry contortions against the cruel tub. She basked in the contrast, swishing her fingertips through the surface of the water. Brady popped to his feet and gently placed his camera on the cabinet again. As he lifted the red-stained Tupperware, Sidney cringed.

"Don't give me that face," Brady said, slowly stirring the fake blood with a large spoon. "This is always your idea."

Sidney let out a little whimper. "I know," she said, pouting.

Smiling broadly, Brady scooped the red liquid and began drizzling the spoon over the water. Thick and lazy droplets slithered through the air and splattered over Sidney, dripping from her skin to turn the water crimson. As the spoon emptied, Brady cocked his head to evaluate the scene. Then he heaped on two more spoonfuls.

"So, what are you planning to do with these blood bath pictures?" Brady said through the lens as he hovered over her.

"I'm writing an article about the best bathroom death scenes in horror," she replied, between poses. "So, the pictures will go into the article. Then I'll use them when I post the article on social media. You know, the usual."

"Luring people like a siren with your bloody nakedness."

The shutter snapped again.

"It gets people's attention. If I can get their

attention, they might click. If they click, they might read. If they read, I might not have to work my horrible, soul-crushing day job for the rest of my life."

The answer felt dead in its rehearsed dance off her tongue. She said it so often when asked about their pictures online. She told herself, as much as she told everyone else, that she just needed the right amount of internet celebrity—enough to be able to support herself.

The shutter snapped again.

"Lift your chin, honey," he said, crouching closer.

Sidney's reflection gleamed in the open mouth of the lens. Her eyes looked wide and lost, searching. She tugged her face to exaggerate the expression. She stared into the black hole until the camera blurred out of focus.

"They do catch people's attention," he echoed, continually turning the focus on the lens. "I'm going to use these and the ones from our butcher shoot at the next convention I go to. Might see about getting into a gallery around Halloween. You know, when people are in the bloody mindset. You could bring your mother. I know they're her favorite."

"I don't know why that woman bothers to follow me on social media. Everything I post just upsets her." Sidney splashed defiantly in the water.

"You're like a train wreck. She can't look away."

"Hey now!" she laughed. "It's not just my mother. People have the strangest reactions to our pictures. Every time you release one, there are the comments, of course."

"Straight guys making jokes about periods."

"Right. But then there is also a rash of messages."

"Honey, I told you to just forward those dick pictures off to me."

"And face Jordan's wrath? I don't think so."

The shutter continued to snap.

"OK, sink lower into the water," he said. "Yeah, get some of your face in there. I know it's gross. You do this to yourself."

Sidney pursed her lips and sunk into the sticky water. She let the horror on her face tell the story Brady wanted to capture.

"I think we got it," he finally said, after another flurry of shutter snaps. "Let me help you out of there."

Brady extended his hands and gripped both of Sidney's. His fingertips pressed into her skin through the slickness of the blood. As she stood in the tub, a strange mingling of water and blood droplets rained back down around her. Once she was upright, naked and dripping, Brady released her and gathered a towel around her. He held her shoulders through the towel and steadied her until she stepped out onto solid ground.

"How long on edits, do you think?" Sidney said.

"I'll have at least a couple done today, just like usual. I know you have that article you want to get posted."

"And you need fresh pictures on your profiles."

"Exactly. Our symbiotic collaboration. I get a cooperative model into all sorts of twisted shit, and you get custom, clickbait media for your articles."

"I think you got the sweeter end of this deal."

Sidney smirked as she stood naked, awkward, and sticky-coated in dried fake blood. Brady responded with a mischievous grin.

"Get showered off," he said. "And we'll see how terrifying you were today. Then you'll help me clean up this disaster."

"Maybe we do need an assistant," Sidney said.

2

SiDNEY PULLED A beer from the bottom shelf of her fridge. She cracked the bottle open, leaving the cap on the counter. Bringing the bottle to her lips, she reached for the bowl of chips with her free hand. She gathered her snacks and migrated to her favorite corner of the couch. As the opening credits of the horror movie flashed over the room, she took another swig and pulled her computer into her lap.

The opening death of the movie screamed through the shifting shadows of her living room as she opened Brady's email and launched the gallery from their photoshoot. Her naked form consumed the screen. Brady had cranked up the contrast, saturation, and clarity on the image, which paled Sidney's skin and sharpened the lines. Her body lay unnervingly contorted in the base of the white tub, her eyes wild and face grimaced. He had enhanced the blood until it almost glimmered.

The blood was the subject, and she was the landscape.

She felt her eyes wander the curves of her own image, critiquing and cataloging. Did she see that bulge Brady tried to obscure? Was her thigh too thick turned unnaturally like that? Were those wrinkles nestled in the blood spatter on her face? The thoughts swelled in her brain, crowding her mind.

She closed her eyes, sucked in a deep breath, and looked at the picture again. She drew her focus out away from the shape of her body to take in the entire image. Brady's composition was perfect, as always. His processing made the image disturbing yet hauntingly beautiful. He made her part of something, and she forced herself to ingest the whole.

She scrolled though the other edits then typed a reply to Brady: *Bitch, these pictures are AMAZING! Release one tonight so I can use it as a teaser for my article?*

As the email vanished into cyberspace, she began her evening ritual of moving through her social media accounts. She began on Instagram. She found it most effective to ease in on pictures. In her first notification, she discovered Brady had already begun posting their pictures.

"He's way ahead of me," she mumbled to herself, smiling.

He had already posted the first picture from their private proofs gallery up on all his socials. Clearly, his favorite. He always processed and posted his favorite image first, unable to temper his joy, unwilling to make their audience wait.

@JaggedRainbowPhoto: @FinalGirlScreams making a blood bath look sexy!

A flurry of hashtags followed Brady's caption. Sidney reposted on Instagram, approved and shared on Facebook, retweeted on Twitter, and shared on every other social media platform she had.

A little taste of what's coming in my next article, she wrote on each post.

With her naked, bloody body cast far across the vast internet, she took a breath and lifted her fingers from the keys. She reclined against the couch cushions and allowed her eyes to trade the laptop screen for the television. She lost herself in the slow-moving pursuit of a serial killer as the notifications racked up on her screen.

Wicked!
That is so HOT!
I love your work. Please check out my page.
That girl needs to invest in better tampons.

"Straight boys," Sidney said, shaking her head as she parsed through the comments.

Johnny has sent you a photo.

"Well, that's a dick picture. Delete."

She tabbed away from her browser and into her active document. The bloodbath in her movie began to overshadow the chocolate-flavored recreation she had posted all over social media. She skimmed the last paragraph in the document, running her finger through the air over the words and mouthing the sentences silently as she read.

Even considering new classics like Final Destination *and* Saw, *to crown the best bathroom scene in horror, we have to circle back to the beginning.* Psycho *is where it started, where the slasher genre itself started, and where this article has to end as well,* she typed.

As she saved the full draft, a familiar message tone chimed from her chat application. She smiled, knowing who waited on the other side of the conversation, the same as every other night.

Oliver: What is the horror movie tonight?
Sidney: How do you know I'm watching a horror movie, stalker?
Oliver: You watch horror every night. Besides, I hacked your webcam.
Sidney: LOL! Like what you see?
Oliver: Always, beautiful.

Sidney smiled and bit her index finger between her teeth.

Oliver: You should come out here so I can show you how much I like it.
Sidney: There is nothing stopping you from coming out here.
Oliver: Only money.
Sidney: Likewise.
Oliver: One day I'll come join you in that blood bath.

Sidney took a breath and caught her lip with her teeth.

Sidney: So you saw the picture.
Oliver: Of course I saw the picture! It's already my home screen wallpaper.
Sidney: It is not! LOL

Oliver: It might be. It's very sexy. Makes me want to lick all that blood off of you. Chocolate, right?

Sidney released her lip from her teeth as she grimaced.

Sidney: It is chocolate, but you don't want any part of that. It tastes like Hershey's and plastic. Disgusting.
Oliver: I would deal with it if I got to lick you.

Sidney grinned again and felt herself blushing in the glow of her laptop screen. As she typed with Oliver, she continued to scroll through comments—a blend of generic hot comments, menstruation jokes, and clickbait advertising. She tallied the reactions in her head. This picture had already attracted more attention than their previous photo. She shared some random horror memes, retweeted from her favorite followers, and commented on horror groups in Facebook. She marched through her evening routine.

As she processed the comments and emails from her website, another conversation notification rang.

Adam: Open my feed tonight . . . BAM! Bloody, naked Sidney!
Sidney: Is that a bad thing?
Adam: No, you look great. But wow.
Sidney: Thank you
Adam: Brave of you to put yourself out there like that.
Sidney: The internet is unforgiving.

Sidney continued to click away on her keyboard, shifting between conversations threads and social media platforms, until the movement of the doorknob snatched at her attention. Sidney looked up as her roommate swung the front door open. Kendra burst through in a wobbling heap of bags. Sidney sat up and set the laptop aside to get a better view.

"Hey roomie," Sidney said, laughing. "What is all that?"

Kendra stumbled a few steps through the door to strip the bags from her shoulders, heaping them at her feet. Her wild mane of hair spiraled out from her head in fat curls, making her presence seem larger and farther reaching. Beneath the layered straps of the many bags, Sidney could make out the meticulous business-casual attire of Kendra's work day, her badge plastered against her somewhere beneath the web.

"Oh, girl," Kendra huffed, "don't even ask. Kids. It's kids."

"But you don't have your kid this week."

"I know!"

Sidney laughed and heaved herself off the cushion. "Oh man, let me help you," she said, reaching for one of the dangling sacks.

Kendra leaned into her assistance, sloughing the bag off into Sidney's grasp. "Thank you," she panted. "We're doing Divorced Moms Club tonight. Hard. How much wine do we have?"

"One, maybe two."

They abandoned the bags in a pile. Kendra navigated through the pile and stomped toward the kitchen. She rounded the counter and stopped, reaching forward to snatch up Sidney's bottle cap between her fingertips. She lifted it toward her face and glared dramatically at it before shifting her eyes to Sidney. Sidney stifled a giggle, pressing her fingers to her lips, and stared back with feigned innocence.

"Really, Sid?" Kendra said, flicking the bottle cap at her. "Every time? Does it have to be every time? Just recycle the damn thing!"

"I was getting to that," Sidney lied.

"You recycle the bottle. Why do you neglect the cap?"

"Because I have this amazing roommate who just lives to throw them at me. I couldn't rob her of that."

Kendra planted her fist on her hip as she jutted it out and rolled her eyes. "Anyway." She flipped her hair over one shoulder, stubborn curls tumbling right back. "I don't know if one or two bottles is enough. And you're going to have to turn that horror shit off."

"Fine, princess. It's just the credits anyway. You're safe."

Kendra popped the cork on the first bottle with expert precision and overfilled two glasses.

"So, how was work?" Sidney asked, sipping deeply.

"Work was a whole other thing." Kendra drank then moved toward the couch. Sidney followed and joined her. "Like, how hard is it to do your job? I swear my people work harder at not working than just doing the work."

"Hard to be the boss lady."

"Exhausting," Kendra laughed, saluting Sidney with her glass. "Like, just do the damn job! Check the patients, fill out the paperwork, stock your cart. These are not the dumbest people. They can do this." Kendra took a breath to take a sip. "Then all of Savannah's shit had to move here tonight. It couldn't wait until when she comes back over here in, like, forty-eight hours. So, I had to go over and see the ex and try to remind myself that I don't want him anymore."

"Which you totally do," Sidney mumbled loudly into her glass.

"I do not!" Kendra shouted, playfully swatting at her then smiling broadly. She used her empty hand to tame her curls behind her shoulders, exposing the tasteful earrings hiding beneath. "But every time I go to that house, it stirs up all this shit in me, and then I pick a fight for no reason."

"What did you pick a fight over this time?"

"The fact that Savannah's room was messy." Kendra averted her eyes into her glass as she answered.

"At his house?"

Kendra nodded as she drank.

"Kendra," Sidney scolded.

"I know! I told you, going over there does something to me, messes with my head."

"Because you still love him."

"Girl, hush!"

Sidney reached forward and folded her laptop closed.

"How are the online boyfriends tonight?" Kendra said, sly in her subject change.

"I don't have online boyfriends," Sidney replied, sipping her wine.

"Sure, girl. What do you call them?"

"Friends. Just online friends."

"You think I don't see you when you're over there

typing away, blushing like a schoolgirl. That is not talking to just a friend."

Sidney smiled guiltily into her glass. "Online flirtations then," she said. "It's not like I'm ever going to meet these guys, or sleep with them, or have some real relationship with them. Just some harmless chatting."

"I wouldn't say harmless. You never know what's on the other side of the keyboard these days."

"Well, I've been steadily talking to Oliver and Adam for months and months, one for over a year. That would be a pretty involved deception."

"You know I always just say to be careful. You get it, girl. Between your online romances and little boy toy, you're getting way more action than I am. The only action I've seen in ages is when my ex wants to do a friendly little relapse. And then pretend it never happened and we're just divorced again. And then another little relapse. And then me going crazy in his house like an idiot." Kendra sighed and rolled her eyes. "Get enough for both of us. Then maybe a little extra."

Sidney laughed, heat swelling color into her cheeks. She pulled the wine onto her tongue to feel the acidity in the flavor bite at her taste buds.

"At least you can get along with your ex," Sidney redirected, tensing her jaw. "Aiden and I can barely be close enough to exchange Cameron."

"Is it better to not be able to quit your ex but also not be with him or to have your ex hate your guts?"

"They both sound pretty stupid," Sidney said.

"That is why we have the Divorced Wives Club."

Kendra raised her wine. The two clinked glasses then drank deeply. Kendra drained her wine and stood to fetch the bottle from the kitchen. Sidney felt her head swim a little and relaxed back into the impending buzz.

"All right," Kendra said, topping off their glasses. "Put on some shit that won't give me nightmares."

"I am not watching reality TV."

"No reality TV for you. No horror for me. We both know we meet in the middle at comedy. That is how this relationship works."

"Ugh, fine," Sidney laughed, "but not romantic comedy."

Sidney sat in her idling car, wringing her hands around the steering wheel. The early morning sun glared through her windshield, glinting along the cracks reaching out across the glass. She squinted behind her sunglasses but kept her fingers gripped to the wheel. The minutes closed in around her, banging away in time with her throbbing heartbeat.

She hated coming to Aiden's.

He still lived in the small house they had purchased when Cameron was learning how to walk—the house in which they had been a family. After all the renovations he had made over the subsequent years, he had said she would have to pry the keys from his cold, dead fingers. If only it was all of those tireless renovations that had ended their marriage.

As time collapsed on her and she ran out of seconds to stall, she took a deep breath and tapped her forehead on the steering wheel. Then she yanked the door handle and forced her steps to the front porch where Cameron used to color with sidewalk chalk in the summer. She poked the doorbell then wrapped her arms tightly around herself, fingertips crawling around her ribcage.

Aiden's shape appeared behind the screen. He extended his arm to open the main door, but his shadow remained faceless as he kept his eyes down. The form did not even hesitate before walking back into the house without acknowledging her. His footsteps thumped in the hallway as he kept his shoulders rounded like an angry and pouting child.

"Cameron," he hollered down the hallway, "your mother is here."

Sidney reached out and let her fingertips touch the handle on the screen door. Her heart pounded harder. She heard it in her ears as her chest tightened, like it always did now at this house. She almost tightened her grip to open the door, then let her hand fall back to her side. She returned her clutch to her ribs and pressed her teeth to the inside of her lips.

She heard Cameron's footsteps slapping the floor before she glimpsed him bounding toward the door. His shoelaces fluttered untied on the ground beside him, and his backpack bounced on one shoulder. Aiden intercepted him in a quick embrace, pressing a kiss into his hair then releasing him.

"Momma!" Cameron cried as he pushed the screen open.

"Good morning, baby," Sidney said, grabbing him in a hug as she walked off the porch.

Aiden slammed the door firmly behind them. She felt the impact echo on her skeleton.

"How was your weekend with Daddy, baby?" Sidney said as they settled into the car.

"Really good!" Cameron clicked his seatbelt and sat up excitedly on the backseat. "We did monster trucks!"

Sidney tried not to let her deflation show on her

face. She stretched her smile tighter and tried to, instead, bask in the presence of her child. She forced the thoughts away of how she spent her time with him at school drop-off and baseball practice and homework while his father got to be fun and bring him to things like monster trucks. Things that made his smile impossibly big, as it was now in the rearview mirror.

"That's awesome, Cam," she managed. "Did Daddy pack you a lunch today, bud?"

Cameron furrowed his brow for a moment then reached over and opened his backpack.

"Nope," he replied.

Sidney felt the rage flicker deep in her chest. She tightened her grip on the steering wheel and pushed thin breaths out between her lips, clutching until the tension dissipated.

"But I have my baseball bag, Mom," he said.

"Did Daddy put a snack and a water bottle in there?"

"Nope."

Sidney continued to strangle the steering wheel. Her breath whistled through her lips as she pulled them taunt over her teeth. She did not realize how tightly she was flinching until her forearms began to tremble. Below her writhing frustration, images rolled unmediated through her mind.

"Momma," Cameron said from the backseat, far away. "Momma? Momma!" Louder until he was shouting.

"What?" Sidney snapped.

"That's the turn! You're missing my school."

"Oh shit!"

Throwing a frantic glance toward her blind spot,

Sidney yanked the wheel and sent the small car careening toward the turn. The oncoming van slammed on its brakes, driver flailing as they skidded by. A horn behind her wailed angrily. On the smaller residential street, she slowed the car to approach the drop-off line as if she had not almost landed herself in the middle of a traffic accident. Her heart banged in her chest as she unwound the tension coiled in her back.

"Momma, we almost died!" Cameron yelled. "Daddy is going to think it's so funny."

The stress knotted back up along Sidney's spine. Quiet fury broiled over her stomach, gnashing unhappily in its hunger. The file of cars crawled along the blacktop, bumpers flirting with each other. Every time her foot pressed on the brake, the irritation swelled in her chest.

"Here, baby," Sidney said, as they approached the curb. "Take this money for your lunch. There are a couple dollars you can use in the vending machine for a snack and a water. Don't forget your baseball bag. I'll pick you up after practice tonight."

Cameron spotted a couple of his friends milling around the planters outside the front of the school. He kept his eyes locked on the group of boys as he snatched the bills from his mother's hand and dove out the door.

"Have a good day," Sidney said to his backpack.

The car door slammed in her face.

"I love you," she said to herself.

She did not have time to wallow in the echo of the slamming car door. She squealed from the curb, avoiding eye contact with the scowling teacher aide in an orange vest brandishing a STOP sign. The line of parents streamed into the gap she left to filter through the parking lot. Sidney retreated back into her mind, coasting to work on autopilot.

She parked her car behind the store and glanced at the clock. With eleven fading minutes between her and opening, she turned off the engine and unlatched her seatbelt. She released a pent-up breath and dug her phone from her purse.

Sidney: Started this morning off with a strong mom fail.
Pick up more wine on your way home?

She knew Kendra would not answer for hours, but somehow it felt better to send the message now, to say it to someone.

Adam: Good morning
Sidney: Monday is already kicking my ass.
Adam: It is brutal. What happened?
Sidney: Just picked up my kid. Ex didn't send him with any food. Almost missed the turn for school and nearly killed us. Now at hell . . .
Sidney: I mean, work.
Adam: That's a hell of a start.
Sidney: I hate this place.
Adam: I know you do. Get more advertisers for your website and get that blog going so you can quit!

Sidney smiled to herself and felt a little farther away than the cell phone store parking lot. A double vibration cued that she had more messages on another platform.

Oliver: Hi sexy
Sidney: Hey there
Oliver: Let me see you this morning.
Sidney: I'm just heading into work.
Oliver: Doesn't mean I don't want to see you.

Sidney opened her camera app and lifted the phone slightly above her head. She let a sly smile tease her lips and stared into the lens. Then she sent the selfie.

Oliver: Gorgeous

Sidney rocked the nail of her index finger along her bottom teeth. The distractions swept her further away until the moments closed in around her. She slipped the phone into her back pocket and went to open the store.

The store sat dark and quiet as Sidney's keys rattled and scratched against the metal doorframe. Sidney shoved the glass door inward, sending jagged reflections of the morning sun violently across the carpet. She sucked in a deep breath of yesterday's recycled air. It tasted the same as it did every morning—like disappointment. She choked a bit on the stale and familiar aroma before falling into the worn foot patterns on the flattened carpet.

As she settled into her shift, the sunlight crawled lazily across the floor, inching toward the base of the display cases until the mechanical chime signaled the opening door.

"What's up, Sidney?" Seth greeted her, letting a heavy emphasis drag out the first half of her name.

"Morning, Seth." Sidney pushed herself away from the counter and clasped her hands in front her waist. "You know you're ten minutes late, right?"

Seth slipped his phone out of the pocket of his impossibly skinny black jeans and lit it up to read the time. The fitted cuffs of his pants strangled his legs down to his brightly laced high-top sneakers.

"Yeah, you're right, boss lady," Seth flashed her a broad smile. "I'm sorry, Sidney. I met this new girl last night. You know how it goes." He continued to flash his childish grin at her as he moved toward the door to the storage room.

"I have to write you up next time," Sidney said, shaking her head.

"Oh, come on," Seth mock-whined. "I wouldn't have to go through all these girls if you would just finally go out with me."

A laugh erupted from Sidney, full and wholehearted.

"Seth, I am way too old for you. Plus, I'm technically your boss."

"So you keep saying," Seth joked. "But think of all the things you could teach me."

"I'm about to teach you with a write-up."

"Yes, ma'am!" Seth snapped to attention, laughing, and disappeared into the back to stow his backpack.

As the door clicked shut behind him, Sidney giggled to herself and shook her head. Seth was borderline worthless as an employee, and she knew his flirtations were a complete farce, yet he had a way of keeping her distracted from the claustrophobia she always felt within these walls.

By the time Seth joined her among the counters of dancing smartphone screens, she had posted herself behind the register, leaning back as she waited for disgruntled customers. Seth already had his nose in his touchscreen. Sidney's phone found its home in her hand. She scrolled through her notifications. An unimpressive number had racked up in the brief morning hour since she left the parking lot.

She tapped her memo app and scrolled through her half-constructed blog post ideas: the tragic devolution of vampires in the horror genre; the best and the worst of the found footage horror explosion; the best indie horror out of this year's film festival circuit; scream queens to watch, the new horror badasses and final girls. She tapped her nail on the edge of her phone case as she formulated the sentences in her mind. Then the phone vibrated against her palm.

Brady: And the likes keep coming!
    Bloody bathtub for the win!
    See you at yoga.

The day dissolved around her, the same as all the others spent under the florescent lights. Eight then nine then ten hours swallowed by monotony. Sidney happily resigned her managerial responsibilities to Seth and practically sprinted back to her car. She had precious minutes to race back before the end of Cameron's baseball practice. The sun began to die in the sky around her as she retraced her near-catastrophic commute earlier in the day.

Sidney threw her car into park and ejected herself

from the seat. She slammed the door behind her, not even bothering to lock it as she leaned into quick steps toward the grass. The cars along the edge of the field were scarce. The pack of children had been reduced to a few stragglers still insistent on running the same dirt they had been playing on for the last hour. Several parents hovered menacingly around the coach as he gathered up stray bats behind home plate. Her heart flexed in her chest, climbed up into her throat. She was late.

Sidney spotted Cameron at the edge of the dirt, his bag slung over his shoulder. His back to her, he stared out at the empty field.

"Shit," Sidney breathed to herself as she walked faster and plastered a smile on her face.

The thick smell of impending rain swept across the lush carpet of park grass. Clouds gathered around the sun's retreat behind the mountains. Sidney closed her eyes as her steps squished across the field and she pulled the aroma back into her lungs. Something about it smelled like her childhood. As she ascended the small slope beside the field, Cameron finally caught sight of her. He did not move to meet her. He made her come all the way to him.

"Hey, Sidney!" one of the lingering mothers said as she approached.

"Hey, Kate," Sidney returned, slowing her steps to loiter beside her.

"You look awfully clean for someone who has been bathing in blood," Kate laughed.

Internally, Sidney rolled her eyes at the shallow quip, yet she smiled.

"Someone has been on Facebook."

"Instagram, but yes. That picture is crazy! I'm just scrolling through my feed of kids at the park and people's lunches and bam! There you are naked and covered in blood. Very bold, girl. I'm just glad none of the kiddos were peering over my shoulder. I wouldn't want to have that talk yet."

Sidney chuckled, good-heartedly. Beneath her shirt, her back muscles contracted.

"Are there more bloody pictures coming?" Kate continued. "You know, so I know to keep my scrolling out of sight of the kiddos."

"Yeah, my friend and I did an entire shoot, and he's been editing a lot of them."

"Oh, how exciting. What are you going to use them for?"

"Just more articles and promotions and clickbait and stuff."

Sidney glanced across the field. Cameron stared into her with his arms crossed, shifting his weight from leg to leg.

"Uh oh," Sidney said. "I'm getting the eye."

Kate looked over at Cameron, smiled, and waved at him.

"He did great today," Kate reported. "He caught the most impressive pop fly."

"Oh, you were here for practice?"

"Yeah, I like to come watch. It's just so important that the kiddos know we are here to support them. Got to be here for every little thing." She paused, leveling her gaze at Sidney. "It matters."

"Well, I'll see you tomorrow." Sidney turned and allowed her eyes to roll freely.

"All week, then the game on Saturday," Kate piped.

"Have a good night, Kate."

Sidney shook the exchange loose as it echoed in her head. Something about the baseball moms inspecting her naked, blood-soaked body made her stomach tense. She pictured them wrinkling their noses, tapping their finger on the bulge Brady had not managed to hide. She heard them whispering to each other about how disturbing and sad it was that she felt the need to post these pictures. Imagining her pictures being consumed seemed more exciting when she envisioned anonymous readers on the internet. She let these real and live comments slide off the back of her brain and turned her focus to Cameron.

"Hey, bud," she said, lightly shaking his shoulder. "How was practice? Kate said you caught a pop fly today."

"You're late," Cameron replied. "All the other moms are here. You're never here on time."

Sidney's heart dropped out of her chest. "I know, bud. I got here as fast as I could after work."

"I'm really hungry, Mom." Cameron hung his head as he began trudging toward the car.

"I bet you are. Did you get to buy some lunch?"

"Yeah, but no snack."

"Well, let's get home and get you some dinner." Sidney tugged Cameron's bag from his shoulder and hoisted it onto her own. "Shit! We still don't have groceries."

Cameron sighed exasperated and tossed his arms.

"Pizza or Chinese?" Sidney asked.

"Chinese," Cameron mumbled.

Chinese, of course. What his father always wanted to order on Friday nights.

4

"**MOM, I'M SO HUNGRY!**" Cameron whined from the couch.

"Baby, the food is finally here. I just have to unbag it," Sidney said, unpacking the steaming boxes onto the coffee table.

"Can we watch a scary movie?"

Sidney hesitated, stalling by continuing to arrange the food on the table and extracting chopsticks and condiments from the brown paper sack. She kept her eyes down on her hands.

"Mom! Can we watch a scary movie?" Cameron repeated, louder and with an edge.

"Your daddy doesn't like it when I show you scary movies," Sidney finally replied.

"Daddy just doesn't like scary movies."

"Also true."

"Please!" Cameron sat up straight and opened his eyes wide at his mother.

Sidney smiled, helpless.

"OK, bud," she said, "but not a really scary one."

"Yes!" Cameron threw his fists into the air.

He popped up from the couch and moved to snatch a box of *lo mein* and a set of chopsticks. He nestled back on the couch cushion as Sidney summoned the movie on the flatscreen.

"What's this one about?" Cameron managed between ravenous bites. Noodles spilled from his greased lips.

"The Headless Horseman."

"The Headless Horseman?"

"Yeah, he's a ghost who chops off people's heads."

"Then why is *he* headless?"

"Cam, just watch the movie. It will answer your questions."

Cameron's eyes widened in the reflective light of the screen. "What's it rated?" he asked.

"R." Sidney shoved a large bite of orange chicken between her teeth, waiting to see his reaction.

"R?" Cameron practically jumped from the couch and dropped his *lo mein*. His fixed scowl from the morning drive and afternoon practice was finally replaced by a dazzling grin.

Sidney basked in the momentary glow of his bliss. She smiled in return. Yet as the bright, unnatural blood splattered over a jack o'lantern face on screen, she felt herself cringe as she gauged Cameron's response. Was it too graphic? Was it too scary? Was she showing it to him too soon? Would Aiden lose his mind when he found out?

She straddled her emotions as the movie climbed through its plot. As heads rolled, she savored his screams and giggles of enjoyment. Yet she also felt the tension of worry, of self-doubt as it wound around her chest. She felt guilty for enjoying his horror indoctrination at this young age, and she felt stupid for doubting something so trivial as a scary movie.

Somewhere in the contradiction, she wasted the night.

After the horseman dove through the Tree of the Dead and the credits rolled, Sidney tucked a protesting Cameron into bed. His breathing grew weighted before she even closed his bedroom door behind her. Clearly, the movie had not traumatized him enough to cost him sleep. She shuffled the Chinese leftovers into the fridge and upgraded herself to another, exceedingly more graphic horror movie, placing her laptop across her legs.

Sidney navigated to her website's dashboard to unleash her article, ignoring the notification counts beckoning her from every window and application. She opened "Blood Baths: The Best Bathroom Scenes in Horror" and clicked the button to publish. Before she could even shift her attention to the accumulated comments and messages, her phone rang.

Only one person ever actually called her phone. Sidney chomped down into her lip without realizing it.

"Hi Mom," Sidney said into the phone. She flinched against the device along her face as it felt unnatural against her cheek.

"Oh Sidney, I caught you. Is now a good time, honey?" Her mother's thin, high voice drew a line along Sidney's nerves.

"Yeah, Mom. I'm just watching a movie and working on my website."

"Watching one of your horror movies?"

"Of course."

"I don't know how you stand that nonsense. Why would you want to be scared and disturbed all the time? How's my perfect boy?"

"Cameron is good. He's sleeping right now. He caught a pop fly at practice today."

"I hope you don't let him watch that scary stuff with you. Too much exposure to violence like that could turn him into a sociopath."

Sidney stifled a sigh. She brought her fingers to her face and rubbed her forehead before pinching the bridge of her nose. "Was there something you needed, Mom?" she said through pursed lips.

"Actually, yes." Her mother cleared her throat. "I got a call from your uncle today about some picture you posted, so I go online to see. Sidney Laurie, why are you naked and covered in blood on the internet?"

Sidney threw her head back and let it bounce on the couch cushion repeatedly. She pinched her nose harder this time, until it hurt.

"Mom, we've been over this." Sidney heard the whine in her voice and how much it sounded like her son when he was hungry.

"I still don't understand, Sid," her mother began her speech. "Getting bloody is for a crime scene. It is not art. You can't say it's art. I know what Brady says, and he's a very nice boy, but there's no reason to produce obscene stuff like that. Honestly, Sidney, are you trying to embarrass me? Aiden could use these pictures in court if he really wanted to."

"Mom, it's not gross," Sidney tried to interject. "And fake blood is not going to cost me custody."

"And you're never going to find a new husband posting naked pictures on the internet. What man wants his woman flashing all her goods all over Facebook?"

"Mom, I don't need a new husband."

"And what are you teaching Cameron? Do you want him to grow up to date women who take their clothes off? Strippers. Do you want him dating strippers?" Her mother's tone contorted in the thick disapproval Sidney knew well.

"Well, if he's going to be a sociopath, it sounds like that might be the perfect woman for him."

"Sidney!" Her mother's voice cracked.

"Come on, Mom. Strippers?" Sidney cradled her forehead in her hand.

"OK, fine. Maybe that was a little dramatic."

"A little?"

"But you see what I mean."

"No, Mom. No, I don't." Sidney squeezed her eyes shut and tried not to let her mother hear the irritation edging her breath.

"Well, we will just have to agree to disagree, dear."

"We have agreed to disagree, Mom, so we don't really need to keep having this conversation. I'm going to keep taking and posting the pictures; you're going to keep disapproving. I don't think we need to go in the same circle every time."

"I just want you to be safe, dear. You never know what kinds of weirdos are out there watching on the internet."

Sidney rolled her eyes hard, gritting her teeth. "I know, Mom. I will be careful." Her voice fell flat as her lips just made the practiced shapes, as her face contorted in all the irritation her mother could not see.

Her mother finally dropped the tired topic and proceeded to babble on about Sidney's uncle's new girlfriend and her cousin's assumed prescription pill problem. Sidney sat trapped beneath her laptop, her phone dangling against her earlobe as the Netflix description page of her horror movie mocked her. By the time her mother released her from cellular bondage, irritation roiled under Sidney's skin. She dropped the phone to the cushion beside her and glared at it, disgusted.

Sidney picked up the remote to scroll to another horror movie in her ever-expanding queue. The thin weight of exhaustion unrolled itself over the length of her skin, packing down on top of her eyelids. She shook her head against the sensation and against the crackling edge of her annoyance, focusing back on the screens shining their truths on her face.

She clicked through internet tabs and parsed the accumulating reactions and comments on her "Blood Baths" post.

This bitch obviously doesn't know anything about horror, but at least she looks good naked.

Psycho is the only movie to consider for best bathroom death scene!

Maybe you should go on a diet instead of sitting on your fat ass watching horror movies.

Great article! I love your story. Come check out my website.

Well written, girl. You know your horror.

You can't write *Final Destination* in the same sentence as *Psycho*. Only *Candyman* can be listed as comparable. The *Final Destination* franchise is just death scene porn.

Get the most followers for your website! Click now!

Looking hot! I want to lick every drop of that
   blood off of you!
That chick would be hot if she wasn't on the rag
   in every picture.
How brave of you to post these pictures! You
   look amazing.

The comments continued and duplicated, branching along the same deeply-worn veins. Horror adoration, sexual innuendo, body judgment, shaming—an awkward blend of tired and flat extremes. Sidney liked and responded to the neutral and positive comments. She lingered on the words, dwelling on the warmth that spread across her chest at the admiration. She read and reread the pleasant responses until the phrases began to lose meaning. Yet she stumbled on the negatives, on the hateful words, on the trolls. Those responses were sharper and conjured a sinking nausea in her stomach. She forced herself to read past them, deleting each entry and blocking their senders on social media.

As she shifted to her draft of her Nightmare Film Festival movie reviews, her messenger chimed.

Oliver: It's been too long since I've seen you.
Sidney: You've never actually seen me.
Oliver: You know what I mean.
Sidney: You saw me this morning.
Oliver: Too long ago. It's been a whole long,
   shitty day of work since then.
Sidney: I'm sorry. Bad day?
Oliver: Make me feel better?

Sidney leaned back and contemplated a selfie. She did not feel attractive. She felt the exhaustion of the day drawing wrinkles in her face. She felt the worry overexposing her son to horror and how much Aiden would hate it creasing deep lines in her forehead as the weight of her mother's judgment accumulated under her eyes. She reached for her discarded phone, and it vibrated in her palm. She had a direct message on Instagram.

Max: Your last article was great, and your pictures are . . .

Sidney tapped her nail on the cell phone case as she nibbled the edge of her lip. She rarely opened direct messages from unknown friends or followers. She had been scarred by too many uninvited pictures of genitalia or generic and disgusting come-ons or indications on how desperately she needed Jesus.

She tapped Max's name to view his profile. A page of bright tiles appeared, Max's face gracing the majority of them. He was attractive. She felt a subtle jolt looking at his images. Pictures of him with his dog on hiking trails mingled with horror memes and movie posters. She swiped back over to his message.

Max: Your last article was great, and your pictures are gorgeous. You're so beautiful, and the blood is so unnerving. It's the perfect contradiction.
Sidney: Thank you, Max! That compliment means a lot to me. That's exactly what we were going for.

Max: It works! It works really well.
Sidney: Thank you again!
Max: You're very unique. A horror-loving girl as attractive as you. And such cool concepts for the pictures.
Who comes up with the ideas?
Sidney: It's really a collaboration between me and the photographer.
Max: Who thought of the blood bath?
Sidney: That was me. To go with my article.
Max: Brilliant. Really brilliant.

Heat flushed along Sidney's skin into her typing fingertips. She felt the words in the shape of her keystrokes, the same way they might feel on her lips and tongue as they leapt out of her mouth. She absentmindedly gnawed on the inside of her bottom lip, bringing more blood to build on the tingling sensation spreading over her. The exhilaration of anonymous flirtation—safely long distance, comfortably a dead end—buzzed on her synapses.

Part of her wanted Max to materialize on the couch cushion beside her to act out all the flattering words he would send, the same way she frequently wished to conjure Oliver or Adam. Yet the rest of her was equally content to recline on the unconsummated tension that could exist in a limbo untainted by real life.

Sidney alternated between the conversation on her phone and draft film review on her laptop, the smile from the compliments still wriggling on her lips when she typed about the cinematography balanced against graphic violence or the believable character arc of the serial killer.

Oliver: Where are you, gorgeous?

She giggled to herself, realizing she had completely forgotten Oliver's request. Max had distracted her mind from its usual multitasking. She lay back against the couch cushions and snapped a quick picture to send to Oliver.

Oliver: There you are. Hello, beautiful. How is your night going?
Sidney: Good. It's been a long one. Still have a lot of work to do.
Oliver: I would love to be there to distract you.
Sidney: You're already distracting me.
Oliver: What are you working on?
Sidney: Reviews from the last fest. Just went through the comments from my last article.
Oliver: Everyone telling you how hot you are naked and bloody.
Sidney: If only just that.
Oliver: You are hot as fuck naked and bloody. Let me come take a blood bath with you.
Sidney: Real blood or fake?
Oliver: Whichever you want.

Sidney's temperature crawled up another degree. Once again, a seething part of her wanted the online personality made flesh beside her.

Adam: Working yourself to death.
Sidney: You know me.
Adam: Don't die. I'll miss you too much.

Sidney: You're sweet, but I'm just a voice in the computer.
Adam: You're so much more than that.

Between the three building conversations, Sidney typed away on her review. She kept her eye on the word count as it climbed toward the optimal length. Enough to fully assess the movie, not too much to lose the reader. She wished she was more of a writer, that the words flowed more naturally off the wrinkles of her brain. She had to dredge the sentences out of her skull and edit them over and over, but her streaming chats distracted her from the struggle.

Adam: How are you?
Sidney: OK
Adam: Just OK? What's wrong?
Sidney: It was just a long day. Late picking up my son from baseball. Then some mom making weird comments about my pictures. Then watched a horror movie with Cameron. I think maybe I just showed him the movie to win him back. Maybe I shouldn't have.
Adam: Was it too scary for him?
Sidney: Didn't seem like it. He really enjoyed it. Oh then my mom called to shame me.
Adam: So there's the real problem.
Sidney: Yeah, maybe.
Adam: What did she have a problem with?
Sidney: Everything. My uncle saw the blood bath pictures. It's gross. I'm going to fuck up my kid.
Adam: Don't listen to her.

You're amazing.
The pictures are art and sexy as hell.
And you're a good mom.

Sidney took a deep breath and let it stretch her lungs. She held it in and released her head back. Then she exhaled in an awkward burst. She drummed her fingers on the edge of her laptop as his words sunk into her brain.

If only he knew her well enough to be trusted.

Sidney keyed in the concluding sentences of her review and opened the gallery Brady had sent from their blood bath shoot. She clicked past the leading image Brady had released first and the selection she had included in her article. A pulsating, defiant instinct had her gravitating to the most graphic and revealing picture of her splayed and stuck to the bottom of the empty bathtub. She wanted to print it out poster-sized and hang it in her mother's dining room.

She took a breath and scrolled deeper into the gallery. She settled on one of the final dry shots Brady had taken. She was reaching unnaturally over the edge of the white basin. Her body contorted in strange angles, and her eyes bugged out from their sockets. Her face was terrifying, yet her bare hip drew a suggestive line through the image, her bloodied skin cresting curves from the edge of the tub. The perfect balance on the line.

Sidney selected the image and began sharing.

5

"**GIRL, YOUR INSTAGRAM** feed is about to give me nightmares," Kendra said as she scraped her spoon along the inside of her coffee cup.

"You know I do that just for you," Sidney replied, shuffling into the kitchen beside her.

"I know you do."

"Yep. I pick a picture, and I think, this is going to get inside Kendra's head. Then I sit up on the couch, listening for you to scream in your sleep."

"I'm not even surprised." Kendra smirked as she sipped from the steaming cup. "Let me pour you a cup. You look like you need it."

"I woke up like this."

"Did you even sleep like this?"

"Not really." Sidney ground her knuckles into her eyes. "I had to get the rest of my reviews from Nightmare Film Fest drafted."

"You don't have to do anything. You're not getting paid for this."

"I'm getting paid a little. Just not enough to live on."

"Either way, it's a side hustle."

"Yeah, and if I hustle hard enough, it can be the main hustle. So, I had to finish the reviews."

"And post creepy ass pictures to put your bloody face in my nightmares."

"Had to do that too."

Sidney reached out and took the mug from Kendra, smiling with a tiny nod.

"Is it strange that I don't hear any children?" Kendra asked.

"Strange, no. But it does mean that neither of them are getting ready," Sidney replied.

"Savannah!" Kendra shouted toward the hall. "You better be dressed up there."

An inarticulate mumble answered her.

"My bet is that Savannah is on her phone and Cameron is still in his pajamas playing a video game," Sidney said.

"That's not even a guess, girl. It's a certainty."

Kendra tugged her pants up and adjusted her well-tailored collared shirt, her necklace jingling as it jostled against her chest. Then she leaned her hip against the counter and lifted an oversized mug slowly and deliberately to her lips. Steam curled from the coffee and disappeared around Kendra's nose. Kendra drank slowly, inhaling deeply as she did, fully experiencing her coffee.

"You're doing it again," Sidney laughed.

"What?" Kendra lowered the mug to the counter.

"Making love to your coffee."

"Girl, I do not get the time to taste the other five cups I pour down my throat during the day. This one, this morning cup, is special." She laughed as she pulled the cup back to her face and closed her eyes, drinking deeply.

Sidney giggled then glared past Kendra to the microwave clock.

"I'll go yell at him in five minutes," Sidney promised.

Kendra adjusted her large watch and gave Sidney a playful look.

"So, I think I have a new internet stalker," Sidney said, redirecting.

"Oh really? In addition to the two online boyfriends you already keep?" Kendra cocked her head.

"Yep."

"Facebook?"

"Insta."

"Now, is he a trick who only talks about sex or a wifey who cares about your day? I know you already have one of each."

"To be determined." Sidney grinned.

"Sure, keep racking them up while I'm over here with just my ex. Just be careful. You never know what's really on the other side of that keyboard."

"I think about that all the time," Sidney said. "OK, that's definitely five minutes."

Sidney set her mug in the sink and sprinted up the stairs to harass Cameron into the bathroom, into his clothes, and into the car. As she reached the top of the stairs, her phone chirped from her back pocket.

Max: Is it wrong that I am completely aroused by how creepy your last picture was?

Adam: Good morning. Remember, you're still amazing.

Oliver: Please tell me you're still in bed so I can come join you.

Sidney smiled to herself and stowed the messages for a later response. Then she hustled her child to school.

***

As she leaned on the counter behind the store register, Sidney pulled her phone back into her palm. No customers milled the flattened gray carpet. Seth leaned over a tablet beside one of the large demo television screens.

Sidney: I think this job is killing my soul.
Adam: It is. But it's temporary. A means to an
    end.
Sidney: I did not go to college to manage a
    cellphone store.
Adam: No one does what they went to college
    for.
Sidney: Still. A high school student could do this
    job.
Adam: Not as well as you do.
    Temporary.
    You won't be there forever. Website, blog . . .
Sidney: Here's hoping.

The hours bled away into a blur of chat threads, upgrading customers to newer phones, and explaining why data package rates had to be so exorbitant. Each customer interaction suffocated her. Each issue she resolved for Seth irritated her. All the seconds and minutes and hours of her shift heaped on her consciousness—wasted. She could not help but count and weigh them.

When she was finally able to strip off her shift with the hideous polo and dress pants she was forced to wear, she exchanged it for yoga pants and a tank top. Brady waited for her outside the studio in the blazing afternoon light, chic sunglasses over his eyes and a rolled mat balancing on his exposed shoulder.

"There's my bathing beauty," Brady said as Sidney approached him. "What's up, Sid?"

"Just another day," Sidney laughed.

They hugged briefly, Sidney's chin nestling into Brady's chest. Then he opened the studio door for her. The aroma of incense saturated the yoga studio, making the air sharp and thick as Sidney breathed. They both slipped off their sandals beside the sign-in desk and moved into the studio to unroll their mats on the hardwood floor.

"So, this blood bath shoot seems to be our most popular yet," Brady said, lowering himself down to his mat. He drew his legs in and leaned forward to warm up.

"Yeah, tell me about it," Sidney replied, crouching down on her own mat.

"There's even been a minimum of menstrual comments. Everyone is just fixated on how hot and creepy you look."

"All thanks to you, sweetheart."

"Your mom call yet?" Brady twisted his spine and raised an eyebrow.

"You know she did. All disapproval. It's not art. It's gross."

Brady raised his hand and gasped. "She did not say it's not art."

"She did. Don't take it personally. She still loves you."

"Still, honey." Brady reclined back on his arms and pursed his lips.

"Then, it was how I'm fucking up Cameron by exposing him to horror and how I'm never going to find a new man posting naked pictures on the internet."

"Um, that is exactly how you find a new man!" Brady laughed.

"Either way."

"So, what did you tell her? Did you defend yourself?"

"It's like talking to a wall with her. We 'agreed to disagree.'" Sidney raised her fingers in air quotes.

"Well, are you just doing it for the attention? The comments? Your online stalkers and boyfriends?" Brady asked.

The question tangled at the edge of Sidney's mind, but she answered quickly, compulsively. "No, I don't think so. I tell myself I am doing it for the exposure and the clickbait, getting people to my website enough for it to be more. I do enjoy the attention, most of the time, but that's more of a happy side effect."

She regurgitated her usual explanation, to the question she seemed to be getting more often than internet comments lately. Like reciting a line from a play she had performed too many times.

"Look, girl, we have fun doing these shoots, right?" Brady said, sitting up again.

Sidney nodded.

"And we produce some badass images, right?"

Sidney nodded again.

"And we're both happy doing it, right?"

Sidney nodded once more.

"Then who actually cares about the rest? Your uptight mom and the baseball moms and the internet stalkers. So, let's just do what we do while it makes us happy."

"Hell yes." Sidney's smile was fierce on her face, but it wavered behind her lips.

The yoga teacher moved through the mats, calf muscles rippling as he unrolled each footstep silently along the floor. He steepled his fingers as he perched on the small podium at the front of the studio. Entrancing, gentle music floated through the air. The studio fell silent except for the growing swell of synchronized breathing. Sidney closed her eyes, surrendering to her practice.

"Now, curl your toes under and press up into Downward-facing Dog," the instructor said, his voice soothing.

Sidney pushed her palms flat into the spongy surface of her mat and sent her hips toward the ceiling and back toward her feet. The sharp edge of the stretch drew a line down the back of her leg, tracing her hamstrings from her hip bones into her ankles. The nerves lit up in a pleasant burn. She inhaled deeply, and as she exhaled, she forced the muscles along her legs to release into the burn.

As she trapped her body in the pose, her mind wandered away from the incoming messages and protests of her flesh. Her deep, yogic breathing fell into a practiced, automatic rhythm, and her thoughts unfurled her insecurities along the front of her brain.

Why did she take these pictures? Was she so insecure that she needed comments from strangers to make her feel attractive?

"Now, send your leg back into Donkey Kick," the instructor commanded.

Sidney raised her leg high behind her, moving the stretch from her hamstring to the front of her hip flexor.

Why did she need these online flirtations? Was it because she had destroyed her marriage to the point where Aiden couldn't bear to look at her? Was it because she didn't trust herself to not do it again?

"Send your leg through and come down into Pigeon," the instructor continued, his voice moving around the studio as he paced among the practitioners.

Sidney drew her raised leg into her chest and folded it under her body. She lowered her chest onto her calf and allowed her body weight to migrate the stretch into the root of her hip joint. She breathed deeply until her forehead met the ground. Her own breath recycled back against her from the mat.

A pigeon, a rat with wings, chasing any crumb. Just as she was online, begging for the clicks, the comments, the reactions, the reads. Posing for the horror trolls in hopes they toss her a few browser cookie crumbs. Why did she love horror at all?

"Press back up into Down Dog, and come to the other side."

Sidney let the questions roll over her mind like a wave. They slipped from her focus, as if dripping from her skull as she lifted it from the mat. She did not find answers between her breaths, but somehow, asking the questions at all unwound some of the tension curling around her chest. As the thoughts surged and receded, her mind fell quiet. Her focus collapsed to only hear the instructor and feel the shape of the poses.

Once outside the studio, Brady hugged Sidney tight and pressed his lips to her cheek. Her muscles radiated in the calm echo of the class. She smiled lazily as she bid him goodbye and headed to pick up Cameron. She grabbed her phone as she walked toward her car.

Tony: Heyyy beautiful, what are you doing tonight?

Sidney rolled her eyes at the banal and immature message yet replied just the same. She knew she would invite Tony over as soon as Cameron was back with Aiden—because sometimes she needed more than messages on the internet. Sometimes, she needed something real.

She slipped her phone into her pocket. First, she needed to hurry home to pick up her son from Kendra and get him to his father.

6

"WE NEED TO TALK," Aiden said. He opened the screen door for Sidney without looking at her.

"Hi Dad!" Cameron beamed, hoisting his backpack and baseball bag.

"Hey, buddy. Welcome back," Aiden said. He smiled broadly and patted Cameron's shoulder.

Sidney's body seized. Anxiety flared over her nerves, knotting up every muscle her time on the yoga mat had unwound. Her glance flitted as her heart pounded loud and relentless in her ears, avoiding Aiden and the way he refused to look at her. He stood frozen, held the door ajar, and stared at the ground.

As many times as she had wanted to walk back into her former home, as many times as she had fantasized about returning to her former life, the threshold felt electric and menacing now. She pressed her teeth into her lips and forced herself to step past Aiden and into the house.

Her heart broke with the sound of the screen settling back into the frame. She had not set foot on these floorboards in months. Aiden had taken down all the family pictures she had hung in the entry hallway—the delivery room when Cameron was born, their wedding in the mountains, backpacking through Spain after college. All the memories erased and replaced with flat, gray paint, though Sidney could imagine the phantom shapes of the frames still on the walls.

She walked slowly down the barren hallway. She wanted to let her fingertips trace the vacant paint but kept her hands curled against her chest. Each step sent anxious waves up her legs. The sensations balled up in her stomach, forcing nausea up behind her teeth. Her head swam in a torrent of emotions.

To no surprise, he had not changed the family room. It always really was his space. The same black couch consumed the floor in front of the large flatscreen. The couch where he had held her hand as she nursed Cameron. The television where they had marathoned countless series after Cameron had gone to bed. The urge to vomit tightened around her throat. She made a hard turn into the kitchen to skirt the swell of memories.

"What the fuck are you doing, Sidney?" Aiden said coldly before she even reached a chair.

"What are you talking about, Aiden?" Sidney replied, dragging a chair out from the table and dropping into it.

"You posting naked, bloody pictures on the damn internet."

"Wait, you don't follow any of my accounts. You blocked me on everything."

"Your shit is public, Sidney. Anyone can see that shit. I've heard about these damn pictures from multiple people. My parents still follow you." Aiden stomped along the length of the counter but still did not look at her.

"What I post is none of your business, Aiden. None of your business."

"Of course it's my business. I still have to share a child with you. I have to deal with it when our mutual friends or his teachers or my parents see you covered in blood and naked on the goddamn internet."

Heat prickled along Sidney's scalp, spread along her skin, causing the anxiety to melt into something else. "That's my problem." Her voice solidified from its wobble." Not your concern anymore. You don't get to decide what I do now."

"I never got to decide what you did, Sidney. As long as we share Cameron, this sort of shit is my business. Maybe you shouldn't get Cameron anymore. Maybe it's not good for him to be around you."

Sidney's heart stopped, and her blood ran scalding through her veins. Her fists clenched until her knuckles trembled white. Her mother's voice echoed somewhere in the back of her mind.

"You can't take my kid away over pictures," Sidney yelled. "Some photography has nothing to do with my parenting."

"But showing him horror movies does." Aiden finally looked into her eyes, defiant, hateful.

Sidney choked for a moment. On his words, on the contempt in his face. "I have never shown him anything inappropriate."

"I don't think you're fit to make that call. If you think it's a good idea to pose naked in a bathtub of blood and then post it for everyone to see."

The anger writhed through Sidney. Her thoughts

stuttered under its pressure. The rage blanked her mind and replaced the rational with an insatiable desire to injure her ex-husband. "You are such a fucking prude, Aiden," she managed.

"Oh, of course. Of course, I'm a prude. I'm not the one who went around fucking other people, so that makes me a prude."

"I did not fuck other people, Aiden!"

"You fucked at least one," he snapped, that hateful gaze burning brighter. "How do I know you didn't fuck more of them? All of them? You're just a desperate and insecure little bitch, trying to find someone to make you feel better about yourself. Posting pictures like this is just pathetic."

Sidney clenched her teeth hard, hearing them grit against each other, and instinctively looked over her shoulder to ensure Cameron was not lurking within earshot. Like she used to do so many times as their marriage was collapsing. "Lower your voice," she hissed. "We agreed we would not fight in front of Cam anymore." Her blood frothed beneath her words.

"Oh, now you care about what we expose our son to," he shouted back.

Sidney lost track of what she screamed at him. The argument was so habitual that the banter become muscle memory. They had had this same fight on repeat since Aiden discovered her infidelity, since their marriage had utterly exploded. Somewhere beneath her outrage, Sidney registered that Cameron could probably hear them fighting again, that he probably had heard them so many times he no longer cared, yet she could not temper her voice. She was sure it continued to echo in her old house long after the door slammed shut behind her.

She pulled her car screeching away from the curb and into a gas station down the street. She could not get to her phone fast enough.

Sidney: Fuck Aiden.
Kendra: What happened?
Sidney: Blowout

Sidney's fingers trembled as she grasped at words to articulate for Kendra.

Sidney: I'll explain in person.
    I'm messaging Tony.
Kendra: Damn, it must have been bad.

Sidney breathed, pursing her lips in an O and exhaling firmly until the fury in her dwindled to a simmer, until she could read the glowing screen clearly again.

Sidney: What is with everyone and these
    fucking pictures?
Adam: What happened now?
Sidney: My ex just went off on me.
Adam: Are you OK?
Sidney: No. Not at all.
Adam: Are you safe?
Sidney: Yes.
Adam: What happened?
Sidney: He invited me in for the first time in
    months.

He said I shouldn't have Cameron. Because
I post these pictures.
He said I was desperate and insecure.
He accused me of fucking everyone.
Adam: Wow.
Sidney: He can't take my kid over pictures. Over
pictures with FAKE blood.

Hot and frustrated tears leaked from Sidney's eyes.
She hastily swiped them away, as if Adam could see
them.

Adam: No, he can't. Not even in the reddest
state.
Sidney: Horror movie people have kids.
Adam: And it doesn't make them bad parents.
Sidney: I am a bad parent.
Adam: You are not.
Sidney: I let him win. I screamed and screamed
at him just like old times. When my kid could
hear.
Adam: Your ex deserved it.
Sidney: But my baby doesn't.

Sidney could not fight the fiery tears burning tracks
down her cheeks. The anger overloaded her brain,
scrambled her emotions. Somehow, crying made her
even more angry, which only caused more sobs to
shake out of her.

Sidney: I need you now.
Tony: Omw

Sidney forced her cries into whimpers and wiped her eyes until she could see enough to drive. She poured her rage into focus. She turned the car home toward distraction. She did not even think as she crossed town.

Tony must have been close. When she pulled into the driveway, she spotted Tony's car already waiting on her curb, the sleek midrange sportscar of a man with no other, more pressing priorities.

Sidney burst into the front door in an unintended flurry. Tony and Kendra stood on opposite sides of the kitchen counter peninsula, both holding beers. They turned startled as Sidney flung the door shut behind her. Kendra's body had been angled away from Tony, granting him only the side of her shoulder, but when she saw Sidney, she turned toward her and stepped past Tony. Tony stood as nonchalantly oblivious as always, beer hovering near his lips.

"Oh shit, honey," Kendra said, knowing. She flexed her lips into a thin grimace but held back her words.

"Hey Sid, you OK?" Tony said.

Sidney shook her head before the words finally formed on her tongue.

"I don't want to talk about it right now," she said.

"Do you want a beer?" Kendra offered.

"Absolutely."

Sidney moved into the kitchen and took the perspiring bottle from Kendra. Her arm near-trembled from the relentless adrenaline dancing on her nerves. She forced it to her lips and gulped desperately at the beer.

"Must have been one hell of a night," Kendra said, watching. "You never chug."

"Later," Sidney said between gulps.

As she slammed her beer, Sidney noticed Tony's eyes moving over her. He stared at her mouth, then let his gaze meander down her neck and over her body. Kendra noted the same behavior and gave Sidney a knowing glance.

"Well, I'm going to head upstairs to watch a movie with Savannah in her room before bedtime," Kendra said as she dumped her beer bottle in the recycling. "You two have a good night. Sid, catch up in the morning?"

Sidney smiled at her gratefully, nodding.

"See you in the morning." Sidney placed her own empty bottle on the counter beside her.

Tony set his bottle down and reached forward to take Sidney by the waist. The frothing tide of her anger tempered at the distraction of his touch. She snuck in a breath before he pressed a kiss to her mouth and closed her eyes to tumble fully into the motions.

"Must have been rough," he mumbled against her neck. "Let's see if I can make you feel better."

"Exactly what I had in mind," Sidney said, leading him to her room.

7

IN THE LATE weekend sunlight, Sidney woke to an empty bed, the sheets still cooling from when Tony had vacated before dawn. She ran her palm along the mattress and arched her back until her muscles awakened. She rolled her eyes closed again to bask in the brief quiet of her mind. Before the thoughts would begin to stir again. As it registered that her son was not under her roof, she dragged herself from the comfort of her pillows.

Sidney stumbled on half-conscious legs, a light ache drawing lines towards her hips. She smiled at the gentle strain in her step and placed her hands on top of her dresser. As the sleep cleared from her eyes, the miniature blue baby booties came into focus. Aiden had given them to her when they returned home from the hospital after she had Cameron. She had tossed and abandoned everything else Aiden had given her when she was forced from their home, yet she could not part with those. She was still the mother of his child. She pulled her eyes from them and dug out a pair of yoga pants.

"Feeling better?" Kendra asked as Sidney dropped onto the couch cushion beside her.

Kendra had piled her curls on top of her head haphazardly, a clear indication that she had no intention of leaving the couch any time soon. She clutched her coffee close, resting the bottom of the mug on her sternum. Her morning talk show babbled across the room from the television.

"I don't know about better," Sidney said, massaging her face with her hand. "As long as I don't think about Aiden, I'm at least distracted."

"I have been waiting. Now, spill."

"Do I at least get coffee first?" Sidney whined.

"Girl, you know I left yours warming in the pot, but I'm not going to pour it for you to get cold on the counter while you're sleeping off sex I did not have."

Sidney chuckled as she hurried to the kitchen to pour herself a matching mug of coffee. Then she sat back down and took a deep sigh in preparation. Kendra paused her show and turned to face Sidney.

"I should have known when he invited me into the house," Sidney started.

"He let you in the house?"

Sidney nodded.

"Well, that shit was a trap."

Sidney smirked and took a burning sip. "Yes, it was. He lost it on me, Kendra. We fought the same as we did all the way to the end. Pretty sure Cam heard it all, just like he used to."

"About what this time?" Kendra propped her elbow on the back of the couch and leaned against her hand.

"The pictures." Sidney looked down into her cup, almost mumbling.

"Oh. The blood bath."

"He said I'm not fit to raise Cam, that Cam should

61

not be with me. On and on." Sidney swirled her finger out into infinity and dropped her head back.

"You know he does not give one shit about those pictures. You started this whole horror modeling thing when you were still together. He didn't care then. Shit, he even bragged about it."

"Maybe he thinks that's where we went wrong."

"We both know that's not true. He's just looking for any way to hurt you because you hurt him."

"Cameron." Sidney hung her head for a moment.

"Bingo," Kendra said. "He doesn't care about the pictures. The pictures are not going to get Cameron taken from you. It sucks and it hurts, but you'll be fine."

Sidney nipped at her bottom lip and nodded. They were just pictures.

"I'll have you know your little visitor caused me to booty call my ex last night." Kendra took the pause to divert the conversation.

"Kendra! You didn't."

"I did. I was lonely! I wanted a bedmate. He didn't answer though." Kendra stuck out a pouty lip.

"You can borrow Tony if you want," Sidney laughed.

"Ha! I don't think he's my type. He may be cute, but I can barely share a beer with the boy. You could not get home fast enough last night." She cackled. "I just didn't want the same empty bed."

"Tony's not my type. He's nice to look at and fun to sleep with, but damn, that boy is dumb."

"And young," Kendra reminded. "And dumb," she laughed.

"And very young. But that makes him safe. No

danger I'll fall into a relationship with him. I don't need to repeat Aiden."

"Just don't waste too much time on the dummy. Sexy or not, he's not worth it. And don't worry about Aiden, girl. He's just bitter. I mean, he's earned that, don't you think?"

"Maybe. I did fuck him over." Sidney began rubbing her forehead again. "Is it too early to start drinking?" Sidney pouted.

"Don't you have yoga with Brady in like half an hour?"

"Yes, I do. He wouldn't judge me if I was buzzed."

"He's probably already buzzed on mimosas."

"Exactly," Sidney laughed. "OK, I'm going! What are you doing today?"

"Nothing!" Kendra smiled broadly at the word.

"Wait, nothing? You never do nothing. You're always working yourself to death then running Savannah all over."

"Not today. I promised Savannah a morning of whatever she wants to watch on Netflix. Right after this show."

"Are you going to be able to do it?" Sidney curled the edge of her lip.

"I'm surely going to try. Otherwise, I'm going to drop dead before any of the patients at work."

"You sure you don't want to join us? We could get brunch after."

"You know that yoga is not for me. Besides, I got Savannah. Now, get out of here. You're going to be late."

Sidney heaved herself in her yoga pants off the couch, leaving Kendra to endure a morning of streaming cartoons with Savannah. Her mind wandered off into the distance as she navigated the familiar route in her car. Outside the studio, she found Brady in his same spot waiting for her. They embraced and moved inside to claim their usual spaces on the hardwood studio floor.

"Honey, it is time to plan our next shoot," Brady declared on the mat.

"Already?" Sidney questioned. "I haven't even finished releasing the last set."

And it was causing her enough problems.

"Details, girl. I think we need to keep the momentum going. I have racked up over 1,000 new followers on Insta with the blood bath. I know you're seeing all kinds of love. Clearly, naked and covered in fake blood is our thing."

"That is not our thing."

"Denial is not cute." Brady pursed his lips. "What should we do next? I know you have ideas."

"I don't have more ideas for being bloody and naked."

"Liar," Brady smirked.

Sidney smiled back, guilty. "OK." Her smile spread. "Maybe a bloody coyote ugly. Like, oops, I woke up, and he's dead."

"Oh. My. God! I love it. We're doing it."

The instructor hushed Brady as she walked between the mats to the podium. Her taut muscles rolled visibly with each step under her matching seafoam green tights and sports bra. Her haphazard bun wobbled as she ambled through the rows of mats on the floor. Sidney and Brady grinned at each other like scolded school children then settled into their practice. Sidney dug through her thoughts and found the calm somewhere between her breaths.

As class ended and the participants began rolling their mats, Brady picked up their conversation exactly where it had been hushed.

"So, are you done stressing about the reactions to these pictures and ready to go hard for it?" Brady said as they wandered out of the studio after class.

"Well, after Aiden threatened custody, it can't really get any worse," Sidney laughed.

"Um, are you kidding me? Over pictures?" Brady giggled. "Does he forget that he mixed up our very first batch of fake blood?"

"I guess he does."

"Oh, honey. Why did you have to fuck around on him? I really liked him before you made him crazy."

"Hey!" Sidney laughed, yet the words stung.

"It's OK. We're all just moving on. And you and I are moving on to the bloody coyote ugly. All in."

"Yes, all in," Sidney echoed. "Let's get fucking creepy. We're using your bed though, right?"

"Sid, the blood washes out."

"We're using your bed though, right?"

"Of course, why would we shoot in your suburban nightmare when I have a loft with huge windows? No offense."

Sidney returned home to an empty house. The quiet was so unfamiliar that she found it unnerving. Kendra had taken Savannah to her Saturday swim lesson—Kendra's way of coping with the fact that she herself could not swim and was terrified of drowning. Sidney took advantage of the rare moment and sprawled out on the couch with her phone and a horror movie.

Max: How was yoga?

For a moment, Sidney's heart seized. How did he know where she was? She scrolled back through her posts in her memory and recalled checking in at the studio with Brady, citing that she was hatching the next photoshoot concept with Jagged Rainbow Photo, planting bait for future reactions.

Sidney: Much needed.
Max: What's the next photo shoot?
Sidney: Bloody coyote ugly
Max: That's hot! I can't wait to see the pics.
    What are you doing now?
Sidney: Just relaxing. I have a live tweet tonight.
Max: Are you alone in the house?

Sidney stopped at the familiar horror movie line, her heart twitching out of rhythm again.

Sidney: No, I'm never really alone.

Something in Max's question prickled on Sidney's brain, yet she ignored it. All her online correspondence walked through the same predictable pattern. After two weeks or two months, most piddled out. Except Oliver and Adam. Surely, Max would not last much longer.

Plus, something in that tingle in her head made the conversation risky, exciting.

Adam: What time is the live tweet tonight?

Sidney: 7pm mountain
Adam: Is Wes joining you?
Sidney: Of course.
Adam: Isn't it cheating to live tweet in person with someone?
Sidney: No! We're both tweeting separately on the same hashtag.
Adam: What's the movie tonight?
Sidney: *Final Destination*
You in?
Adam: Always.
Though I would rather be there with you. Instead of Wes.

Sidney smiled to herself as she glanced back to the flickering light of the death scene on the screen. She placed her phone on her chest and folded her hands on top of it until it vibrated again.

Oliver: Hey sexy!
Did you go to yoga without me?

Sidney silently reprimanded herself for the yoga check-in. The post had few likes for how many people were apparently paying attention.

Sidney: You aren't into yoga.
Oliver: I would be into yoga with you. I'll fold you into all kinds of positions.
Naked, of course.
Sidney: Of course.
Oliver: Let's do a private session.
Sidney: Sure, come on out to my house.

Oliver: I wish. It would be way better than working here. Scrolling through your pictures.
Sidney: Poor baby. Don't those ever get old?
Oliver: Pictures of you? Never. I'll never not want to look at you.

The day passed lazily over Sidney. She should have been updating her website in preparation to launch her new blog. She should have been drafting her first round of blog posts. She should have been proofing her festival horror movie reviews. She should have been responding and posting on social media. She should have been cleaning the house around her. She did nothing. She allowed the aftermath of all her recent drama to sedate her and lay on the couch messaging faceless strangers on the internet.

After the sun had retreated from the sky, Wes's knock rattled the door.

"Hey, Wes," Sidney smiled as she pulled the door ajar for him. "Come on in."

"Hi Sid," Wes replied, shouldering his laptop bag and stepping in past Sidney. "How long until the live tweet starts?"

"Twenty minutes," she replied. "Plenty of time."

Wes shuffled around the coffee table and settled into his favorite spot, the same spot Kendra loved to occupy when she was home. He meticulously placed his bag on the cushion between him and Sidney's seat, gently extracting the computer. He sat up on the edge of the couch and looked between the empty coffee table and Sidney.

"Do we have the customary snacks?" he asked.

"What do you think this is? My first live tweet? Of course we have the customary snacks."

Sidney moved into the kitchen and returned with a heaping bowl of chips and a bag of licorice bites. She deposited both on the table then circled back to extract two cold beers from the fridge. She placed them down forcefully enough to hear the glass clunk against the wood.

"Better?" she mocked.

"Much better," Wes laughed. "Now, I'm feeling the vibe. It's only better in October when we have Halloween snacks."

"October is coming. Which reminds me, we need to talk about the Telluride Horror Show."

"That's right." Wes leaned back and rubbed his hand over the stubble advancing across his chin. "It's almost time. How was Nightmare?"

"It was good. Really good." Sidney snagged her beer and dropped to the cushion beside Wes's bag. "It's a little more commercial than Telluride, so it has a bigger setup, more swag but less of the, I don't know, culture. I saw a lot of good movies. Some we'll have to watch later."

"When are you posting your reviews?"

"This week. I just finished drafting them but was too lazy to proofread today."

"You're allowed to take a day off, I guess," Wes shrugged. He grabbed his own beer and a handful of licorice, easing back against the couch.

"So, Telluride," Sidney redirected, "you're a yes, yes?"

"Yes. I mean, I think so."

"You think so? Your wife will let you out?"

"Pam might have some stuff planned for us, so I'll have to check with her. Otherwise, yes. I'm a yes."

Sidney rolled her eyes and smiled as she took another swig.

"Does Pam want to come with us?" Sidney asked.

"No. God, no." Wes shook his head violently.

"She doesn't have to watch horror movies. She could go hiking or whatever. Telluride is a cool town."

"I know. And she knows. She always does a spa weekend when we go to a fest."

"So, if we drove out on Thursday," Sidney pressed, "we could do all horror Friday, Saturday, and Sunday then drive home Monday. We could get a good deal on a room at the same place we stayed last time."

"I did like that place. I like being able to walk to everything."

"Including the bar!" Sidney raised her beer.

"You do not need to get as drunk as last year. You think just because we live in Colorado you can't get affected by that extra altitude."

"We were fine."

"I was fine," Wes laughed. "You were too hungover for morning movies the next day."

"Well, I'm going. It would be nice to not go alone."

"I'm probably going with you. If not, you could always invite one of your online boyfriends." He pressed his fingertip into his chin then grinned and pointed at her. "Or you might see one of your stalkers there."

"Funny you should mention that." Sidney sat back and pulled her laptop across her knees.

"Oh, no. What?" Wes rolled his eyes and did the same with his computer.

"One of my online 'boyfriends' is talking about coming to the fest." Sidney used her fingers to quote boyfriends. "I'm sure he's full of shit, but that's what he's saying."

"And you're not alarmed by this?" Wes squinted his eyes and turned his face near profile to her.

"No." Sidney hesitated. "I mean, maybe. I've been talking to this guy for almost two years, near daily. If he is full of shit, he is very committed. I don't think he is. But maybe the risk is part of the excitement?"

"You write about horror, Sidney," Wes said firmly. "You know where this story ends. With you in fifteen pieces in the mountains outside Telluride."

"Oh, stop being so dramatic. You'll be there to protect me."

Wes let his jaw drop.

"Oh, I see what this is about," he said. "You don't want a horror buddy at the fest; you want a stalker chaperone."

"Never! Always a horror buddy. If you happen to be a stalker chaperone, you know, even better. Can't it be both?" Sidney chuckled.

"Are you going to hang a sock or a tie on the door of our room if shit gets serious, like in college?"

Sidney cackled a bit and reached forward to gather a handful of chips. She crunched them loudly as she smiled over at Wes. He continued to shake his head, turning his attention to the laptop screen. He adjusted his glasses and smoothed his beard before placing his fingertips gently on the keyboard.

"Oh shit," Sidney mumbled through chip fragments. "It's time!"

She gathered the remote and conjured the movie onto the large flatscreen.

"What are we watching again?" Wes asked. "These tweets are all starting to blend together."

"*Final Destination.* Follow-on to my discussion of the bathroom death scene in my last article."

"Carnage candy," Wes laughed. "How could I forget the bloody, naked bath?"

"Not you too!" Sidney gasped.

"Sid, you posted naked, bloody pictures on the internet. What did you expect?"

"Less reaction, I guess. I didn't think they were that shocking. Or at all sexy."

"Well, you're desensitized. Didn't you post them for reactions?"

"Online reactions," Sidney clarified. Her face darkened as her tone thickened. "I did not really expect to discuss them with everyone in my real life."

"Real life, digital life. Where is the line anymore?" Wes weighed his hands in the air, like tipping scales.

"I sure see that now. It did boost my website traffic too."

"Then I guess it worked," Wes smiled.

"OK and . . . now." Sidney pressed the play button on the remote and sent *Final Destination* pouring into the living room.

Sidney and Wes sat one cushion apart on the couch, both in identical stances with their laptops balanced across their knees. Sidney shimmied lower into a slouch on the cushion, drawing the computer closer as she placed the remote aside.

"What's our hashtag tonight?" Wes asked as his fingers danced over the keyboard.

"Hashtag FDlivetweet, hashtag horrorlivetweet,

hashtag finaldestination, hashtag youcantcheatdeath, hashtag finalgirlscreams," Sidney answered.

"Why don't you copy all that into a chat for me?" he laughed.

Sidney rolled her eyes as she complied. She opened Twitter in one window.

Let the #livetweet begin! #FDlivetweet #horrorlivetweet #finaldestination #youcantcheatdeath #finalgirlscreams

She added an iconic image of Devon Sawa and clicked the Tweet button. Then she opened the #FDlivetweet thread in another tab. Her own initial tweet appeared, followed by Wes's. Steadily, more of her usual Twitter horror lovers weighed in.

@L1v1ngDead1te: We're at it again! Pushing play on #FinalDestination with @finalgirlscreams! #FDlivetweet, #horrorlivetweet, #finaldestination, #youcantcheatdeath
@ChuckysBabysitter: Yes! One of my all time favorites! Great choice, @finalgirlscreams #FinalDestination #FDlivetweet
@Romero4eva: It is time to face Death! @finalgirlscreams @L1v1ngDead1te #finaldestination #FDlivetweet #horror #horrormovies

"I really do love this movie," Wes mused beside her. "Even if it is just death scene porn."

"The first one isn't just that. I think the first one is legitimately decent horror, but the rest of the franchise is definitely just that."

"Same as *Saw*."

"Exactly."

As death began to claim characters on the screen, a chatter of excited tweets rolled up Sidney's browser tab. She and Wes liked, commented, and retweeted appropriately, expanding their watching session beyond the confines of the two of them on the couch. Other voices joined them in detached synchrony.

Sidney kept the #FDlivetweet thread refreshed.

@Romero4eva: #FinalDestination is based on a woman changing planes based on her mom's intuition! #truestory #FDlivetweet #horrorisreal

"Holy shit," she mumbled between popcorn bites. "Did you know *Final Destination* was actually loosely inspired by real events?"

"I had heard that," Wes replied, typing. "But did you know it was originally supposed to be an *X-Files* episode?"

"No! How do I not know all this?"

"This is why we live tweet, Sidney."

Beyond the tweet thread, Sidney's direct messages and chats began to sing.

Oliver: Hey sexy! *Final Destination*, huh?
Sidney: Of course. Join us?
Oliver: Only if I can have you in person.
Sidney: Come on over.

Adam: Love this movie. Watching along with you.
Sidney: As always. Thanks!
Adam: Say hi to Wes for me.

Max: I know what you're doing right now.
Sidney: What's that?
Max: Watching *Final Destination* with @L1v1ngDead1te.
Sidney: All of Twitter knows that.
Max: What's your favorite death scene?
Sidney: The bathroom
Max: Kinky girl into strangulation.

Sidney tapped her fingertips on the keys at the last message. Something in the words made the back of her jaw flex. She clicked away, not caring he could see she had read what he had sent.

Allison: Hi girl! It's @ChuckysBabysitter from the live tweet. I hope you don't mind me messaging you directly. This movie was such a great choice.
Sidney: Hi! No problem at all. I think this movie will always be one of my favorites.
Allison: I have to admit I have been following you for a while but didn't think you'd ever answer me.
I loved your bathroom death scene article.
But I think *Final Destination* may have the best bathroom death scene.
Sidney: It is my favorite scene of this movie.

Allison: You definitely know your horror. And make your own with those pictures!
Sidney: Thank you!

On the television, another teenager met their fate. Sidney tensed, despite the many times she had already seen the often-emulated jump scare.

Wes looked over at her, raising an eyebrow. "How can you startle so easy? You have this movie memorized," he laughed.

"Gets me every time," Sidney said.

"You startle like a little girl."

"I do! Keeps it fun though. Can't let myself get too desensitized."

"This is why you are my favorite person to go to a haunted house with."

"So you can laugh at me," Sidney glared.

"Yep."

Wes lifted his beer to drain the bottle and pulled the bowl of chips to the cushion between them. He crunched loudly then wiped his fingertips on the napkin beside him before typing again. The tweet threads and conversations continued to scroll between Sidney and the movie.

@ChuckysBabysitter: The Bus! Gets me every time! #finaldestination #FDlivetweet #finalgirlscreams
@HorrorL0ser: BOOM! #youcantcheatdeath #finaldestination #FDlivetweet

Allison: That scene is so infamous. I remember my jaw dropped when I saw it in the theater.

Max: If you had to die in a horror movie, how
    would you want to go?

Max's question branded on her brain. The tweets
and responses and questions continued to pour in but
dissolved into a chatter. Her mind continued to circle
back to, *If you had to die in a horror movie, how
would you want to go?* She needed to speak in the real
world to hush the echo from the internet.

"I think I have some new stalkers," Sidney said.

"In addition to your online boyfriends? Can you
support more stalkers at this point?" Wes replied
without looking away from the screens.

"Yes and yes."

"You don't have to answer them, Sid," he said,
flatly.

"I know that." Sidney slid a little further into her
recline.

"Do you?" Wes turned and gave her his eyebrow
again. "You don't know these people. You don't have
to interact with them."

"Isn't that the point of social media? To be social?"

"You're posting and tweeting. That's social. You
don't have to direct message. What are you going to do
if your website takes off like you want? You won't have
time to personally and individually talk to your entire
audience."

"True." Sidney paused to let his words roll around
her mind. "But right now, I do. I need something to
pass the time at my shit job."

"And the nights when you don't have Cameron."

Sidney winced at Wes's words, accurate as they
may be.

"Ouch," she said, softly.

"You know I didn't mean it like that," Wes said in a gentler voice.

"I didn't think you would be one to judge me for having an online life." Her voice grew smaller. "Since you're tweeting right beside me."

"I don't judge you," Wes returned in his normal voice. "That would make me a huge hypocrite here. I'm merely commenting that you don't have to engage all your stalkers. You never know who is on the other side of the keyboard."

"So I keep hearing." Sidney half rolled her eyes.

"So you already know. Who have you attracted tonight?"

"One girl who seems really into my website and this movie." Sidney felt that vague tension return to her jaw. "And one new guy who just asked how I would want to die in a horror movie."

"That's a little creepy. Not the single white female, but the dude."

"Could be creepy." Sidney shrugged off the tightness between her teeth. "Or it could be a perfectly legitimate horror question. Maybe I should blog about it."

"Don't give him the satisfaction. It will just encourage him."

"I'm trying to encourage him," Sidney returned. "I'm trying to encourage them all so I can quit my stupid day job."

"Hashtag horror hustle. Hashtag soul seller." Wes lifted his fingers and crossed them to form the hashtag symbol.

"Wow, I didn't know you were this stupid," Sidney giggled.

"Hashtag fuck off."

Sidney: I think I would like to have my head cut
    off. Quick and effective.
Max: I was not expecting that answer!
Sidney: What were you expecting?
Max: Strangulation
Sidney: No that's just my fetish

Sidney flinched at her own message and quickly typed again.

Sidney: Kidding!
Max: Sure, you are.

Sidney felt herself flush, giddy and nervous in the conversation. She glanced over at Wes to ensure he didn't see it on her. His eyes remained locked on the glowing screens in front of him. Physically beside each other on the couch yet wandering off apart in cyberspace.

Oliver: What are you wearing?
Sidney: Clothes
    (lamest line ever, btw)
Oliver: I'm too tired to be clever.
    Show me?
Sidney: Maybe after my company leaves.
Oliver: Date?
Sidney: Ha! Not for a live tweet.
Oliver: Good. You're supposed to date me first.
Sidney: Sorry. No online dating for me.
Oliver: You'll make an exception for me.

Another excited flare skittered across her nerves. She hesitated in it before typing her response.

Sidney: Oh, will I?
Oliver: Yes

Allison: How did you get the idea for your article about Lovecraftian influence in modern horror?
Sidney: Wow! You have been reading for a while.
I saw a movie at a film festival last year that really had that vibe but did it so subtly.
Allison: It was very good.
Sidney: Thank you!
Allison: Can I ask you something?
Sidney: Sure.
Allison: Is it scary to post your pictures on the internet?

Sidney paused at the question for a moment, lightly nibbling her bottom lip as she considered.

Sidney: Sometimes.
The internet is full of assholes.

Sidney hesitated to type the last of the answer then pressed Send anyway.

Sidney: But it's also exciting.

The movie finally concluded, and the credits scrolled over the screen. Wes and Sidney took the time to tweet the customary wrap up and thank you sentiments, tagging each other. Sidney set her laptop on the coffee table as Wes began to pack his into his bag.

"Another successful live tweet," he smiled. "This one was pretty popular. A lot of interaction on the thread."

"I know! It was fun. Thanks for coming over to do it with me."

"Every time."

Wes shouldered his bag and walked toward the door. Sidney stood and followed. The door opened itself, and Kendra and Savannah burst in. Kendra had a heap of grocery bags gripped in one hand. Savannah tangled her little fingers in the other. Savannah's small eyes drooped under the late hour.

"Wes!" Kendra boomed as she released her daughter's hand. Savannah hovered by the door, rubbing her tired face. "So good to see you."

Kendra hurried across the room, and Sidney chased her to help her offload the bags.

"Hey, Kendra," Wes said.

Kendra gave Wes a quick hug and looked to the television.

"Look at my amazing timing to miss the entire horror movie," she laughed. "What was it tonight?"

"*Final Destination*," Sidney answered. "It's not that scary. You would have been fine."

"And have nightmares about Death stalking me? No thank you!" Kendra countered. "There is enough death in my life already."

Wes gave Sidney and Kendra light embraces and departed. Sidney closed the door gently behind him.

Savannah had not moved since Kendra had released her hand. She stared distantly as she lingered.

"Oh, tired girl," Kendra laughed.

Savannah looked at her mother lazily.

"What did you do to her today?" Sidney laughed, reaching down to jostle Savannah. Savannah animated, laughing and playfully swatting at Sidney's hand.

"Oh, you know," Kendra replied, "the usual. All the things."

"What happened to nothing?" Sidney laughed.

"I have a project due this week," Savannah said through a yawn. "I'm building a pyramid."

"A pyramid?" Sidney gaped. "How big?"

"This big!" Savannah threw her arms as wide as she could. Kendra popped a hip and widened her eyes at Sidney.

"So, we had to get supplies. And food. You know, we're always out of food."

"It's like we have two kids in this house," Sidney joked.

"And two women who like to eat!" Kendra laughed. "Oh, I got more wine too."

"You did do all the things."

"Mommy, I'm tired." Savannah drooped as her voice wavered into a whine.

"OK, baby, OK." Kendra gathered a sleepy Savannah into her arms, giving Sidney a conspiratorial smile, and whisked her off to bed as Sidney returned to the conversations blooming across her laptop screen.

Max: If I was going to kill someone in a horror movie, it would be strangulation.

FOLLOWERS

Sidney: Now who has the fetish?
    But it can't be me. Don't you know? I'm the
    final girl.

THE BASEBALL CRACKED against the metal bat in a resounding *ting* Sidney almost felt vibrating down her own fingers. The tiny white dot careened into the clear blue sky, arching high above the uniformed children spread out over the diamond. Cameron stood stunned for a split second, staring in amazement at the ball's flight, before the yelling of his coaches stirred him. He flung the bat as he leaned into his sprint toward first base.

Before she realized it, Sidney was on her feet, clapping her hands hard and shrieking her son's name. She yelped excitedly as he slid into second base. Safe.

Still throbbing with pride, Sidney sat back down on the bleachers. She turned and caught Aiden's glance. He sat a couple rows down and away from her, peering out from beneath his baseball cap. Out of habit, he smiled back at her, mingled in the parental moment. Then he caught himself and snapped his eyes back to the field. Sidney felt the smile turn heavily and fall from her cheeks.

"Sidney!" Kate waved, as she and another mother climbed up the bleachers. "Cam sure got a hold of that one!"

Sidney bristled at the unsanctioned nickname for her child but returned the grin and slid over to make more space.

"Hi Kate," Sidney said. "Hi Maggie. How are you guys?"

"Our boys are up," Kate said. "That always makes it a good day."

Kate lifted her water bottle, plastered with school spirit stickers, and took a long sip. She faced the game attentively, talking out the side of her mouth.

"Sidney, it feels like we haven't seen you around in so long." Maggie smiled gently beneath her sunglasses.

"Yeah," Sidney mumbled. "Work has been crazy. How about you, Maggie?"

"Oh, so busy. I've been working really hard potty training Brextyn. It's like a full time job."

Kate laughed and nodded in affirmation. Sidney forced her lips awkwardly up and turned back to the game. After the next batter launched a line drive past the shortstop, Cameron ran hard around third base. The outfielder fumbled the ball, and the base coach urged Cameron around toward home plate. Sidney launched back onto her feet, hopping on the metal plank beneath her. Cameron dove toward the catcher and emerged from the cloud of dust, beaming as the referee called him safe. Sidney cupped her hands around her mouth and cheered at the top of her lungs.

"Way to go, Cam!" Kate shouted, as they sat back down on the bleacher. "Oh, his hard work is really showing, Sidney. Aiden must practice with him all the time."

Sidney's skin contracted, tugging the hairs along her neck to attention. She bit at the inside of her cheek until the pain signal distracted her, making sure to grin pleasantly as she did so. Her phone trembled against her thigh, neglected. With her son off the field, she capitalized on the opportunity and brought it to her face.

Oliver: Thinking of you this morning.

Below the message, a closeup of an erect bulge in his shorts loomed. Sidney near choked on a gasp, half giggling as she pressed the phone screen into her chest before Kate could steal a phallic glimpse. Her cheeks flushed with a light heat, deeper than the sun toasting her. She composed herself before lifting the phone again, angled away from the other moms.

Sidney: The mom army nearly got an eyeful of all that.
Oliver: Well, it's just for you.
    Where are you?
Sidney: Baseball game
Oliver: Now, you owe me one.
Sidney: You'll have to wait until I have less witnesses.
Oliver: Tease.
Sidney: You like it.

Oliver responded with another picture of himself, no shorts impeding her view. Sidney laughed to herself and escaped the conversation thread.

Adam: How's Saturday?
Sidney: My kid is kicking ass at baseball.

And I'm stuck in the cheap seats with moms talking about potty training and my ex pretending I don't exist.
Adam: Well, that's 50% good.
Sidney: I'll take what I can get.
Adam: You deserve more than 50%.
Sidney: You just don't know me well enough.

Sidney exited the conversation before Adam could reply.

"Oh, Sidney!" Maggie said, out of nowhere. "I spent some time on your website this week."

Internally, Sidney flinched. Her fingertips flexed against her phone case, and she held her breath in anticipation of yet another round of questions and criticisms.

"Thanks, Maggie." Sidney released the phone to her lap. "What did you think?"

"You are into some dark stuff." Maggie's voice dropped a bit. "But it's all very well researched and interesting. I read several articles while Brextyn was down for his 1:15 nap."

"And all those pictures," Kate chimed in.

"Yes!" Maggie clapped her hands. "The bathtub ones specifically. Sidney, you look amazing! How do you do it? I can barely get time to brush my hair in the morning."

By not having enough money to buy food, Sidney thought to herself.

"Um, I do a lot of yoga with the photographer," Sidney mumbled.

"Well, keep it up. It's working. You look great," Maggie repeated.

Sidney smiled back thinly and nodded.

"Oh, there's my little pumpkin butt," Kate said, gesturing to the field. The women returned their focus to the baseball diamond.

Once the attention abandoned Sidney, she snatched up her phone. She wanted to talk to anyone but the baseball moms surrounding her.

Allison: I watched *Final Destination* again today. That was such a fun live tweet! Plus, I was so happy to talk to you.
You don't mind me messaging you, do you?
Sidney: Of course not. I'm glad you enjoyed it.
Allison: Can I ask you another question? Do you mind?
Sidney: Shoot.
Allison: What movie made you fall in love with horror?
Sidney: *Scream* lol

Sidney smiled at the memory of her first horror love and switched conversation threads.

Max: I want to see what your insides look like.
Sidney: I'm not sure if that's sexual or serial killer.
Max: Can't it be both?
In either case, I'm kidding.
Maybe.
Good morning.

"So, what's the next photo shoot?" Kate asked between plays. "I'm assuming there's a next one."

"We haven't decided yet," Sidney said, keeping the bloody coyote ugly concept safely tucked in her brain. "I usually come up with an article idea. Then we base the shoot off that concept. I haven't come up with my next article since I've been working on launching my blog."

"What's the difference between a website and a blog?" Maggie said.

"Websites are meant to be more static, kind of like reference material. Blogs are a more fluid flow of content that has comments, categories, and subscriptions. With how many articles I have been adding to the website, it only makes sense to just branch a blog off of it," Sidney said.

"Don't you work at a cell store?" Kate asked.

"Manage. Yes." Sidney answered automatically, before remembering the details were none of their business. Internally, she flinched at how her answer must have sounded.

"Girl, you're in the wrong business," Maggie said.

"That's why I'm trying to get out of it."

"Well, if bloody bathtub pictures get you there." Kate lifted her water bottle, as if to salute the idea. Sidney felt her skin crawl in prickles again.

After the final inning, the moms congratulated each other on their sons' win and diverged from the bleachers. Sidney took a deep breath, shoving her phone and her hands into her pockets as she turned to meet Cameron outside of the dugout. Where Aiden was waiting.

"Hey, Aiden," Sidney said, as she approached him. "Cameron did great today!"

"Sidney," Aiden replied, curt. He kept his shoulders

turned to the gap in the fence where Cameron would emerge.

"Look, Aiden, I know you hate me. And maybe you should. But we have to get along around Cameron. He can read all this between us."

"How can I not be embarrassed to be seen with you? All these parents looking at your naked pictures on the internet." Aiden kept his eyes behind his sunglasses and turned toward the field.

"Are you fucking kidding me, Aiden?" Sidney managed to spit the question out through her bewilderment.

"No, Sidney." He chewed on her name before he dropped it from between his teeth. "No, I'm not fucking kidding you."

"And why do you suddenly give any kind of shit, Aiden? You used to help with these shoots, remember? You never cared then." Sidney's anger writhed through her veins, making sweat swell along her hairline.

Aiden stood silent for an infuriating moment. He hooked his thumbs through his beltloops and tugged on them. Sidney caught sight of Cameron moving towards them, still smiling broad and proud.

"Aiden?" Sidney insisted.

"Back then, everyone didn't know you were fucking someone else."

He did not wait for her reply. He left her in the wake of his words, slapped a grin on his face, and hurried over to hug his son. Sidney hesitated a moment, chewing back the sobs welling in her throat, blinking back the angry tears threatening in her eyes. She shook her head hard then hurried across the field to congratulate her son, awkward with Aiden beside her.

Adam: If it helps at all, I think you're amazing.

***

As the evening absorbed the day, the chatter of the Divorced Wives Club filled Sidney and Kendra's home. Sidney attempted to gulp her wine subtly. She tried to hold the line of Adam's chat in her mind.

If it helps at all, I think you're amazing.

Yet all she kept hearing was Aiden.

How could I not be embarrassed to be seen with you?

Everyone didn't know you were fucking someone else.

His words twisted around her brain until she felt the weight on her chest. That same dreadful, crushing weight she felt when she woke up in a foreign bed. That same choking tension she had gagged on while her marriage collapsed. Even with chatter and giggles engulfing her, she only heard Aiden's vile tone echoing through her bones.

"Sid, you OK in there?"

Kendra reached across the table and cradled Sidney's forearm in her hand. Sidney startled involuntarily and attempted to shield it with a smile. When she looked directly into Kendra's bright eyes, Aiden's voice resonated a little quieter in her.

"There are no sad faces at Divorced Wives Club," Kendra continued, giving Sidney's arm a squeeze and raising her wine glass.

Sidney brought herself back to the room around her. Kendra's wide and intent eyes came into focus first, but Amy and Carla stared at her too as they all sat around the kitchen table. Amy slouched back in her chair, dangling a wine glass in one hand as the other meandered through the short, spiky hair on her head. An entire monochromatic palette clung to her body in form-fitting layers, all shades of black and gray to match the silver color beginning to invade her dark hair. Carla leaned forward with her elbows tucked awkwardly against her sides. Her jeans had stopped fitting after her divorce, and she pressed her arms into the overflow of flesh pinched by the pants. Her breasts were stacked precariously close to her drooping chin, but she forced a smile through the layers of makeup she applied even to sit in this house.

"Um, I'm pretty sure Divorced Wives Club is founded on sad faces." Sidney squinted at Kendra. "I'm pretty sure every divorced wife here has completely fallen apart and cried her eyes out at Divorced Wives Club. That is where we started."

"Well, that is not where we are now," Amy said, sitting up and raising her glass to clink against Kendra's. Her thin arm spiraled out from the gray shirt cleaving to her.

"No more tears over stupid men or stupid decisions." Carla brought her glass to the collective, smiling hard enough to crease her makeup.

"Oh, you bitches," Sidney laughed. She rolled her eyes and saluted the group, relieved for an excuse to drink deeply.

Sidney placed her glass down on the table, nervously shifting her hands between her discarded silverware, spinning her empty plate on the table in front of her, trying to keep the sound of her ex out of her ears. The three women stopped, wine glasses still suspended from their fingertips, and watched her expectantly.

"Well," Kendra said, "spill. What's going on?"

Sidney whimpered pathetically and practically thrust the lip of the wine glass past her teeth. Her muscles tensed against the anxiety, against making the pain real with words. Six eyes just stared at her, blinking over the warm haze of two bottles of wine. Amy returned to relaxing coolly in the chair, yet her stare remained engaged. Carla fidgeted in her seat—uncomfortable in her ill-fitting clothes, in her flesh itself—but never took her attention from Sidney. Kendra simply waited, calm and comfortably perched in her knowledge that Sidney not only needed to spill, she wanted to.

"Ugh, fine," Sidney finally said. "It was Aiden today."

The group took a collective eyeroll punctuated by more pulls from their glasses.

"Cameron had this amazing game today," Sidney continued. "Great hits, great runs. Just awesome. So, Aiden and I are waiting for Cameron after the game. He's a total dick, so I tell him we need to pull our shit together in front of Cameron. Then he just goes off on me about those fucking pictures again."

The synchronized eyeroll ascended into full on groaning and dramatic flopping.

"Girl, he's just jealous," Carla said, subtly tugging at the waistband of her jeans.

"Most people who get cheated on are," Sidney mumbled into her wine glass.

"Most people who get cheated on get cheated on for a reason," Amy commented.

"So, I reminded him how he used to be all about this horror modeling," Sidney continued, "how he used to help me and Brady with the blood."

"What was his response to that?" Kendra asked, tapping a fingernail against her glass.

"He said he was embarrassed to be seen with me. He said back then, everyone didn't know I was fucking someone else." As Sidney paraphrased the verbal assault, she felt the noise roar inside her skull again.

"Look." Kendra's hand returned to Sidney's forearm. "We all know he's just mad about the cheating. He's just coming after you with those pictures because that's your art, part of your heart. Just like he's using it to come after you with Cameron. Your heart."

"Exactly." Amy and Carla both nodded firmly.

"Doesn't make it hurt any less," Sidney murmured, barely hearing herself over the Aiden in her brain.

"Good thing we are here to distract you then," Kendra smiled warmly. "Not like Tony can . . . but distraction nonetheless. And we're going to start by filling that glass!"

"Oh, how is the boy toy?" Amy asked, plunging into the current of the blatant topic change.

"The same," Sidney half-giggled. "Mindless fun."

"I need mindless fun," Carla mused. "Why is it that you have boy toy boyfriends and online boyfriends while we have . . . "

"Exes," Kendra chimed in.

"We have exes," Carla laughed. "Some of us did, in fact, stop fucking ours."

"It's because Sidney posts naked pictures on the internet," Amy said from above her wine glass.

"Hey!" Sidney shouted. "I thought we were supposed to be making me feel better."

"I'm kidding!" Amy pushed Sidney's shoulder playfully. "Mostly. I'm also jealous."

"That's so stupid." Sidney rolled her eyes and wrapped her arms around her body. "Look at me. I'm a fucking disaster. My life is a sad mess."

"We're all a mess," Kendra said. She revitalized Sidney's glass then moved to fill the other three. "I did not plan to have a roommate in my 30s. Or to be sleeping with the man who left me. Yet here we are!"

"Let us live vicariously through your mess, Sid," Amy said. "Tell us all about your online escapades."

"Escapades?" Sidney scoffed. "I don't know about escapades. But sure. It's not like I have secrets out on the internet." She took a deep breath as the drama receded, as she diverted herself into distraction. She sat straighter to deliver her stories. "So, in real life, I have Tony. He's fun because he's young, and he's safe because he's dumb. I would never end up dating him, poor thing. Then, I have my two constants online. Oliver just wants pictures and to talk about sex, but Adam is more 'wifey'. He actually gives a shit about my day and me. Or pretends to. Then, after this bathtub set, I got Max, who admittedly is getting a bit creepy. And my very first female stalker." She paused to let them react before continuing. "Allison seems quite taken with knowing everything about me."

"Wow!" Amy exclaimed, Carla and Kendra laughing along with her.

"And none of this ever freaks you out?" Carla asked. "These people following you online, maybe becoming obsessed with you."

"Not yet, no," Sidney lied. "Sometimes, it's exciting. I guess I'm a bit of a closet exhibitionist."

"There's no closet involved when you're naked and bloody in the bathtub," Amy cackled.

"Sometimes, it's strangely comforting," Sidney continued. "Being able to connect with people in a detached way, in a safe way where you might not get as hurt as you would in person."

"Disconnected connection," Kendra echoed.

"Yeah, something like that." Sidney nodded. "I mean, I know how the internet works. I try to be smart about it. I know that there is no such thing as actual privacy, that privacy settings can be a lie, so I post things knowing they could go to anyone. I don't check in everywhere I go, definitely not to places I go routinely. I don't post pictures of Cameron anywhere associated with my horror work or indicate where he goes to school or plays sports. I tell these people online things but not things that would help them find me."

"Damn, girl," Kendra cut in. "You've thought this out."

"Yoga," Sidney replied, quickly.

"That makes sense," Carla replied. "But you are more out there, more of a target because of your social media presence?"

All six eyes turned to Sidney.

"I guess so, but with everyone online, most people on social media, am I really that much more of a target? No more than I was before the world was online."

"What are all the platforms you're on?" Carla said.

"I don't know, Sid," Amy countered. "People are weird. The internet makes them weirder. Or lets them fully release their weirdness anonymously. You're deliberately posting provocative pictures for attention, as is the right of any woman, but what if you attract the wrong attention? I mean, isn't that the bullshit world we live in?"

"Thank you!" Kendra threw up her hands. "I tell her that shit all the time. Don't I, Sid?"

Sidney released a controlled breath.

"I just have to find the balance between exposure and safety," Sidney said. "Enough to get my website and blog lofted but not too much for things to go *Single White Female*."

"I would feel much better if you'd just cut off the stalkers," Kendra said. "Help me sleep at night."

Sidney smiled at Kendra's words, forcing a playful and polite nod, yet her hand itched to respond to those stalkers. The thought of ignoring them, of leaving the conversation threads unanswered, caused the loneliness that lived at the pit of her stomach to spread and blossom, reaching its dark arms up into her chest—even as the women she knew and considered her closest friends continued to chatter right beside her.

"**OK, JORDAN,**" Brady said, leaning toward his husband with a sly smile creeping across his face. "We need the blood to look like 'oops, I killed my one night stand' and not 'my maxi pad overflowed'."

"How am I supposed to know what a maxi pad blowout looks like?" Jordan asked. He planted his feet squarely and crossed his arms over his chest.

"Sid?"

The two men whirled around to Sidney, standing in the bright sunlight of their loft apartment. Sidney startled at their attention, still holding the spa robe wrapped around her naked body. Brady moved in wild and sweeping gestures while Jordan followed him in methodical and measured steps, gently guiding Brady back to focus.

"Well, this got awkward," she giggled.

"Educate us on wayward blood flow," Brady said, brandishing his camera over the bed.

Sidney laughed again and stepped forward to join them.

"OK," she started. "Well, obviously all that blood would originate low. So maybe keep ours up more around the pillows. And lots of splatter."

"Not too much splatter," Brady snapped. "This is our beautiful home."

"But it all washes out," Sidney mocked. "Maybe just bloody up his side of the bed. Then, on me, all blood needs to stay north of the equator. Also, mostly on the front side."

"And, Jordan, honey, I'm actually going to have you lay on the floor and flop your hand up on the bed, so there can't be any confusion that there is another body in play."

"Oh! I get to be a blood assistant and a victim," Jordan said, rolling his eyes.

Brady and Jordan exchanged playful, bratty expressions, which terminated in Brady looking Jordan over as if he were food.

"Please, pour some blood on this bed to keep you guys from screwing before we do this," Sidney joked.

"What, Sid, you don't want to watch?" Jordan asked.

"Exhibitionist. Not voyeur." She smiled.

"Don't worry, Sid," Brady said, taking test shots around the bed. "You'll be naked soon enough."

Brady continued to orbit the bed, contorting himself to seek out the perfect light and the best angles. Jordan stepped forward hesitantly. He stirred the spoon through the blood then raised it timidly before plunging it back into the crimson liquid.

"You can't really fuck up blood spatter, love," Brady said from behind his lens.

Jordan smiled to himself then lifted the spoon over the sheets to let it drizzle slowly into a puddle on the white fabric. "You're sure this washes out?" Jordan lifted his second spoonful.

"Every time so far," Brady replied between shutters.

"Why do you have white sheets anyway?" Sidney asked.

"Girl, I bought these for the shoot. Then Jordan here got all infatuated with how 'clean' they look," Brady laughed.

Jordan's posture went rigid as he resumed bloodying the scene, becoming more comfortable and confident with each stroke. He applied a spatter then stepped back to evaluate the addition, briefly pressing his hand against his chin and squinting his eyes. Then he stepped forward to adjust the scene. The stark liquid practically vibrated in color contrast on the sheets. The splattered droplets dripped and soaked in, permeating the fabric in terrible patterns. Jordan retreated to assess his work once more then moved forward to smear his hand through the puddle and off the edge of the bed.

"Like I was groping at the edge of the bed," Jordan explained, his smile widening in an echo of pride.

"Babe, that's perfect!" Brady moved in to kiss him. "All right, honey, your turn." He turned to Sidney.

Sidney dropped the robe out of frame and let Jordan splash and smudge the fake blood over her face, chest, and arms. Then she tangled herself in the sheets. Before she could even finish properly censoring herself with the top sheet, Brady started clicking away.

"So, the blog is live," Brady said, leaning in close enough for her to see her own eyes wide in the reflection of the lens. "Bring your fingers to the corner of your mouth. Yeah, just like that."

"It is," Sidney answered, frozen in the pose.

"How did that go? Tilt your head down. Yeah, make your eyes look a little more menacing."

"Really well, actually. I saw an uptick in traffic for a couple weeks, got some solid responses in comments to start. Before it plateaued off like it always does."

"Oh, honey, that's fantastic. Making progress."

"Thanks a lot to your pictures, I think." Sidney made an effort to look into Brady's eye through the camera.

"I do what I can, honey." Brady moved the camera aside to give her a wink. "Jordan, baby, I need you to limp wrist it a little. I want you to look dead, just kind of flopped up there. So, what's next? Aside from these already creepy and sexy bloody coyote ugly pictures."

"Telluride."

"The horror film festival?" Jordan chimed in from the floor.

"My favorite one," Sidney mused. "It's small enough that the people are friendly and humble. Telluride is gorgeous, especially in the fall. You should come with us one year."

Sidney peeped over the edge of the bed to see Jordan wrinkle his nose.

"OK, Brady," Sidney corrected, "you should come with us. You could offer horror mini sessions or try and sell some of our prints."

"I do like the sound of that," Brady said. "You going with Wes?"

"Yes, as always."

"That boy come out yet?"

"Wes is not gay."

"If you say so, honey. At least you have nothing to worry about with him, alone in a condo after a horror movie."

"That's because he's married."

"Or it's because he likes dick." Brady laughed at himself. "OK, I want you to get on your stomach, pinup style. To keep your ass away from the blood, let's put your chest there. Baby, you can get up now. You did great."

Sidney peeled herself from one location in the sheets and stuck herself down in the next.

"Yes, OK, perfect," Brady continued. "Now, prop your chin up on your bloody hands and cross your ankles. You know the pose I'm talking about? I want to get a hint of ass in there. Right there! Now, make it creepy."

Sidney seized her muscles to maintain Brady's exact positioning. She let the blood smear against her cheeks from her slickened hands. She closed her eyes briefly, letting all expression fall heavily from her face. Then she snapped her eyes open, intense and sharp. She stared into Brady's lens until her vision wobbled in focus.

"Shit, she is so creepy," Jordan whispered over Brady's shoulder.

"Isn't she though?" Brady admired. "She's got those creepy eyes down. OK, now on your back. Hang your head and your hair where Jordan's hand was and pull the sheet over the business."

Sidney ripped her skin away from the fabric.

"I'm starting to stick here," she said.

"Don't worry, honey, we're almost done."

Brady hunched down and shot up from the floor level, where Jordan had crouched. Then he pulled a step stool over and shifted the view to above her, capturing her entire body tangled in the bloodied sheets. After stepping down carefully, he leaned in close, until the lens practically smudged against her nose. The shutter flurried before Brady moved the camera aside to expose his grin.

"Done!" he beamed. "I love them already!"

Sidney separated her skin from the drying fake blood, pulling gently to discourage it from clinging to her flesh. She discarded the modesty sheet then awkwardly shuffled across the mattress.

"There's a towel already in the bathroom for you, Sid," Jordan said, as Brady scrolled through pictures on the camera beside him. "Don't worry about the floors. Hardwood is easy to clean."

Sidney wiped her hands thoroughly on the top sheet then padded stickily across the floorboards. The fake blood on her feet stuck to the hardwood, and she peeled each tacky footprint from the floor. On her way, she snagged her phone from the top of her bag. After closing the door behind her, she snapped a couple quick, suggestive photos to send off to Oliver and Adam. Then she stepped into the steam and washed the roadmap of blood droplets off her skin.

When Sidney emerged from the bathroom, she had her phone glued to her face, catching up on correspondence and notifications.

Adam: Whoa!
Only you could look that good bloody.
Sidney: I don't think that's true. Plenty of women look amazing bloody.
You're just saying that because I'm naked haha.

Oliver: Come over and let me wash your back. I
 think you missed a spot.
Sidney: I'm already clean. Thank you.
Oliver: Then let me make you dirty again.
Sidney: I just did a photo shoot about killing a
 guy after I slept with him.
Oliver: I'm willing to take that risk.

"You talking to your boy toy?" Brady asked.

"Not right now." Sidney blushed as she looked up from her phone. Then she kept swiping over the screen.

"She's blushing," Jordan pointed out.

"Must be the online boyfriends," Brady said.

"Online boyfriends? Plural?" Jordan asked. "I'm impressed."

"I told you what she was into," Brady replied.

"Wait, what?" Sidney lowered the phone.

"Yeah, but I didn't know she was juggling multiple dudes on the internet," Jordan said.

"He asks for my rejected dick picks," Sidney confessed.

"Traitor!" Brady gaped.

"Shit, as if I wouldn't know that," Jordan laughed and pecked Brady on the cheek. "So, Sid, you're living in Cougartown then also harvesting admirers off the internet?"

"When you say it like that, I sound fucking ridiculous." Sidney's cheeks grew even warmer.

"Or amazing," Brady contradicted. "It's all perspective, honey."

"And we think you're amazing," Jordan agreed. "Did you see yourself rolling around all sexy in that blood? No wonder they're banging down your inbox."

"I don't know. Sometimes, I think—" Sidney let the words fade out of her mouth as the pictures she had just sent flashed over her brain.

"Don't be shy now, honey," Brady said, motioning for them to sit on the couch. "We both just stared at you naked for over an hour."

"I did not stare." Jordan raised his hand.

"Well, I know what I'm doing with Tony. I know I'll never care and never get hurt."

"That's what toys are for," Brady nodded.

"The rest—I think, sometimes, that they all might be a game. A way to feel better about myself, a way to boost my self-esteem. Maybe like the pictures and the comments. Maybe people are right. Maybe I'm just posting and chatting as bait for compliments and interest because I'm insecure. Damaged from Aiden," Sidney lowered her head. Her phone continued to seize in vibrations in her hand.

"Whoa, Sid," Brady replied. "I didn't expect you to go all heavy psychoanalytical and shit."

"Sorry." Sidney forced a smile.

"Do you actually connect with these people online?" Jordan said.

"A couple of them, yes. We've been talking long enough that it would have to be a really elaborate lie now. I can tell them things without risk of ever having to see their reaction. The rest are more like conversations to fill the quiet."

"It sounds like you know what you're doing," Jordan responded.

"Do what makes you happy," Brady said. "Post your pictures. Have your boyfriends. Everyone else is too busy being miserable in their lives."

"Does it make me a horrible person that it makes me feel better?" Sidney's smile was genuine now.

"Well," Jordan said, "it does make you one of us, so maybe?"

Sidney lingered in the conversation a little longer, steadily monitoring the constant notifications vibrating from her phone. Then she finally collected herself to head home.

"Well, gentlemen, it has been a wonderful, bloody, soul-baring day, but I need to get out of here and prep for the party. I'll see you tonight?" Sidney hugged them both tightly.

"The blog launch celebration? Of course, we'll be there!" Brady assured. "Just make sure to have the drinks ready above all."

Sidney hurried down the stairs from Brady's apartment and out onto the street. She found her car and tossed her armload onto the passenger seat. She pulled the car door shut behind her and tugged out her phone again before turning the ignition. She found a flurry of notifications from a new name: Jack. Jack liked most of her Facebook profile pictures and had begun following her on Instagram and Twitter.

This picture is amazing!
I saw this movie three times. In the theater. One of my favorites.
You have the creepiest eyes. Well done!

His comments saturated her notification feeds.

Max: I've still been thinking about your insides.

Sidney flinched at the message, feeling her guts tighten. She went to type a response then backed out of the conversation. The thought of replying made her chest heavy, so she simply navigated away.

Allison: I watched *Scream* last night. I can see why it made you love horror. Which is your favorite death?
How did the photo shoot go today? Do you have any behind the scenes pictures?
Any big plans this weekend?

Again, Sidney went to reply but hesitated. Suddenly, it felt like pressure, like a chore. Instead, she sent Adam and Oliver the same message before driving home.

Sidney: Photo shoot was killer! Now, to go celebrate my new blog.

10

"**THANK YOU ALL** for coming." Sidney's voice quivered slightly as all eyes found her.

Her heart pounded happily at the sight of all the faces crammed into her home. Friendly smiles turned toward her, yet the attention caused her mind to flicker at the same time. She took a deep breath and licked her lips.

Her eyes darted around her party, flitting between guests. She had to consciously slip a breath into her speech and slow her focus between each attendee. She stood on the edge of the kitchen, facing out into their dining room. Kendra perched on the first chair, both shoulders facing her, back aligned in effortless posture as always. Amy and Carla squeezed in behind her, Carla absorbing all the color between the two as she compulsively tugged down the hem of a too-short red dress and Amy reclined in plain gray.

"We are here tonight to celebrate the launch of my new blog, *Final Girl Screaming*. All of you are my inner circle, my support system. My lovely roommate, Kendra, who puts up with me constantly watching horror movies. Which she hates."

"Yeah, I do!" Kendra chimed in, toasting Sidney with her cocktail glass.

"We have my wine drinking mommas, our Divorced Wives Club, who keep me sane. There are the boys who get me all bloody and take pictures of me."

"I didn't know you were doing toasts, honey," Brady answered. "When do I get a turn?"

Brady and Jordan leaned against the wall, Brady standing forward and shifting his weight to one side as he spoke. Jordan casually crossed his arms over his chest, smirking at Brady's words. At the far end of the table, directly across from Sidney, Tony sat quietly, nursing a beer bottle and watching her speak.

"Hush, you," Sidney giggled. "This is my party. Anyway, you all know who you are and why you're here. I just wanted to say thank you for all the times you've helped me or put up with my bullshit. I wanted to keep this party relatively small, but to celebrate, we are going to play a murder mystery game."

"Spoiler alert! Sidney's the killer," Amy shouted. Polite laughter rippled through the room.

"So sorry, cheater," Sidney laughed, "as the host of the party, I am the one person who cannot be the killer."

"This game is obviously rigged," Brady chuckled, leaning towards Jordan but speaking for everyone.

"For the purposes of tonight," Sidney continued, "I am your victim." She reached into the box sitting on the table in front of her and brought the card in front of her face. "The victim." She stopped, looked around the room at her guests, and pointed at her own chest with a smile. "The victim, Sidney, was discovered in her kitchen during a dinner party. One or more of her party guests killed her during the festivities. Her body was discovered in the kitchen. The cause of death was strangulation."

Sidney pulled a braided cord, alternating in red and golden strands, from behind her back and stretched it out long between her hands, displaying it for her audience.

"The murder weapon," she continued. "Each of you has a character card. One or more of you is the killer. If you are a killer, your goal is to avoid detection. If you are not a killer, your goal is to discover who the killer is by interacting with and questioning your fellow party guests. From this moment on, you are all in character. Good luck!"

"Are we allowed to lie?" Brady asked, his hand shooting up like a schoolboy.

"Of course you would ask that," Jordan said beside him.

"Deception is encouraged," Sidney answered. "However, it can't be too convincing. We don't want this game to go on forever. And I'm holding dessert ransom until you guys find the killer."

"Oh, this sounds so fun," Carla murmured. "Sid, did you write this game?"

"She can't answer you. She's dead now," Amy laughed, bumping Carla's shoulder and trying to peer at her character card.

Sidney stifled a laugh and shook her head no. She dropped the script card back in the box and sat back to observe her party unfold. Kendra gathered her wine glass and stepped back from the group, reading over her card and surveying the actions of the others as she sipped calmly. Jordan immediately divorced himself from Brady's side to indulge his competitive nature. Carla continued to nudge Amy's back as she attempted to read Amy's card sloppily.

Against her better judgement, Sidney had included Tony to fill the player cards and have the six required suspects. She peered at him from the corner of her eye, careful to not let him catch her. He looked dumbly between his card and the other guests, eyebrows knitted on his forehead. A strange blend of irritation and pity flitted through her.

Sidney shook her head and laughed to herself. It felt good to be the watcher for once.

"Hello, my name is Doctor Monroe," Jordan said, walking up to Kendra. "I tried to resuscitate the victim before declaring her dead. Obviously, that means I did not kill her."

"Except you would know exactly how long to strangle someone to kill them," Kendra countered, sipping her wine from the side of her mouth.

"A doctor would have chosen a better method. Who are you?"

"Amanda Hugginkiss," Kendra stumbled over a giggle in the syllables. "I'm the victim's nosy neighbor. I see everything she does, everyone who comes to this house. She was quite the little hussy." Kendra stopped to shoot Sidney a sneer. "I saw her go into the kitchen with that other floozie over there." Kendra threw a finger in Brady's direction, her grin spreading.

Jordan popped a hip toward Kendra. They shared a chuckle. Then he sauntered over to Brady. Brady had stolen a cardigan from Sidney's coat rack and brandished it as a shawl. He tossed his head back and forth dramatically, fanning his fingertips toward his face.

"Hello, my name is Doctor Monroe," Jordan started.

"A doctor!" Brady squealed, tossing his hands up. "Oh, thank the lord! I have been positively having heart palpitations with all this drama. And the tragedy. Oh, the tra-ge-dy!"

"Um, calm down, ma'am?" Jordan choked on the words through his own laughter.

"Yes, ma'am!" Brady shrieked. "I am Madame Delphine. I am the victim's wealthy, southern aunt."

"Of course you are." Jordan caught himself. "Well, Madame, please tell me what happened. Were you in the kitchen with the victim?"

"Yes, naturally." Brady grasped one of the cardigan arms and flipped it around his neck like a scarf. "I was instructing her on how to properly serve a dinner party. I couldn't very well allow my own niece to feed her guests dog food like this." Brady gestured grandly at the empty plates littered over the table.

Jordan cupped his hand over his mouth and bent over, gripping his own cheeks tightly. Then he pursed his lips and arched his back with his hands on his hips. The chuckles rippled out of him, gaining volume. His eyes scrunched up behind his cheeks as he laughed harder. "Sid. Sid," he managed between guffaws. "I can't, Sid. I just can't with him. Will you look at him?" He looked over at Brady, who again theatrically adjusted the cardigan. "I can't even look at him! I know who the killer is. I want to make my guess."

"All right, Doctor Monroe," Sidney said, standing. "Make your case."

"It's him," Jordan said, motioning to Brady. "Her!" he instantly corrected. "It's Aunt Madame Delphine."

Brady gasped wildly and clutched his hand to his chest. "State your proof, sir!" Brady demanded.

"Well, aside from the fact that it is always the crazy, old, southern aunt, Brady's lying," Jordan answered. "I can always tell when he's lying because he won't make eye contact with me when he talks. And this bitch has been whipping her hair back and forth since I walked over here. Hasn't looked at me once."

"That's not evidence!" Brady argued.

"He has made a claim," Sidney said. "You have to tell us if you're the killer."

"Fuck!" Brady threw the cardigan to the floor then regained his gentile, southern composure. "Yes, honey. It was me!"

The room burst into a wave of laughter and applause. Sidney raised her glass high, and her guests imitated as they all saluted the end of the game. Brady lifted an arm high above his head and twirled dramatically for his audience.

"That might be the shortest murder mystery game ever," Sidney concluded. "Next time, Jordan doesn't get to interrogate Brady."

"I can't get away with shit with this one," Brady said.

"Honey, that's exactly what you need," Kendra replied.

Sidney moved around the room, collecting cards and congratulations, chattering with her closest friends. Tony watched her move through the room, patient on the couch, nursing his beer. The drinks flowed until voices boomed higher and eyelids drooped lower. Finally, a parade of Ubers began revolving outside the house, and the party dwindled down to Sidney, Kendra, and Tony.

Before the door had completely closed behind the

last of the departing guests, Sidney felt Tony's hands creep around her waist. He drew her into him, gathering her into his arms. By the time his chin nestled against her neck, Kendra had awkwardly taken notice.

"Whew!" she said, stretching unnaturally. "I am going to have such a hangover tomorrow. I should get to bed so I get some sleep before Savannah gets back tomorrow."

"Goodnight," Sidney managed to call before Tony's mouth swallowed hers.

***

In the blistering morning sun, Sidney stood on Aiden's porch where she, Cameron, and Aiden used to place their carved jack o'lanterns every Halloween, where she used to take Cameron's picture in his costume before they set out trick-or-treating down the street. Her sunglasses were not dark enough. The light blared in on her eyes from all sides, radiating back into her skull, rattling her brain where it rested dehydrated against her forehead. She still felt Tony all over her skin, and somehow, that made standing on Aiden's porch more uncomfortable.

"Mommy!" Cameron's voice came from behind the screen door. It shattered the ominous weight that had bloomed over her.

Sidney smiled broadly, even though it hurt her head, as Cameron pressed the door ajar for her. Her heart seized a bit as she crossed the threshold but unfurled again when her baby jumped into her arms.

"I missed you," Cameron said, in a perfect voice.

"I missed you too, baby."

Aiden's footsteps came scraping down the hallway

114

behind them. Sidney clutched Cameron's shoulders for another second then stood to face Aiden.

"How was your party?" Aiden mumbled, walking past her.

"Good."

"Must have been. You're late."

"You said 9."

"It's 9:10."

Sidney pursed her lips to prevent her response. She breathed through a tight and thin mouth.

"Thanks for keeping him the extra night, Aiden," Sidney said, curtly. "I really appreciate it."

"I'll always take extra time with my son." Aiden finally shot a fierce gaze into Sidney's eyes, so sharp she could have used her sunglasses again.

"Speaking of, can we talk about the Telluride schedule?"

"You taking off on your son again? Sure." Aiden squared his posture and crossed his arms.

"Aiden!" Sidney whispered harshly, looking down at Cameron.

"When do you leave?" he said, unfazed.

"Thursday during the day."

"So, I pick him up from practice Thursday and handle Friday. Then I have my normal weekend."

"And drop him at school Monday too," Sidney reminded.

"Easy. I'll handle it." Aiden moved to walk back down the hall.

"I'll get you a list of everything he needs for those days."

"I said, I'll handle it."

Sidney opened her mouth to reply but found no useful words on her tongue. Aiden stood, staring at her, daring her response. At her silence, he gave a small scoff and moved toward Cameron. He kissed him on the forehead and tousled his hair before disappearing back down the hall. Cameron snatched up his bags and followed Sidney to the car, turning to wave back at his dad.

Before starting the engine, Sidney checked her phone.

Adam: How was the party, beautiful?
Sidney: Great! We had a lot of fun.
    The murder mystery was a success. Over fast though.
Adam: I'm so glad it went well.
    How do you feel? I mean, for a dead woman lol
Sidney: Hungover hehe. So partially dead.

Sidney swiped from Adam's words to Oliver's.

Oliver: Show me your hangover.
Sidney: Who says I'm hungover?
Oliver: Are you?
Sidney: Yes lol
Oliver: Show me.
Sidney: It looks ROUGH.
Oliver: I don't care.

Sidney slyly lifted her phone, attempting to subtly capture a selfie.

"Mom, what are you doing?" Cameron barked from the backseat, shattering the illusion of her escape. "Can we go now?"

"Nothing," Sidney replied, sending the picture and dropping the phone.

As soon as Cameron dumped his bag inside the front door, he sprinted into the house.

"Savannah! Savannah! I'm home," he called as he disappeared into the house.

Sidney heard the mumbled voices as Savannah and Kendra greeted Cameron. Then Cameron and Savannah's footsteps began moving excitedly over the floor. Sidney cradled her head and dropped to the couch, gathering up her phone again. She knew Kendra would be down to chat momentarily, after the childish excitement died down and she had changed into something baggy and comfortable. For now, she took the moment alone, not at work, not on Aiden's porch.

Max: Are you ignoring me?

The message made Sidney's head pound a little harder as her heart quickened in her chest. She stared at the words for a moment, unsure how to proceed.

Max: Did I freak you out with the insides thing?
    I was only kidding.
    I know you like *Scream* from your articles.

Sidney took a deep breath and brought her fingers to the touchscreen.

Sidney: No, not at all.
    Just really busy here.
    How are you?

Max: Oh good. Glad you're still there.
　　If I lost you, I would have to come find you.
　　Kidding again!

Sidney threw some half-hearted emojis into the conversation and backed out of the thread. She felt that tightness return to the back of her throat, that subtle nagging pressure on her chest. She responded out of habit and felt regret trailing her messages.

Allison: Your blog is amazing! I love it so much!
　　I didn't know how it could be different from your website, like what it would really add. But it worked!
Sidney: Thanks, Allison! That's very sweet of you.
Allison: What are friends for?

"Oh, we're friends now?" Sidney murmured to herself. "OK, girl. We can be buddies."

Sidney parsed her notifications from all her social media platforms when a new message popped up on Twitter.

Jack: Hi Sidney. I don't know if you answer direct messages.
　　I just wanted to say that your work is amazing.
　　The website and the pictures.

"Well, hello Jack," Sidney said, again to herself. "Phone is just blowing up today."

Sidney: Hi Jack! Thank you! I really appreciate the compliment.
Jack: Whoa! You actually answered.
Sidney: Hehe. Yes.
Jack: I really love your website. I've read all of your articles.
Sidney: Thank you.
Jack: And the pictures you post. They are so sexy and creepy.
Sidney: Thank you again.

Sidney took another breath on the couch to bask in the hum of the compliments. The sweet words were hollow and shallow, but they felt smooth rippling over her mind. Pleasant instead of jagged and cutting. She would take that sensation where she could get it, even if it was in the glow of her phone screen.

11

I THINK THE only reason you bring me to this thing is so that I can drive while you play on your phone," Wes said from the driver's seat, the jagged mountain edge of the Colorado scenery sliding across the car windows.

"I'm not playing. I'm working," Sidney replied, her eyes still glued to her phone.

Wes shot her a glance from behind his sunglasses.

"Fine," Sidney agreed. "I'm mostly working. Playing a little bit."

"Have to keep those stalkers engaged."

"Stalkers and readers. You know these festivals are a huge bump for me."

"Oh, I know." Wes snaked a piece of licorice out of the bag and snapped it between his teeth. "I would be tweeting too. If I wasn't, you know, driving you."

"Driving us," Sidney giggled. She momentarily set her phone down on her lap. "Damn, I'm so excited. Telluride Horror Show is my favorite horror fest."

"Mine too. Not that I've been to as many as you."

Wes smiled as he stared out the windshield. Anticipation vibrated between them and filled the cab of the car. Sidney allowed her eyes to wander out the window. The trees climbing the hills around them had already surrendered to fall, igniting bright gold in the crisp sunlight. The hours stretched out ahead of them as the road wound between the rolling hills of yellow aspens that climbed up to mountains.

She lifted her phone to the window and snapped a quick picture of the fall trees blurring by, then flipped the camera to capture a selfie with Wes driving.

@FinalGirlScreams: Headed to the #TellurideHorrorShow with @L1v1ngDead1te! Mere hours away from all the #horror we can take! #roadtrip #horroraddicts #filmfestival

She added the photos to the tweet then uploaded the pictures with similar sentiments on Instagram and Facebook, making sure to tag Wes and the horror show properly.

Adam: So I have a surprise for you.
I wasn't going to say anything, but then I thought it might be creepy if I didn't.

Sidney's heart quickened in her chest at Adam's messages.

Sidney: Well, tell me! What is it??
Adam: I'm coming to the horror show.

Sidney held her phone in shock. She felt her mouth fall open yet continued to stare at the message. She was not sure how she felt until she started typing.

Sidney: Telluride? Really?!
Adam: Yeah. I'm at the airport now. I'll get in
     late tonight.

"Holy shit," Sidney breathed out loud before she could type her reaction.

"What?" Wes said, gnawing on another stem of licorice.

"Adam is coming to Telluride."

"Adam, like, your longtime Insta stalker?" Wes stopped chewing and shot Sidney another look from the edge of his eye.

"Facebook," she corrected.

"Whatever."

"Adam's not a stalker. We're legitimately friends now. We've been talking for years."

"Online," Wes corrected, sitting up straighter. "You've never seen him in real life. Have you ever even talked to him on the phone?"

"Not really. We've exchanged videos a couple times."

"And you don't find this creepy?" Wes's eyebrows crept up from behind his sunglasses, rolling hills reflecting off the lenses.

"Wesley, you need to calm down."

"Don't pull *Wesley* on me."

"This is a film festival. He's not showing up at my front door. This is a public event with a lot of people. It's a horror show; he loves horror. He's talked about coming for years."

"Oh, Sid, you poor naïve girl. He's coming to see you."

Sidney blushed reluctantly. "Maybe that too."

"Does he want to sleep with you? Like, is that the kind of online thing you have going?" Wes wrinkled his nose.

"Possibly." Sidney shifted in her seat, drawing her legs up onto the dashboard. "There is definitely flirtation in our relationship. Attraction. But he talks to me about my day, cares about how I feel about things. So maybe just friendship."

"Do you want to sleep with him?"

"Possibly." Sidney laughed as she repeated herself. "I don't think I could decide without meeting someone in person."

"So, the sock on the door thing is actually going to happen?" Wes snatched up another licorice stick. "College style? You'll hang a sock on the door if you guys are humping in our condo? No! It's a horror festival, so obviously, you need to hang a sock with a foot in it on the door."

Sidney burst into laughter at the visual that flashed up at his words. She covered her mouth and nose with both hands. "You are getting way ahead of me here. Right now, I'm not humping anyone."

"Oh, this is going to be so awkward for me. The third wheel at the horror show." Wes shook his head sadly, but a smile teased his lips.

"Or you'll love hanging out with Adam, and he will be a fantastic addition to our little horror crew."

"He can hold your bags while I drive you around."

"Hey now!" Sidney snapped, chuckling again.

Sidney: Holy shit!
That's amazing. We're finally going to meet.

Adam: Yep. In the flesh.
Sidney: Message me when you get in so we can
    meet up.

The slight fluttering in Sidney's chest pressed harder against her ribcage, ascended to full-on flapping. She felt the smile taking over her entire face. Suddenly, the car felt too small and the ride too long. Excitement crawled along her skin, twitched along her nerves in a rhythm nearly forgotten.

Max: So you're headed to the horror show?
Sidney: On the way now.
Max: A whole weekend of horror movies?
Sidney: Yep. We managed 12 last year.
Max: That's impressive in 3 days!
    I bet the shows run late.
    Are you walking around the mountains alone
    in the dark?
Sidney: In town. And not alone. But the walks
    home are definitely creepy.
Max: I would love to catch you alone on one of
    those walks.
    Drag you off into the bushes.
    Then we could have some real fun.

"Fuck," Sidney breathed. Her palpitating anticipation dropped like a weight into the pit of her stomach.

"Oh no," Wes responded. "What now? Another online boyfriend showing up in Telluride?"

"No. One of my stalkers is getting creepy." Sidney reached down into the bag and pulled up a piece of licorice, nibbling on it nervously.

"Just one?" Wes waited for her to respond, but Sidney just stared at him. "Creepy how?" he finally said, his tone leveled.

"He's just gotten really weird. First, he was talking about seeing what my insides look like. You know, quoting *Scream*. Then, he just said he wanted to catch me walking alone at Telluride and drag me into the bushes to have some fun."

"Sidney!" Wes's voiced boomed against the glass.

"What? I can't tell if he's kidding or not."

"About rape and/or murder? Block him."

"That seems excessive," Sidney started.

"No, Sid. Block him. Stop answering his messages and block him. That is nothing but red flags," Wes said, firmly.

"I've never blocked a friend before," Sidney replied quietly.

"Seriously? What do you mean by 'friend'?"

"Someone I actually talk to in private messages, have an online friendship or whatever with."

"Well, this is the perfect time to start. Do it." Wes turned and glanced down at her phone before returning his eyes to the road. "Do it right now."

Sidney glared over at Wes like a scolded child, yet she still lifted her phone. Opening the conversation with Max, she found the block option and pressed her fingertip against it. The application confirmed that Max would no longer be able to send her messages or see her activity.

"There. Fine," Sidney said.

Wes relaxed beside her, sinking back into the seat. A mixture of pressure and relief alternated over Sidney's thoughts. She felt the trailing edges of the unnerving anxiety conjured by Max's messages, but he was blocked now. The problem had been closed by the tap of her finger.

Sidney rolled her eyes back out the window, watching the scenery continue to whip by. She pressed her fingertips into the edge of her phone case, flexing against the anxiety that crawled under her skin. She shoved the echoes of Max's messages out of her mind, the weird cringe she felt at the thought of blocking him, about what he might think. She turned her mind to the idea of meeting Adam. That thought brought its own fluttering anxiety, but it was pleasant. It unrolled a smile back across her face. She touched at it with her pinkie as she mused.

Oliver: How far to Telluride?
Sidney: Couple more hours. Over halfway there.
Oliver: I wish I was going with you.

Sidney hesitated a moment before typing her response.

Sidney: Me too.

"You know," Wes said as he chomped into another piece of licorice, "if you're going to look at your phone the whole drive, we could at least go over the movie lineup."

"But then I would have to ignore all my stalkers." Sidney smiled out of the corner of her mouth.

"I'm sure they'll be able to survive. I mean, they're going to have to last full hours all weekend while we're in movies. You might go into withdrawals."

"Shut up," Sidney laughed.

She leaned toward her thighs, propping her phone against her knees.

Allison: I can't wait to read all your movie reviews! I hope you have so much fun in Telluride.
Allison: @L1v1ngDead1te looks like a good road partner.
Sidney: He is the perfect horror buddy.
Allison: Are you guys dating?
Sidney: God no. We've been friends forever.
Allison: Are you married?
Sidney: Divorced.
Allison: Seeing anyone?

"Hello, Sidney!" Wes called. "Movies?"

"Right," Sidney replied. "I got distracted."

"Of course you did," he laughed.

Sidney left Allison waiting and switched over to the browser on her phone. She navigated to the festival website and queued up the lineup of films.

Never Hike in the Woods, a fan film honoring the masked franchise killer who stalked a lakeside summer camp. *The Rest Will Come*, a horror-comedy on the terror of online dating. *At the Mercy of the Demon*, a documentary examining sleep paralysis. *The Black Leather Glove*, Giallo in the shadow of Dario Argento. The list was exhaustive, with more compelling options than they would have opportunity to see.

"So, solid movies the entire weekend. Just like last year," Wes summarized.

"Exactly. This is why we go!"

"I'm going to need more licorice." Wes snapped another rope between his teeth.

Sidney slipped back into her messages.

Sidney: Kind of.
Allison: What does that mean?
Sidney: I have a guy I sleep with.
Allison: A fuck buddy????
Sidney: Yeah, I guess so.
Allison: Do you think you'll end up with him?
Sidney: No, that will never happen.
    What about you? Family?
Allison: I'm a single girl right now, but I have my
    eye on someone.
Sidney: Oh yeah?
Allison: Yeah, it's only a matter of time.

The two lane highway wound between the tall walls of rock until the mountains formed a ring around the town ahead of them. Telluride emerged from the trees, hugged by the jagged peaks. Wes navigated through the simple streets and under the huge banner reading *Horror Show*. He parked them in the familiar lot of the condo from the previous year, and they finally stood to stretch their stiffened limbs.

"We made it," Sidney exclaimed, pulling her arms high above her head until the stretch burned down her back.

She felt herself smiling, giddy, and turned to see Wes mirroring the same euphoric expression. Telluride was always their vacation. This horror show was always their escape.

***

Wes set the key cards on the kitchen counter as they walked into the condo.

"This looks exactly the same as our room last year," Wes mumbled. "Flashbacks."

"I imagine we're dealing with a finite number of floor plans," Sidney replied. "Worked great last year."

"Well, I'm taking the same room as last year," Wes said as he gathered his bag and moved across the living area. "Especially if you're going to be bringing your stalkers home with you."

"Hey, no one said that is happening."

"Sure, sure."

Wes disappeared into his room to unpack. Sidney picked up her bag and did the same.

Adam: Layover. Halfway there!

Something quivered in Sidney's chest again as her skin prickled. Her muscles felt anxious, happily twitchy. She tried to brush the smile off her lips with her fingers. She sent Adam a happy dancing gif and slipped her phone into her back pocket, tucking her online life away to be overshadowed by the real life around her.

She heaved her suitcase onto the bed and began extracting the contents. She stacked her brush, jewelry, and other toiletries on the adjoining bathroom counter. She set the suitcase open on the chair perched in the corner. She extracted her outfit for the next day, a screen printed shirt reading "I heart horror" with a bloody anatomical heart in place of the word and a pair of distressed black skinny jeans.

Settled in the condo, Wes and Sidney stepped out

from their unit and across the parking lot into the blazing mountain fall day. A thin, crisp edge played on the air, even through the warmth of the beating sun. The bright light set the yellowing aspen leaves ablaze on their branches as their fallen comrades cracked under Sidney's boots. She took a deep breath that felt only like autumn and Halloween, and nostalgic bliss stirred in her chest. A foreign sense of peace crept in, and she forgot entirely about the digital world stowed in her pocket.

As they walked along the narrow sidewalk, brittle leaves dragged their rough edges along the concrete on the light breeze. They crossed a bridge with a dehydrated creek babbling beneath before intersecting the pedestrian trail. They turned onto the gravel as it weaved through the increasingly skeletal trees.

"Breathe that fall mountain air," Wes mused, sucking the air in audibly.

"I love it here," Sidney echoed.

"You love it anywhere you're not working."

"Well, I mean, true. But especially here. I'm so ready to just watch horror for three days."

"Blood and guts and more blood and more guts." Wes bounced his steps to accentuate each word.

"Death scenes and jump scares," Sidney continued.

"And, of course, a couple artsy, slow burn, international horrors."

"To balance things out, naturally. It can't be all splatter porn."

"Well," Wes raised a finger, "it could be." He laughed. "But it won't be."

As they moved onto the main street of Telluride, Sidney began spotting her people. Distinct from the quintessential local mountain resident donning a beard and flannel, the horror fans strode the leaf-scattered streets like aged goths. Black shirts with blood splatter printed on them. Familiar faces of the famous horror movie killers emblazoned across a chest. Industrial jewelry. Thick black boots. Wildly unnatural hair colors. Sidney felt vanilla in such a crowd, but she was not alone. Some already wore their festival passes dangling around their necks.

Wes heaved the thick wooden door open and held it for Sidney. She stepped through into the old hotel bar with a smile widening on her face. The room breathed with the seething exhalations of the small crowd, their conversations mingling into one writhing sound. Sidney felt the group energy in the air infecting her, thick with the collective anticipation and excitement.

"Welcome to the Telluride Horror Show," a purple-haired pixie said from behind red glasses. "Can I get your last name, please?" Then she stopped and narrowed her eyes at Sidney. "Wait, I think I know you!"

"Oh, do you?" Heat flushed to Sidney's cheeks.

"Yeah, yeah," the pixie continued. "You run that one website. *Final Girl Screams.* I loved your bathroom death scene article. Almost didn't recognize you in clothes."

Sidney laughed nervously as the warmth swelled on her skin. She let her fingers cover her cheek to obscure the color.

"Thank you," Sidney smiled.

"Here you are, Sidney," the pixie said as she handed Sidney her colorful pass on a lanyard. "I'll be looking for your movie reviews after the fest."

Sidney thanked the pixie again and shuffled her way through the bodies to find Wes.

"Aw, look at the blushing celebrity," Wes joked.

"I am not a celebrity," Sidney said as her cheeks cooled.

"You just got recognized in public. I think that might qualify you as a celebrity."

"Ew." Sidney crossed her arms over her lanyard.

"Isn't that what you wanted?"

"Real life attention is different than online. I'm so awkward in real life," Sidney said.

"Yeah, you are," Wes laughed. "But you can't have it both ways."

"We have one hour to the first movie," Sidney said. "We might as well walk down and get in line now."

"Might as well," Wes smiled.

12

"**HOLY SHIT,**" Wes exclaimed as they pushed out of the crowded theater and into the crisp mountain night. "Did you see that decapitation?"

"Of course I saw that decapitation," Sidney said, taking long strides to match his excited pace.

"It was so slow," Wes continued. "So visceral. That's why horror still needs practical effects. CGI couldn't capture all the textures of flesh and bone and veins that way."

"I agree completely."

"And the way the eyes just sort of twitched and went dead. Amazing. Just amazing!"

"So, you liked that one then?" Sidney joked.

"Strong start. It was a very strong start." Wes finally caught up to himself and slowed his steps. "So, now what?"

"Oh shit!" Sidney threw her hands up.

"What?"

"Adam," she exclaimed. "I haven't checked my phone."

"You haven't what? Are you sure you're OK, Sid?"

Sidney playfully shoved at Wes's shoulder as she extracted her phone from her back pocket. It had snuggled against her so long it left a dent in her flesh. Her anxious fingers pulled the screen to her face.

"He's here," Sidney breathed, in some strange mix of excitement and fear.

"OK," Wes replied. "Now, what?"

"We're meeting him at the hotel bar, and we'll go from there."

"Oh, how exciting," Wes replied, flatly.

Sidney's heart banged against her ribs in a crescendo as they traced the gravel trail through the darkness. The creek trickled and slid over rocks beside them, but Sidney could not make out the water in the dark. Their footsteps crunched on the pebbles, louder than in the daylight. The night became the sound of their footfalls, the low creek, and their thin breaths. Sidney couldn't tell if the swimming sensation around the edge of her mind was from anticipation or the altitude.

They circled back to the hotel bar where they had started. Horror fans milled around a large bonfire and wandered through the dark street. More people in the gothic uniform talked in amplified tones in the biting heat of the bar. The warmth burned the chill on Sidney's cheeks, but she also felt her own heat radiating up to her face.

"So, where's your boyfriend?" Wes said, as he shimmied out of his quilted base layer coat and tugged the beanie from his head. Compulsively, to mask the edge of the question, he stroked his beard down into place.

Sidney let her eyes roam over the crowd until they settled on one face. He was already smiling at her, the same half smile from his profile pictures online. He looked the same as the many pictures she had seen—but also somehow different in three dimensions. Larger and smaller at the same time, more real and more surreal. Her mind reeled to bend around the contradiction. But, without thought, she smiled back and moved across the bar toward him.

"Sidney," Adam said as she approached, his grin unraveling in full. "It's so good to finally meet you in person."

"Oh my God, you too, Adam," Sidney returned. She wanted to say he looked better than his pictures, but it sounded too much like bullshit in her head. Surprisingly, he did look even more attractive in all three dimensions.

She continued walking right into him until they embraced. He hugged her back tightly until she had to pull back. She smiled at him then stepped back to encourage Wes closer.

"This is my friend, Wes," she said, gesturing towards him with her eyes lingering on Adam.

Wes stepped forward to offer his hand, which Adam shook heartily.

"Living Deadite, it's really nice to meet you too, man," Adam said. "It's not every day I get to meet two people I follow in person." Adam pressed his hand to his chest. "Zombie of Elm Street."

"Right!" Wes exclaimed, snapping his fingers. "You're always in on our live tweets."

Adam stood and offered his barstool to Sidney. Sidney took the seat graciously and leaned over the bar to order a round. She handed the boys their drinks, and they stood around her stool.

"So, what have you guys seen so far?" Adam asked.

"We just went to the opening movie, *Never Hike in the Woods*," Sidney replied.

"Any good?" Adam asked.

Wes went rigid in excitement beside him. Sidney laughed into her beer.

"Go ahead," she said. "Tell him."

"I don't know," Wes wavered. "Wouldn't that be spoilers?"

"No," Sidney said, "just be adequately vague."

"Yeah, go for it," Adam agreed.

Wes poised for delivery, setting his beer on the bar behind Sidney. He brought both his hands up to accentuate his point.

"This movie literally had the best decapitation scene. Ever."

"Whoa!" Adam stepped back. "That's a pretty big claim. Like better than *Evil Dead 2*?"

"It holds up," Wes nodded and brought his beer back to his lips.

Silence threatened to swell, but Adam quickly cleared his throat. "What's on the agenda for the rest of the night?"

"Well," Sidney started, "there's an audience participation showing of *The Rocky Horror Picture Show*, but Wes actually hates that movie."

"Wait, isn't not liking *Rocky Horror*, like, horror sacrilege?" Adam asked, looking to Wes out of the side of his eyes. Wes looked toward the ceiling as he drank.

"Yes, it is," Sidney said.

"But how do you not love *Rocky Horror*?" Adam continued.

"It's the singing," Wes said. "The singing is just so stupid."

"That's the best part!" Adam's eyes widened.

"Right!" Sidney punctuated with her hand.

"Well, if you want to go, I'll go with you," Adam said to Sidney.

"Hell yeah. You can still come with us, Wes."

"Absolutely not," Wes replied. "I'm going to finish this beer. Then I'm going to go tweet my ass off about decapitation in horror."

***

Wes gave the two of them a small salute in the dark as he turned toward their condo complex. Sidney and Adam continued along the shadowed street, following the other late-night movie goers creeping toward the venue. They gathered popcorn, newspaper, rice, and toast and headed to their seats in the filling theater. The crowd chattered loudly, unlike the normal, silent homage to the silver screen.

"When was the first time you saw this movie?" Adam said as they sat.

The thick seats folded down and creaked under their weight. Dim lights peeked out from the thick curtains lining the wall. The wide, gray screen loomed anticipant in front of them.

The actors ran madly up and down the aisles, shrieking as their steps ground popcorn into the flattened carpet. They paused to mock and interact with the patrons. Magenta swung her wide hips as her frizzy hair bounced on her shoulders, dragging her feather duster over any face within reach. Riffraff loomed in a corner, leaning out menacingly as new people entered the theater.

"Sleepover in junior high," Sidney answered between bites of popcorn.

"Ha! What were your first impressions?"

"I was confused but very intrigued. You?"

"My mom showed it to me, of all people." Adam smirked.

"How old were you?"

"Early high school, I guess."

"That seems weird," Sidney giggled.

"It was. But my mom was weird. The best kind of weird—a horror lover. I have some strange stories. I'm surprised you never live tweeted this one."

"Everyone live tweets *Rocky Horror.*"

The lights dimmed around them as the massive lipsticked mouth consumed the screen. Sidney settled back into her chair and drew the bucket of popcorn to her chest. She felt Adam settle beside her. He leaned closer, and his arm lined up along hers. Her nerves ruffled in her chest.

The movie crashed and sang through the theater as the crowd cheered, laughed, and shouted. "Damn it, Janet!" echoed against the walls until the floor seemed to vibrate. Sidney lost herself in the familiar scenes and shouting out the right lines at the appropriate times. She only kept track of how close Adam was to her as they watched and participated.

Once they finally burst from the humid theater, the cold edge to the air was welcomed. Sidney's cheeks ached from laughing, and her voice felt ragged in her throat.

"How could your boy, Wes, not be into that?" Adam laughed as they walked.

"I have no idea. There is clearly something wrong with him."

"More wrong than enjoying it as much as we did."

The streets of Telluride were quiet, the sounds of horror lovers shuffling off to their lodgings fading into the dark. The farther they moved from the theater, the heavier the quiet of the night weighed down on them. Sidney gathered her hoodie tighter around herself, folding her arms in tight to trap in her own warmth. Adam kept his steps near her until they reached the path again.

"This is where I turn," Sidney said, pausing her steps.

"Let me walk you to your condo," Adam said as he turned to face her.

"No, it's totally fine. This is Telluride."

"Well, maybe there's not a psychotic serial killer, but there might be a bear or something."

"Says the boy from the big city."

"Here, let me walk you." Adam moved to start walking in Sidney's direction.

"Nope," Sidney asserted. "I'm fine. We will meet before the first round of movies in the morning."

Adam smiled at her words then looked down to the shadowed gravel under his boots. Sidney stepped forward and extended her arms to hug him. Her arms hovered in the night; then he gathered her tightly into him. She felt the intensity of his embrace as the stubbled heat of his cheek radiated against hers. Consumed by the sensation, she melted into him, into how safe and easy it felt. Then her mouth was on his. The kiss somehow ambushed her. She was not sure if he had initiated it or she had, but she dove into it without hesitation. She let her breath tangle completely with his, pressing her face hard into his. She finally had to pull herself back from Adam and bid him goodnight.

A giddy smile lingered, intoxicated, across her lips. The blush flooding her cheeks was obscured by the darkness around her. The echo of kissing Adam tangled her so tightly she nearly forgot herself. When her awareness truly returned, she found herself completely alone on the dark path. The creek gurgled steady and familiar below her. She had not even heard him walk away.

She had not realized how black the night was, the moon completely obscured by a thick layer of silver clouds. She searched the sky for any pinpoint of light but was greeted only with the abyss above. Suddenly, her isolation solidified on her skin. Her footsteps scraped, near-deafening, against the quiet around her. The flush faded from her nerves as her heartbeat climbed up out of her chest.

She had not been alone all day, but she suddenly felt too alone.

Sidney snatched the fear in her mind. She realized she had marched herself right into a horror movie trope. What had she been thinking, deciding to walk by herself?

"This is some white girl in a horror movie shit," Sidney scolded herself under her breath. "At a horror festival no less. Sure, I'll walk myself home. It'll be just fine. This isn't basically asking to end up in the opening body count."

Sidney shook her head at herself and forced her breathing slow and steady, attempting to wrangle her heart rate. She told herself it was fine; she was fine. Everyone was drunk or in their room, and she only had to make it the two blocks to her condo.

"Famous last words," she mumbled.

The sound of her own steps overtook her hearing. Her brain reeled around the sound, reaching out to make sure it was the only noise. Yet below and behind the scrape of her shoes on the rocks, another sound menaced. Dull, steady, moving with her. Once she noticed it, she could not unhear it. Her chest tightened again.

Sidney stopped walking and held her breath in the dark. She strained to hear, to look with her ears through the black around her. Nothing. Silence only massaged by the moving water beside her.

She shook her head hard to dislodge the fear and stomped her steps deliberately down the trail.

As soon as she fell into stride again, the low rubbing sound returned, following her. Her steps quickened before she could even think, and the sound rubbed closer and louder on her heels. Tension escalated to fear on her skin, pulling it taut as the small hairs stood rigid. She whirled around to confront the noise. It ripped louder then disappeared.

As her bag swirled around her waist with the sound, she realized she had been the origin all along. Her messenger bag swiped along her hip as her legs alternated in steps. Sidney nearly laughed at herself and felt the pressure blow off of her with the cold breeze. She shook her head yet again and started walking.

"Fuck," Sidney breathed to herself.

As soon as she relaxed back into her peaceful night walk, something moved in the water below her. She heard the splash ripple through the gentle rapids. Then another followed it, the way footsteps echo each other. The foliage on the bank of the creek whined and bent as something moved through it.

Sidney did not stop to investigate. She did not hesitate. She clutched her messenger bag and sprinted the last block to the condo door.

15

SIDNEY PEELED HER dehydrated eyes open as the early morning sun pierced into her room. As her consciousness surfaced, she felt the thin, uncomfortable wake of all her drinks from the previous night. The high-altitude air she heaved during her run through the dark exacerbated the hangover spreading through her. Her head ached along the back of her forehead, the painful pressure begging her to close her eyes again.

When she allowed her eyes to drape shut again, her subconscious swelled over her like a dark flood. Adam emerged first. The feeling of his arms around her through her hoodie, the sweet abrasion of his rough cheek. She dissolved back into that moment as sleep rolled on top of her. The night replayed through her mind until she was back alone on the trail, hearing something large step through the water. She snapped back awake when that something shoved through the branches to get to her.

Sidney groaned and dug her fists into her eyes, her heart pulsing through her eardrums. She heaved her head off the pillow and herself into full consciousness. Once the room stopped swaying, she clawed for her phone. All of her apps were inflated with notification counts. A flood of comments on her arrival at the festival rolled with jealousy and shared excitement.

Adam: Good morning, beautiful

Sidney smiled and pressed the phone briefly to her chest before continuing. The feeling was dangerous, infectious.

Oliver: I miss you
    So distracted with your film festival.
    I hope you're having fun.
    But not as much fun as you would have with me.

Oliver's words did not conjure the same reaction, and Sidney swiped her way into Allison's thread.

Allison: How is the horror show??
Sidney: Great so far.
Allison: How many movies have you watched?
Sidney: Two. The opening show of *Never Hike in the Woods* then *The Rocky Horror Picture Show.*
Allison: I love *Rocky Horror!*
Sidney: Most of us do.
Allison: Who all are you there with?
Sidney: My horror buddy. Then a friend from the internet actually came out here to meet me.
Allison: Oh! A friend or a stalker?
Sidney: Friend lol
Allison: More than a friend?
Sidney: Maybe . . .

Sidney smirked and hopped conversations again.

Jack: Hello, Sidney. I hope you are having a great time at the Telluride Horror Show.
I can't wait to read your reviews so I know what to watch later this year.
Isn't it a little scary to be up in that mountain town at night?

Having addressed all her notifications and messages, Sidney forced herself to kick off the blankets and stand on the matted carpet. Her head swam as she brought herself upright then leveled back out. She toddled her way into the scalding spray of the shower and washed off her hangover.

Sidney returned to her room wrapped snugly in a towel and moved toward her suitcase. She looked to the arm of the chair, where she had laid out her clothes for the day when she had unpacked. The arm was empty. She stepped forward and dug through the suitcase. The clothes were not folded within. Sidney's eyebrows knitted as she struggled through the fog in her brain.

"What the hell?" she whispered to herself. "They were right here. I put them here. Then we were out all night."

Sidney reached down to clutch her towel as she spun in futile circles. She stomped back to the bathroom to twirl in the steam of her fading shower, puzzled. The clothes had effectively vanished. She stopped dumbfounded in front of the dresser, her perplexed reflection staring back from the dormant flatscreen TV screen. The first drawer hung slightly ajar.

"There's no way I was that drunk," Sidney mumbled as she stepped forward.

She slipped her fingertips into the opening and tugged the drawer open. Her outfit, complete with shirt, pants, bra, panties, and socks, sat neatly folded in a small fabric pyramid. Stunned, she simply extracted the clothes and began pulling them over her damp skin.

"Very funny with my clothes," Sidney greeted Wes as she walked into the kitchen.

Wes stood in front of the stove, stabbing at a mass of congealing yellow with a spatula. Steam from the pan fogged up his glasses. He turned, confused at her words.

"What are you talking about?" he said, lifting the spatula from the eggs.

"Didn't you hide my clothes last night?"

"Um, no. After you abandoned me, I came here, posted, tweeted, and passed out. Slept like a damn baby."

Sidney frowned at Wes, but he continued to look back at her, blankly innocent.

"How is the wide world of the internet?" he redirected. "I know that's the first thing you checked when you woke up."

"Guilty," she admitted. "It continues to go on without us. It is a bit creepy that everyone knows where I am and keeps asking about what I'm doing when I haven't talked to them about it."

"That's the consequence of posting and checking in everywhere you go."

"All for the sake of promotion," She threw up her hands.

"How was that awful movie?" he asked.

"Awesome. You really missed out."

"No, I didn't. I see you made it back to the room and slept alone."

"I did," she laughed. "But some scary shit happened to me on my walk home."

"Wait, that creep didn't walk you home?"

"He insisted, but I told him I was fine."

Wes laughed in his throat. "Just like a white girl in a horror movie."

"Yeah, so when I was walking along the trail, something was in the water."

Wes stopped stirring and turned to her. "In the water? What, like fish?"

"No, asshole," she laughed. "Something was walking through the creek then coming through the bushes on the bank towards me."

"Holy shit. Are you sure? Are you sure you weren't drunk and scaring yourself?"

"No, I'm sure. I scared myself earlier, but this was real."

"Well, no more walking alone like first reel bait. Deal?"

"Deal," she agreed.

"You want some eggs?" he lifted the pan from the burner and tilted the steaming mass toward her.

***

After breakfast, the vivid Colorado sun burned Sidney's eyes through the fluttering aspen leaves. The morning carved sharp lines down her brain with the painful sunlight. As they walked, Sidney clutched her water bottle close and chugged at it. Adam stood ahead of them, at the same point in the trail where he had kissed her goodnight hours before.

"Good morning," Adam said, as they approached.

Adam reached out and shook Wes's hand. Then he wrapped himself around Sidney for a brief hug. Sidney felt flittering excitement surge along the length of her skin.

"So, where do we start?" Adam continued. "I'm stoked for my first day at a horror film festival."

"Has Sidney communicated the plan to you?" Wes said, feigning seriousness. "We spent crucial hours on the drive perfecting our agenda."

"He's not serious," Sidney laughed.

"Oh, I'm very serious," Wes countered. "We take horror film festivals very seriously. Can't you tell from Sidney's hangover?"

"You're hungover?" Adam tipped his sunglasses to look at Sidney.

"A little," she answered, glaring at Wes.

"Conveniently for Sidney, we are beginning our day light, with a horror comedy. Nothing too heavy or traumatic until she recovers."

"Lead the way," Sidney said.

Wes nodded and turned to direct them back to the main street and toward the venues. Adam fell in step beside Sidney, smiling at her from the side of his mouth. Sidney still managed to find the chill in the air euphoric, the smashing of leaves under her feet making her grin. Autumn infected her and only made her heart palpitate harder.

She didn't think about the internet. She didn't think about her website or blog. She didn't think about

Aiden. Guiltily, she didn't even think about Cameron. She didn't think. She was simply there on the street with her mindless happiness. She felt both free and at home, even if it unnerved her to have to find it so far away from her life.

Before she realized it, Adam reached over and took her hand. She let him.

"It's tradition to start the mornings with a Bloody Mary," Sidney said as they approached the hotel.

"I'm down," Adam said.

"Sidney also has a bottle of booze in that bag of hers," Wes ratted.

"A girl on a mission," Adam joked.

"Always. Plus, a little hair of the dog just to be safe," Sidney answered.

Sidney replaced the thin layer of headache with the haze of a gentle buzz and the acidic bite of spice, tomato, and vodka. The previous night fully slipped from her consciousness, to be filed in memory. As they moved into the theater for the first screening, Sidney settled comfortably between Wes and Adam. She dug through her bag to extract a box of Junior Mints.

"Breakfast of champions," Adam snickered.

"Hey, it's a horror fest. There are no dietary rules."

"That's right. Vodka chased with chocolate. So healthy," Wes laughed.

Sidney reached into her pocket and lifted her phone.

"Must be time to check on the stalkers," Wes commented.

"To be fair, my message volume is about half of what it normally is."

"Why is that?" Wes asked.

"Because he's here," Sidney giggled, gesturing to Adam.

"Hey," Adam said, "I'm not sure if I'm offended by that or not."

The lights around them smothered down to shadows as the screen ignited. The mumble of the crowd silenced. All eyes turned to fixate on the large Telluride Horror Show logo. A few motivated morning patrons let out isolated whoops. Sidney flattened a Junior Mint against the roof of her mouth with her tongue as the opening credits snuck across the screen.

The scenes danced in front of them, and the crowd reacted and participated more actively than in a normal movie theater. Less animated than *The Rocky Horror Picture Show*, the attendees cheered and yelled aloud for each gruesome and hilarious death scene. As Sidney took in the comic violence, she found herself writing titles and snippets of her future review in her head.

The Rest Will Come: Online Dating Will Drive Anyone to Murder

With the parade of douchebags she has to endure, the audience can't help but cheer on our protagonist as she dispatches them in inexperienced and hysterical methods.

If The Rest Will Come *franchises, it will join the ranks of* Final Destination *and* Saw *in searching for the cleverest methods of execution.*

When the closing credits rolled, Sidney found her chest light with satisfaction. Her cheeks ached faintly from laughing. The positive movie review was already half drafted in her head. She whipped out her phone to swipe the sentences into her notepad app before they dissolved on her brain.

"Well, I know you loved it," Wes said to Sidney.

"I did," Sidney replied, still swirling her finger over her phone.

"Writing your review already," Wes continued.

"Of course."

"It was pretty damn funny," Adam contributed. "Especially when she fell out of the damn trunk trying to dump the body."

"I think it may have cured me of my curiosity for online dating," Sidney said. "Oh, I need to write that down too."

"Um, Sid, you kind of did online date," Wes said.

"What do you mean?" Sidney asked.

Wes lowered his chin to look at her wide out of the tops of his eyes. He dramatically raised his finger and flicked it between her and Adam.

"That's not the same," Sidney argued. "That's social networking."

"What exactly is the difference?" Wes said.

"Intention," Adam laughed.

"I call bullshit," Wes replied.

Adam and Sidney looked at each other awkwardly and laughed.

"That's right," Wes said. "No argument."

After the house lights rose and the theater was illuminated again, the three remained in their seats for the Q&A session with the director, three actors, and author of the original novel. Sidney kept her phone in front of her face, ignoring her notifications and messages to take notes. She had every intention of hazing her memories through the remainder of the weekend. The notes would resurrect the details when she was back on her couch drafting reviews and articles.

Sidney raised her hand, and the man in the Telluride Horror Show hoodie with the microphone on the stage gestured to her. Sidney stood slowly and cleared her throat.

"This question is for the author." Sidney dug deep to project her usually docile voice. "You probably get this question all the time, but what inspired this story? I mean, do you have a really horrible online dating history?"

A low wave of laughter rolled over the crowd. The author smiled as she looked down at her boots and ran her fingers through strands of her orange hair.

"I do get this question all the time," she chuckled. "But no, this book actually does not contain any of my personal dating stories. Instead, it's based on a compilation of all my friends' terrible dating stories. I would listen to them complain about their online dating adventures, and I was like, how do you not murder people? Hey! What if you murdered people? And that's how the book happened."

Sidney smiled and nodded gratefully before sitting down and tapping more notes.

After the session had concluded and they had filed out with the rest of the crowd, they stood on the leaf-littered sidewalk in the blinding sun. The three stood in a triangle. Wes extracted his printed movie schedule and held it in the center of their shape.

"OK," Wes said, placing his fingertip on the print, "we can do Scandinavian vampires, which is also showing again tomorrow. Or, we can do Canadian zombies. Looks like this is the only showing we can swing for zombies."

"I vote Canadian zombies. I'm curious to see if they

actually eat anyone or if they are just too nice about it," Adam offered.

"Seconded," Sidney said.

"After that, we are definitely going to the one about the haunted sex toy shop," Wes continued.

Sidney opened her mouth to speak.

"Silence," Wes said, lifting his hand into the air. "We're going. And that gets us to the late showing. We can do an homage to Giallo or a documentary on sleep paralysis. I won't vote since I'm enforcing the sex toy one."

"Giallo," Sidney said, as if there was no alternative.

Both looked to Adam. He shrugged and nodded with a smile.

"Did you pack food?" Sidney asked Adam.

"No," Adam replied. "Was I supposed to?"

"Oh yeah," Wes said. "There's no time for meals here."

"Hardcore," Adam laughed.

"As many movies as we can cram in!" Sidney laughed. "We can run by our condo and snag some more food on the way to Canadian zombies."

Sidney shouldered her messenger bag. Together, they walked at a quickened pace to the condo then to the vintage movie theater for the next film. Canadian zombies were not, in fact, too nice about anything. Haunted sex toys vibrated terrifyingly until the plot wandered off into the utterly ridiculous. Wes laughed so hard tears streamed down his cheeks. He clapped wholeheartedly at the closing credits. And the Giallo film paid all the proper homage to its inspirations of Argento and Fulci, reserving an avalanche of gore to reward its audience's patience through the mystery.

After each movie, Sidney diligently swiped in her notes, though they made less sense as she drained the bottle in her bag.

By the time they concluded their viewings, the day had long disappeared under the heavy night. The sky was clear, and the moon seemed larger and brighter as it illuminated the streets.

"Well, I am done for the night," Wes said as they stood outside the last venue. "I need to slam down some tweets and crash out now if I'm going to do this again tomorrow."

Wes slipped the glasses from his face and tipped his head back to the night sky. When he exhaled, Sidney could faintly make out the cloud of his breath in the cold.

"What about you?" Adam asked Sidney.

"I would be interested in a drink and some late night munchies," she replied.

Intoxication hummed happily on Sidney's nerves, keeping her mind quiet. She didn't want to stop. She didn't want that wave to recede yet.

Wes saluted them goodnight before disappearing down the trail turned silver by the moonlight. Adam reached out and gathered up Sidney's hand. They moved in the opposite direction toward the bar. Sidney felt herself relax as Wes wandered out of sight. She could embrace how good it felt to let Adam touch her without risking Wes's judgement. She clutched Adam's hand tightly.

Festival attendees crowded the entire establishment. All had the glazed-over expression that happened after having their brains assaulted by upwards of eight hours of horror imagery. Their faces were a mix of exhaustion and exhilaration. The voices muddled into a high roar that consumed the room. Adam gently placed a palm against her back and followed her through the huddled bodies. They managed to snag a cramped table in the corner. They waited for a cocktail waitress to locate them. Sidney slipped her phone into her palm.

"Holy shit," she breathed as she illuminated the screen.

"What?" Adam asked.

"So many messages."

"Well, you have been offline for, like, a whole day."

Oliver: I miss you.
Let me see you.

Allison: Canadian zombies? What are those like?
Are you having a good time?
What has been the best movie so far?

Jack: I love Giallo. How did the homage hold up?

Kendra: Miss you, girl! Drinking a glass for you.
Though I doubt you need it . . .

"It's just so weird," Sidney said, to her phone screen.

"What is?" Adam asked.

"It's like they're following me. The way they can talk about things I'm doing that I've never directly told them."

"Uh, they are following you. Virtually following you."

"You know what I mean," Sidney laughed, turning her phone face-down on the table. Her fingers lingered on top of the device until Adam reached across and rested his hand on top of hers.

The waitress finally appeared, took their order, and returned with full beers. The crisp foam nibbled on Sidney's lip as she took a deep gulp. "Oh, I forgot to tell you what happened last night," she said, licking her lip and placing her beer back on the coaster.

"Last night? When?" Adam asked from around the rim of his beer.

"After we split up."

"You mean, after you went summer camp counselor in the first reel on me? After you refused to let me walk you home?"

"Yeah, then," Sidney dismissed. Then she felt a swell of the panic from the previous night and blurted out, "Something came at me."

"Something?" Adam straightened in his chair. "What do you mean came at you?"

"Well, I was walking along the trail, psyching myself out. I creeped myself out with my own bag swishing on my back." Sidney paused to sip her beer. And for effect. "Then I heard something walking through the creek, coming through the branches along the bank."

"What?" Adam snatched his hand back and rubbed his face. "See, you should have let me walk you. Did you see it? What did you do?" His questions came in a fury with his widened eyes.

"No, I couldn't see it. I just ran. Sprinted to the condo."

"Did you trip?" The smile returned to Adam's lips.

"Nope." Sidney smiled back, feeling heat again in her cheeks. "I made it all the way home and am still alive to tell the tale. Guess I'm a little better than one of those camp counselors."

Chatting and laughing casually through horror trope jokes, they finished their beers and emerged from the still seething crowd into the cold night.

"So, you're letting me walk you home tonight, right?" Adam said.

"How about you walk me to your condo?" Sidney replied, her words emboldened by the alcohol swimming in her bloodstream.

"Yeah?" Adam's grin spread wide across his face, shining in the darkness.

Sidney nodded and allowed him to gather her under his arm. He kept her tucked close to him as they stumbled down the trail and into his hotel room.

***

Adam snored lightly on the sheets beside Sidney. He snoozed facedown in the pillow, his narrow, bare back catching the moonlight streaming in from the bedside window. Sidney slid herself up, soundless, and turned over her shoulder to smile at his sleeping form. She felt the instinct to lay back down beside him, to curl safely into his body. Yet something about that instinct conjured a tense anxiety on her skin. She wrestled with herself for a moment before snatching her clothes as she left the bed.

The haze of the alcohol hugged Sidney's consciousness. She straddled the line between her fading intoxication and threatening hangover as she had to put thought into her movements. Her heart thumped in her chest long before she reached the gravel trail along the creek. It started pounding the second she considered lingering on the sheets. It rattled her ribs in some contradiction of regret and purpose. She told herself she was hurrying home to not worry Wes, yet something in the terrible rhythm of her pulse chanted that she did it to run from herself.

Her skin prickled as her hurried steps scraped along the dirt. She wrapped her arms tightly around herself, and her messenger bag bounced violently against her side. She knew to ignore the rubbing sound this time. Yet that knowledge did not stop all her senses from reaching out in desperate caution.

Calm down, she told herself. *You were fine last night. You'll be fine tonight. You can already see the condo. Just breathe, Crazy.*

The parking lot of her condo expanded as she drew closer. Gradually, she loosened her grip on her own hoodie. She breathed slower and slower. Then the deep splash rippled up from the creek beside her.

Sidney seized. Despite her vigilance, her fear strangled her. Her steps ground to a stuttering halt as her eyes scraped through the darkness. The second plopping splash brought her awareness back to her flesh. By the time the branches whined and snapped, her legs had instinctively started to run toward the dim lights on her condo.

But not quick enough.

The sound moved through the darkness unimaginably fast: a second set of feet threw crunching slaps on the gravel. Small stones ricocheted out into the night. Sidney found herself clawing through the air, groping into the night, hoping it would propel her forward. Even over her own ragged gasps and banging nerves, she heard the footsteps gaining on her.

Two hands materialized out of the black behind her, seizing handfuls of her hoodie. Fingertips dug into her and yanked her from her run. Her hands splayed out into the impact as she tumbled violently to the dirt. She felt the gravel bite and scrape into her palms, felt the horrible burn as friction rubbed through layers of flesh to blood.

As she collided with the ground, a body fell on top of her. She felt the weight on her the same way she had just felt Adam on top of her. She kicked against the pressure and dug her nails in the dirt trying to scramble out from under it. Hands groped on her again, grabbing at her arms, hips, legs as she squirmed, her muscles and lungs burning painfully.

She gulped at the air but found it infected. The pungent aroma of disinfectant burned at her nostrils, practically manifesting artificial lemons on her tongue. The acidic bitterness made her choke. Tears welled in her eyes, from the panic and the burn.

She felt nothing. She only kept bringing her eyes back to her condo, her safety. Her attacker climbed her body, gripping and wriggling up her, working to pin her down. Sidney kicked her legs, thrashed wildly. Her mind was blank, primal, disconnected from her frantic flesh, detached from the attack. Distantly, she felt the rocks digging into her hip as her attacker pressed down harder on top of her.

Somewhere, beneath the flurry, her hand fought its way to her bag. Her fingertips groped through the contents until they wrapped around the handle of the empty vodka bottle. She permitted her attacker's hands to roll her to her back. She swung her arm around with the movement to crack the bottle against them.

The heavy *thunk* of the collision echoed in the night. The sounds of their struggle faded into the muffled groans from the body on top of her. Her attacker's hands released to cradle where the blow had landed. Without thought, Sidney capitalized. She heaved the bottle back up and slammed it into the form again.

Her attacker appeared faceless and vague in the dark, shrouded by the licking edges of shadow. The dark shape of something human grabbed at her, yet no matter how Sidney squinted at the darkness, no details came into focus. The movements, the sounds were familiar. She knew a person was on top of her. Who that person was meant nothing to her in that moment. As her attacker howled and rolled off of her, she dropped the bottle. She scrambled to her feet and ran the same sprint as the previous dark night, her panic turning her vision into a blur.

14

SIDNEY'S HANDS TREMBLED as she cupped the steaming coffee mug on the breakfast bar in her condo. She gently touched her palms to the mug then retracted as the heat singed the scabs that had hardened there. Exhaustion lay heavily on her muscles, the painful drain of all her flight response adrenaline, yet her mind sprinted in several concurrent and colliding circles. Her thoughts whirled as she stared blankly into the dark liquid in front of her.

Her eyes drifted out of focus, her memory assaulting her in staccato bursts. The weight of her attacker climbing up her. Her heartbeat banging so desperately in her ears. The gravel grating against her and digging into her palms as she clawed. The lights of the condo parking lot so far away. She was back in that moment when Wes opened the door, and her arms flinched so hard she nearly spilled the coffee on herself.

"Just me," Wes said, gently.

"Was there anything out there?" Sidney said in a shaky voice.

Wes answered by holding up her empty bottle. Unbroken and unmarked.

"Nothing else?" she asked, more firmly. She stood and padded toward him, reaching out to touch the bottle.

"Nothing. Not even a sign of a struggle. Just the trail." Wes retracted the bottle. "You OK, Sid?" His brow furrowed deeply as he stared hard at her.

"Yeah, I'm fine." Sidney blinked her eyes hard and shook her head a little. The words did not ring true in her mind, but she did not dare voice that.

Wes dropped the bottle into the recycling and tipped his head at her.

"What?" Sidney asked.

"Do you think it was Adam?"

Sidney's phone vibrated loud on the counter, interrupting Wes's question. Instinctively, Sidney glanced at the notification.

Adam: Where did you go?

Sidney pictured the message that had flashed on her phone screen in the early hours. Still left unanswered.

"No," Sidney said automatically, wrapping her arms around herself and returning to her perch by the coffee. "Why would it be Adam?"

"Why would some guy you met on the internet come all the way out to Colorado to meet you? Maybe he was mad you pulled a coyote ugly on him."

"I don't think you know what coyote ugly means."

"Well, you know what I mean."

Sidney conjured up the sensation of Adam's mouth moving along her collarbone, his hands sliding up her back. She thought of his weight on top of her, so different than the violent crushing on the trail. She inhaled, remembering Adam's soft and salty smell with no artificial edge biting at the back of her throat. She nibbled the edge of her lip without realizing it.

"I don't think it was him," she said.

Wes reached toward Sidney, and she shrank back instinctively. When she realized she had snatched her arm away from him, she looked up at him remorsefully. Confusion, maybe hurt edged Wes's features before softening. Sidney gave him an apologetic look as she extended her hand to take his.

"I'm not convinced. Sid, you should call the cops. We should have called the cops last night."

Sidney slid her hands up the side of her face as she gently shook her head.

"Why not? You got assaulted."

"Nothing really happened. I made it home," Sidney shrugged.

She had made it home, she affirmed in her mind, sandbagging the thought repeatedly against her sea of doubt. Nothing had really happened to her—only to her attacker, when she smashed the bottle over their head. She had not left wounded, aside from some scrapes on her hands from when she fell. She was fine, she replayed in her head before she responded.

"What the fuck, Sid? That doesn't even make sense. You got attacked, and the guy—" Wes hesitated, "maybe Adam . . . " he paused again, "is still out there."

"It wasn't Adam. It's fine. I'm fine. I just want to pretend it never happened. OK?" Sidney heard herself getting louder.

"Well, that's some stupid victim shit if I've ever heard it."

Sidney's mouth fell into a flat line. She turned cold eyes up to Wes.

"OK, I'm sorry," he backpedaled. "I guess it is up to you. So, what do you want to do now?"

"We meet Adam. We go to movies all day. And we go to the closing party."

"So, basically, like it never happened."

"Basically."

***

Sidney's steps slowed as they moved onto the trail. Wes said they could have taken the sidewalk, but Sidney refused. Part of her needed to see it. The trail looked different in the daylight, smaller and innocuous. As she stared desperately at the trail, her chest tightened around her throbbing heartbeat. She could not even make out where her attacker had taken her down. She only knew it was the stretch between the last cross street and the condo parking lot. Wes was right; there was nothing.

After they crossed the first street, the tension in her chest uncoiled. Her shoulders retreated from their position hugging her earlobes. She glimpsed Adam in the distance, shifting anxious on the trail, watching for them. The echo of fear on her nerves was instantly drowned out by a stabbing guilt.

Sidney wondered if she should have stayed with Adam. Why did she leave?

Wes stiffened protectively beside her when Adam came into view, his steps scraping curtly along the gravel. The uncomfortable flutter in Sidney's chest intensified with each footfall beside her.

She should not have left. Why did she leave?

Up ahead, Adam smiled when he saw them

approaching, yet he continued to shuffle his feet back and forth beneath him. His hands dug deep into his pockets. Sidney forced a smile onto her face to hide the anxiety flexing on her cheeks.

"Good morning," Sidney said as they reached him.

Wes looked Adam up and down from behind his sunglasses and turned away. Adam registered Wes's attitude, frowning briefly, but then he focused on Sidney. He smiled, genuinely, then hesitated a breath before stepping forward to kiss her. Sidney reached out to grasp his arm and guide him closer. He pressed his lips gently against hers then grinned more confidently. Wes looked at Sidney then began walking toward the main street, Sidney and Adam trailing behind.

Adam leaned toward her. "Hey, why did you leave last night," he said, soft enough for the words to get lost in the wind before they reached Wes.

"I'm really sorry about that," Sidney said, looking over to briefly meet his eyes. "It had nothing to do with you."

"That's a relief," Adam's laugh came out slightly strangled. "Because I had a great time with you last night."

"I did too. And then I freaked out." Sidney had always told him the truth online. In real life, it seemed to leap off her tongue naturally just the same. The freedom surprised her yet was seductive.

"That's OK." Adam smiled again. "What's up with Wes? Is he pissed at me or something?"

Sidney stopped walking, putting her hand to her forehead.

"Oh shit!" Sidney gasped.

"What?" Adam nearly stopped walking.

"I haven't told you yet. I should have led with what happened last night."

"What happened?"

"When I ducked out on you last night, I got attacked on the way home."

Adam stopped and snagged Sidney's elbow to drag her to a halt beside him.

"What do you mean attacked?"

"When I was walking home, someone came out of the creek again and tackled me." Sidney shrugged, but her words still quivered.

"Holy shit, Sidney! Are you OK? What the hell happened?" Adam took a step closer to her. His fingers lingered on her arm.

Sidney glanced up the street. Wes stood on a corner, looking back at them with his arms crossed.

"I'm fine," Sidney said, casting her eyes to her shoes. "It's fine. They came out of the creek, chased me down, and tackled me. I cracked them in the head with my empty bottle and ran to my condo."

"Oh fuck." Adam seemed closer still. "Did you call the cops?"

Sidney shook her head. Her eyes scanned Adam's head for a wound or a lump until she caught herself and looked down.

"No? Why not?"

"I didn't want to. I'm fine. I just want to finish the fest today and go home."

She would not waste her treasured time, her reprieve from the crushing repeat of normal life on police reports and questions she did not want to answer. She wanted to pretend it never happened, and if she could get them to stop hounding her on the topic, maybe she could melt back into the festival and let the attack fade away like a waning nightmare.

Adam did not reply. He wrapped his arms around Sidney. She pressed her face into his chest.

"Wait," Adam said, pulling back from the embrace. "What does that have to do with Wes?"

"He kind of thinks it was you," Sidney answered.

"He what?" Adam snapped backward to see Sidney's face. "He thinks I attacked you?" His face contorted in disbelief and outrage.

"Yeah, a little. I told him I knew it wasn't you, but he thinks it's weird to travel to meet someone on the internet."

"Really?"

"He just doesn't get it," Sidney smiled.

Adam's face softened again. His eyes dilated, relieved and inviting.

"Are you sure you're OK?" he said.

"I'm fine," Sidney said again. If she said it enough, she could make it true.

By the time they caught up to Wes, he was tapping his foot impatiently on the concrete.

"Hey, man," Adam said as they approached Wes. "Look, I didn't attack Sidney last night."

Wes spun towards him, arms still pinned around his chest.

"Is that an actual line from *Scream*?" Wes replied. "It sounds very Billy Loomis."

Sidney laughed awkwardly between them. Adam cracked a half smile.

"It might be, but I still didn't attack her. I just want you to know that," Adam said.

"Not to belabor a trope at an actual horror film festival," Wes replied, "but isn't that exactly what the stalker-slash-killer would say?"

"Yeah, but out here in real life," Adam smirked, "it's just the truth."

Wes and Adam stared at each other for a long moment that seemed to accentuate the mountain chill. Their sunglasses mirrored themselves back to each other. Sidney noted Wes scanning Adam's head for injuries, evidence of being bludgeoned with a bottle. Then Wes jerked his head to nod a little, and the edge of his lips curled up. Without any more words, they all walked on to the theater in an awkward truce.

The first theater was dimly lit. The darkness cradled Sidney as she took a seat between Adam and Wes. Adam's arm draped over their shared armrest, allowing his fingertips to trace along the top of her thigh. She scarcely noticed the touch as she allowed the images shifting in front of her to monopolize her focus.

Onscreen, the last victim cautiously crouched behind a tree in the dark, struggling to suppress his breathing. His eyes flitted around him, as the movie score crept unnervingly through the air. Sidney's back muscles tightened into knots around her vertebrae. The character startled as a branch snapped behind him. As he whirled around, he saw the lumbering form of the killer approaching methodically. The victim broke out into a run, branches snapping against his flailing arms, his gasping breaths drowning out the background music.

The killer closed the distance to his victim. He snatched his prey and sent him tumbling to the dirt.

As the victim collided with the ground, Sidney felt the sharp gravel digging into her hands, pressing into her back. The scabs on her palms seemed to contract. The killer seized his victim and dragged him closer, flipping him to his back to expose his vulnerable points. Sidney felt the weight of the attacker crushing down on top of her, the desperate burn in her frantic muscles.

Sidney stopped breathing. She didn't notice until her heart knocked a reminder on her ribcage. Her hands climbed up her legs, over Adam's touch, to ball tightly against her stomach. Adam turned his eyes from the screen and faced her.

"Sid, are you all right?" he whispered into her ear.

His breath on her neck caused her ribs to tense. She saw the distant light of the parking lot mocking her in the distance, burning tracks along her vision as her head thrashed back and forth. As her fingers wrung themselves, she felt the canvas of her bag and the smooth glass she searched for.

Sidney threw herself forward, digging her elbows into her knees and grinding her fists into her eyes. She heard the death on the screen but kept her sight obscured by her hands. The crowd around her rippled in cheers and laughter as the death gurgle sputtered in the speakers. She shifted her hands to her ears and cupped them to muffle the sounds.

Adam reached over and moved his hand over her back. She recoiled at first then relaxed into the touch. She focused on the motion against her skin, pulling herself out of the memories with the sensation. She finally pulled her head back up and forced a smiled at him in the dark.

The remainder of the movie blinked past in a blur.

Sidney allowed her eyes to fall out of focus as her mind swam with thoughts. She was relieved when the credits rolled. Wes pressed the theater door open, showering Sidney and Adam in glaring sunshine. Sidney flinched into a hard squint. Adam's hand gently caught her shoulder as they moved past the crowd.

"Sidney," he said, almost whispering to her. "Are you OK?"

Sidney turned to face him and plastered a wide grin on her face.

"What do you mean?" she said. "Yeah, I'm good. It's bright out here."

Adam leaned in closer. Wes finally noticed they were no longer in step with him and turned back.

"Sidney," Adam said again, her name heavier on his tongue.

Wes stepped beside Adam and assessed them both.

"I'm good," Sidney said forcefully, smiling first at her hands then at both men. "That final climax was pretty intense though, huh? I liked that one."

Adam tilted his head at her. Wes narrowed his eyes.

"Cliché but effective," Wes agreed.

Sidney stared at them expectantly until Adam finally relented and they resumed crunching the leaves as they walked down the sidewalk.

They took in a block of horror shorts on mother issues that could have made Oedipus blush. The day vanished outside while they sat entombed in the velveted walls with the screams echoing from the speakers. Twilight crawled into the afternoon by the time they walked toward the last venue for the final screening. The approaching night was sharp on the air, causing their breath to bloom in front of their faces.

Wes's suspicions had clearly waned as he chatted with Adam about how disturbing it was to pervert the base relationship of mother and child. Adam talked with his hands, swirling them through the dim air between them. Sidney allowed herself to trail a couple steps behind them, content in her silent observation, dragging out the fading moments of the festival.

The Horror Show had horded an unnerving gem for its final screening. The line teemed as it crawled out from the front doors, and once the crowd was seated, it breathed as one massive organism hungry for one last dose of carnage. The energy swirling in the air mirrored the opening movie, the same anxious excitement and shared anticipation. Sidney took a deep breath and held it in to enjoy it one more time, to put horror back where it belonged—onscreen.

The crowd around her vanished as the theater went dark. The world reduced down to her single chair and the giant screen glowing in front of her. The moving light captivated her vision, stimulated her brain into compliant focus. She almost felt the transcendent calm that came from escaping into the screen, yet an anxiety nibbled at the edges. Her consciousness kept running itself over the wound on the back of her brain, keeping it open.

As the plot and characters spiraled into dimension across the flat screen, Adam's hand found hers again. In the dark, the same way his fingertips seemed to gravitate toward her in his hotel room. Her nerves contracted as the world around her flesh ticked away. She felt a phantom flash of the warmth of his skin against hers.

Somewhere along the echoing sensation of his

body against her own, it dawned on her that the fest was not the only thing ending that night. As Adam's fingers weaved between her own, she realized he would be gone tomorrow. She would be gone tomorrow. Wes would drive her back through the Colorado mountains to her bullshit job and her mediocre performance as a mother.

The panic at that suffocating idea swam through her veins. She clutched Adam's hand and leaned over the armrest toward him. In the light of the horror movie in front of them, she could make out the same wide, startled yet grateful smile as he pulled her close to him. She breathed deep and didn't smell burning disinfectant and fake lemons. She inhaled him, that sweet and salty aroma that would now trigger the flashbacks on her flesh.

"It's not over yet," Adam whispered into her hair, near reading her mind. "She hasn't even seen the killer yet."

Adam nuzzled briefly against Sidney's cheek, releasing her from the sinkhole in her brain. Her attention unfurled and reached back into the dancing shapes in the light. The heroine had not seen her killer yet, but not for his lack of trying as he loomed in the bushes outside her window. A strange flutter slapped at Sidney's lungs each time the woman failed to notice the threat, something like the fear she had experienced on the gravel path, shrink-wrapped in excitement. The conventionally conjured fear felt alarming.

Sidney writhed against the contradiction and snuggled into Adam until the credits rolled.

Applause replaced the darkness as the lights came up. The audience stretched and shifted but lingered longer in their seats. No next screening to run to. The momentum and excitement of the fest had dwindled as time seemed to slow and thicken.

"Are we doing last call?" Wes said, squinting against the lights.

"What's last call?" Adam asked from the other side of Sidney.

"It's the closing party of the fest at this bar down the street," Sidney answered.

"You cannot end as up as hungover as last year," Wes said. "The drive home was miserable."

"You sure you're up to it?" Adam asked Sidney.

"Yeah, I'm fine." Sidney nibbled on the sentence. "I'll be good. Let's do this."

The trio finally pried themselves from the last set of theater seats and filed out among the other weary watchers. Half the crowd dissipated out into the night. The rest shuffled in clusters to the glowing sign of the saloon.

Wes broached the crowd as Sidney tailed him. They pushed through the mass of the same faces they had been passing anonymously for days, the awkward blend of the familiar and unfamiliar passing over them in waves. The bodies packed in between the thickly wooded walls. The groups of people branched out from the long bar with glowing taps along the wall. They all smiled warmly in vague recognition.

As a group of flannel-clad, bearded men vacated a corner table, Sidney swooped in to claim it. She wrapped her fingertips around the lacquered edge of the wood. She felt a strange, deep itch climbing in her limbs. She shook it off and tried to wash the sensation away with deep gulps of her beer. Something about the buzz of the crowd, the ambiguous and seething blend of voices, grated along her nerves.

"Back to reality tomorrow," Wes said, raising his glass.

Sidney and Adam instinctively raised their glasses and clinked them together. Sidney took another desperate pull from the beer. She felt like something was moving nearby; something in the crowd was setting her nervous system on edge.

"Adam," Wes started, the alcohol beginning to curl in his words the way Sidney recognized. "I can honestly say it was good to meet you. I'm glad you joined us."

"So, you don't still think he assaulted me?" Sidney joked.

"Well, I guess not. Would be a good twist if he had though. I mean, clearly, I would have to die before the big reveal since I was the one who suspected him. Saw his true nature," Wes said.

"Clearly," Adam smiled.

Sidney drained her glass and stepped away from the table to navigate to the bathroom. As she stepped away from her chair, the zing of anxiety cinched tighter around her lungs. She felt her skin more acutely, as if all the hairs were pulling to attention. She pushed herself through the crowd and slipped into the bathroom to stare at herself in the mirror.

In the garish light of the bathroom, her features looked gaunt. Yet even beyond the poor lighting, her face seethed. Her lips pulled tight and thin. Her eyes loomed wide below her arched forehead. She did not completely recognize the reflection that met her or the feelings coursing through her.

Sidney relieved herself and splashed water on her face until she could tell herself she felt more normal again. When she emerged from the bathroom and back into the sea of bodies, the faint yet harsh lemon scent carved its way through her senses. Light and vague on the air, her brain nearly ignored it, yet something deeper in her flinched.

"Hey!" the foreign voice boomed from beside her. "You're from that *Final Girl Screams* site. You post all those crazy blood pictures. I've read your stuff."

Sidney turned to find the voice bellowing from the fluffy beard of the man behind her. His lean face drew up into a broad smile beneath the plumes of facial hair, and his rounded black glasses encased excited eyes. Sidney fought the urge to shrink back and directed the impulse to instead spread a warm smile across her cheeks.

"Yes, I am," Sidney replied.

She brushed her cheek as if she were blushing and briefly cast her eyes down as she tucked her hair behind her ear. The motions happened automatically, practiced. The smile on her face felt immobile as it lingered.

"I really love your work," he continued. "Those pictures in the bathtub were just haunting. The blood was so convincing. It was fake, wasn't it?"

The pictures. Always the pictures.

"Of course it's fake." Sidney added the giggle at the end of her confirmation.

The beard continued to talk, but the words started to dissolve from Sidney's hearing into the mumble of the crowd enveloping them. Sidney inhaled naturally, compulsively through her nose, and her chest seized.

The pungent edge of disinfectant ruffled through the hairs along her nostrils. It tunneled through her sinuses and into her brain.

The beard still fluttered in the breeze of her admirer's empty words as Sidney whirled around. Her eyes scanned the crowd around them. The laughs echoed deafeningly through her head as she saw flashing teeth and stretched grins blur around her. Beer splashed in glasses swirled in sloppy grips.

Sidney could not repress the startle as a touch glided across her back. She jumped and snapped her head around.

"Oh, I'm sorry," the girl said as she tried to push through to the bar.

Sidney tried to smile reassuringly, but anxiety tightened her features.

"Are you OK?" the beard asked.

Again, Sidney tried and failed to be cordial. She opened her mouth to say she was fine and continue the conversation with him babbling emptily about her pictures, yet her mouth fell agape. She managed to spit out an "excuse me" as she whirled away from him. She didn't even try to compose herself before she fumbled through the crowd.

Sidney reached out her arms to swim through the bodies. Adam and Wes were out of reach on the distant shore. She bumped and jostled the innocent bystanders comprising the ocean that swallowed her. She fled the scent, the aroma that burned through the blistered memories she had tried to shove out of her consciousness. Her body moved instinctually, full flight.

She almost reached the thick, wooden edge of their

table. Then the disinfectant grew stronger, closer. Adam locked eyes with Sidney before the panic seized her. She vaguely registered him nudging Wes and gesturing to her. A grip snatched her wrist, and the smell swelled to overtake her.

The narrative in her mind abandoned her. Her consciousness transitioned into action as she ripped her arm away and plowed through the crowd. *Run*. It was all she could think to do.

***

"Sidney! Sidney!"

Sidney did not hear the voices chasing her in the dark. She could not hear anything over her pulse clobbering through her eardrums. Her shoes pounded the concrete as the streetlights washed over her then dropped her back into the night like waves on the tide.

"Sidney! Sid!"

Her breath became more ragged, more desperate as exertion intersected her adrenaline.

"Sid!"

The fraction of her name finally registered below her base survival drive, her traumatized responses. Her strides stuttered and hesitated on the sidewalk. She stomped to a heavy stop directly under a streetlight so she could feel it bathing her, wrapping her up away from the dark. She doubled over and planted her hands on her knees as she heaved to catch her breath. There did not seem to be any oxygen in the thin air.

Adam and Wes trailed her, still jogging even as she halted. In the harsh shadows sliding over their faces in the night, she could see their concern, an echo of the fear that drove her from the bar. Adam reached her first, his pace a little heavier than Wes's. He let his hands find her shoulders.

"What the hell happened?" Wes panted.

"My—my—my—" Sidney gulped at her breaths. "My attacker."

"What?" Wes said, more clearly. "Wait. What are you talking about?"

"My attacker was there," Sidney said.

"What? He was there? You saw him?" Adam released her shoulders and stepped back. Adam and Wes aligned side-by-side to examine her.

"Yes," Sidney stammered. "I mean, no." She hesitated, choking on her own words. "I smelled them. Then they grabbed me, and I just . . . I just freaked."

"Smelled?" Wes said. "What do you mean, smelled?"

Sidney bit her lip and wrung her cold fingers around each other.

"When I got attacked on the trail, they smelled like—I don't know—cleaner, disinfectant. That gross, fake lemon shit. It was strong, distinct." She paused again. "That's how I was sure it wasn't Adam."

She flitted her eyes to Adam, embarrassed. Adam consoled her with an innocuous smile.

"We should go back," Wes said.

"Wes, no." The panic welled back up into Sidney's throat.

"But he's there. We could report him, what he did to you."

"No!" Sidney's shout startled them all. She took a breath and tempered herself. "You can't arrest someone for a smell. No. I just want to go. Can we just go?" Sidney's fingers picked and squeezed at each other. "I want to get out of here."

Both men looked at Sidney with a myriad of expressions on their faces. Concern, irritation, fear, frustration, pity. Sidney glanced at them but found their perplexed expressions repulsive. She cast her gaze down, vibrated in her fear, and chewed her lip more compulsively.

"Of course we can go." Adam broke the terse moment and wrapped his arm around her, bringing her close along his side.

"Yeah, Sid, yeah," Wes echoed reluctantly. "Let's go get our shit together. We can leave whenever you want."

Sidney released a relieved breath and leaned into Adam.

"Thank you," she said softly into Adam's chest.

Wes moved up beside them, and they walked back to the condo, one on each side of Sidney, supporting her.

***

By the time the sun crested the horizon, Wes had driven them far from the ring of peaks cradling Telluride. The miles raced behind the car, growing the distance between them and the awful moments in the town. The aspens reflected across the windows as the car moved past them, but Sidney did not see them. She rested against the glass, the cold biting her forehead, and stared blankly at the scenery. Not seeing any of it.

She sensed Wes glancing over to check on her, but her head felt too heavy to rock toward him. Her entire body became as weighted as her head, thick and catatonic. Her flesh drifted far away and forgotten, leaving the thoughts surfacing as the only reality.

Artificial lemon disinfectant, that smell laced and

danced through every figment in her mind. As it spiraled into her thoughts, she found herself back on the dark trail, foolishly alone. She saw the condo light mocking her in the distance. She relived the gravel pressing into her. She saw that menacing presence so close it could have been in the backseat behind them. If she could feel her body, it would have been wrapped in anxiety.

Then the surge receded as memories of Adam climbed up to take their place. First, she relived the feeling of his skin, the way he smiled unadulterated at seeing her. Yet those pleasant, impulsive responses thinned and stretched as her brain attempted to apply logic to hindsight. The colors in her memories turned gray as awkwardness infiltrated her affection.

What had she been thinking meeting up with a stranger from the internet? Why had she jumped into bed with him immediately? Did she even know him, online or in Telluride? And what happened next? Where did they go from here as they were currently traveling in different directions across the country?

But didn't he know her? Didn't he honestly know her better than anyone in her real life? She had also told him everything, unfiltered and uncensored. Hadn't they truly connected so much that he was willing to travel across the country to meet her, to be with her? What did the medium for connection matter?

The last turn on the circle of her mind curved her home.

What would she tell Cameron about her trip? Would she lie to him and tell him she had had a great time? Would she tell him the truth about how his stupid mother almost got herself killed for horror movies and sex? Would Aiden be able to see it all on her? Would the story confirm what a loser his ex-wife was?

Her heart contracted tighter with each revolution of the mental rollercoaster. Somehow, in the blur, the echoes of her attack gradually became the least of her worries as real life swelled up around her.

She had forgotten her phone, cradled neglected in her palm. It vibrated sporadically, yet, just like with Wes's wellness checks, she could not muster a response. Between all the three-dimensional living and near-dying she had been doing, her online life was woefully neglected. She had made sure to check in at all the screens and post festival pictures. She had replied to her network. For the most part, she had been disconnected and plugged into the festival and Adam instead.

Her friends and followers were waiting for her reviews, or so she would have once hoped. Oliver, Max, Jack, and Allison were waiting, some more patiently than others. They could continue to wait through this drive. Just like Wes. She needed and could allow herself to get lost for these hours so that she could function when she stepped out of the car and back into her life.

"Are we going to talk about any of this, Sid?" Wes finally said, his concern obviously overtaking him.

Sidney let out a long slow breath and finally forced her eyes toward Wes. His head bobbed gently with the texture of the road as she glanced over at him. She cast a heavy look at him, trying to answer him with her eyes.

"Come on," he said. "You haven't taken a bite of a single piece of licorice. Realistically, that could mean you're dead."

A smile nearly teased the edge of Sidney's mouth, but it felt like too much work. She groaned as she peeled herself from the car seat and rubbed her hands hard over her face.

"What should we talk about?" Sidney finally croaked.

"Aside from the fact that we always debrief the fest on our drive home, a whole lot more happened this time. Most importantly, the attack you didn't want to report or talk about. Also, you know, Adam. As a whole."

Sidney breathed hard and mashed on her face again.

"Besides the near-death experience, I thought it was a good fest." Sidney attempted to keep her voice level.

"Ha! Nice try, Sid. That is our lowest priority topic."

"Fine." Sidney felt herself almost half-smile again. "Tell me what a stupid decision you think Adam was."

"Well, I did think it was super creepy to meet him there, but I guess the guy kind of grew on me."

"What?" The smile finally broke through Sidney's depressive paralysis. She felt some of the weight shed from her muscles, release her from its restraint; she felt a little more in her body in the car beside Wes.

"I mean, I did think he attacked you for that minute, but other than that, he seemed all right. He knew his horror and seemed to really give a shit about you."

"So glad knowing his horror was first on that list."

"Sid, it is a horror festival. Priorities."

That made Sidney actually laugh.

"Now, how do you feel about it?" Wes continued.

"Fuck, I don't know." Sidney breathed out hard.

"OK." Wes paused and waited. "Keep saying words."

"I feel conflicted. I've always really liked him. We always connected. And the time physically with him was great, aside from what happened after. That's where my instincts are. But my brain says, where do we go from here? What happens now? And maybe this is a terrible idea, hooking up with some stranger from the internet."

"All valid," Wes nodded. "You insisted he was not a stranger. Now, he's a stranger from the internet?"

"Ugh. I don't know."

"The Adam thing will sort itself out. Don't go all Sidney on it and overthink it to death. But we have to talk about this attack, Sid."

"I don't want to," Sidney grumbled and covered her face with her hands.

"I know you don't want to, and that's the problem. Why don't you want to talk about it? Why didn't you want to report it? Why are you just running and pretending it didn't happen?"

The embarrassment burned on Sidney's cheeks, and the sensation repulsed her. It felt so sickly familiar, the way it seemed to scorch her from her tender center out to her skin. She wished she could smother the words. Her muscles itched to run from them. She chomped on her bottom lip before answering.

"It's not that big of a deal," Sidney stammered. "I mean, I'm fine."

"Oh, don't be that fucking victim." Wes shot her a cold glance from the side of his eye, and she knew what kind of victim he meant. She knew what kind of victim he was familiar with.

"I'm not a victim," Sidney near-snapped.

"Ah." Wes's eyebrows popped up then floated back down. "That's what it is, isn't it?" he said, calmer now.

"What is?" Sidney said on impulse, already knowing the answer.

"You don't want to be a victim. You don't want people to see you that way."

Sidney choked at his words. They embedded in her brain, burrowing deep before spreading out. They found scars worn in the same pattern from all the horrible ways people had seen her before. Cheater, liar, selfish bitch.

"That's not what it is," Sidney denied. But maybe it was.

"Then what is it? You got attacked, so you report it. You don't just leave the attacker out running around in the dark."

"I don't know." The words felt so familiar that they could have worn grooves along her tongue.

She didn't know. She didn't know why the idea of telling the police, telling anyone about the figure in the dark chasing her down and tackling her to the dirt stacked a pressure on her chest that made it hard for her to breathe. She didn't know why the suggestion of reporting the incident made her limbs feel as trapped and desperate as they had while fighting off her attacker. Yet the squelching sensation was undeniable and simply screamed, with no justification, that she should not walk that path, that she knew the terrible place it went.

"I don't know what to do with that, Sid. I really don't." Wes's voice became distant, resigned. "You know it's the wrong thing to do, but you don't know why."

The hot tears sliced halfway down Sidney's cheeks before she realized she was crying. She hadn't felt the typical stinging swell of emotion overtake her face and tingle through her eyes. The tears had just crept out and started falling. She reached up and tried to subtly flick them away, the traitors.

"Can we just drop it for now?" Sidney managed. "That window has closed anyway."

Wes responded with silence, but Sidney noted the flexing in his jaw as his thoughts twitched over his features. He reached over and quietly began eating the neglected licorice.

Conversation died out, and they spent the last hour or so riding in silence. Before she was ready, the car's tires rolled into her driveway. Wes's irritation at Sidney had dissipated. As he helped her unload the car and hugged her goodbye, she felt the affection and concern radiating off him. It was comforting somehow.

Each step from the car up the driveway felt farther from Telluride, farther from the Horror Show, farther from that burning disinfectant smell, but also farther from Adam. She marched the entirety of the trip from the forefront of her consciousness, back towards memory. By the time her fingertips slid over the doorknob, it had dwindled down to an aching echo on her nervous system.

"Well, look who survived," Kendra said from the kitchen before even glimpsing her roommate.

Sidney chuckled to herself at the irony of the greeting, but the smile slipped from her cheeks with the guilt that she had not told Kendra everything yet and she would have to relive the whole mess again shortly, over a bottle of wine. Or two. She should have told her when it happened; she knew that more now as she confronted the idea of explaining why she had not.

"Barely," Sidney replied, giggling a little in spite of herself.

"Get in here. How was the trip?"

"How was your weekend with an empty house?" Sidney redirected.

"A house is never empty with Savannah bouncing off its walls." Kendra chuckled. "It was lonely without you guys, of course. We went to see my mom. You know going to the facility drains me. Too much like work."

"Oh, did you survive?"

"Clearly, I did," she laughed. "But how was *your* trip?"

Kendra rounded the counter of the kitchen and hurried across the living room toward Sidney. She hesitated and tilted her head at the sight of Sidney's puffy, splotched visage. Then she smiled and gathered her in a quick hug.

"Not that great?" Kendra inferred from Sidney's appearance. "Oh wait, you met Adam there! How did that go?"

"Are you going to pause to let me answer, or are you going to just keep on with the questions?"

Sidney chucked her bags onto the sofa, placing her laptop and phone gently on the coffee table.

"Fine, fine," Kendra laughed. "First one. How was the trip?"

"It was a mixed experience," Sidney said, as she dropped down beside her bags.

"Well, what does that mean? Start with Adam. The suspense has been killing me. You practically dropped off the world while you were out there. If you don't message, you must be dead."

Sidney smirked again. Kendra sat on the couch, drew her legs under her.

"Adam was . . . " Sidney searched for the word. "Great. Adam was great."

"So the connection was there in person?"

"Yeah, it was. It was like we had always known each other. It was no different than all those years online." Sidney felt herself smiling.

"Did you sleep with him?" Kendra leaned forward slightly, raising an eyebrow.

Sidney nodded.

"So, you slept with your longtime online boyfriend who might actually be a decent guy, and it went well. This is huge. How could this be a mixed trip? Was the festival a total bust or something?"

The warm smile dropped from Sidney's cheeks. She felt her own face fall as she shifted uncomfortably. Her teeth parted several times. Her lips opened, but she did not find words on her tongue.

"Jesus, Sidney," Kendra said. "What is it?"

"It's not a big deal." Sidney shrugged.

"It looks like a big deal." Kendra leaned in closer, bringing her hand to Sidney's shoulder.

"So, the night I went home with Adam, I kind of had a Sidney freak out after we slept together."

"Not entirely surprising."

"I decided to just leave in the middle of the night and get back to my room."

"Why?" Kendra interrupted.

"I'm not sure. That's not important though. As I was walking the trail back, I got attacked."

"Attacked?" Kendra nearly shot up to standing with the word.

"Sit down, Kendra. I'm fine."

"Fine? What do you mean 'attacked'?" Kendra returned to her cushion yet remained rigid.

"I was walking down the trail, and someone came out of the creek beside the trail. They chased me down and tackled me. I'm not sure what they intended to do, but I managed to bash them with an empty bottle and run off."

"Hell yeah, you did," Kendra said. Then she sat processing for a moment. "What did the police say? Did they catch the guy?"

"I don't know that it was a guy."

"Did they catch the person? The perpetrator. Your attacker."

Sidney took a deep breath and looked down at her lap, where her hands had tangled themselves together.

"I didn't report it," Sidney mumbled.

"You what?" Kendra launched back to her feet. "How could you not report it?"

"It wasn't a big deal."

"Stop saying that! That's what you said when you cheated on Aiden. That's what you say every time something happens with Aiden. These things are big deals."

Sidney rolled her eyes then returned her gaze to her lap.

"I already went through this with Wes."

"I'm sure he agrees with me." Kendra popped her hand on her hip.

"As usual."

"Well, that ship has sailed," Kendra breathed, returning to the couch. "Is that it?"

"Kind of." Sidney still did not look up.

"Kind of?"

"I think the attacker came at me a second time."

"Sidney, what?"

Sidney reached out and snatched Kendra's wrist before she ejected off the sofa again.

"Whoever attacked me smelled like cleaner. It was so strong I could taste the fake lemons. That's one of the reasons I could tell Wes that it was not Adam."

"Wes would think that."

"I smelled it again at the bar at the last party. Then someone grabbed me."

"Was it the attacker? Did you see him?" Kendra's eyes grew wider with each question.

"I don't know. I panicked. I just ran. Wes and Adam chased me down."

"Please tell me you reported it then."

"Reported what?" Sidney finally looked up at Kendra. "A smell? What would I tell them at that point?"

"What if it was one of the guys from online?"

Sidney avoided the question, looking away. She and Kendra sat for a moment, awkward in the quiet. They both stared gently at the carpet at their feet.

"So, that pretty much ended our weekend," Sidney

resumed. "I freaked out so bad that I just wanted to go. Wes and Adam got me back to the condo. We packed up, slept a little, and drove back here."

Sidney smiled at Kendra, knowing it was forced and knowing Kendra could see it. Concern wrinkled Kendra's brow, the way it always did when Sidney had told her about a recent episode with Aiden or a new internet friend. The contortion of her features also hinted at disappointment, and those edges cut at Sidney as she tried to ignore them.

"The fest itself was really good." Sidney elected to talk over the awkwardness. "The movies were really solid. Great Q&A sessions. Fun crowds. I actually got recognized several times. For my pictures and not my words, of course, but still."

Kendra acknowledged Sidney, but Sidney knew her mind was firmly fixed on that trail where Sidney had been attacked. Perhaps part of Sidney's mind still lingered there too. The conversation died between them, suffocated by all the things they didn't want to say.

Sidney gathered up her bags and dragged them to her room, closing the door quietly behind her. She took a long, slow breath to settle into the solitude. It was comforting to be alone, to not be answering questions about how stupid she had been, to not have to perform, to not have to be OK or not. She closed her eyes and inhaled again before finally gathering up her phone.

Adam: Just landed. Miss you already, beautiful.

The natural grin consumed Sidney's face. She bit at the edge of her lip as she typed in response.

Sidney: Just got home. I miss you too.
Adam: How was your drive?
Sidney: Long and awkward.
Adam: Why awkward?
Sidney: Wes lectured me a lot about not reporting the attack.
Adam: Well, he's not wrong . . .
Sidney: . . .
Adam: It is your choice to make though. I'm just glad you're safe. Home far away from whoever it was.
Sidney: Me too.

Sidney could have lived in the conversation thread with Adam. It felt safe there, like the way his heartbeat thumped in her ear as she lay on him before fleeing his bed. Already, he felt so far away and that night felt so long ago.

Oliver: You're back! FINALLY
Sidney: Hi Oliver. It was only a few days.
Oliver: A long few days without seeing you.

The instinct to send a selfie for his appreciation snapped into her fingertips. She acknowledged the feeling and ignored it.

Sidney: I posted plenty of pictures.
Oliver: Not the same when they're not for me.
Sidney: How are you? How was your weekend?
Oliver: Boring without you.
Sidney: Haha, lies.
Oliver: How was the festival?

Sidney bit her lip and looked at the blinking cursor in the field. She could lie here in the threat. She could omit. How would he know? He wasn't there to know she was false. She could give him whatever slice of truth she wanted, and for some reason, that made her want to give him all of it unfiltered. Yet when she brought her fingertips to the screen, she recoiled.

Sidney: It was a great festival.
Such good horror movies this year!
Oliver: Good good.
What are you wearing?

No question of authorities or reporting. No statements or judgements on what she should have done. Answering the question with how she wished it had been made her feel lighter, made the darkness of the memory slightly lighter.

Sidney took the time to acknowledge Jack and Allison, giving them shallow overviews of her weekend with promises to talk more later. She forced herself onto all her social media platforms, remarking how sad it was the festival was already over and how she couldn't wait to return next year.

Could she wait for next year? Her ribs flexed when she typed about future trips. Could she go back like it never happened, pretending it never happened as she had tried the last days after the attack?

She checked off all the mental boxes for her online life and pulled herself into bed. Her own sheets and pillows welcomed her. Her muscles fully relaxed for the first time since she had heard movement in the dark creek beside her. She let out a weighted exhalation as she sank into her nest. The exhaustion unfurled across her, spreading out like the blankets on top of her. She had never felt so ready for sleep.

Yet sleep did not come. Even as every cell in her body tumbled toward oblivion, her mind kept her tethered to consciousness. She returned to the terrible circle her thoughts had spiraled through on the drive home. Attack, Adam, reality. Each revolution seemed to bring her closer to Hell. They all marched her toward an unrested dawn.

"**M**OMMY!" CAMERON SQUEALED, bounding down the hallway as Aiden opened his front door.

Cameron's smile stretched so wide and so bright that Sidney did not even acknowledge Aiden. He was a doorstop, nothing more.

"Mom, you're back," Cameron said as he reached her. Sidney let Cameron plow into her midsection and truly felt the tightness in his hug. She didn't even care to see if Aiden watched. "I missed you," Cameron said.

Sidney could see that he really had. Maybe he had talked to Aiden about how he missed his mom. Maybe he had made Aiden listen to how great she was, for once. Sidney smiled openly in front of her ex-husband for the first time since their marriage had ended. Aiden was mumbling something as Sidney turned, her arm still around Cameron's shoulders, and walked down the driveway. But she didn't hear it. She happily shut Cameron's door behind him and dropped into the driver seat.

"How was your trip, Mom?" Cameron said from the backseat. His voice surprised her. The inflection at the end seemed foreign when he was not asking for something.

"It was good," Sidney replied. "Wes and I went to a lot of movies."

"Were they scary?"

"Some of them, yeah. Some of them were scary. Some of them were great. There were a couple bad ones too."

"Can I watch any of them?" Cameron asked excitedly, catching her eyes in the rearview mirror.

"Not yet," Sidney laughed.

Cameron pursed his lips and shook his head. "What else did you do?" he asked.

Sidney chewed at her lips without realizing it. She thought of Adam first. His hand on her thigh during the movies. His lips on her neck in the dark. Yet those memories instantly twisted into the attack on the trail. Disinfectant cleaner and the sound of the creek babbling calmly beside her frenzy.

"Not really anything, baby." Sidney choked on the words. The lies felt awkward and bumbling on her tongue, made her mouth feel full and uncomfortable.

It never would have crossed her mind to tell Cameron about Adam. She already kept him insulated from the very idea of Tony. The thought of having to tell him about some future partner pooled a heavy dread below her stomach. The subject of a stepparent was not a bridge she wanted to think about crossing.

She definitely could not tell her 10-year-old son she had been assaulted while walking in the dark in the mountains. Even with the attack safely in the past, it would scare him. He would worry about his mother. It would show him the ugliness of the world she was unprepared to explain. It was not as easy as dismissing the fiction in a horror movie on the screen.

Abruptly, Cameron ran out of questions or interest. He hummed to himself and snapped his fingers arrhythmically until Sidney pulled over to deposit him at school. Even as she turned her tires towards work, even as the things she had not told her son echoed in her brain, she still smiled at how happy he had been to see her, how tightly he hugged her, and how curious he had been about her trip. She bathed in the moment, reliving that simple joy. Her heart swelled with how much she had missed him and how complete she felt at his proximity. Her mind filled with curiosity at how his practice was over the weekend, what he ate, if Aiden kissed him and tucked him in the way he liked—the same things she wondered every weekend he was away, only stronger. Yet the car door closed behind him, and he turned to wave goodbye to her from the other side of the window.

Her euphoria carried her to the front door of the store. The key scraped through the lock. Daylight illuminated the dust particles in the air, and they danced in front of cell phone covers and chargers. At the sight, the levity receded from her chest, an unhappy weight replacing it. The pressure of discontentment.

Sidney turned on the lights and prepped the store then settled behind the counter with her phone.

Adam: I miss you.

She reread the message to which she had woken. She could read those three words over and over all day.

Adam: Back to work today. This Monday hurts more than usual.

Sidney: Just got to the store. It really is the worst.
I have to write all my reviews this week too.
Adam: You got this.

An hour passed in quiet solitude, with only the mumbling and flashing of the promotional videos filling the store. Apparently, no one needed an upgrade before lunch on a Monday morning.

Allison: I can't wait to read your reviews from the fest! How did it go?
I've never been to a film festival before.
Sidney: The fest was really good this year. A lot of good movies.
I have a lot of writing to do.

"Hey Sidney."

A familiar voice startled Sidney from her conversation threads. She jerked up embarrassed, feeling unprofessional. Tony strode across the flattened carpet. Sidney's heart clenched, fluttered, then resettled before he reached her counter.

"Tony," Sidney greeted, trying to infuse the name with some sort of excitement. "What brings you in here?"

Tony looked toward the ground before sweeping his eyes back up to her, sly smile on the edge of his mouth—a look that had worked on her numerous times. His face remained attractive. She could still make out the shape of his chest under his shirt. She still knew his scent and how he tasted. Yet the customary swoon was missing, the swell of questionable decisions, the repeated pattern that landed them on the nearest horizontal surface.

She looked flatly at a man who was far too young for her, whose conversation skills encouraged her eyes to roll in their sockets. Instead of an option, he looked more like a mistake.

"I need an upgrade." He grinned, skinning his phone from his back pocket and wagging it between his fingertips.

She realized he knew that look worked on her.

Sidney spared Tony her rehearsed assessment of each current phone model, subtly tailored to encourage the customer to favor the most expensive and least reliable option. She let him guide her to the phone he claimed to want and pulled up his plan details on the computer.

"I saw you were in Telluride over the weekend," Tony said as she took his new phone out of the box.

"Yeah, for the Horror Show," she replied without looking up.

"You didn't post as much as you usually do. How was it?"

"Stalking me online?" Sidney joked, squinting at him gently. Tony leveled that smile in return. "Yeah, I was in movies most of the time. Film festival and all."

Sidney placed his new, functional phone in his hand and collected the discarded device behind the counter. She extended her hand for his credit card.

"Is there no friendly discount?" His smile again. "I mean, I have seen you naked."

"As has half the internet," Sidney replied, less amused than he was. "If anything, I should charge you more."

"I feel like we haven't hung out in forever. Not since your party." Tony planted his elbow on the counter and leaned closer to her.

Tony's words seemed slow and heavy to Sidney. His proximity lacked the normal promising excitement. Instead, the back of her brain climbed down into her pocket to guess at what messages might be waiting for her there, reaching into her online life to escape the moments in the present.

"I've just been really busy," she replied, coolly.

"I'd like to spend some time with you." Tony reached out with his index finger and let it draw a line down the nerves on the side of her hand.

Adam: I miss you.

Sidney looked down at the frisky digit and smiled to herself, almost with detached amusement. Tony had always lingered since their first encounter, but she had consistently reached out for him. This felt like the first time he reached for her.

"Yeah, we can do that soon," Sidney said, drawing her arm back gently. "I'll message you."

Sidney did not move around the counter to escort Tony to the door. She knew from the way he kept glancing at her mouth that he would try to kiss her. She pretended to be entering data about the sale into the computer and sent him off with a friendly wave. He hesitated for an instant at the threshold then turned to glance back at her through the glass before climbing into his gleaming car.

Oliver: I still haven't seen you.

Sidney scrolled through her album and selected a neutral selfie from before her trip to Telluride. She did not want to show him herself now—post-Adam, post-attack—yet she was not sure why.

Oliver: This is not from today.

Sidney read the message preview, and her brow furrowed. She swiped the notification aside and did not open the conversation. She did not want to reply, and she did not want him to see that she had read the message.

The work day bled into evening. As twilight hinted in the sky, Sidney hurried out to her car and then headed to the baseball diamond. Cameron seemed less impressed with her than he had been in the morning, but she was on time picking him up, and that was enough of a victory.

After practice, Cameron babbled incessantly about some collaborative computer game Sidney had never heard of then devoured four slices of pepperoni and pineapple pizza. Then he disappeared to play that same game. Before the end of the night, she forced him through homework and into bed.

With Kendra and Savannah out for the night and Cameron snoring away in his bedroom, the house felt cavernous and empty. The rooms stretched wider in their vacancy. The air thickened with the quiet. Sidney found herself standing between the kitchen and living room for a moment, clutching her cold beer bottle and absorbing the emptiness of the house around her.

Then she snapped back into reality. She positioned

herself on the couch, pulled her computer across her lap, and gathered up the remotes.

She scrolled through streaming platforms and servers. She read familiar descriptions. She paged through her watchlists. Yet she found herself utterly uninspired. Hours, days, a lifetime of horror revolved past her eyes, but it seemed to have lost its flavor.

Did she want to see high school kids chopped up by a deranged serial killer? Did she want to watch a woman wash off the blood and execute her revenge? Did she want to see a demonic spirit overtake the body of a young girl in the country? Did she want to watch hillbilly cannibals ensnare ignorant road travelers? Did she want to see a brilliant psychopath show the woman he obsessed over how to live?

Somehow, instead of the welcome distraction, all these divergent dark paths led right back to the trail in Telluride and all the ways that moment made her mouth go impossibly dry.

Sidney dropped the remote beside her on the cushion and threw her head back with a sigh. She felt trapped, unable to find refuge in her usual places. She swirled her hands over her face as her laptop screen glowed at her, mocked her. When she lifted her head again, the edge of her sight caught a strange shape in the window beside the couch. Her brain latched on to the vague figure, and she turned her gaze to articulate it. Whatever it was moved rapidly, and her focus sharpened as her heart expressed interest.

Sidney looked and looked at the window, now just a black square in the wall reflecting her own dumb face back at her. The neighbor's dog barked. Sidney thought she heard something move against the house, a muffled crunch on the rocks perhaps. Her heart stopped pounding and seized instead.

Cautiously, with her arms curled up toward her chest, she rose from the couch. She rounded her spine to crouch toward her arms as she took exaggerated, careful steps to the window. She looked behind her for no reason before leaning down and casting her gaze into the night. Black greeted her at first, but as her eyes strained into the darkness, she made out nothing.

Absolutely nothing.

Sidney released the breath bundled up in her chest, not realizing how much it had been burning and knocking at her lungs. She rolled her eyes at herself as her heart settled back into her chest. Uncomposed, she sloppily tossed herself back on the couch and pressed the button to watch whichever movie she had last viewed.

Adam: Good morning, beautiful.
    I miss you.

Sidney smiled to herself, reading the messages through bleary eyes. She felt relieved to hear from him, to read the affirming words, like an addict getting a fix.

She lay on her back in bed as the dawn painted along her ceiling. No alarm waited on her phone since it was the weekend, but she had been watching the light creep into her window, developing the room out of the darkness. The hours had dragged out above her. She had counted the seconds tick off as her mind refused to plunge into sleep, as her brain flexed hyperaware of every noise and creak inside and outside her room.

Sidney let a heavy, frustrated breath dribble out of her lips and lifted the phone to her face to read Adam's messages again. She typed *I miss you too* into the field then tapped the delete button until it disappeared again. The cursor blinked, mocking her.

Sidney ran her fingertips along the vacant sheet beside her. She turned her head to look at the empty pillow. Part of her wished Adam occupied the bed with her. When she read his words, the back of her mind tumbled open and dumped her into the bed in Telluride beside him. She wanted to feel the warm, rough touch of his hand sliding up along her bare spine, pulling her close to him.

Yet the echo of his touch wandered. Though she tried to cling to the moment, to the feeling of him, the past unfolded against her will. She felt herself foolishly slip from their tangled sheets and walk out in the autumn night alone. Her heart pounded in her chest as the flashback leaped ahead to the figure rushing out from the shallow water. Immediately, she felt the panic of her attacker on top of her.

She flinched and shook the tendrils of memory from her mind. She snapped back from the warmth of the bed she had shared with Adam, back to her empty bed where she cuddled against the frosted edge of breaking morning. She rolled onto her face and ground it into her pillow, whining to herself. She knew she needed to respond to Adam. And the other messages she had been neglecting. He could see she had read his greeting and had not replied. She didn't want him to read anything into it.

Sidney: Hey there
     How are you?

Sidney pressed Send then hesitated for a moment. She nibbled at her lower lip in the light of her phone.

Sidney: I miss you too.

She quickly backed out of the conversation before

she could see he was typing a response. She did miss him. She wanted him beside her now. Maybe she would feel safer then. Maybe she would have slept through the night instead of flinching and opening her eyes wide at every miniscule sound. She just wished that her pleasant memory of him was not perverted by the awful decision she had made immediately afterward.

Allison: Are you OK?

Sidney smirked at the question.
"How did you know, Allison?" Sidney said to the empty room.

Sidney: Yeah, I'm OK.
Allison: Why are you up so early? It's early there, right?
Sidney: I haven't slept yet.
Allison: Someone keeping you up?
Sidney: Only myself.
Allison: Then what's wrong?

Sidney retracted her fingertips from the screen and chomped at her lip again. She had skimmed over the story with Adam and Wes. She had given Oliver a light rendition. She had adamantly avoided the event with Cameron. Yet her attack bubbled inside her brain; it frothed in her mouth, around all the words she didn't say. Couldn't it be safe to talk about it here, with this virtual stranger, in a world that didn't feel entirely real?

Sidney: Something happened in Telluride that's
  been keeping me up.
Allison: Did you meet someone?
Sidney: No
  Well, yes but that's not it.
Allison: Oh so what happened?
Sidney: I got attacked.
Allison: What? What do you mean attacked? Are
  you OK?
Sidney: I was walking down a path at night, and
  someone attacked me.
Allison: OMG! Are you OK?

Allison's insistent questions were somehow comforting. When real physical people asked Sidney if she was OK, she cringed. Yet here, filtered through the small, flat screen, it felt safe and more like a lifeline, something reaching out to keep her from floating away into the dark figments of her fear.

Sidney: I think I'm OK.
Allison: That's not very convincing. Tell me the
  whole story.
Sidney: I was walking back to my condo at night
  on this path along the creek. When I got
  close to my condo, someone came out of the
  creek and attacked me. They tackled me
  down. I managed to clock them with a bottle
  I had in my bag. Then I ran away.
Allison: Oh my God! That's so scary! Did you
  call the cops?

Sidney stopped and rolled her eyes. The cop question again.

Sidney: No.
Allison: Why not?

Sidney rolled her eyes harder. She hated that question even more. She wanted to again say that it wasn't a big deal, that she was fine—but that was not really true. Sidney took a deep breath and blew it out against her phone.

Sidney: I didn't want to.
Allison: Why not?
Sidney: I didn't want that attention.
Allison: What do you mean?

That attention. That judgement. Those whispers behind her back at how stupid she was or what bad decisions she made. The same as it had been as things fell apart with Aiden.

Sidney: I didn't want to be a victim.
	I watch victims all the time. I write about victims all the time.
	I guess I didn't want to be that cliché.

There it was. The truth.

Allison: Still. You should have called them.
Sidney: Maybe.
Allison: So why is it keeping you up now?

Sidney: I don't know. I keep thinking I'm hearing or seeing things.
Allison: Like what?
Sidney: Like someone is in the house or outside the house.
Allison: That's probably pretty normal after what happened.

Somehow, Allison's last message calmed Sidney. She had not entirely accepted why she had refused contacting the authorities. She just knew the idea made her stomach sink and her skin crawl harder than it already was under her fading panic. It felt good to type it out of her brain, look at her motivation and see its shape. It made more sense than she expected. And Allison had not judged her.

The day had spread fully into Sidney's room as she typed and swiped on her phone. In the bright daylight, the sleepless night and all its unnerving noises felt more like a dream—though she would have had to sleep for dreams to unwind in her brain. All her fears felt flat and foolish in the light.

Even though there were sounds in the house now, Sidney's pulse remained flat and level. The sounds were familiar, the bumping and shuffling of the life within their walls. Savannah and Cameron's voices bounced along the walls as the footsteps battered the carpet. Kendra's muffled yelling pushed up against Sidney's door.

Sidney groaned as she stretched. Her weary muscles objected to the movement, to the very idea of hoisting her body from the sheets. She could not leave Kendra alone taming the little monsters downstairs.

"Mom!" Cameron yelled.

He skidded his steps along the floor and barreled into her, wrapping his arms tightly around her waist. Sidney closed her eyes to relish the embrace as she pressed her hand between his shoulder blades. Then Savannah came running up beside him, and they were gone bounding down the hall.

"Well, good morning," Kendra said from behind the open fridge door.

"Morning," Sidney groaned. Her voice sounded foreign and gravelly.

Kendra snapped up from behind the door, her eyebrows knitted above her nose.

"What?" Sidney croaked, attempting to clear her throat.

"You look awful." Kendra held the orange juice suspended in the air beside her.

"Hey," Sidney laughed. "Yeah, I didn't sleep last night."

"You look it. Why not?"

Sidney nipped at her lip quickly, before she caught herself. She felt the honesty she had typed out to Allison well on her tongue then swallowed it back down.

"Just restless, I guess," Sidney lied. "I have so much to write up from the fest. I feel very behind. I spent most of the night writing articles in my head."

"But you never got up and just wrote them?" Kendra asked.

"No, I kept telling myself I would just fall asleep any minute."

"Well, girl, let me flip on the coffee for you."

Sidney smiled wide. "Thank you. I surely need it.

Going to try to catch up on my writing today. Where are you headed, dressed and done with coffee already?"

"My mom." Kendra's smile slid from her cheeks.

"Oh no. Is she worse?"

"Not really." Kendra kept her eyes down on the orange juice now balanced between her hands. "She's just getting really confused some days, and that makes her very agitated. You know Mom."

"I do." Sidney smiled. "She's got that controlling streak about a mile wide. Thankfully, none of that passed on to you." Sidney playfully rolled her eyes.

"Thankfully." Kendra cracked a grin and looked up at Sidney, her eyes less heavy.

"What can I do?"

Kendra placed the glass on the counter and swept her fingertips along her eyes to ensure her makeup was in line. She jostled her curls and looked at Sidney again.

"I don't know. Pick up Savannah if I get stuck there long?"

"Of course. Just let me know and I'll make it work."

"Thanks, girl. I just wish visiting her wasn't like going to work. I wish I didn't want to manage everything around her. I wish I couldn't see the staff the way I see my people."

"You mean, you wish you didn't want to control it?" Sidney added a gentle giggle.

"Ha! Pretty much. I'll try not to control it and want to control it today. Maybe that will help." Kendra's eyes drifted downward again.

"I hope it does." Sidney nodded.

Without a word, Kendra walked over and hugged

Sidney. Sidney gripped her tight for a long minute, clutching until she felt Kendra withdraw. Then they shared a smile before Kendra moved to gather her things.

Sidney's phone buzzed in her hand.

Adam: What's wrong?
Sidney: What do you mean?
Adam: You don't seem like yourself. You OK?
Sidney: How can you tell that over message?
Adam: Just can.

Somehow, Sidney knew he was smiling as he typed that. The same expression found its way onto her face.

Oliver: Where have you been, beautiful?
Sidney: Nowhere, just busy.
Oliver: You haven't had the time to flirt with me.
Sidney: I'm sorry.
Oliver: I miss you.

The words did not read the same coming from Oliver. Oliver had always been a fun flirtation, yet that did not stimulate Sidney right now. Something in her chest seemed closed, but she wasn't sure what that was. She didn't think she wanted to terminate the relationship, but she felt flinchy at his requests.

"Your phone is blowing up as usual," Kendra said, handing Sidney a steaming coffee mug.

"Always," Sidney grinned. "Thank you so much."

"Adam?"

"Yeah. And the stalkers."

"Always the stalkers. Just be careful with those

weirdos, Sid." Kendra stopped for a moment, chewing on her next thought. "Do you think the person who attacked you was one of your online stalkers?"

Sidney went rigid, setting the coffee cup on the counter to not drop it at her feet.

"Do you think it was Adam? Like Wes did?" Sidney shoved the questions out between her teeth.

"No, no." Kendra waved her hands dismissively. "No, Sidney. I mean, do you think it was one of the other randos who messages you? Someone who would know you were at the fest?"

Sidney wrapped her arms tightly around her stomach.

"Well, honestly, anyone could know I was there," Sidney said, staring down. "I post and tweet about it publicly in real time. I figured it was safe because it was a festival full of people and I always had Wes with me."

"Except alone on a trail in the middle of the night."

"That was unplanned. Definitely didn't post or message about that." Sidney sucked in a deep breath then let it escape. "I suppose it could have been any of these people who message me. It could be anyone who just follows me. The internet is full of stalkers. People who spectate on social media, never posting or commenting or interacting, the same way they spectate on real life."

"Or it could have just been some random person."

"Exactly."

Sidney finally looked up at Kendra. Kendra had started to lean in. Sidney knew she would next be reaching for her shoulders.

"They definitely followed me while I was there," Sidney said. "I heard something in the creek the night before. Then, when I was alone, they came out of the creek. But whether I knew that person or they stalked me online, I really have no idea."

"Man or woman?"

"I honestly don't know. Bigger than me. Stronger than me. But it all happened so fast."

"So you didn't get a look at him at all?"

"You know, I didn't call the cops so I could avoid questions just like this," Sidney said.

"And you should have called the cops!" Kendra playfully shoved her shoulder.

"Yeah, I probably should have." Sidney rubbed her hands over her face and retrieved her coffee. "But enough about that part of the trip. I need to write about the rest of the fest."

"Are you going to include this in your recap?"

"And invite the 'you got what you deserved' comment shit storm online? Absolutely not."

Sidney raised her mug to salute Kendra and Savannah as they hurried out of the house. Cameron briefly appeared in the doorway to negotiate his way into more computer game time—an easy sell, since it enabled Sidney to work. Then Sidney moved her laptop to the couch and the TV.

Five hours later, Sidney had drained an additional four cups of coffee and produced three reviews and two articles. Cameron had only surfaced for sustenance. She felt the weight of her torso compacting into her hips as her lower back whined at the inactivity. Her arms dragged heavily on her wrists as they pressed into her laptop. She willed her fingertips to keep dancing nimbly over the letters on the keyboard, yet they stumbled through typos.

Sidney shifted the warm laptop off her legs and onto the cushion beside her. Maybe Kendra was right and she should surrender and get a proper desk. Kendra kept telling her she could still watch horror movies while writing from a desk. Snatching up her phone and her empty mug, Sidney moved to the kitchen.

As she placed her mug in the sink and replaced it with a glass of water, she checked her phone notifications. Conversations with Jack, Tony, and yet unknowns called out to her with red indicators. It felt unnatural to ignore them. She toyed with the idea of making excuses to pacify her online personas. Yet her heart hovered somewhere low in her ribcage, heavy as it pressed on her diaphragm. Her brain did not wind down the normal paths. All paths ended up in the dark in Telluride.

Sidney shook her head hard. It was fine. She was fine. Telluride and the dark trail and the creek and the figure were hours away. No one was here, besides her distracted child. No one was coming for her. She needed to shake it off, get back to work, and get back to normal.

The computer game had been gracious enough to distract Cameron all day, but Sidney could not hide from being a mother forever. Sidney hoisted herself off the couch and disconnected from the internet. She shepherded Cameron through the bath and bedtime routine, making sure to fully engage with him before tucking him in tight. She caught herself kissing his head two or three times extra. She shut the light and dragged the door closed behind her then returned to her screen until her eyes dried out and her vision grew blurry. By the time she closed the laptop, she near stumbled, bumbling with all the thoughts pouring out of her head and onto the virtual pages.

Her mind was blissfully empty, quiet the way it was right before she drifted off to sleep. Her body moved on autopilot as her brain hummed in steady static. She mechanically changed her clothes in her bedroom, convinced that she would find sleep on her pillow this time.

She drifted into the bathroom, practically tangled in sleep as she moved. Her fingers crawled along the counter toward the cup that held her toothbrush. When her hand found nothing, she looked down at the empty cup. Confusion roused her cognition. She stood up straighter and scanned the counter. Her eyes found the missing toothbrush lying flat on the opposite side of the sink.

She stood staring for a long time, looking between the toothbrush and where she should have found it. She pursed her lips before nibbling at them, perplexed.

Sidney reached with the opposite hand and lifted the toothbrush to her face. She ran her fingers along the bristles. They were damp—too damp from the morning use. She was sure she had replaced it in the cup. Maybe Cameron moved it while he and Savannah were playing or while he was getting ready for bed himself. It had to have been Cameron. Sidney told herself she would scold him in the morning, yet something snagged at the back of her mind, pulling her farther away from sleep.

***

Sidney's phone alarm shattered the morning. Apparently, she had slept, if only for those fleeting

215

moments as the night died. Yet there was no protesting against Monday, and she dragged herself painfully from the sheets. She staggered down the hall before swinging Cameron's bedroom door open and flicking on the light.

"Cameron," Sidney shouted through her morning breath. "Get out of this bed. Now!"

"But Mom," Cameron whined, throwing the blankets over his head, "I'm just so tired."

"So am I, baby. Out of this bed."

"Nooooooo."

Cameron burrowed deeper into the bed, attempting to tunnel away from his morning obligations. His muffled grumble belabored his protest. Sidney threw her head back in exasperation and massaged her forehead. The same dance every morning.

"Cameron," she said again, in her Mom Voice.

Cameron responded with more stifled whines. Sidney reached down and snatched the edge of the blanket. She yanked hard until she unearthed her willful child and the blankets piled on the floor beside his bed.

"Mom!" Cameron shrieked, popping up on the mattress rigid and angry.

"Out of this bed," Sidney repeated as she turned to walk out the door.

As Sidney padded down the hall, she heard her son grumbling, yet his laments were at least migrating towards the bathroom. She waited until she heard the door click behind him; then she hurried down the hall to hustle herself ready. Once she donned her loathed polo, she marched back to motivate Cameron.

"Are you dressed?" she hollered down the hall.

"Yes!" Cameron whined back.

"I'm coming to check," she threatened.

She heard Cameron's disproportionately heavy footsteps scramble to corroborate his embellishment. She smeared makeup over her face and hurried down to meet Kendra in the kitchen.

"You look less dead," Kendra greeted.

"Good morning to you too," Sidney replied.

"Those kids getting ready?"

"Hell no. Do they ever?"

"Not without yelling."

Sidney moved around Kendra as she packed school lunches, kicked off the coffee pot, and waited to fill their mugs. Once she had a steaming cup, she extended it to Kendra.

"There is not enough of this in the world right now," Kendra mused as she inhaled the steam. "Two people called out last night. One quit."

"I know. I was here with your daughter, remember?"

"Ah, yes, of course you were."

"When did you finally get in?"

"After 2."

"Oh damn." Sidney toasted her.

Kendra took a deep sip, scalding her tongue, and winced.

"Oh, girl," she said, pressing her finger to her lip. "Remember that Savannah and I will be gone the next two nights."

"Right, that thing with your aunt."

"Yep. Two nights of being interrogated as to why I don't just resolve things with the ex. For Savannah's sake of course. And because I'm not getting any younger. And because you and I can't continue like two divorced lesbians forever."

"We absolutely can live like divorced lesbians forever," Sidney laughed.

"That's what I tell her. I ask her if she would rather Savannah and I live all alone, if she would really want me to do it by myself until some other guy, who most likely would screw me over, showed up."

"Does she have an answer?"

"Not really," Kendra smirked. "She just says our homosexually suggestive relationship will scare off any prospects."

"Little does she realize that would instead lure the wrong prospects."

Kendra dissolved into giggles, lifting her mug to her lips so that her laughter echoed against the coffee.

"I tell you, she's as bad as my mom was before she started slipping," Kendra shook her head.

"She's just picking up the slack," Sidney laughed.

Sidney drained her mug and set it in the sink. Then she gathered up her purse and coat.

"Cameron, we gotta go!" she shouted.

Sidney flipped her keys in and out of her palm, letting them bounce against the scabs on her palm, and tapped the toe of her shoe on the carpet. She heard no sounds of life moving punctually toward the door to leave for school.

"Cameron, NOW!" she yelled louder.

"You know you're going to have to go get him," Kendra said from behind her. "You have to every morning."

"Is it too much to dream that he will one day learn

and get his shit together without me screaming?" Sidney sighed.

"Yes. Yes it is."

Kendra looked into her empty mug then shuffled toward the coffee maker for a refill.

Sidney tossed her head back in a huff and stormed back toward Cameron's room. When she reached his door, she slapped her hand into the frame. Cameron and Savannah lay sprawled on his rug, playing with cars.

"Are you kidding me?" Sidney shrieked. She was yelling before she even realized it, the words tearing out of her throat louder than she ever would have intended. Yet the words came like an avalanche. "What are you doing? You don't hear me calling you? We have to go! Now!"

Cameron looked at her, dazed, then leaped to his feet. He stood there on the rug, just looking at her wide-eyed. She felt the anger surge up in her again.

"Shoes! Put on your shoes now!" Sidney threw up her hands, keys rattling against her fingers. She stomped down the hall as the rage throbbed through her legs and pulsated at her temples. Cameron mumbled to Savannah and chased after her.

Sidney continued to seethe as they began their morning commute. Cameron sat in the back, rigid at first. By the first intersection, he had forgotten his mother's screaming fit and resumed talking and singing to himself. His normal sounds bristled against Sidney's agitated brain initially. Then they permeated her tantrum, wore down to her logical reason. The wave of anger crested and receded to unearth guilt like shells embedded in the shore.

Sidney took a deep breath and let it swirl out from her lips. An apology swelled on her tongue, but she let it deflate and trickle back down her throat. She didn't want to disturb Cameron's happy, carefree game by dragging him back to her shouting about shoes.

The weekday routine swallowed Sidney. She dropped Cameron off at school, telling him she loved him as she silently promised herself she would be a better, calmer mother tomorrow. She picked up more coffee to water her empty stomach and reluctantly dragged herself to work.

She was relieved to pull into an empty parking lot. No Tony there to awkwardly greet her this time. For once, she was happy to open an empty store and sit alone in the quiet.

She lasted about five minutes listening to the devices in demo mode before her fingertips crawled into her pocket. Her frantic morning had left her inboxes neglected, and the notification counts reflected that. Even as she had withdrawn from online life, online life had not yet withdrawn from her.

Adam: How is your day going?

Oliver: Where are you, gorgeous? Do I get to see you again?

Jack: How is it back home? How are those reviews coming?

Allison: Hey girl, how are you feeling? Any better?

Brady: BITCH, stop avoiding me! We need to shoot.

Wes: Hey Sid, just checking in.

Sidney smiled to herself, warmed by all the contact. She read over the message previews repeatedly, not touching them to indicate she had read them just yet.

Sidney: Well, I lost it and yelled at my kid.
Like I always do.
So I don't feel super awesome about myself.
Now I'm at work. Yay.
Adam: But you have the best job ever and you love it.
Sidney: Haha

Against her best efforts, Sidney did laugh at his sarcasm. She found it easier to infer his tone after having met him in person, having assigned mannerisms to the words and phrases she knew.

Sidney: Thanks for checking on me.
I'm good.
Wes: I don't believe you . . .
Sidney: I'm fine!
Wes: Liar . . . haha
Sidney: I'll give you live tweet proof of life soon.
Wes: Deal!

The thought of doing a live tweet seemed daunting, but she also knew Wes would diligently keep checking on her until he was satisfied.

Sidney: I don't know about better.
Allison: What do you mean?
Sidney: I don't know.
    I feel very paranoid maybe?
    I keep thinking I see or hear things outside.
    I'm not sleeping great.
    I have just been freaking out over stupid stuff. Like my kid moving my toothbrush the other night.
Allison: Are you sure your kid moved it?

Sidney flinched for a moment, not wanting to consider that question, not wanting to abandon the safety of her explanation.

Sidney: He had to have. No other explanation.
Allison: Of course. That must be it.
Sidney: I just want to feel normal again.
Allison: It's not like anyone has been in your house. Don't worry.

Sidney wanted to believe Allison. She wanted to think she would get back to normal again. If she reflected objectively, she could tell herself nothing had really happened in Telluride. She had gotten tackled by some crazed shadow in the dark and had escaped. She was fine and far away now. Things were fine, normal.

Sidney: Tonight will be a good test.
Allison: How do you mean?
Sidney: It will be my first night alone. No roommate, no kids.
Allison: You got this, girl!

Sidney took a deep breath and opened her camera app. She lifted the phone to reflect herself from the flattering downward angle. She was going to feel normal again; she was going to be normal again. She pressed a normal, coy smile onto her cheeks. She opened her eyes and stared into the tiny camera. She snapped the shot, reviewed it, and forced herself to send it to Oliver.

Oliver: There you are!
  Beautiful
  I missed you.

Oliver's compliments did not resonate as they had before. They did not inspire a warm flutter in her chest. Yet she did still smile genuinely and did, in fact, feel a little more normal. She even responded to Jack, whom she had been avoiding since Telluride for reasons she could not quite articulate. She shot him vague and obscure apologies to keep him on the hook until she was herself again.

Everyone was a potential website visitor.

Adam: You still don't seem quite yourself.

Sidney sighed as she read the message. Adam's perception and persistence felt misplaced. Digitized. Part of her felt guilty for omitting so much of herself right now, yet part of her wanted to keep that fresh disfigurement safely out of his view. She liked him, more than she cared to accept, and she wanted him to continue liking her. She already felt stupid and weak enough for getting assaulted after leaving his bed. She wanted to go back to his bed and stay beside him, never wandering off in the dark to find a stranger on the trail.

She chewed at her lip as she lifted her phone to reply. Her fingers twitched in objection, yet she tapped the keys through the resistance.

Sidney: I guess I'm not yet.
Adam: What's wrong?
Sidney: I think I'm still a little shook up from Telluride.
Adam: I thought you said you were OK.
Sidney: I thought I was. Then I guess it started to sink in.

Sidney shook her head, feeling stupid as regret laced its way through her thoughts. In the empty store, she kept her eyes on the screen, watching the icons dance as Adam typed his reply. Her lip began to tear beneath the constant tugging of her top teeth.

Adam: So, what's going on?
Sidney: I'm just not really sleeping.
    I'm scared sometimes.
Adam: Scared of what?
Sidney: I'm not really sure.

Lies.

Sidney rolled her eyes at herself. She could just flay open her heart and confess the truth to Allison, some online persona she had never met. Yet knowing Adam in real life, having had his hands move over her actual body, had her virtual tongue in awkward knots. Every time she typed, she felt more stupid and remorseful. She should have continued to keep her madness tucked back in her physical head.

Adam: Are you just still upset or do you think
there's something to be scared of now?
Sidney: I know there's nothing to be scared of
now. Whoever it was is far away.
I think it just got under my skin.
I just need some normal life.
Adam: That'll happen. Just need some time.
You want to hear something good?

The anxiety eased in her chest. She smiled at the idea of something else, something good. Sidney leaned forward on the counter, propping herself up on her elbows and holding her phone closer to her face.

Sidney: Yes, please.
Adam: You haven't complained about your ex
since before Telluride.

Sidney shot back up and let the phone dangle from her hand. He was right. Aiden had not crossed her mind in any moment she was not actually with him. She would have to see him when she brought Cameron to him after practice, yet she had not spared a moment dreading it. It was a strange void in her brain, unfortunately filled by something more malicious.

Sidney: Wow, you're right.
I think I have you to thank for that.

And it was true. Partially true, at least. As she walked in the dark away from Adam's hotel, Aiden had been the farthest thing from her mind. Now, when she turned to the empty pillow beside hers, she projected Adam's face from her memory.

At Adam's words, Sidney's mind wandered to earlier in that night, to long before the trail in the dark. She saw the unmitigated smile that stretched his face when he saw her for the first time. She felt his hand tentatively reaching for hers in the dark of the movie theater. She heard their laughter as they fumbled into his hotel room after the bar. She felt his hand pressing, heavy and unconscious, into her bare back. Relief spiraled out from the pleasant turn in her train of thought.

Sidney messaged her way through the hours of her shift. So few customers broached the door that only the security cameras were there to witness. When Seth wandered in half an hour late, she did not even lift her eyes from the screen.

"Hey, boss lady," Seth said, almost cautiously. "Sorry I'm late. I met this—"

"Don't worry about it, Seth," Sidney dismissed. "I'll write you up next time. For being late. And for not stocking the shelves before the end of your shift. And for not properly entering your returns."

"Whoa, Sidney, what the h—"

Sidney ditched her phone on the counter and lifted both her hands gently. She let her gaze wander to his sneakers, laced in bright green below his tight pant legs.

"Sorry, Seth," she said, finally lifting her eyes. "I

mean, you do need to stop being late, but I didn't mean to come for you."

A smile finally broached Seth's lips, softening his face to the boyish flirtation usually on his features. For Sidney, and for any female customer who walked through the door. The smile of a man accustomed to his looks doing most of his negotiating. Sidney suddenly thought that aging would be hard on him, when his strongest tactic began to wither and fade, revealing everything he had been hiding behind it.

"Go ahead and get out of here, Sidney," he said, stretching the grin wider and sweeter. "It looks like you need it."

Sidney left the conversation where it died, pushed the glass door open, and hurried to her car. She sped over to Cameron's practice then to Aiden's porch.

As she ascended the tragically familiar steps, she thought of Adam's messages. A slideshow of his face flickered over her mind, replacing the montage of screaming, crying memories with Aiden. When Aiden opened the door, she did not even gauge his body language. She did not look at him to see how he was looking at her. She simply handed him Cameron's bag and retreated off the porch, light and untethered. She thought she saw Aiden watching her, puzzled, as she walked back to her car.

As the road rolled under her tires, Sidney was almost alarmed as the tension uncoiled from her lower back. She gently pressed deeper into the upholstery of her car seat. Her fingers formed loose rings to maintain control over the steering wheel. As the sun reclined behind the horizon and the light diffused across her windshield, calm felt foreign on her nerves.

Her mind rattled almost empty with only a few musing thoughts about Adam and the writing she would plow through in her isolation ahead.

By the time she approached her own front door, the day had died in the sky above her, bleeding out in purple and orange along the now-dark jagged edge of the western horizon. She moved mechanically, practiced, absentminded, as she unlocked her door and stepped inside her home.

She moved through the house in the dark, memorized steps navigating the floorplan in her brain. She drifted past the couch, flipping on the first light, and dumped her keys on the kitchen counter. She stripped her purse from her shoulder and shrugged off her coat.

The chill in the air surprised her. She brought her arms around herself against the cold and squinted around the room.

It took her longer than it should have to realize the window above the couch was open and the screen was missing. Once her mind wrapped around the sight, her ribcage flexed and heart throbbed. Her skin tightened as her goosebumps rose. She felt colder. She stared at the window, noticing the pillow on the couch was tipped from its usual position, the cushion depressed with a footprint.

Sidney flinched back until she bumped into the counter. She clung to her own arms, wrapping her shoulders in tightly, curling herself into a ball. Wide-eyed, she took a step forward, a step deeper into the house. Was she alone? Was that really a footprint? Was there someone in the house?

She made it ten steps into the hallway before

reason surfaced beneath her panic. The thought crystallized in the forefront of her mind. She did not want to be a white girl in a horror movie. She knew better. She was smarter than this. You do not go investigate the strange noise. You definitely do not go see if the burglar is still in the house.

With her intelligence restored and active again, she snatched her purse and keys. She fled the house and hurried back to her car in the dark night.

17

"**TELL ME AGAIN** where the other residents are," the officer spoke in a dreadful monotone, her eyes reflecting the flatness of her tone.

"Kendra, my roommate. She and her daughter are with Kendra's aunt," Sidney repeated. "My son is with his father."

"And you were coming from work and dropping off your son." The officer looked at her pad as she spoke.

"Right. I opened the door and walked in like usual. When I turned on the light, I realized the window was open and the screen was gone. Then I ran out here and called."

The officer stopped talking and tapped her pen on her pad. She did not make eye contact with Sidney, did not acknowledge her. Her curly hair was wrangled into a bun at the base of her skull. She wore no makeup and no jewelry and towered above Sidney with an intimidatingly calm presence. Her partner, a pale and slight man who appeared to be drowning in his uniform, moved up behind her. She nodded at him then stepped aside so he could face Sidney in parallel.

"We've secured the house," her partner said, his voice much less commanding. "You'll have to give us an inventory of anything you see missing. As far as we can tell, the perpetrator only got to one room. We're assuming you interrupted the burglary when you got home. Must have fled out the same window while you were out in your car."

Sidney's chest tightened with each phrase that tumbled from his thin lips. She stared at his mouth as he spoke, forcing herself to see the words that drifted farther away.

"Do you have somewhere you can stay tonight?" the female officer asked, finally making gentle eye contact with Sidney.

Sidney startled then forced an awkward smile.

"Yeah, I have somewhere I can go," she replied.

"You can come back tomorrow to look over the scene," her partner said. "Also, have someone fix that window and change all the locks. Standard precautions."

Sidney nodded, tears caught in her throat, strangling her words. She left the officers still talking in her driveway as she slowly pulled away in her car. She did not sink into the seat; she perched so rigidly that her muscles trembled along her back. Her hands wrung the steering wheel, sliding in her own sweat. Her mind teemed with thoughts, impregnated by her fear, warped by her panic. The fading adrenaline in her veins burned and ached in its decline.

When Brady opened the door, he did not say a word. He did not ask a question. He simply swallowed her in his arms and held her close. Jordan stepped up beside him and wrapped the two of them in a firm group hug. Sidney cuddled into their tight embrace as it encircled her. She gripped the fabric of their shirts. She felt safe and never wanted to let go.

After a long hug, the three disentangled. Sidney swiped her cheeks and smiled warmly at the men. Brady draped his arm around her and guided her to the couch. He placed her squarely on a cushion and sat across the coffee table from her. Jordan joined them, expertly juggling three stemless glasses of crimson wine. The deep liquid barely wavered with his level steps. He placed a glass before Sidney and sat down beside Brady.

"Thanks for putting me up, guys," Sidney said quietly, staring at the way the dim light reflected off the surface of her wine.

"Of course, Sid," Brady dismissed. "I'm so glad you called us. You know you can always come here. Did you tell Kendra?"

Sidney nodded. "Yeah, I called her before I left. She flipped but was glad I was coming here."

"We're just glad you didn't actually see the burglar," Jordan said. "Could have been way worse."

"I almost did," Sidney mumbled.

"How do you mean?" Jordan asked.

"I had a white girl in a horror movie moment."

"You were going to investigate the strange noise?" Brady's eyes snapped open.

Sidney lifted her glass and nodded as she sipped. Both men shook their heads.

"I caught myself," Sidney said. "I saw the open window. Then I started walking deeper into the house to investigate. Then I realized that was stupid and ran out to my car to call the police."

"I'm glad you called the police this time," Brady replied. Jordan nudged him.

"They think the person was still in the house and I

interrupted. They said things only looked disturbed in one room," Sidney continued, before gulping at the wine. She reached forward and replaced the glass on the coffee table. Her fingertips gravitated toward each other nervously, and she began picking at her nails and tugging at her cuticles. She stared toward the legs of the coffee table but did not focus her eyes enough to see them.

"Oooh, we should do a break-in shoot!" Brady suddenly said, excitedly. "Use this awful night for inspiration."

"Brade," Jordan said softly.

Jordan reached over and placed his hand on Brady's arm. They looked at each other. Brady read Jordan's expression then softened his own. The creative enthusiasm drained from the edges of Brady's face. Then they both turned to Sidney, sympathy weighing their features.

"Brade, look at her."

"Oh honey," Brady said, "you're really shook up."

Jordan stood and skirted the coffee table to drop down beside Sidney. He pressed his palm into her shoulder and draped his fingertips down the top of her bicep.

"Sid, why are you so upset?" Brady asked. "I mean, I know a break-in is scary, but no one was home."

"Thankfully," Jordan added.

"And it doesn't sound like they got the chance to take much. For what it is, I think you got very lucky."

"I know. I know it doesn't make sense," Sidney said, her voice strained and wavering.

Sidney rubbed her hands over her face, smearing the light tears into her skin. Brady got up and slid onto the cushion beside her. She found herself ensconced between her friends again. Brady stroked her back gently.

"It's this," Sidney continued, flipping her hands limply. "And it's Telluride. I know they're unrelated, and I know this is just some random break-in. It's just so much at once, so close together. I feel so violated. I feel so exposed. I don't feel safe."

"You're safe here, girl," Jordan said, firmly.

"You can stay here as long as you need. You know that," Brady said.

Sidney chewed on her lip and picked at her fingers as her pause dragged out into a silence. Brady and Jordan released their touch but stayed with her, quiet and patient. The words were on her tongue, but she didn't want to hear them out loud.

"Sid, honey," Brady said. The familiar sharp edges of his voice fell off, and his tone came across gentle and soft. "Just say whatever you're chewing on."

Sidney immediately released her lip from her teeth and shook her hands apart. "I don't know," she stalled. "I just . . . " She took another deep breath and resisted the urge to nip at her bottom lip again. "I just don't feel like myself."

"How so?" Jordan asked.

"Everything makes me nervous now. Normal stuff that has nothing to do with getting attacked in Telluride or having my house broken into. I'm trying to just go back to normal, be normal, but I don't feel normal."

"I think all of that sounds pretty natural, Sid," Jordan said. "I mean, you're shook up. You got attacked. Someone was in your house. Yes, it could have been worse. Yes, you're fine. But it's still going to take some time to fade, to get back to normal."

"And that's OK," Brady echoed, nodding gently.

Sidney forced a smile that felt strange on her face. She snatched back up her wine. She closed her eyes and tipped the glass up until she drained it. Her mind throbbed, pregnant with thoughts, worries, and the echoes of Brady and Jordan's words.

"Let me get you a pillow and blanket for this couch," Brady said, standing.

"I have to go back to the house tomorrow. Will you guys come with me?" Sidney asked.

"Shit, honey, I have a client in the morning," Brady said.

"I can go, Sid," Jordan replied. "I'll go with you."

Sidney allowed them to tuck her in on the couch. She cuddled down into the pillow and wrapped the blanket in her hands. She pulled her fists into her chest. Even if sleep would prove elusive, she felt safe in the apartment with Brady and Jordan snoring softly nearby.

***

"Did you sleep at all last night, love?" Jordan said from behind his sunglasses.

Sidney leaned heavily against the passenger side window of Jordan's hybrid SUV. The answer to his question weighed on her muscles, made her want to melt into a puddle in the early morning sunlight. She whimpered and shook her head, grinding her hair against the glass as she did so.

"Oh honey." Jordan rubbed her shoulder. "That's not surprising. You must be exhausted."

He retracted his hand and reached to the center

console. He extended the travel coffee mug towards her. She looked to him, and he nodded at her sideways, keeping his eyes on the road. Sidney took the offering and sipped at it a bit desperately.

The coffee was warm, perhaps a touch scalding on her tongue, yet the bite brought her back to her body. She told herself that it would wake her. She willed the caffeine through her veins. Yet it was their arrival into her driveway that quickened her pulse, that stiffened her muscles, that woke her back up.

The house looked normal and unassuming, even without her or Kendra's cars loitering on the curb. Kendra knew, had screamed panic and anger and confusion into the phone when Sidney actually called her. It was never good when it was a phone call. But Kendra's car would not be here, Kendra would not have to actually deal with it for another day.

Sidney wanted the house to look like their home, to feel like the center it usually did. The place she shared with Cameron and Kendra and Savannah. Home. All these months, she thought she had been lamenting the loss of her home with Aiden. She thought this had been a sad and temporary displacement. Yet glaring through the sun at her own front door now, she realized she had made a home here. She had not seen this until it had been disrupted, threatened.

Before she noticed, Jordan had parked the car and moved around to open her door. She looked up at him, puzzled under her sunglasses, before she remembered herself and stepped out to follow him.

The key scraped loud in the lock, and the door seemed heavier as Sidney pushed it open. She walked through her front door and hesitated on the carpet. She brought the keys to her hand and tracked the grooves with her fingertips, staring at the window and the couch. Taking a deep breath, she traced her steps from the previous night. She echoed the memory until she stood in her footprints on the carpet where she noticed the window. The police had slid the glass closed before they left, and no screen filled the pane on the other side. Sidney's chest flexed with the aftermath of her panic from the night before.

"That's where they came in." Sidney forced her voice to be steady. "I got to about here before I noticed. It was colder than it should have been, so I looked at the window. Then I took a couple more steps before realizing I needed to get the hell out."

"I'm glad you came to your senses." Jordan stepped up beside her. "Do you want me to go first?"

Sidney chomped on her bottom lip for an instant.

"No, the police went through the house last night," she replied.

"We'll go together." Jordan offered her a gentle smile that she could not help but mirror.

Sidney picked up where her path from the previous night had doubled back and went sprinting back to her car. She walked through her point of no return, down the hallway, and up the stairs. Everything appeared normal, untouched, regular. Sidney expected to see footprints staining the carpet, pictures askew on the walls, something out of place. Yet her journey to her room was alarmingly unaltered.

Sidney reached out and pressed her bedroom door open, letting it swing fully into the room and craning her neck in after it. Finally, she saw the violation, the evidence of her intruder. Her room, unlike the rest of the house, displayed the motions of the burglar. Her dresser drawers hung ajar, their contents dangling out. A heap of clothing clung to the hangers piled outside of the closet. Her bedspread had been yanked down to expose her sheets.

Sidney stood stunned in the doorframe. Jordan had ambled farther down to peer in the other bedrooms. He returned and peered in over her shoulder.

"Oh wow," he breathed over her. "So here's where he went."

They both stepped forward into the room and stood among the debris, circling their gazes in disbelief.

"Why only your room?" Jordan asked.

"The police said I interrupted them when I came home so they fled," Sidney replied, flatly.

"Still a strange place to start. Why not the living room where he came in? With all the electronics."

"I have no idea."

"Is anything missing?"

"I'm not sure," Sidney said, stepping forward to investigate.

Sidney glanced over her heaped clothes. She riffled through her disheveled drawers. Everything appeared to be present, if not in place. She moved to her nightstand. She picked up the clock from the floor and replaced it. She snatched up the couple of books and restacked them beside the clock. Her fingers combed the carpet. Her eyes scoured the corner of the room. The tiny baby booties were gone.

"Cameron's baby booties," Sidney said, softly. "The

little fake baby shoes Aiden gave me when I had Cameron are gone."

"Are you sure?" Jordan said. "Are they not just under the bed or something?"

Sidney dropped to the ground, letting the carpet fibers tickle her cheeks. Only shadows greeted her under her bed.

"They're not under here," she replied.

"They might still be in here." Jordan planted his hands on his hips then looked the room over again. "Or he took them. Shit, I don't know."

"Maybe they'll turn up when I clean this up."

"Do you want to clean it up now? Or do you want to get the fuck out of here?"

"We might as well just do it now," Sidney said. "We have to wait for the locksmith anyway."

"Perfect," Jordan said, snatching up a handful of hangers. "It will give me the overdue chance to purge this wardrobe of yours."

***

"When does Kendra get back?" Jordan asked, later, as they stepped out onto the porch.

Sidney followed him and pulled the front door closed behind her, sliding her fresh key into the changed deadbolt.

"Tomorrow morning," she replied.

"How does she feel about all this?" Jordan cleared the steps and ambled down the driveway, flipping his keys in his fingers.

Sidney smiled to herself briefly.

"She freaked out. You know Kendra. She was worried about me, lectured me. Then she was pissed someone was in our house. She's making sure I do all the things I need to do. Change the locks, follow up with the police."

"We did all that today. So, are you going to wait for her before you come back?"

"If that's OK with you and Brady. Aiden said he would handle Cameron. Figure one more night of wine with my boys."

Jordan stopped walking and swooped his arm around Sidney's shoulders.

"White or red, honey?" His eyes smiled beneath his sunglasses.

18

THE HOUSE LOOKED restored with the new screen, locked window, and cleaned mess. The house even felt normal with Kendra and the kids back within its walls. Their energy filled the looming vacancy Sidney had felt the night she interrupted the break-in and the morning that followed when Jordan escorted her back to her ransacked room. Yet below Sidney's casual smile, as she sat on the couch beside Kendra and listened to their children play through the hallway, her heart and mind were at odds. Her brain reasoned that the danger had passed and life was back to normal, yet her heart could not relax in her chest. Her anxiety, warranted or not, nibbled at the edge of her brain in the quiet moments between her and Kendra's words.

Donning fluffy pajama pants, Kendra folded her legs beneath her as she piled her curls on the top of her head. She loosely gathered the tresses before winding a rubber band around them. When she released her hands, the strands fanned out like the pointed leaves of a pineapple. Her stem bobbed as she turned her head from side to side. With her hair contained, Kendra slipped out a nail file she kept tucked under the couch cushion and began filing the edges of the nails she had chipped at work, though Sidney was never sure how an administrator could regularly chip so many nails. Perhaps she chewed them when she was nervous instead.

Sidney curled up on the couch cushion, drawing her legs into her chest. She held the wine glass in one hand and let it dangle against her knee. She was acutely aware that her own body depressed the same spot where the intruder had left a footprint upon entry. Her soft couch now felt stained by that echo, permanently disrupted by the brief violation.

Kendra leaned forward and tilted the wine bottle to spill more wine into Sidney's glass. She looked at Sidney as she did it, stared into her. "You OK, girl?" Kendra asked. "You just don't seem yourself. Like, you seem normal, but something is just off."

"Yeah, I'm OK." Sidney shifted her legs and lifted her wine glass to her mouth. "It's just been a weird couple of weeks."

"It really has! Between that creep on the trail in Telluride then a creep in our damn house this week. If they weren't half the state apart, I'd say you finally got yourself a real-life stalker."

Sidney nearly choked on Kendra's words. She tried not to let her falter show, sipping casually on her wine. "And Tony showed up at my work," Sidney said to skew the subject.

"Eew, what?" Kendra wrinkled her nose.

"I don't know," Sidney laughed a little lighter. "He's never done that before. We've always been more casual."

"You mean, you slept with him because he was dumb and pretty."

Sidney nodded.

"Well, you messed that up when you invited him to that dinner party," Kendra said. "You crossed that casual line. Dum-dum probably thinks you're Facebook official now."

"Man, you really don't like him."

"You don't even like him. He was fine for play, but now you have an actual man."

Sidney smiled broadly before she could temper it. "Adam," Sidney said, still grinning.

"Yes, Adam! Your original stalker. How is Adam?"

Distraction felt pleasant, the way she drifted away from the tension lining her mind. If she could focus on just Adam, not the walk home after him, she still experienced the buzzing thrill of her attraction to him. "Worried about me, I think," Sidney answered.

"We all are a little bit."

"I'm fine," Sidney insisted.

"You say that, but it's OK to be shook."

"I'll be shook later." Sidney leaned forward and placed her wine glass on the table. "I need to watch a movie or write an article or something tonight. My site has been dormant for too long. I'll lose loft if it goes stale too long."

"I think this might be an appropriate time to take a horror break." Kendra pursed her lips and tipped her glass toward Sidney. "Now, that you've had a taste of it in real life."

"OK, first off, none of those instances were horror. I'm fine. Nobody died."

"You keep saying that. 'I'm fine.'" Kendra rocked her head side to side on the syllables, mocking.

"I am fine. A bizarre couple of weeks." Sidney

forced a shrug and reclaimed her glass. "Little scary, I will give you that, but life goes on."

"Life, yes, but I think you could take a horror break. Watch other movies. Write other articles. Do other things. Just, like, a little bit."

"But why? Horror is kind of my brand," Sidney tried to sound neutral.

"I mean, I don't know why you like any of that stuff anyway, but do you really want to watch more stuff designed to scare you and give you anxiety after what is happening in your real life?"

"Maybe I want to see how much worse it could be," Sidney joked. "There's definitely not a horror movie where someone just gets attacked in the woods and lives or just has a mother memento stolen."

Kendra's laughter was a relief. Sidney smiled against the rim of her glass, trying not to hear the deformed echoes of what Kendra had said bouncing around her mind. Her skin crawled and tightened as her nerves started to itch again.

They drained their glasses. Sidney trailed Kendra into the kitchen and placed her empty glass beside Kendra's in the base of the sink. They both knew the deep red of the wine would stain the cups, yet they left them with remnants swirling at the bottom until morning. Kendra flashed Sidney the parting smile she always bestowed when fleeing Sidney's horror movies, a mix of pity, confusion, and affection. Sidney found herself clinging to the last attribute, wishing for Kendra beside her on the couch a little longer, her gentle interrogation a little deeper. But she would have had to give up horror for that.

Sidney decided to forego the follow-on pour she

usually had after Kendra retreated. She did not like the way the weight of the alcohol let her distorted thoughts unfold across the length of her. She kissed Cameron goodnight three times before he finally shooed her out of his room, and she was left alone in the living room, holding the remote.

As she pulled her laptop on top of her legs, Sidney had the immediate urge to draft an article about her little taste of horror in real life. She could feel herself typing the words before the embarrassment seized her again. She didn't want to tell people what had happened, either time. The story tasted as bitter and felt as deformed and unnatural on her tongue as the times she had to explain the dissolution of her marriage. Something about the details of her own scare made her feel inexplicably insecure in her love of horror. She figured a movie review would be the easiest, since the film would do the majority of the thinking for her.

She queued up her watchlist and began to scroll. She browsed past any stalker tales or home invasion movies. She might be telling herself that her experiences were not horror, but she didn't need to blatantly assault her clearly wounded mind. She wanted to watch something familiar, a film that had worn paths in the gray matter of her memories, a movie where she knew all the jump scares; but she only reviewed movies new to her. She had to brave the theatrically unfamiliar.

Maybe the couch would have still felt safe if she wasn't curled up on the shoeprint of the intruder.

Sidney took a deep breath. She was just watching a movie. Just a horror movie. No different than the thousands she had watched before it. She knew it could not hurt her. Horror was on the screen, not in her real life. She couldn't go confusing that line now, not when she was finally on the precipice of hosting a successful website. She could not stop now.

She closed her eyes and mashed the button on the remote. The typical eerie music spiraled out from the speakers and curled through the air and into her ears. The ominous score was comforting in its familiarity, in all the pleasant memories forged in the vibrating soundtrack to a horror movie; yet there was something else flowing beneath that sensation. Something tight and unnerving.

"It's just a fucking movie," Sidney whispered to herself, queuing up her website and blank document. "Get over it. It was just some creep on the trail. Get over it. It was just some asshole that took your baby booties. Get over it. They don't get to do this to you."

Her own last sentence resonated through her chest. They did not get to do this to her. Such small threats and violations did not get to change her mind. She rooted herself down in the cushion, pressing past the footprint so that her own weight erased it. She allowed the familiar plot arc of the movie to feel like home and began triaging her avalanche of messages.

Adam first. Always Adam first now.

Adam: Are you OK, beautiful?
  I'm still worried about you.
Sidney: Yeah. I'm sorry for not being so responsive lately.
Adam: No problem.

I mean it sucks, but I just want you to be OK.
How is it back in the house?
Sidney: Good. Kendra and the kids are here, so
it feels normal.
Mostly.
Adam: I'm so glad you're not alone there.
But I wish I was there too.
I would feel better there.

Sidney smiled to herself, glancing up from her computer screen to see a young girl gutted across the TV. She caught herself assessing the realism of the blood and edges of the wound, just like old times.

Sidney: Me too.
When do you think you could come visit?
Adam: I have to build up vacation time after
Telluride.
You?
Sidney: About the same.

The distance between them felt further as she typed it. She distracted herself by scrolling through her social media notifications. The counts were relatively low, a nagging report that she had not uploaded a photo recently. She knew the photos snagged interest on the visual platforms, but she could not even bring herself to post an old picture. It felt too exposing right now. She wasn't ready.

Allison: How are you, lady?
Sidney: Eh, OK.
How are you?

Allison: Oh, I'm fine. Tired from work.
  What's the matter? Aside from all the things.
Sidney: Haha. Just all the things.
Allison: You can tell me. Safe space.

Sidney lifted her fingers off the keys, cracked her knuckles. She felt like she had been repeating the same woes endlessly, but it had only been in her mind. The cyclical worries and denials had been locked in her skull, only getting louder in their own echoes. The only thing she had been repeating aloud was that she was fine, and that lie only made the symphony in her head spin faster.

Sidney: I'm trying to be OK.
  I don't know if it's working.
Allison: How do you mean?
Sidney: Like it was hard to start watching a horror movie tonight.
Allison: So? You had some scary shit happen. Why not take a horror break?
Sidney: I can't take a horror break. I made horror my life. I can't just take a break from it.
Allison: Why not?

The question almost punched Sidney in the chest. Because she did not have an answer. Though indulging in her genre was currently uncomfortable, the idea of forsaking it, even temporarily, also stirred anxiety between her ribs. It was more than just her website going stale, losing loft, or risking followers. Something deeper than that.

Sidney: I don't know how.
    Horror is where I went after my divorce.
    All in. When I started my website. When I found me.
    I don't want to have to find new things.
Allison: We're talking about a break, not quitting.

Taking a break felt like quitting.

Allison: Should we distract you instead?
Sidney: Yes, please!
Allison: Let's talk about boys.

Sidney rolled her eyes to the empty room, but a smile did fracture her anxiety, caused it to recede from the back of her throat.

Sidney: Hehe
    What about boys?
Allison: How are things going with the new one?
Sidney: Good. I really like him.
    Long distance though.
Allison: Have you done long distance before?
Sidney: No.
Allison: Do you want to?

Sidney stopped, ran her thumb across her bottom lip before she chewed at it. Then she replaced her fingers on the keys.

Sidney: Yeah. I think I'm willing to try it with him.

Allison: What about the other one? The young
    guy?
Sidney: I might have to give him up. He's fun,
    but it was never going anywhere.
Sidney: My roommate was actually just telling
    me today that I should end things.
Allison: Are you exclusive with the new guy?

Sidney hesitated again. Why was she telling Allison all this? Why was it so easy? It made sense to have this same conversation with Kendra. Kendra shared her home, participated in her life, commiserated in her pain. But who was Allison? Just some persona on the internet.

Sidney's online life was an exercise in abstract realism. The conversations and relationships she cultivated there felt closer, more intimate as they only echoed against the walls of her cranium, undisturbed. Yet those echoes also shrouded it all in a dreamlike haze, a blur between reality and imagination. Somehow, it felt safe online—like whispering gently in the dark away from witnesses and accountability. Yet, somewhere at the back of her mind, she knew that darkness was full of dangers. She reassured herself that though the digital may feel less tangible, it created far more evidence—traces that could be preserved indefinitely in cyberspace.

The writhing thoughts ballooned anxiety below her ribcage. The tension swelled until it bubbled up in her mouth. She chewed on it a moment then started typing again.

Sidney: Not yet.
Allison: Then why end things?
Sidney: My roommate thinks I need to end
things to give the new guy a real shot.
Maybe she's right.
Allison: I don't know. You might not want to let
him go too early. The long distance thing
may not work out.

Sidney's lip slipped around under the pressure of
her front teeth. She let the ideas roll around her
thoughts, circling until the repetition made them
smooth.

The characters in the movie continued to make
survival-incompatible decisions and meet their messy
fates. Sidney was almost relieved that the movie was
not very good. Flat characters, predictable plot twists.
It practically advertised the jump scares before the
music seized. It was easier this way.

Oliver: Where are you?
Sidney: I'm sorry. Lots of shit going on.
Oliver: What's the matter?
Sidney: My house got broken into.
Oliver: No shit! What did they take?
Sidney: Not much, thankfully.
Oliver: Scary.
Come here. I'll protect you.

Sidney rolled her eyes to herself. The end credits
loomed as the violence accelerated into a crescendo on
the screen. The music blared to indicate the danger,
the struggle, the suspense. Sidney wasn't sure if she

didn't care because the movie was bad or because her mind was simply broken tonight. She was too lost in herself to invest in two-dimensional twits begging for the knife.

As she opened the blank document to begin her dissection of the largely disengaging and disappointing film offering, she noticed a new friend request. She took a quick skim of Dylan Tate's profile. They shared several friends who followed her website and he had posted a couple of horror-related articles, including her own. She accepted his request, and a direct message immediately appeared in her inbox.

If experience had taught her nothing else, she knew it was most likely a picture of his penis.

She opened her inbox. Surprisingly, the message preview did not say photo. The opening characters seduced her with writing compliments, and she opened the message.

Dylan: I really love your writing. I follow your website. I love how you put all your reviews and genre articles alongside your horror photography.

Sidney's fingers leapt to the keys to express her gratitude, to invite more of the compliments that spread a warm smile over her lips. Then she flinched. The fact that Dylan was a stranger, a figment on the internet, suddenly leapt to the front her mind in large, blinking letters. She always knew this about the people she interacted with on the internet. It always echoed along the back of her mind as they chatted. Yet now it resounded against her frontal lobes.

She pulled her hands into her chest. Then she picked sloppily at her nails, just staring at his message. She had opened the message; he could see that she had read it. Now, she was an asshole if she didn't respond. She typed a quick thank you, with an exclamation point for gratitude, and closed the message before he could respond and she could read it.

Slamming the laptop closed, Sidney retreated to her room. The room someone had broken into to steal the tiny shoes her ex-husband had given her when their son was born.

19

THE DAYS BLED into weeks, gradually eroding Sidney's anxiety. Each uneventful day that passed lulled that nagging, chewing sensation at the back of her brain. Every time the morning broke and nothing happened, it became easier to inhale against the weight crushing down on her chest. Complacency unraveled over her like a familiar blanket.

The sound of her attacker's steps ripping across the gravel trail faded back into her memory to be replaced by the chorus of promotion videos on the screens at work. The footprint on her couch cushion was replaced by the curve of her constant seat as she jammed away at her laptop. She stopped dreaming of finding tiny, blue baby booties on her pillow and started dosing off as she composed new articles in her mind until the darkness swallowed her into sleep.

Adam: Good morning, beautiful.

The same message greeted her every morning. She fixated on the idea of meeting up with Adam again.

"Divorced Wives Club tonight?" Kendra asked her as she poured two mugs of coffee.

"I still have Cameron tonight," Sidney replied, tucking her shirt into her dress pants.

"I have Savannah too. I'm proposing a mini session. You, me, and Merlot."

"And a horror movie?" Sidney smiled at Kendra out of the side of her mouth.

"No, ma'am. Romantic comedy?" Kendra held out the mug, still steaming.

"Hell no," Sidney laughed into her coffee. "Never."

"Well, I guess we'll have to find some other compromise."

"Action movie with hot guys who can't act?"

"Perfect!"

"OK, I have to pick up Cameron from baseball, per usual. Should I grab some dinner on my way home?" Sidney slurped on her coffee again as she started gathering her purse and keys.

"Sure. I would love not to cook."

Sidney nagged Cameron into the car and felt the small, daily heartbreak as he jumped excitedly out to his friends without a kiss or an "I love you". She dragged herself into the parking lot and through the cloud of her resentment and atrophied motivation. She got herself behind the counter, the same as every work day before and what seemed like every other day laid out in front of her.

It was nice for these to be her problems again.

Typical of the start of her shift, the store hung idle as the sunlight crawled through the windows and across the flattened carpet. Sidney turned everything on, organized everything, then perched behind the main register, leaning back against the counter and bringing her phone to her face.

Sidney: Ugh, another work day begins.
Allison: I know, right!
   This shift cannot end fast enough. I need a drink.
Sidney: You and me both. After I pick my son up from baseball, my roommate and I are having a wine night.
Allison: So she can tell you to drop your fuck buddy?
Sidney: Ha! Possibly. She really seems to think so.

Sidney seemed to agree with her. Between all the drama in her real life and Adam in her virtual life, she suddenly realized she had not messaged Tony. She had not really even thought of him since he had showed up in her store.

Sidney: Maybe she's right. Maybe it's time.
   It was never going to be a real thing.
Allison: I would wait to see. You never know with people.
Sidney: Maybe.
   What about you? Dating anyone?

Sidney suddenly realized how one-sided her conversations with Allison had always been. A spire of guilt jabbed through her chest. She had been so selfishly consumed by her own life, happy to pour every detail into a willing outlet. It had taken her this long to consider the person on the other side of the digital persona.

Allison: Yeah, I have a boyfriend. We started
     casual, and I thought he was just a toy. But
     we've been together a couple years now.
     That's why I say you never know!
Sidney: Well, that's good to know.

Sidney let the idea of escalating Tony to a relationship play through on the theater of her mind, but she found herself laughing it away once she tried to picture having a single deep conversation with him. Before she could even broach envisioning him helping her parent Cameron, the fantasy had disbanded.

She could see Adam there though. His movie played much longer, and more graphically, on her mental screen.

Dylan: Your last article was great! What do you
     think is the best of the hillbilly horror genre?

Sidney skimmed the message preview. She still had not answered Dylan. She had not even opened the conversation thread since that first message. His doting compliments tempted her, but even in her regained comfort, new virtual figures unnerved her. Better the devils she already knew.

Oliver: I miss you so much, sexy.
     Please let me see you again.

Sidney depressed her bottom lip beneath her front teeth. As boredom drummed in her fingertips, she decided to distract herself with some flirtation. It had been ages since she had dropped him a selfie, and what was one more in the library he already had in their thread? One more step back toward normal. Perhaps next would be shooting with Brady again.

She lifted the phone to the right angle and slipped a coy smile across her lips. She awkwardly pressed the shutter and sent the photo off to him. Absently, in the back of her mind, she wondered when this would feel like betraying Adam, currently still just another figment on her phone.

Oliver: There you are!
    I feel so much better.
    Still sexy as always.
Sidney: Thank you.
Oliver: How are you, love?
Sidney: Pretty good. Things are getting back to
    normal.
Oliver: So glad to hear that.
    I really missed you.

Did he? Sidney wondered. And if he did, what did that say? She let the conversation die off in pleasantries and bleed off from her mind as well. He could fade safely into the back of her mind and the internet for now.

The sun continued to slide over the carpet and crawl along the walls. Customers rotated in, asserting there was no way they could have used that much data in the billing period or that they had a screen protector on when they dropped their smartphone but it clearly failed. Seth arrived to split the customer support load. Then the day vanished as uneventfully as it had begun.

Sidney's lower back tightened as she finally dropped into the driver's seat of her car. The muscles communicated their outrage at standing for so many hours. What felt like wasted and fruitless hours. Yet the farther her car rolled away from the store, the more relief flooded into her—now that she was staring through the glass of her windshield rather than her phone screen.

The sun flirted with the horizon as she pulled into the school parking lot. She looked across the grass to the baseball diamond. Practice had clearly dispersed already, but players and coaches remained scattered over the area. A couple of boys continued to lob a ball at each other. The adult figures bent and stood repeatedly as they gathered discarded supplies.

Sidney hurried over the withering grass. Her shoes pressed deep into the leaves as the wind tangled through her hair. She squinted out in front of her. All the figures were anonymous at this distance, but she could not identify Cameron yet. As her eyes moved from body to body, her heart and pace quickened. By the time she could discern their faces, she could see her son was not among them.

She could not breathe. There was no more air. She could not hear. She had gone deaf. Then air slammed back into her lungs as the sound crashed back into her ears. The sensation surged over her instantly. Her heart did not seem to pump anymore. There was nothing around her as long as she could not see her child. She gagged on the panic that filled her mouth. Her fingers tingled and clenched, anxious. She strove to shove the dread down, tried to unearth rational thoughts from the fury spinning in her head.

She told herself he was here. He was always here. Where would he go? The coaches were right there. He was fine. She would find him. He was fine. She found herself mouthing the words, willing them to be true.

No matter how many times she repeated the affirmations to herself, they fell on a deaf mind. Her brain seized around her fear and only frantically searched over and over the baseball diamond, dugout, and field around her. Each revolution that did not locate him only accelerated the panic that now nauseated her.

"Coach!" Sidney shouted, her voice strangled.

"Oh hey, Ms. Gray," Coach Bradford waved to her as she jogged up to him. "What are you doing here?"

"What do you mean?" Sidney fought back the tears menacing in her eyes.

"Cameron already got picked up. Pretty sure he's with his dad."

"Aiden? No, it's my night. Aiden shouldn't be picking him up." Sidney's hands strangled each other, wrapped together in front of her stomach.

"Well, you might want to tell him that."

"You're sure it was Aiden."

"Looked like him, but they were pretty far away when I saw them leaving."

"What car did they leave in?" Sidney could barely see. Rage now infiltrated her fear.

"Didn't see."

Sidney wanted to shriek in his face, demand to know why he hadn't been watching her child. That was his job, wasn't it? How could he just let him leave? Instead, she choked on false gratitude and sprinted back to her car and her phone.

When Aiden answered, she could barely speak. She shouted his name, and it erupted from her lips unmitigated.

"Sidney?" Aiden's confused voice responded. "What the hell? What's wrong with you?"

"Do you have Cameron?" Sidney managed to yell the only question that mattered.

"What? No. Why would I have Cameron? It's your night."

Aiden kept talking, but Sidney could not hear it. His tone hardened, the words became harsher, but she could not care.

"Aiden, he's gone," Sidney interrupted and silenced him. The line momentarily went dead in her ear, long enough for her to hear her heart hammering. "I came to pick him up from practice, and Coach said he already left with you."

Another stunned silence dragged into eternity.

"I—I—I don't have him," Aiden stuttered. "Sidney, I don't have him. Where the hell is our son?"

"I don't know! I wasn't even late. Do I call the cops? Do I call the cops now?" Sidney's lip was bleeding from her teeth chomping desperately at it, but she did not notice.

"Where are you?"

"Baseball field."

"I'm in the car now. I'm coming."

The call died in Sidney's ear. She held the phone suspended for a moment, vibrating in her fear.

Sidney: Cam is gone.
Kendra: WHAT?
Call me! NOW!

She couldn't call Kendra. She could barely type, much less speak. She had to reserve her composure for Aiden.

Sidney: Can't.
    He's not at practice.
    Coach said he left with someone.
Kendra: I'm coming to you.
Sidney: No, wait.
    Aiden is coming.
    I'll tell you what we're going to do.
Kendra: I'm putting Savannah in the car now.
    We'll drive around the neighborhood.

She wanted to be with Kendra, doing something. She knew she could not leave, but she could not stay in the car either. She could not breathe in there, the way the windshield crushed down on her failure, the way the doors encapsulated her solitude. She could only think about Cameron, about all the terrible things that could be happening to him.

She had watched movies about what could be happening to him. She had written articles about the cinematic portrayal of what could be happening to him.

Suddenly, it felt more like her fault.

She paced back and forth across the edge of the field in what looked more like a sprint. Her arms flailed around her body, overloaded with purposeless energy. The field was clear, no figures haunted the diamond. She debated whether she should have gone back to the coach, told him Cameron was gone, but what could he have done? He had let her son walk off with a stranger. He was less than worthless; this was his fault too. She could deal with him later, when she was holding her baby again.

She felt inept in wasted moments. She was tortured over multiple lifetimes before Aiden's car screeched in beside hers. She caught his wild, frantic eyes through the reflection of the sky on the windshield. Immediately, instinctively, she shrank back, curled into herself. If he did not hate her enough before, he would never forgive her for this. For losing their child.

Aiden stormed through the grass. Sidney flinched and took a step back. The blow she expected, the one she deserved, did not come. He plowed into her and wrapped his arms around her. The familiarity of his embrace, the desperation is his grip enveloped her, and she finally let herself weep. She sobbed hysterically, driving apologies between her cries. When both their bodies finally fell still again, he released her. She could not hazard his eye contact.

"What do we do, Aiden?" she said quietly through her tears, sobs shaking her words.

"I don't know." Aiden stepped back, infected by the same panicked energy. He thrust his hands into his hair and tugged on it. "I don't fucking know. Cops. Where is Coach?"

"He left. He said Cam had left, and I ran to the car to call you. He packed up his stuff and went back into the school."

"You let him leave?" Aiden's wide eyes found hers, but the rage behind them was not for her. "Did you tell him?"

"What could he do? He let Cameron go with

someone . . . someone he thought was you . . . some man." Sidney flinched at the words.

Aiden turned toward the diamond, whirled back to face the car, turned back to Sidney. "Cops. We call the cops," he said.

Sidney's phone was in her hand before he finished talking, 911 ringing in her ear. Her composure fractured with the operator. She unleashed a blur of words and syllables, talking over the calm voice on the other end. She felt Aiden's arm slip around her shoulders and remain there until the squad cars joined theirs in the parking lot.

20

JUST GO HOME. They had been told to just go home.

Sidney and Aiden had told the same story and answered the same questions, described their son on repeat. They had texted the most recent photos to the officers as the AMBER alerts began chirping on their phones describing their own boy. They had watched the coach, beset by officers and questions of his own. They had filled out the missing person report, tears threatening to blind Sidney as she scribbled. Now they were supposed to let them do their jobs, let them send out a BOLO and set up checkpoints, let them question the others from baseball practice. And just go home.

The words had not made sense when the officer said them to Sidney and Aiden. Sidney stared at him dumbfounded, knowing he was saying words but unable to discern what they meant. They held no meaning at a time like this. They sounded like instructions to do nothing, but she could not do nothing. When she did nothing, she only inventoried all the awful things her child could be going through at that moment.

Aiden gathered her by the shoulders and guided

her to his car. He deposited her in the passenger seat and drove mechanically and silently beside her. She would not have been able to drive. Her mind did not reside within her body.

"Aiden, we can't just go home and do nothing," Sidney said, bitterly.

"We aren't doing nothing. Text Kendra. Have her meet us at your place. Then we'll decide how to search for him," he answered her.

His words buffered the edge of her panic. She felt it continuing to seethe through her, yet at least it had a direction. At least they would be doing something.

Then silence consumed the car. The quiet was thick, infected with all their worry. Any words they managed would have been wasted. Neither of them wanted to speak the horrors they were imagining for their child. Saying them aloud might tempt them to come true.

Like watching horror seemed to have.

As Aiden pulled into Sidney's driveway, his headlights swept over the front porch. Sidney could have sworn she saw her boy sitting there, baseball bag and backpack heaped beside him.

"Is that Cam?" Aiden said beside her.

Sidney snapped up in her seat and looked at Aiden.

"You saw him too?" Sidney said.

"I thought so."

Aiden stomped the break and slammed the transmission into park. The car continued to idle as they both ejected themselves from their seats, leaving the doors ajar behind them. Aiden took larger, faster strides and beat Sidney up the drive. He had Cameron seized in a constricting hug by the time Sidney reached them. She hesitated a breath, but Aiden reached out and snatched her into a shared embrace.

The tears poured down Sidney's cheeks silently, watering her son's hair. Relief burned through her eyes as her entire body sizzled with adrenaline. She clung to them, her child and her ex, and lost herself in the feeling of their bodies—present, real, alive, and safe—against her. She did not let go until Cameron started to whine and squirm between them.

"Where the fuck were you?" Aiden boomed, kneeling before Cameron and clutching his shoulders too tightly, the euphoric bliss draining from him. He never cursed around Cameron, much less at him.

"Mom's friend gave me a ride home. I've been here," Cameron's voice squeaked against his fear.

"My what?" Sidney shouted. She seized Cameron's shoulders from Aiden, angry but happy to be touching his real, safe shoulders again.

"Your friend. He said you got stuck at work and wanted him to take me home. He took me here and dropped me off." Cameron's eyes welled. Sidney knew the look, her son's fear of being in trouble. "But no one was home."

Sidney took a deep breath to calm herself. She forced her shoulders down. She willed her features to soften.

"Cam, honey, you're not in trouble," she said, gently. "We were just so worried about you, baby." She looked to Aiden, who automatically nodded in agreement. "We just need to know what happened."

Cameron visibly deflated a bit. His eyes swam back up as the tears receded.

"This friend of mommy's," Aiden started, "have you seen him before? Did you know him?"

"No," Cameron said, sheepishly.

Aiden threw up his hands and spun around in frustration.

"Then why the fuck would you go with him? Cam, you know better!" Aiden shouted. Cameron shrank away from the volume.

Sidney placed one reassuring hand on Cameron's shoulder and raised the other to calm Aiden. Aiden jostled his son a bit then nodded, returning to a nonthreatening stance.

"Aiden," Sidney said, "you should call the police. Let them know we found Cam. That one gave you his card, right?"

"Yeah." Aiden started searching his pockets. "Yeah."

Aiden stepped forward to gruffly and firmly embrace Cameron again. He held him tight, and Sidney watched him breathe in the scent of his son's scalp, the way he used to when Cameron was an infant. He closed his eyes as he inhaled, and Sidney was sure he was back at that early moment. Then he pulled out his phone and stepped down the drive to inform the police.

Sidney stood and guided her son to his feet. She gathered up his bags for them and got them both through the front door, spying Kendra's headlights pull up beside Aiden's car as they moved inside. She eased Cameron to the couch and sat down beside him, refusing to release his hand, savoring how tangible it felt in hers.

"Cam, baby," she started slow, "I didn't send a friend to come get you. I wasn't tied up at work."

Cameron's face contorted. His eyes went wide

before his mouth started to drop and expose his lower teeth. He gawked at her, confused, the awareness of the situation finally infusing fear into him. Sidney wanted to clutch him to her again, protect him from all the things that could have happened to him, from all the things that did happen to him in the preceding hours in her mind. She just gripped his hand tighter.

"So, I need to know about this guy," Sidney continued. "The police will be here soon. They're going to have a lot of questions. But I want to know about the guy who took you first."

Cameron took a deep and shaky breath.

"He was just a guy," he said, snot dribbling from his nose. He sniffed in hard and swiped the back of his hand across his face. "I was waiting for you, like I usually do, kind of by the parking lot. And he came up like he knew me."

"Did he tell you his name?" Sidney said.

Cameron shook his head, eyes in his lap. "He just said, 'I'm your mom's friend.'"

"What did he look like? Was he young? Old? Tall? Short? White? Black? Asian?" Sidney felt the questions firing off her tongue.

Aiden cracked the door, disrupting Cameron's concentration. Kendra and Savannah came flooding in after him. Kendra's arms were already moving in circles over her head.

"Oh, Cameron, baby," she yelled, hurrying around the coffee table to hug him firmly. "I am so relieved! Baby, I was so worried about you."

Savannah trailed her mother and quietly sat on the other side of Cameron, slipping her small hand into his other one. Cameron looked over at her and smiled.

Aiden rounded the herd and perched himself on the armrest beside Sidney.

Kendra stood with her head cocked, her fingertips clutched against her chin as she stared at Cameron and Savannah's tangled hands. Her eyes welled with all the tears Sidney had felt threatening in her own sinuses. Kendra released her cries and the relief and fear they signified down her cheeks as she glanced back at Sidney. Sidney's tears followed the example until they were both weeping.

Aiden noticed Kendra's emotion across the room first. Her eyes bobbed and swam in tears. Then he looked across to see Sidney just as consumed. They both quivered on the precipice of a breakdown. He pretended to not see the impending emotional storm, averted his eyes before their tide threatened to pull him under. Sidney stood and marched directly to Kendra, burying herself in her embrace. Kendra's curls enveloped her as they clutched each other, their sobs causing them to quiver in a sick unison.

"Thanks, girl," Sidney breathed into her ear.

Kendra held onto Sidney until both their tears waned, until their breathing fell back into the normal rhythm. Then she leaned back with tear-drenched cheeks and smiled, nodding.

"Always," she whispered, just for Sidney, before letting her go.

Sidney smiled through her drying tears and returned to her chair. The thought that she could not survive any of this without Kendra flitted through her already surging mind. She could not wait to tuck the children back into normalcy, see Aiden out, and have their normal debrief on the couch. Where they would figure out life once again.

Aiden anxiously fidgeted beside Sidney, bringing his hand to his chin then crossing his arms then standing then sitting back on the armrest. Sidney took a deep breath and tried to make her voice as gentle and unassuming as possible.

"What did he say to you, Cam?" Sidney resumed.

"He said, 'Hey, Cam.' He called me Cam. Then he said, 'Your mom is stuck at work and sent me to take you home.'" Cameron's voice continued to waver softly. "I asked if you wanted me home by myself, said I didn't have a key yet. He said, 'but her roommate is home, isn't she?' And I said 'Yeah, Kendra will be home.' Then I went with him."

Sidney felt Aiden tensing beside her. His forearms flexed and released in time with the pressure building in her chest, the anger that had been allowed to blossom since they had their son back under their gaze. She wanted to reach out and take his hand in hers. It felt like the natural answer, but she knew they were no longer there, no longer sharing that space. He might have been able to embrace her in their terror, but they would never be there—a couple—again.

"Did he take you straight home?" Sidney continued.

Cameron nodded cautiously.

"What did he say to you in the car?"

"Nothing, really." Cameron looked to his lap, at his hand entwined with Savannah's. "He asked about how baseball was going. He asked how often I got to see my dad. If I liked school. Then we were here. I got out. He said goodbye and drove away. Kendra wasn't here, so I just waited on the porch."

"I was out looking for you, baby," Kendra said. She

gave Cameron the loving look she always gave him, even when she was irritated with him, the look she only gave to him and Savannah.

Cameron looked up at her, smiling, with tears threatening again.

"You're OK, baby," Sidney reassured. "You're OK now."

Kendra gave Sidney a slight side nod and stepped up to Cameron. As she approached, his composure wilted. The tears began bubbling from his eyes as his face reddened. Kendra shook her head no to him, shushing without a sound as she wrapped both him and Savannah tightly against her chest. Sidney could hear the fumbling apologies Cameron was spitting against her chest, but they dissolved against the embrace. When she leaned back, she wiped Cameron's cheeks until they were dry then bonked him on the nose. He let out a stifled laugh. Kendra kissed him on the nose then guided Savannah towards her.

"Savannah, honey, we need to let Cameron talk to his parents," Kendra said.

"No, I want Cam," Savannah protested, pulling away from her mother and wrapping herself around his arm.

"He'll be here in the morning," Sidney reassured, sitting back beside Aiden. "You two can play all morning, I promise."

Savannah looked to her mother, who nodded, before relinquishing Cameron's arm. She squeezed him in a tight side hug before begrudgingly trailing her mother upstairs. Cameron watched them both leave before sheepishly turning back to his parents.

The police came and went. The questions swelled

then faded. The house bustled then emptied. Aiden offered to drive Sidney back to her car, but she refused to leave Cameron. Kendra could take them in the morning.

Aiden and Sidney put Cameron to bed together, as they used to when they shared a house and a life. Sidney watched with bitter observation at how happy it made Cameron, how much calmer and more content he seemed in their familial completeness. As they closed his door softly, Aiden's steps slowed on the carpet. He tapped his fingertips together as he shifted his weight forward then back. They stood in the hallway awkwardly, frozen the way they were the first night they put Cameron down alone in his room as a baby.

Sidney's fingernails picked at the paint of the doorframe as she stared down at the texture of the carpet.

"I'm sorry, Aiden," she said, genuinely. "Sorry for today. Sorry for before. Sorry for everything." And softer, "You were right."

"I know it wasn't your fault, Sid."

He hadn't called her that since her infidelity surfaced.

"It would be easy to be mad at you," he continued. "I'm usually mad at you, but it wouldn't have been any different if it was my night. I would have come to get him at the same time and found him gone just the same."

Sidney smiled her gratitude at the floor.

"But this guy said he was my friend," Sidney pressed. "He clearly knew about Cameron and Kendra and where Cameron would be. He has to know me."

"Maybe. Maybe even from the internet." Aiden swallowed. "But I know you're pretty careful about what you post. Because I watch."

Sidney's eyes snapped up and caught his for an instant.

"Trust that we'll figure it out," Aiden continued. "But, for tonight, our boy is safe. And right now, that's all that matters."

Aiden stepped forward and squeezed her shoulders gently. He looked at her solemnly then stepped around her and departed.

Sidney remained rooted outside Cameron's door for a long time. Kendra smiled at her and brushed her hand along her back as she moved past her to escort Savannah through the bedtime routine. When Savannah was safely tucked in, Sidney followed Kendra back downstairs. They poured the wine reserved for their Divorced Wives Club session, yet they did not speak. Words seemed worthless. They sipped in silence, sitting close enough for their shoulders to support each other, their appreciation of a quiet house with two sleeping children resonating wordlessly between them.

When Kendra moved to retire for the night, she topped off Sidney's glass, hugged her tightly, then smiled as she left.

Sidney felt utterly alone in the room. The thought of sleep was unrealistic. Her mind crawled and teamed with all the *what ifs* of the evening, of all the ways her life had almost completely fallen apart, of all the things she had almost lost. Her adrenaline hangover burned over her, sizzling down her nerves and itching on her skin. She shifted in search of a comfortable position.

She did not know what else to do but remain agonized on the couch.

Finally, when the current in her mind subsided enough, she reached for her phone. She told Adam and Allison, at a high and comfortable level for how raw she felt, what had happened and ignored Oliver and the rest. Yet a new message caught her eye.

[Facebook User]: How is your son?
He's quite the baseball player.
Such a nice kid.

The deep, primal fear resurged in her, riding the driving wave of protective anger. The ambiguous "Facebook User" moniker meant the profile had been created and deleted. A ghost profile designed to remain anonymous. Proof that this person did know her, had come for Cameron because of her.

In the center of her rage, guilt created a sinkhole in her chest. She had done this to him. She and Aiden had almost lost their child because of her.

Sidney slammed the laptop closed. She lifted it in her hands to throw it across the room when she heard something scratch against the window behind her head. Dropping the computer to the cushion beside her, Sidney rushed the glass. A dangerous blend of fury and fear blanked her mind. She pressed her face against the window and saw a shape move in the darkness. She heard it crunch along the rocks lining the house as it fled.

This time, she did not hesitate. She did not question if she should hide the events. Sidney snatched up her phone and called the police back to her house.

FEAR DEVOURED THE following days. Long after the police questions, paranoia reached its tendrils up through Sidney's thoughts. Exhaustion condensed her mind, reducing its capacity and allowing twisted perceptions to blossom in neglect. Everything seemed hard. Everything became a threat.

"Mom," Cameron whined, "I can't miss practice tonight. I can't keep missing practice." He stomped down the hallway after her, half dressed for school.

"Baby, your daddy can't be there tonight, and I'll be at work," Sidney said. "You know we have to be there now, after what happened."

"You guys don't have to be there. I'll be fine, I promise. I'll never go with someone again, I promise." Cameron slammed his feet with each syllable.

Sidney stopped walking. She planted her hands on her hips before turning and leveling her face with her son's.

"Baby," she said in a heavy and slow tone, "you got taken. Someone took you. Horrible, horrible things could have happened to you."

"I know, Mommy," Cameron looked to the ground and traced at the carpet with his toe. "But I won't do it again."

"It's not your fault." Sidney took his face in her hands. "But it really scared me. And Daddy. So, we're just not ready to leave you alone yet."

Cameron sighed exasperated and rolled his eyes. "But I'm not a baby! If I keep missing practice, they won't let me play." Cameron's whining returned.

"Well, your coach let you leave with a complete stranger, so if he has a problem with you missing, he can come to me," Sidney barked.

Cameron let out a yell and stomped angrily back to his room.

"We're leaving in 15 minutes," Sidney shouted after him.

"Are you going to come babysit me at school too?" Cameron yelled back.

Rage flared over Sidney. She balled up her fists and shook them in Cameron's direction. Then she forced herself to turn and continue walking downstairs.

"Screaming match already?" Kendra said as Sidney walked past her bedroom.

"Every morning now," Sidney replied, leaning through Kendra's doorway.

Kendra propped herself against her dresser, rummaging through her jewelry box. Pictures were tucked into the mirror frame that reflected her face back to Sidney. Her bed was already made with the comforter tucked crisply beneath the pillows. Her shoes and blouse lay anticipant across the foot of the bed. All the drawers were properly closed and doors securely seated. The space sat neat, clean, and organized up to the far door that hid the disaster that was the bathroom she shared with Savannah.

"Girl, he just doesn't know how scary it was. How

real it was," Kendra said, fingering an earring then shoving it through her lobe.

"I know." Sidney rubbed her hands over her face. "I know he can't, but I can't yet. I just can't."

"I know. And he'll understand one day." Kendra pushed the matching earring through her other ear and dropped her arms as she faced Sidney. "So, I found three other places for us to look at. Are you still sure you want to keep living together? This is your out right here."

"Oh, I'm sure we stay together. I cannot handle two divorces," Sidney smiled. "We just need to be in a different place. A place whoever took my fucking kid doesn't know about."

"I'm onboard, girl. We're keeping our babies safe. Look over those links at work. They're in our thread."

"Thank you," Sidney said.

Through a flurry of sighs and rolled eyes, Sidney got Cameron off to school. Dropping him off piqued her anxiety, especially considering her new distrust in their employees' diligence. She scarcely noticed that Cameron did not say goodbye as he exited the car. She simply breathed through her seething hatred of the coach who had let her child wander off with a complete stranger—a stranger who apparently knew her enough to deposit her son safely on their porch.

Sidney turned her tires towards work, yet as she approached the parking lot, she radically changed course. If the person who took her child knew where Cameron went to school and played baseball, he surely knew where she worked. She needed to concentrate on getting out of the house, where he knew they lived.

Instead, Sidney pulled into a supercenter parking lot and queued up Kendra's links.

Adam: Sidney, I am worried about you.
Anything from the cops? Your ex still being cool?
Sidney: I'm sorry.
Adam: Don't be sorry. Are you OK?
Sidney: Not really.

Not really was the truth. She was not really OK. She was, perhaps, the furthest from OK she had ever been. Maybe even further from OK than when she had cheated on Aiden or when he had found out and confronted her or when her life had fallen apart because of it.

Adam: I know you're not, and you shouldn't be.
I just want to help.
Sidney: Thank you.
I don't know what to do.
I don't know what I did wrong. I don't know how to keep us safe.
Right now, I just need to move to a new place.

That was all she knew. She might not know much else, but she could control that one, first thing.

Adam: What you did wrong? You didn't do anything wrong.
You didn't ask to get attacked in Telluride.
You didn't ask to have your house broken into.
You didn't ask to have your son taken.
Those are things that happened to you, not

what you asked for.
It's not your faul*t*.

Sidney could only wonder how it had not been her fault, how she had not invited it. She had to click through listings for new places to live because she had made their home unsafe. Adam's itemized reassurances read more like her list of offenses. No matter what he said, she had done something to invite someone to attack her on a dark trail in Telluride and break into her house to steal her child's symbolic shoes then take him from baseball practice. It could not be as simple as loving horror. What had she done to bring this upon them? There was no real way to invite horror into real life. Was there?

Sidney had started crying at some point. By the time she took a break from her touchscreen, she had to wipe at her cheeks. She shook her head hard, hoping to dislodge the sadness that pooled in the base of her skull, and started calling the numbers on Kendra's listings.

When the calls were finished and showings were lined up, she returned to her messages.

Tony: Heyyy.

It somehow seemed fitting that Tony initiated conversation with a useless salutation and nothing more.

Sidney: Hi Tony.
Tony: How are you?
Sidney: Shitty. Really fucking shitty.

Tony: I'm sorry. Are you OK?
What's wrong?

Sidney did not know how to respond. She did not know what to tell anyone anymore, three-dimensional or otherwise. What was safe? What was a risk? Where should she focus her fear?

Sidney: Um, everything.

Sidney did not intend to direct her rage at Tony, yet she found it pointing his way nonetheless. Somehow, it felt right to unleash on the person she used, now for a new purpose.

Tony: I'm sorry. Are you OK?

Again.

Sidney: Not really.
I'm sorry. It's not your fault.
I'm just a mess.
Tony: Can I help?
I miss you.

Sidney briefly entertained the idea of how distracting having him on top of her might be, but as the scenario played out in her mind, she found herself shuddering. If she wanted to be with him, he would have to be where she lived, and that thought strangled her.

Sidney: Not right now. Thanks, Tony.

Tony: Can I see you?
    I miss you.

    Again.

Sidney: Maybe after things calm down.

Instead of working, Sidney evaluated new living arrangements. She and Kendra both had adored where they lived. That part of town spoke to them. Yet it was too close to the crime, too near the perpetrator's knowledge. Sidney swallowed her contempt and drove away from the mountains, towards places where no one who knew them would think they might live.

Sidney: I miss you.

    Her turn to say it.

Adam: I miss you too.
    Do you need me there?

Sidney knew the answer but also knew their financial limitations.

Sidney: Yes.

    She hesitated then continued typing.

Sidney: But it's OK if you can't get out here.
    I know how it is.
Adam: Let me see what I can do.
    I want to help. I want to see you.

Sidney spent her shift evaluating rental properties instead of scrutinizing customers' wireless plans. She considered square footage and number of bedrooms instead of data rates and wireless coverage. She fixated shamelessly on getting out of the house where he knew where they were, even knowing her bank account might suffer for it.

*****

Sidney stood in the empty kitchen of a vacant house, drumming her fingertips on the counter. The kitchen had enough space for Kendra's cooking binges and a large peninsula perfect for morning coffee. Two bedrooms were located upstairs and two in the basement. The kids would balk at being separated by floors, but it would give Kendra and Sidney the illusion of more privacy. The neighborhood bordered on suburbia, but the fences were high and the streets well lit.

There was a neighborhood watch, and the house had an actively monitored security system.

Sidney: I think I found our place.
Kendra: Why aren't you at work?
Sidney: Finding a place is more important right
    now.
Kendra: We can't afford a place if you don't
    have a job.
Sidney: It's fine. Just today.
    But I think I found the place.
Kendra: Which one?
Sidney: Maple Street.
Kendra: Oh, I liked that one online.

Sidney: Neighborhood is a little Stepford, but maybe that will make it safer?
Kendra: Maybe!
Sidney: Check it out after work?
Kendra: Yeah, girl. After I get Savannah.
Sidney: Sweet!
I'm going to take Cam to baseball since I skipped work.
Let me know!

Sidney lingered a moment longer, wandering quietly through the empty rooms, imagining their life here. There would be no large window behind the couch for an intruder to step through or for a prowler to lurk below. They could put the television down in the basement where no one could spy on them. The walls felt new, unblemished, far enough away to be a fresh start.

Sidney: I think I found a place.
Adam: Oh yeah? Already?
Sidney: Called off work today.
Adam: Do you feel better?
Sidney: I'll feel better when I move.

Sidney took one more look around what she had decided she would tell Kendra was their future home before moving toward the door.

Adam: What if I came to help you?
Sidney: Help me move?
Adam: Yes. What if that is when I came to visit?

Sidney stopped walking and clutched the phone in both hands. The smile stretching her face almost felt awkward, unfamiliar. She didn't think she had truly smiled since before Cameron had vanished from the baseball field. Maybe the last time she had smiled had been in Adam's bed.

Sidney: That would be amazing!
   I would love to see you.
Adam: Let's plan on it.
   I'll figure it out with work.

Sidney took a deep breath and released it slowly. It felt like the first time she had truly exhaled in days. As she drove back across town to retrieve Cameron's baseball supplies, her mind wandered. She began cataloging the rooms of their house, mentally assessing how to most effectively pack them. She made note of things to nominate for dismissal, largely Cameron's neglected toys. Then she pictured Adam, helping them load the boxes into the truck, leaving all the drama and fear behind them.

She could start over. It could be OK again.

She hurried up her driveway distracted, her steps lightened by future possibilities and knowing Cameron would be thrilled to attend practice. Even if it included his mother helicopter-parenting around the perimeter. She slapped her foot on the concrete step and something crunched beneath her weight. She snapped from the edges of her fantasies and looked down. Two small baby booties laced together with a shiny ribbon lay cracked beneath her shoe.

22

"**Mom, i don't** want to change schools!" Cameron shouted deeply, projecting his voice from his belly in an attempt to sound like his father. In his rage, he nearly succeeded.

Sidney leaned against the counter bordered with colorful paper pencils, massaging her forehead. She flinched at the similarity and at how his voice carried through his school office. She leaned down to shush him, quelling her desperation.

"I know, Cam, baby," Sidney said. "But it's the only way we can be safe."

"We're already moving! Why isn't that enough?" Fat tears spilled from his eyes to dribble down his angry cheeks.

Sidney reached out toward him, to calm him, to quiet him, to comfort him. He retreated away from her, growing in his anger and stomping hard. He pulled back until his heels butted into the thick, large wooden chest that served as the lost and found, sleeves and legs of abandoned clothes reaching out desperately for their neglectful owners.

"I wish it was enough, baby." The guilt thickened in Sidney's throat. The attacker, the thief, the kidnapper—whoever—was clearly after her. That made it all her fault. "But someone broke into this house. And someone took you from baseball practice at this school. We have to go somewhere they don't know about. We should leave the city."

"No, Mommy," Cameron shrieked, desperate.

"No, baby. I wouldn't take you from your daddy, but we have to do at least this."

"I don't want to!" Sobs strangled Cameron's words, reminding her of his toddler voice.

Sidney opened her mouth to respond but did not know what to say, did not know how to make it better. Perhaps there was no way to fix this, but she had to keep him safe. Starting over was all she knew how to do.

Cameron stormed down the hall, his cries fading into the distance, leaving his mother sitting in the office at his school. She dropped the transfer paperwork to the chair beside her and crushed her fists into her forehead. The remorse broke her heart, leaving her chest feeling heavy and achingly vacant. When she composed herself, she smiled weakly at the administrative assistant as she handed over the completed paperwork. Then she hurried down the empty hallway after her son.

She heard the dying whimpers of Cameron's fading tears before she saw him. Her ears would always know the way her baby cried, always be able to pick his pain out of anything. She turned her head and then her feet to the sound of her son's sadness.

Cameron sat on the floor, pressed against a wall of cubbies in the hallway. Sidney could see his shoes peeking out from the edge of the row, his legs getting too long to be tucked out of sight. She smiled in the painful way she only could when his hurt was equally heart-wrenching and adorable.

"Cam, baby," she said as sweetly as she could.

"No, Mommy." Cameron's sobs were so thick Sidney felt them in her own chest, heaving on her diaphragm. "I don't want to go. I don't want to go to a new school!"

"It's not happening today, baby. Not until after we move. Not until after break. Baseball season will be over then." Sidney crouched down and sat on the battered carpet beside Cameron.

"But I don't want to leave my school, my class, my friends." His voice climbed with each item in the list.

Sidney leaned forward and gathered Cameron's wet cheeks in her hands.

"Tonight, all you have to do is go to your daddy's," she said.

Cameron looked at her with wide, wilting eyes. She could see the fear tucked behind his irises, along with the start of resentment. She had imagined it there since the day she betrayed his father, but looking at it now, she knew it had started here. She felt everything his eyes were telling her, and it cut her, but she forced a gentle smile through and pulled him into a hug. He resisted at first then melted into her.

***

When they arrived on Aiden's porch a few hours later, he opened the door wide to allow Sidney to follow Cameron inside. He didn't move but permitted her to brush past him on her entry.

"What's wrong, bud?" Aiden called as Cameron stormed down the hall and disappeared into his room. The door slammed as his answer.

288

"We turned in the transfer paperwork before we came here," Sidney explained.

Aiden nodded and rubbed his hand over his mouth.

"It's what we have to do," he said. "It's what the police said to do."

"I know. I know." Saying it twice made it more convincing to herself. "Are you sure you shouldn't relocate too?"

Aiden shook his head. "They haven't messed with me yet. They might not even know about me or where I live. Plus, I have my guns if they do."

Sidney nodded, fighting back the tears at the necessity of this conversation. "He'll be all right," she told herself more than Aiden. "The change will be hard, but he will be fine."

"Yes, he's tough. We just have to keep him safe."

Sidney looked at him, and their gaze confirmed their agreement.

"What are you and Kendra doing tonight?" Aiden asked.

"Packing. Drinking wine and packing. Savannah is at her dad's, so we're just going to stay up until it's done."

"Well, good luck." Aiden moved to escort her to the door.

"Thanks," Sidney smiled. "So, I'll pick him up Sunday night."

Aiden closed the door gently behind her, and Sidney lingered on the porch for a breath. She stared at the house, thinking about her angry son and feeling the guilt circulate through her like blood. Two breaths later, she felt just as uncomfortable, so she shoved her hands into her pockets and walked to her car.

Two breaths in the driver seat and she still hated herself. She sighed and let the self-loathing bloom, starting the car then shifting it into gear. She tried hard not to think, and failed, as she drove the familiar route back to the house they would soon be leaving. The house they had to flee because of her.

As she arrived home and parked behind Kendra's car, Sidney reminded herself that she would not have to walk through that door many more times, that her hours in these walls were now numbered, that they were on the precipice of starting over. Yet again. She took deep breaths through the itching weight on her skin and turned her mind to the daunting task ahead.

She jammed her key into the lock and turned. The door was always locked now, even when one of them was home. She imagined it would be at the new house too. The small blue baby shoes would ever be a figment on their front mat, stolen then returned, hovering unnervingly in their minds. It would be their token, warding them towards caution.

"Kendra," Sidney announced herself, locking the door behind her. Nothing answered her. "K, where you at?" she shouted louder as she stepped deeper into their house.

She stepped forward, shedding her purse and keys on the counter. She traced her usual steps into the house. Instinctively, she looked to the window. It was still seated; the couch remained undisturbed. She walked to the spot on the carpet—where she had realized there was an intruder in her home—and froze. That same sensation of violation swept over her. The house felt off, as it had that night.

"Kendra," she called again, the name quivering at the edges.

Before she took another step, Sidney snatched her phone and punched 911 on her phone app. Yet she waited to initiate the call, locking the screen and keeping the phone in her hand. She leaned against the hallway wall and closed her eyes, breathing.

She was being ridiculous. She knew she was being ridiculous. It was just all the stress getting to her. They were almost out of here. It was almost behind them. She just needed to calm down.

Sidney shoved herself off the wall and called her roommate again. Her car was out front, but perhaps she was not home? Or maybe she had started packing in the garage? Yet that terrible crawling feeling on Sidney's nerves persisted. She needed to lay eyes on Kendra, not unlike the way she had needed to hold Cameron after he had been snatched from the baseball field.

She continued to repeat Kendra's name as she ascended the stairs. The lights blazed from nearly every room, as if someone was home packing the contents, as if Kendra was there. She pushed Kendra's bedroom door open first but found the room half packed, with boxes neatly stacked along the perimeter. Yet it was empty. The same for Savannah's room. Cameron's room remained darkened with the door shut, but when she pressed in and flicked on the light, it was vacant as well.

She stopped in front of her own door. The only room violated during their break-in. Light crept through the crack between the door and its frame. Her fingers twitched nervously as her pulse quickened. The anxious feeling swelled to consume her. She reached a shaking hand toward the door then retracted it to pick hesitantly at her nails.

Something was wrong. Something was so very wrong.

"Kendra," she called, sheepishly.

That same unnerving sensation crawled through her, separating her skin from her muscles with a stretching energy, that same electricity that vibrated in her bones when she had noticed the open window. She caught the sensation and tried to shake it away. It could not be happening again. She unlocked her phone and looked at the numbers waiting.

Biting at her lip, she locked the screen. She told herself there could not be someone in the house again. Everything was secure; she knew that. Yet her pulse refused to heed the thought.

She thrust her hand forward, desperate to override her fear, and shoved the door open. The door careened recklessly into the room and clattered against the wall inside. Sidney shrank back as the sound echoed through the continuing quiet around her. She saw the shape on her bed before she even broached the threshold. She stopped breathing and clapped her hands over her mouth.

She willed herself into her own room, staggering in forced steps, shambling against her denial. Her fear strangled her muscles, preventing her from moving, yet the imperative in her brain shattered through its efforts. She had to see; she could not do anything else until she had seen. She didn't know how she could be crying without breathing, but she heard her own sobs as if they belonged to someone else.

Because no one else in the house was making any sound.

Kendra's body sprawled over the mattress. Her

hair billowed across the blanket, untamed in a way Kendra never allowed it to be. Her limbs splayed out, arms tossed over her head to rest near the nest of hair, legs draped heavy with unusual weight.

Sidney's legs failed her before she reached the bed. Her knees buckled and dumped her to the carpet. She collapsed clumsily, too anguished to brace herself with her hands. Her face collided hard with the unforgiving fibers, but she scarcely felt the impact. Her breathing belonged to someone else; her body and its pain belonged to someone else. She did not inhabit her skin in this moment because this moment could not be happening.

As she forced a shaking hand over the edge of the bed, her fingertips tangled in Kendra's curls. The wild strands snared her fingers. The touch sent a frantic pulse dancing distantly on Sidney's nerves. She recoiled from the gentle touch of Kendra's hair and drew all her limbs close, wrapping into a messy and awkward ball on the floor. Then she unfolded and crawled closer, her eyes reluctant on her own bed.

Sidney did not have to touch the body to know she was dead. Kendra simply did not look like *Kendra*. Whatever had animated her, whatever had made her who Sidney loved had gone, leaving her eyes vacant. Kendra's chest sat terrifyingly still, her wide eyes fixed on the ceiling. Her mouth hung open slightly, neat white teeth peeking from the still and parted lips. As if she had something to say. As if she had one more word of comfort or advice for Sidney.

The pain radiated from inside Sidney, from every memory that had Kendra in it, from every time she had hugged her when she felt hopeless, from every laugh they had shared within the walls that now confined them in this terrible moment. As she stared agape into Kendra's dead face, her brain lit up with flashes of Kendra alive. Kendra laughing with her whole mouth. Kendra pursing her lips and shifting them to the side. Kendra closing her eyes when Savannah nestled into her chest. Kendra clutching Cameron after they had found him. Kendra looking intently into Sidney. Yet, with every blink, the living face vanished, and the death on the bed stared back at Sidney.

Shuffling on her knees to the edge of the mattress, Sidney wrapped her fists in the edge of the comforter. Kendra's eyes remained rooted to the ceiling above. Thin red lines snaked unnaturally over the white orbs. A red and gold braided cord coiled around Kendra's neck, pulled so tight the strands had flattened and distended. Discoloration blossomed out on the skin below the ligature. She did not look like herself, more like a perverted echo of the woman Sidney knew, the roommate whom she loved.

Part of Sidney felt compelled to climb into the bed beside Kendra, cling to her immobile corpse. She wanted to embrace her. She wanted to wrap herself around her and weep all over her until her grief reanimated Kendra. The impulse quivered in her muscles, burned on the edge of where her thoughts had died. Yet her fingertips remained entangled in the blanket. She twisted the fabric so tight that her arms trembled. She could not bring herself to move.

Then her cries began. The sounds were soft at first, foreign and distant as her breathing had seemed. Then they built in a crescendo through her body as they rattled her ribs and tore through her throat. Her mouth gaped uncontrollably as screams ripped out and breaths heaved in to refuel them. Her body became the tears and the sobs, no thought or control existing beyond them. They racked her until she felt hollow.

She lifted her arm to touch Kendra's face but found her hand so heavy. Disoriented, she looked to her palm to find her phone still cleaved there. The sight of it confused her. She scarcely remembered what the shiny brick was meant to do. Why did she have it? Why was it in her hand when her hand should be resuscitating Kendra? She examined it dumbly for a long moment before dropping it to the carpet. As she watched it tumble against the fibers, she snapped back to herself and snatched it up.

Sidney managed to unlock her phone and send the emergency call. She blubbered into the receiver. Her words poured out of her lips in an incoherent blur. Roommate dead. Address. Help. She only heard the operator repeat to not touch the body, to not touch anything, and stay on the line. She cried until the action felt so repeated that it became her new normal.

She was the only one left there, breathing in sobs and screaming her sounds in the empty house.

25

"**SIDNEY, HONEY,**" Brady said from across his apartment, "he's here."

Sidney went to sit up from the couch but found herself so heavy. Her muscles trembled weakly, depleted at the thought of moving her own weight. Her head itself seemed to be packed with lead. Or that was the heaping exhaustion from not sleeping for more than an hour straight in a couple weeks.

Sleep felt like betraying Kendra, but waking up felt even more sinister.

Sidney heard the two sets of footsteps move toward her over the hard floors and wrenched herself upright. Adam smiled at her—gently, cautiously—as he followed Brady. Sidney's hands swept over the face and hair she had not washed in days. Her cheeks felt tender from the endless flood of tears. She did not even know if she had brought a brush to Brady and Jordan's apartment.

"I told you I didn't want you to come," she said, her voice like gravel in her own mouth.

"Then why did you give me the address?" Adam joked softly.

"Because I knew you would come anyway."

"I told you I would help you move."

Sidney's face dropped, and her eyes fell to her lap. She bit into the cracks she compulsively kept opening by chewing on her bottom lip. She picked at her cuticles, already woven together in scabs.

"I'm going to run to the store, Sid," Brady interrupted.

Sidney looked up at him and nodded half-heartedly. Brady reached out to shake Adam's hand then softly patted him on the back before he escaped the apartment. All her grief must have made the small space suffocating.

Adam stepped forward, slower than he wanted. She could feel the restraint in his movements. She wished he did not have to be cautious with her. Part of her wanted to leap into him, the way she had imagined so many times since Telluride and maybe even before, yet that part was paralyzed by all her pain. At the end of every moment, Kendra's unblinking eyes were all she could see.

He lowered himself down beside her.

"Come here," he said, gently.

Sidney shifted closer to him as he opened his arms. He drew her into his chest as he leaned back on the couch. She had not intended to collapse on top of him, but at the comfort in his touch, she unraveled. Her head pressed into his chest until she could hear his heart thumping at her ear. He ran one hand soothingly over her head and along her hair. She felt him breathing her in as he kissed her scalp.

"I'm so sorry, Sidney," he said.

Kendra's eyes again.

Sidney squeezed her eyes shut but only saw

Kendra's face more vividly. She burrowed down into Adam, feeling his arms clutch her tighter. He waited calmly until the tension dissolved from her muscles again and she was able to lift her head. She planted her chin on his chest and looked up at him with her tear-stained eyes.

"I missed you," he said.

Sidney swam up his body and took his face in her hands. She kissed him sloppily and tried to remember how much she had wanted to all the days before she found Kendra. He kissed her back but let her pull away when she was done. She replaced her head beside his comforting heartbeat.

"I'm sorry you have to be here for this, when I'm like this," Sidney stammered.

"I don't have to be here," he said, firmly. "I chose to be here. I want to help you through this, Sid."

"I don't know if I can get through this," she said, honestly.

"I know you don't want to." He continued to stroke her hair. "But you can. For Cameron."

Sidney cried into Adam's shirt. "I'm sorry," she repeated.

"What are you sorry for? Sid, this is not your fault. None of this is your fault."

"It is." She cried harder. "It has to be. It's because of me, so it's my fault."

"Nothing you did made someone attack you on the trail or break into your house or take your child or . . . " His voice trailed off.

"Kill my roommate," Sidney choked.

They fell briefly silent. Adam squeezed her tighter again.

The seconds ticked loudly between them as Sidney's mind floundered to make thoughts. She should be thinking. She should be reacting. Yet she felt lost and paralyzed in the black that had blossomed around her heart, seized her entire mind. Finally, Adam's words permeated through that darkness enough for her brain to process them.

"I had forgotten about Telluride," she finally said. "Do you think it's all the same guy?"

"I don't know. Probably not. I don't care as long as you're safe." Adam's heart rate accelerated below her ear. "But you didn't cause any of this, Sidney."

"I had to have." Sidney shot up from his chest, suddenly sitting with impassioned ease. "With all this stuff online. With all this horror. I invited it in."

"No," Adam said, sitting up beside her. He lifted his arm, and she leaned under it. "Nothing you did invited any of this. Watching some movies, taking some pictures, and writing some articles does not equal all this."

"But it attracted someone."

"Yeah, me." Adam smirked at her. "We don't even know if this is related to your online work. What have the police said?"

"Nothing yet." Sidney deflated at those words, the weight of her depression spreading back over her like a terrible blanket.

"Let the cops figure out who this is. Let's get you in a safe place for you and Cameron."

"Cameron is never going to want to live with me again." Sidney's sobs flared again. "He's heartbroken over Kendra. And Savannah . . . " Sidney choked on her name.

"It's too much," Adam soothed. "I know it's too much."

"Aiden already moved all of the stuff out of the house. I couldn't go in there. He just put it in storage for me."

"That was nice of him."

Sidney nodded. "I know it's good that Cameron has been staying with him full time, but I miss him so much. And Brady and Jordan have to be sick of the weepy girl haunting their gorgeous studio . . . I just couldn't stay with my mother."

"I doubt they mind."

Sidney's phone chattered in vibration, causing the glass tabletop to hum in front of them. She startled violently then stared at the device.

"Do you need to check that?" Adam asked, gently.

"No," she said vacantly. "Everyone has been checking on me," Sidney half-scoffed. "Everyone in the *real* world who knows about Kendra. Wes, of course. Carla and Amy have been messaging me nonstop since they found out."

"They're worried about you."

"I guess. I haven't seen my son in days. I haven't been to work since it happened. They've been understanding so far, but I think that's running out. I'm going to get fired if I can't get my shit together." Sidney dropped her head from his shoulder into her own hands.

"Then let's get your shit together." Adam ran his hand along Sidney's spine. "You have so many great people around you, helping you."

"I've had better," Sidney said, dryly. She didn't have to look at Adam to see his face fall.

"I know you have." He pressed his mouth to her hair.

"I'm sorry," Sidney said again. "I know I'm being depressed and contradictory. It just hurts so much. I loved her. I cannot deal with her being gone. And Savannah—" Sidney could barely say her name. "Kendra was such a good mother. Savannah deserved to have her mother. What is *she* going to do now?"

Adam said nothing. There were no words to say. He simply held on to her as the sobs racked her body again. He wrapped around her until the cries faded into whimpers and dwindled back into breath.

***

The cardboard dust coated Sidney's hands. She could smell the strange musty mix of boxes and tape crammed in her backseat. At least it was not snowing, and the winter sun beat down warmly through the window. Adam's hand played at her knee, but when Sidney let her fingers run along his, she only felt the particles of the boxes spread over her skin. Every time she inhaled, the odor of moving saturated her brain and she could only hear Kendra's voice.

"Divorced Moms Club becoming official today, girl," Kendra said from the passenger seat beside her. "Today, we start over. We're going to find our new life together."

Kendra smiled wide from beneath her obnoxiously large sunglasses.

Sidney could almost see her in the reflection of the window. She stared vacantly at the houses and skeletal trees whipping by the glass. Her own shape distorted behind her tears until she could tell herself it was Kendra, desperately excited about their move, selling the dream with everything she had.

Sidney's diaphragm flexed, and she bit down hard into her lip. She snatched her fingers away from Adam's and rubbed her palms against her jeans, hoping to wipe off the memories.

Sidney's phone vibrated against her hip. She reached for it to skim the notifications.

Group conversation
Amy: Sidney, are you OK?
   Are you still moving today?
Carla: We could come help.
   Or bring wine after.
Amy: Yeah. Raise a glass to Kendra.
Carla: I'm so sorry, Sid. Let us be there for you.

The tears stung at Sidney's eyes. She blinked them back hard.

Wes: Sid, please answer me. Do you need anything?

Mom: Do you have my grandson back yet? A boy needs his mother in times like these.

At the last, she tossed the phone to the floorboard.

"Another of your online boyfriends?" Adam laughed.

Sidney smirked, half-heartedly. "My mother."

"So, she was so supportive that you had to throw your phone down in shock?"

Sidney's smirk threatened to spill into a smile. Then she sighed and mashed her cardboard-dusted hands into her face.

"Ha! Not exactly," she said from behind her palms. "What does she have to say?"

"Oh, the usual. Passive aggressively how this is all my fault."

Adam's voice dropped. "Sidney, you know this is not your fault."

"So you keep telling me. She makes sure to check on me, tell me how I should be with my son right now. She gets her jabs in. This must be so hard on me, but I really always surrounded myself with horror, so how is this any different? I can't expect to invite strangers and monsters into my life and not get hurt."

"Whoa, what? Strangers and monsters?"

"Yeah." Sidney smacked her lips. "That's what horror fans are, don't you know? And people on the internet." Sidney paused as her throat tightened. "That's what her daughter is."

"Well, I guess I'm a monster too."

"We know you're a monster," Sidney managed to joke, though the attempt to push the humor into her cheeks hurt.

"A scary stranger from the internet," he chuckled.

"Oh, I haven't even told her about you."

"No? Should I be offended?" Adam slipped his hand from her knee and back to the steering wheel.

"No. I'm just not ready to deal with her bullshit. She can't handle me watching horror movies. She hates that I expose Cameron to anything horror. She's still mad at me for ruining my marriage, says I destroyed my family and traumatized Cam. She thinks posting articles and pictures on the internet is somehow like prostitution."

"Wait, what? Prostitution?"

"She's convinced my side job is going to get me attacked by some internet stalker," Sidney continued. "She won't say it out loud, but she doesn't like Brady and Jordan, blames them for me being naked on the internet." Sidney took a deep breath and puffed it out, glaring down at her phone. "I could go on."

"That's a lot."

"My mom's a lot."

"I can see why you didn't want to stay with her."

"I don't think I could have survived it right now. She would have said how Kendra's death is my fault, and I would have broken right there."

"Kendra's death is not your fault, Sidney," Adam said, firmly.

"So you keep saying. My mom wanted to help me move, wanted to bring Cam. I just couldn't take her being all judgy with Brady and Jordan, and I know she won't react well to you."

"We can deal with that another time."

"If you're still around," Sidney mumbled, compulsively.

"What do you mean?" Adam's voice changed, and he became rigid in the driver's seat beside her.

"If we make it, for all the normal reasons." Sidney began picking at her nails and looked down at her hands. "Or if you can't deal with me for all these new, horrible reasons. Or if you get killed like Kendra." She choked on the last sentence.

"Whoa, Sid." Adam turned his eyes off the road and to her. "You're spiraling. I'm not going anywhere."

"Don't say that. That's as bad as saying, 'I'll be right back.'"

"This is not a horror movie, Sidney. Everything is not a horror movie."

"About a month ago, I would have agreed with you."

Adam sucked in a deep breath but did not use it to form a response. Instead, he leaned toward the window and massaged the stubble spread across his jaw with his fingertips. Sidney let her words die on the dashboard and allowed their fading sound to be overrun by the clicking as she picked her nails.

The silence had become deafening by the time the tires rolled to a stop in front of the small house. As Sidney pulled herself from the car, she heard the doors slam from Jordan's car parked behind them.

Brady's immaculate shoes scuffed along the curb as he walked up beside her. He gathered Sidney under his arm, and she burrowed into his chest, smelling his sweet, crisp scent. He smelled like his spotless loft. He smelled the same as when Kendra was alive. She closed her eyes, wanting to dissipate into his aroma, merge and mingle until she was merely particles in the same memory. Instead, she felt him gently patting her shoulder, calling her back to her nerves being chilled by the sharp edge on the air.

"It's a really cute house, Sid," Jordan said beside them. "Perfect for you and Cameron."

The unexpected tears burned Sidney's eyes. Her and Cameron. Not Savannah, who now stayed with her father full time as he kept her as far as he could from Sidney and Cameron and the household they had shared. Not Kendra, who now rotted beneath Evergreen cemetery. Right now, not even Cameron—who had to hide from her with Aiden because she had brought horror into their home, because she could not get herself together enough to be his mother.

Sidney opened her mouth to respond, to feign some kind of agreement, yet no sound came out. Her lips hung awkwardly agape, hung around an unconsummated sob. Brady quietly hugged her tighter into his chest.

"It's OK, Sidney," he said, her full name so foreign on his tongue. "This is a fresh start. This is a safe place. Plus, we're going to make it fabulous."

Brady took a step toward her new front door, pressing his arm into her back to guide her forward.

THE NEW HOUSE was too quiet, as if the boxes lining the room absorbed the sound and sucked up the air around Sidney. She felt like she could not breathe so alone, in such oppressive silence. Sidney stood uneasy inside the front door, shoes squeaking on the tile under her, fingers fidgeting in her keys. She did not know how to be alone in this new place, *her* place. She could not stand how loud it all seemed in silence.

Cameron and Savannah not giggling as they ran through the hallways chasing each other.

Kendra not in the kitchen pouring a glass of wine and talking about her ex-husband.

No one. Nothing. Just unfamiliar rooms filled with Sidney's possessions hastily crammed into wilted boxes.

When Brady and Jordan ran out of enthusiasm for moving furniture and even free pizza could not rekindle them, Sidney had told them she would be fine. When she kissed Adam goodbye in the departure drop-off lane at the airport, she had told him she would be fine. She was not fine. Nothing in the world around her was fine anymore.

She had thought she wanted to be away from them. She had thought she wanted to be alone.

The pity radiated off Brady and Jordan when they looked at her, so palpable to her that she felt exposed and vulnerable. They felt bad for her, and it was potent enough to blot out anything else they felt for her, anything else she ever was. She was not Sidney to them right now; she was Kendra's death.

Adam's concern had made her nauseous. His gaze was so soft and so attentive as it constantly assessed her. It should have comforted her, yet it felt intrusive. Her skin prickled knowing he judged her every mannerism, knowing he saw her consistent failures. She could not pretend to be fine. Adam could see that, and that sight exhausted Sidney.

She had ignored the incessant messages from Wes, Carla, Amy; forced a blind eye to them constantly checking on her despite how the avoidance made her twitch. Them caring about her pain and wellbeing somehow only made her ache for Kendra deeper and more pervasive. And she felt selfish in her grief. She did not want to share the loss or bridge the memories with anyone else, as if it would cost her more of Kendra.

Yet now, it was too quiet. Now, she was too alone.

Her shoes had not moved from the entryway tile. She had not even bothered to slip her feet out of them. She awkwardly shifted her weight from side to side as her fingers continued to weave through the metal rings holding her keys. The keys chimed against each other, and their tinkling became deafening. Sidney heard her own breathing quicken as her heartbeat throbbed in her ears.

The harder her heart pounded, the more anxious and agitated she became. The clothes confining her skin pressed and itched. Her nerves vibrated in the anxiety while her mind whirled too fast for thoughts to manifest into words. Steadily, she was choking on her own breaths.

When she realized she was staring at her hands knotted in her keychain, she lifted her eyes. Tears blurred her vision when she glanced into her new house. She did not see the empty room with haphazard furniture and stacked boxes; she saw her old house. She saw her place with Kendra.

"Girl, get in here," Kendra's voice said from the kitchen. "It's wine time."

The tears overflowed from Sidney's eyes at the echo of Kendra's voice in her head. She knew she was not in their old house; she knew Kendra was not in the kitchen. Yet she sobbed hard as she stepped forward, her keys tumbling and clattering to the tile behind her.

"I'm going to give you a heavy pour tonight," Kendra's voice continued. "Going to give my 'mom pour.' None of this two sips in the bottom of the glass. We are using this entire wine glass, just like Mom used to. Now, I see why she did though."

The sound of Kendra's laugh shattered Sidney's heart. It stopped thudding in her ears; it felt like it stopped entirely. Her feet continued to move mechanically, shuffling her across the memory. The phantom kitchen drew closer. Just a little further and she would be able to see Kendra behind the counter, administering her Mom Pour. If she could see her through the tears.

"No, girl, there's no such thing as too much,"

Kendra giggled. "There's no such thing as too heavy a pour. I promise we'll feel better after these."

Sidney smiled and grimaced at the same time. There was no such thing as too heavy a pour. She knew that now. Kendra had taught her that, from the aftermath of Aiden kicking her out to when they found her abducted son.

One more step and Sidney could almost see around the corner, almost glimpse Kendra whose laugh infected her ears. As her foot moved forward, she bumped her leg into a box in the real house, in the real moment. She lurched forward, cascading back into reality and her empty new house as she tumbled onto the carpet.

The floor hit her harder than it should have for how slow she had been moving. Yet her depleted muscles did nothing to save her. She flopped to the carpet, smelling the unfamiliar aroma puff up from her impact. Not her, not Kendra, not Cameron, and not Savannah. She inhaled strange dander and the leftover smell of carpet shampoo that worked to mask it.

Kendra's voice vanished, and only the sound of her own sobs replaced it. Instinctively, she drew her knees into her chest and wrapped her arms around herself as she cried. She let the grief pour out of her until her phone vibrated hard in her pocket.

Adam: Made it home.
Miss you already.
How are you?

Sidney could see that same perplexed look on his face in the words on her screen, and she only cried harder. She lifted the phone to reply but could not see through her tears. When the wave finally subsided, she drew herself up sloppily and mopped her cheeks with her hands.

Sidney: OK. Just unpacking.

She forced herself to type the lie, shoving down the outburst swelling in her throat and ignoring the inflated notification counts on all her apps. Her conversations swelled bloated and unmonitored. The topics in those messages were no longer distractions; they had crossed over and entangled with her real world. She looked up at the kitchen that was not theirs, where Kendra was not pouring wine, and found herself too heavy to stand.

Adam: Liar.

"Fuck," Sidney breathed, though the word came out mangled.

She rubbed her hand over her eyes, digging too hard against her eyelids. The pain was somehow comforting. When she pried her eyes back open, she looked over the boxes. The task loomed, daunting, making her muscles feel more weighted. She glanced down at the phone lingering in her hand. She had been ignoring it for days, drowning in the trauma of reality.

She propped herself against one of the menacing boxes and brought the screen to her face. She almost hesitated, almost locked the screen again to block out everything she had found on the internet. Yet then she looked around her sad little reality. She could not stay here in her life. Just the sight of it threatened to collapse her chest. She let her cheeks slacken as she escaped from the sad, empty house and into the flashing, scrolling virtual world.

Her notifications had exploded in her neglect. Her eyes were filled with hearts and upturned thumbs and numbers circled in red. The online attention brewed the familiar warmth in her chest, the safe affirmation that soothed her tattered ego but did not require her to face real interaction. The corner of her lips twitched toward a smile at the *Where have you been?* and *I miss your posts* messages.

Sidney felt a pleasant distance from her reality. For an instant, she forgot where she was sitting and why she was there alone.

She stayed out of the inboxes peppered with queries from her real-life friends and moved over to her social media inboxes, swiping through the messages that echoed the comments and posts to her profiles.

Then her heart seized again.

[Facebook User]: You can't hide from me.

Sidney flinched so hard that she dropped the phone to the carpet between her feet. Her phone bounced then rested against her shoe, screen shining down to illuminate the threads. Her breath panted rapidly through her lips until her chest was heaving. She pushed herself harder back into the boxes, hands groping waywardly.

Then she shot upright, eyes wide. She crept along the floor on her hands and knees to the front door, making sure the deadbolt was locked. Then she scrambled to the front window and arched her back, peering out of the pane and into the black night. Her panicked face reflected back to her on the glass.

When she saw the shape of her own expression, the nausea returned—the same nausea she felt at Adam's caring eyes. She took a long, slow breath as the realization cascaded over her mind. The sick feeling in her gut was not a flinch away from Adam. Instead, her system seized in response to her. She disgusted herself.

Rage flickered in her chest as her emotions collided and her internal pendulum swung away from paralytic depression. She shot to her feet and stomped back across the carpet, snatching up her phone. She took a screenshot of the message then paged away from it.

Her automatic reaction was to want to show it to Kendra, to ask Kendra if she was overreacting. The reaction brought the dark wave over her mind again and the tightness in her stomach. She pursed her lips against the tears and sent the image to Adam.

Sidney: Am I being paranoid here?
  This is creepy, right?

Sidney forced herself to remain standing, willed herself not to crumple around how much she wanted to talk to Kendra, how the void in her life now felt consuming, how this new place felt like Hell. She moved through the foreign house and switched on every light. She pulled a beer from the fridge, knowing it would weaken her mind and further loosen her feelings, and cracked it open. Taking a large swig, she opened the box at the top of the stack in the kitchen.

She knew she should wash the plates before putting them in the cabinet. She knew they were covered in the dirty newspaper they were wrapped in. She did not care. It took most of her restraint to place the dishes in the cabinet rather than smashing them on the floor, stomping her feet on the shards until they bled.

By the time the phone buzzed on the counter, she had tossed the empty box aside.

Adam: Of course that's creepy.
Your internet stalkers are always creepy.

Sidney set the phone back down. He did not think this was her real-life stalker, Kendra's murderer. He thought this was just another, unrelated internet stalker. She had her answer. She was paranoid and crazy.

Kendra could have told her that.

Sidney's phone continued to twitch and beckon from the countertop as she plunged into boxes and beers until she could barely stand. When the discarded box pile stood taller than the packed boxes, she finally trudged up to bed and faceplanted onto the hastily covered mattress. She scarcely formed concluding thoughts before the darkness took her.

The darkness in her dream smelled like the mountains, the air clean with a crisp edge drawing on Sidney's cheeks. She heard her footsteps on the gravel as she followed the shadowed trail. A distant streetlight at the cross street spilled a yellow light down the path, yet as Sidney approached it, the darkness between stretched and elongated. The beacon grew smaller as the fall night swelled heavier to swallow her.

Sidney hesitated, squinting at the shrinking streetlight in disbelief. She shuffled on the gravel, the soles of her shoes grinding on the stones. The instant of silence suffocated her until the sloshing steps through the creek shattered the moment. Sidney whirled around but only saw darkness, hearing the rippled steps moving closer from the black beside her.

Sidney turned to launch into a sprint toward the waning light. She managed two leaping strides before she stumbled on something, on nothing, and careened to the ground. The gravel dug into her cheek, her palms, her knees. She scrambled back to her feet, staring back at the black as the watery steps continued to stomp closer.

She went to run again, yet her feet tangled on the dark and shapeless air, and her face slammed into the dirt. When she screamed into the dirt, she tasted the blood in her mouth. As she pumped her legs back underneath her, a hand seized her ankle and yanked it back away from her. She lurched forward but did not meet the trail again.

Instead, Sidney fell through the path, plunging and twirling through the darkness, and flopped down on her bed beside Kendra's lifeless body. Her face planted into the comforter, compressing the fabric before she bounced up to settle against Kendra's shoulder. As if they were cuddling. Kendra's skin was sickly cool, unnatural, and Sidney recoiled violently away from her. She spiraled from the mattress and collapsed into sobs on the tragically familiar carpet.

Sidney wailed harder than she had ever allowed

herself. She howled inhumanly until her cries consumed the room, deafened her. When she ran out of breath, she finally lifted her head and peered trembling over the edge of the mattress.

Sidney squinted through her tears at Kendra's profile. Then Kendra's head jerked to face Sidney, and her eyes snapped, enlivened. Sidney gasped and plastered her hands over her mouth. Kendra's jaw opened slowly, the dry skin splitting. Her mouth drew agape then began closing again, opening and closing over and over. It took Sidney a while to see through her horror that Kendra's lips were moving in twitching shapes. She was speaking unconsummated words.

Sidney took a huge gasp, inhaling the swollen edge of the nightmare and coughing in her dark bedroom. Reality sharpened around her, the air feeling weightless and time ticking steadily around her. She floundered in her consciousness and groped at the blankets twisted around her waist. She frantically scanned the room around her. The shadows were foreign, and the windows had moved around the wall as she slept.

Where was she?

Her heart shuttered in her chest before reason coagulated from the fog in her head. She was in a new room, her new house. She was right where she had fallen asleep after her frantic unpacking. Right back in the nightmare her life had become.

She flopped back on the mattress. She puffed a breath out over her face, yet her heart continued to flap behind her ribs. She could still hear the watery steps coming toward her from the shadows across the room. She could still feel the grip tighten around her ankle. She could still see Kendra's silent, wagging mouth.

She snatched the empty pillow beside her and wrapped herself around it, scrunching her eyes shut to make the room darker. Still, she only saw Kendra's corpse failing to speak. Now, she heard Kendra's voice in her head.

It's your fault. You did this to me. You killed me, Sid. You did this to Savannah.

Kendra's dead lips mouthed all the words Sidney had been hearing in her own skull for days. The fear, the twitching anxiety coiled in Sidney's chest released in a wave, washed away by the thick and oppressive sadness. As her body became heavy with her pain, she sobbed into the pillow she clutched close.

When the tears finally ebbed, Sidney wiped at her eyes and reached for her phone. She needed to be anywhere but alone in this bed. The screen nearly blinded her, but she squinted until the words came into focus.

Adam: How is unpacking going?
I guess you're really busy.
Are you OK?
Goodnight. I hope you get some rest.

Sidney had not realized she had ignored him for so long. The task had consumed her and her desperation to lose herself in it. She went to reply, tapping the cursor into the text field, then let her fingers hover uselessly above the letters.

She wanted to say she missed him. She wanted to say she wished he was here with her. She wanted to say anything sane and normal, yet all her fingers wanted to type were the words she imagined Kendra's dead lips had mouthed to her.

She could not find the words to answer Adam. She could not bring herself to browse social media or triage her email. She dared not risk sleep and bait more nightmares. Instead, she stomped downstairs to unpack more boxes.

25

"**M**OMMY!" Cameron hollered as Sidney opened the front door.

"Cam, baby." Sidney dropped to one knee so that she could swallow her son in a hug.

With Cameron pressed into her chest, Sidney closed her eyes and took the first real breath she had in days. When she exhaled, her shoulders finally lowered. She melted into him, and when he went to release her, she clung to him an extra second longer. The house around them instantly felt smaller, less cavernous and vacant.

"Hey, Sidney," Aiden said as he stepped in behind Cameron.

"Hi, Aiden." Sidney finally released Cameron, her fingertips still lingering on his shoulders. "Thanks for bringing Cam over."

Aiden awkwardly stuffed his hands in his pockets and moved his eyes around the living room. "It looks good in here," he said. "You've already unpacked a lot."

"I couldn't really sleep."

Aiden nodded but did not step further into the house.

"Cam, buddy, I'm going to put your bag right here,"

Aiden leaned the backpack against the nearest wall, "and I'll see you in a couple days."

Cameron gave his father a quick side hug, and Aiden waved to Sidney as he retreated out the front door, closing it behind him.

"Can I see my new room?" Cameron smiled broadly then hesitated. A shadow twitched along his brows, and he curled into himself.

"Of course you can," Sidney said. "But what's wrong, Cam?"

Cameron crossed his arms and bit at his lip.

Sidney stepped forward and wrapped an arm around him.

"Is it OK to be excited?" he asked quietly.

"About your new room?"

Cameron nodded, pinching his eyes shut.

"Yes. Why would it not be OK?"

"Because Savannah isn't here." Cameron's voice strangled on her name. "And Kendra is . . ." His voice trailed off.

Sidney dropped back down to her knee and snatched Cameron to her chest, stroking her hand along the back of his head. She caught herself shushing softly through her lips and rocking him side to side as she had when he was much smaller. Yet he somehow felt far more vulnerable now—now that it seemed clear she could not defend him from the life around them.

"Yes, it's OK to be excited," she finally said into his ear. "It doesn't mean you miss Kendra and Savannah any less. It's OK to still be happy."

She said the words to her son but felt they were more for herself.

"And you'll see Savannah again," she continued, even knowing the last statement was probably a lie.

Cameron nodded in her arms and sloppily wiped his face. Sidney released him and stood again, tilting her head to stare down at him.

"Do you want to see your room now?" Sidney asked.

Cameron nodded, slowly and still looking down. Sidney's chest became heavier just watching the weight of emotion on his small body. Impulsively, she wanted to seize him in another hug, but her logic restrained her. Instead, she watched him gently and attentively. She felt the sinking stone in her stomach, the familiar guilt dragging down her center, the relentless thought that she had done this to him. This was her fault.

She took a deep breath and pushed the thoughts aside, drove her focus down into her son. She took his small hand in hers and felt the swell of nostalgia at all the times his even smaller hand had been in hers. Now, it somehow felt false. Now, she could not consider herself his safety and comfort. The blurred sensation brought tears tingling through her sinuses, but she blinked them back hard.

She turned her face so Cameron would not notice her struggle and guided him down the hallway. As they navigated the new pathways of the unfamiliar floorplan, Cameron's chin finally abandoned his chest. His eyes explored. He looked childishly curious again.

"So, I'm right here," Sidney said, as they reached the top of the stairs.

Cameron stepped forward, releasing her hand, and peeked his head into the room.

"It's bigger than the old house," he said.

"Little bit." Sidney smiled. Painfully. "And your room is right here, next to mine."

"I'm right next to you this time?" Cameron's smile grew.

"Yeah, there are only two bedrooms here."

"Just you and me," Cameron murmured, only half-heartbroken.

As he dropped the phrase, Cameron moved smoothly into his new room. He did not hesitate at the threshold; he spoke with nonchalance then walked right through it.

"Mom!" Cameron shouted excitedly when he fully stepped into the room. "It's all Spider-Man!"

He bounded into the room and threw himself on the bed wrapped in its new comforter and sheets, adorned with the new character pillows. He stared up at the new pictures hung meticulously on the walls around him.

"It's all new!" he exclaimed.

"A new room for a new start."

Sidney had told herself the same thing over and over as she stood in the checkout and then again as she emptied her checking account to furnish this room, to pretend at this fresh start. A start like she had once made with Kendra.

Cameron hopped up from the bed and sprinted over to her, colliding with her midsection as he wrapped his arms around her and squeezed.

"Thank you thank you thank you, Mom! I love it so much!"

Sidney pressed her hands into his back and tumbled into their embrace, the moment inflated by his joy. This is what she had purchased with all her money, the fleeting feeling in this split second. The hug ended, and Cameron hurried back to his bed, snatching up the near life-sized Spider-Man and clutching it instead. Yet he was still smiling, so it was still worth it.

"Are you hungry, buddy?" Sidney asked.

"Yeah, starving," Cameron answered without looking up. "Dad said you would feed me dinner."

"And I will. Frozen pizza?"

"Sure."

Sidney left Cameron tossing Spider-Man across the room and jumping after it. The sounds of his role play voices echoing down the hall almost made this strange and unwanted house vaguely feel like a home. She found her way to the kitchen that did not have a peninsula heaped with Kendra's purse and keys and opened the cabinet that did not have Kendra's beloved morning coffee lined on the bottom shelf. She tossed the pizza on the rack in the oven and sat up on the countertop, pulling her phone from her back pocket.

The tears clouded her sinuses but had not yet formed in her eyes, but she felt them menacing. She tried to remember the last time that haunting tingle did not writhe under her cheeks. The past couple months seemed to have passed in a blur of tears.

Sidney: Hey, sorry. Busy day.
Adam: That's OK. How's it going?
Sidney: Cam is home. Mostly unpacked.
Adam: You've done a lot since I left.

Sidney glanced across the kitchen at the wine glasses perched behind the glass door. The sedation of just a glass of wine could bring a layer of calm to her mind, could temper the storm of sobs menacing in her throat. Yet even the thought was saturated with memories of Kendra. She had not drunk a glass of wine at home without Kendra since before she left Aiden's house. The tangled thread leading between the series of memories looped around her throat to strangle her.

She shook the awful energy out of her hands and occupied them instead by unlocking her phone.

Allison: Hey girl, I haven't heard from you in forever!
Where have you been? You OK?
I hope you're doing OK. Here if you need me.

Allison's message thread had inflated unattended through the move. Sidney had nearly forgotten about her since Kendra, Adam's visit, and the move. A spire of guilt extended in Sidney's chest before her persistent sadness weighed down to crush it flat.

Sidney: I'm so sorry. Didn't mean to ghost you.
Things have been rough lately.
Allison: Oh hey!
No problem! I was just worried about you.
Sidney: Thanks
Allison: So, what happened? Are you OK?

Sidney looked at the question. It was the only question she had been answering lately. Everyone who hugged her breathed it into her hair. Every conversation with Adam was initiated with it. She had heard it so many times that the combination of syllables had lost all meaning, dissembling into irritating sounds.

She never really answered with the truth—that she was not OK, that her mind had become a minefield of fear and flashbacks, that she saw Kendra's dead eyes every time she blinked, that she thought her heart might sink low enough to stop beating in her chest. She always regurgitated some version of, *I'm fine*.

She was not fine. She did not even know what fine looked like. Yet she could not say that to the people who knew her in her real life.

Sidney took a deep breath and gathered up the phone, putting both hands to work on the keyboard.

Sidney: No, not really. I'm pretty much a disaster.
My son kind of got abducted.
Then my roommate got murdered.
We had to move to a new place.

Sidney stopped and reviewed her list of traumas, watching the dancing dots below her words that indicated Allison was typing. What could she be typing? How could you respond to all that? Sidney realized that Allison probably thought she was full of shit. Sidney's stories and drama since Telluride read unbelievable, like the lies of a bored troll on the internet looking to entertain herself. She scarcely believed what had happened to her, especially when reviewing it in full, so how could she expect Allison to?

She juggled the phone between her palms as she

waited for Allison to call her a liar, to finally not seem so receptive and interested. Maybe it was Allison who was really full of shit in this strange virtual shadow game with a stranger.

Allison: HOLY SHIT!
   Oh, girl, I don't even know what to say.

"Yeah, me either," Sidney mumbled aloud before she realized it.

Sidney: Me either.
Allison: OMG! Is there anything I can do?

There was nothing Allison could do. Or Adam. Or Brady and Jordan. Nothing would bring Kendra back. Nothing would undo what Sidney had brought into their lives.

That thought seized in the back of Sidney's throat, and she jumped down and thrust her hand through the cloud of memories to grab a wine glass. She pulled the bottle from the counter and poured absentmindedly, stopping short of the rim. The sour edge of the wine caused her jaw to flex, but she took several long swallows.

"Mom!" Cameron hollered from upstairs. Some things did not change in a new house.

"What?" Sidney yelled back automatically.

"Can we watch a scary movie?"

Sidney flinched at the question and furrowed her brow at her own involuntary reaction.

"Not tonight, Cam," she managed. "Let's do a funny movie."

"But you don't like funny movies."

"Tonight, I do," Sidney said, mostly to herself, thinking of her compromise comedies with Kendra.

Sidney took another chug of her wine and watched the pizza on the oven rack. At the mention of a movie, she tossed a bag of popcorn into the microwave. As the cheese wilted on the crust and kernels exploded in the bag, she moved through her overflowing inboxes.

Oliver: Where are you, beautiful?
    I miss you.
    You can't leave me hanging like this.
    I know you're reading these messages, you dumb slut.
    So, you're just done with me then? You're just one of those girls.
    You could at least answer me and tell me, whore.

Sidney glared at the escalating rage in his words, her anxiety popping in symphony with the popcorn in the microwave. The anger surged through her fingertips as she typed her response then deleted it. Then typed a new version then deleted it again. Then typed more. Her irritation sent her thoughts from a weighted fog into a pointed fury.

Sidney: Hi.
    I have had a lot of shit going on.
    I have a life, and it went to hell.
    So, here's me saying I'm one of THOSE girls before I block you.
    Don't message me again.

She tossed her phone to the counter and yanked the oven door open as the cheese bubbled and oozed over the edge of the crust. She stomped across the ceramic tile she hated compared to the hardwood she had left and snatched a cutting board from the cabinet beside the stove. At least the cutting boards were where she wanted them now, rather than up with the dishes as Kendra insisted.

She forced restraint into her arms as she guided the pizza onto the board. Aggressively, she divided the pizza into slices. She snagged the popcorn before it burned and dumped it in a bowl. Then she slid her phone into her back pocket and gathered her wine. She dropped dinner on the coffee table and returned to grab a drink for Cameron.

"Cam! Movie time!" she shouted up the stairs.

As she listened to his heavy steps drop from his bed and move through the hallway, she checked her phone again.

Oliver: Sidney, I'm so sorry!
    I didn't mean it like that.

"How else could you mean it?" Sidney rolled her eyes to herself and kept scrolling.

Oliver: I just like you so much, and I missed you.
    I have been hurt and played by so many women on here.
    Please forgive me.

Sidney did not block him, but she did not respond

either. She opened the thread to be sure he saw the indication that she had read his words. Then she backed out of the conversation and set her phone facedown beside the pizza.

Her nerves seethed behind the smile she gave her son. She could feel the tightness in her face as she attempted to smooth it from her expression. Her irritation rolled in a current beneath her surface, but she chose to focus on having Cameron home. He sat down beside her on the couch, but she gathered him under her arm and dragged him into a cuddle, the way they used to watch TV when he was much younger. He whined in protest for a breath but ultimately melted into her and pulled a blanket over both of them.

Comedy almost felt foreign on her screen. Sidney noticed herself searching for the familiar threads in the movie. She evaluated the characters for victim or killer potential. She waited to see who would die first. The assessment happened automatically behind her thoughts, and she had to remind her mind that they were touring outside her country of horror.

It should have felt refreshing. It should have been a distraction. However, horror no longer felt so far away. Horror no longer felt like the fantasy. It felt too close and too real to be distraction. The change and difference made her think of it all the more. The images that used to spirit her away from her life and her problems now only served to call them back up to the forefront of her mind.

She took a deep breath and forced the practiced thought patterns off their rails. She shoved the echo of Oliver's words from her skull. She just stared blankly at the screen, not really ingesting the film, concentrating instead on the weight of Cameron's body alongside her. She took a deep breath and inhaled the moment because, in this moment, she knew exactly where Cameron was.

After the movie credits had rolled and Sidney had tucked Cameron and Spider-Man into bed, she finally returned to her phone. It felt heavier with all the messages she knew had accumulated. She had apparently built enough loft that even in her recent neglect, she was attracting attention. She recognized and cringed at the first notification: Oliver (6)

She sighed and tapped the notification to launch the conversation.

Oliver: Oh now you're just going to leave me on
    read?
    WTF, Sidney?
    You think you're better than me?
    You think you can do this to me?
    I know where you live.
    I'll show you can't do this to me.

26

THE TRAIL GREW darker as Sidney ran across the dirt in a panic. She craned her neck to glare at the creek behind her. When she turned back, the night blotted out the light to consume her. The nightmare became only the sound of her crunching footfalls. She sprinted blindly into the black. Then the streetlight appeared. She leaped toward the light, and when her foot landed in the circle of illumination, the ground went liquid beneath her. Her shoe vanished beneath the gravel like quicksand. Before she could stop it, her other foot followed.

The ground swallowed her feet, slurping greedily to her waist. She could not move her legs or fight against the pressure crushing her beneath the surface. She screamed and howled into the empty night, clawing desperately at the dirt as it climbed her body. As the edge reached her chest, something crashed down on top of her, pushing her deeper into her struggle.

Kendra's limp and lifeless corpse landed on her head, blocking out the streetlight above and accelerating her descent beneath the ground. As the light waned and the pressure grew, Sidney coughed and sputtered to breathe. She groped against Kendra's body, failing to heave it off of herself. It only became heavier until the gravel and pebbles rained in on her head. Then the ground came crushing in on top of her.

Then she was falling. Kendra's limp limbs flailed and spun above her, somehow visible even in the dark. Sidney landed hard on her back, coughing at the impact and curling around herself. Kendra landed across her this time, slamming into the dirt beside Sidney. Kendra's head turned, and her dead eyes stared into Sidney.

The hole smelled wet and earthy. Particles of soft soil clung to Sidney's skin, and wispy roots stretched out from the walls around her. When Sidney finally looked up, she noticed the hole cut the falling light into a perfect rectangle. Sidney stared up at the dark clouds above before shovels penetrated the sky and turned to dump chunks of dirt down on them.

Sidney opened her lips to scream, but the dirt filled her mouth. Before she could scramble to her feet, she was buried in the crushing black again.

Sidney bolted up in her bed, gasping. Her arms shot out around her, frantically pushing against the figments of Kendra and the heavy soil heaped upon her grave. It took Sidney three desperate breaths before she saw her new bedroom around her. Foreign as it may still feel, it was decidedly more familiar than the dark shapes in her nightmare.

Orientated, her breathing and pulse regulated. She felt jittered by her fading fear, but the images quickly stepped back into the shadow of her subconscious. What she did remember became hazy compared to the real morning pouring in through her senses.

She reached over and disabled her impending phone alarm, ignoring the stack of notifications. She saw Oliver's name among the ignored and could not bring herself to see what the night had emboldened him to type. She dragged herself from the sheets and stumbled downstairs to reestablish a morning routine in this house with Cameron.

At first, she lost herself in the tasks of making coffee and Cameron's lunch, disappeared beneath the motions of applying her makeup and hounding Cameron to locate his shoes. Yet, once they were finally settled in the car, once she started navigating the new route to Cameron's new school, that familiar tightness returned to her chest.

"You OK, Mom?" Cameron said from the backseat.

Sidney had not realized she gnawed on her bottom lip or sat up straight to pull herself close to the steering wheel. At Cameron's words, she retracted her teeth and rubbed the back of her hand along her lip to check for blood, leaning back into her seat. The recline suddenly felt unnatural.

"Yeah, Cam, I'm fine," she replied. "Why do you ask?"

"You seem nervous all the time now, Mom."

Sidney flinched at the truth. She had hoped that Cameron being away with his father had spared him witnessing her undoing.

"I know." Sidney did not know what else to say. "Things have just been very hard lately."

"Because of Kendra?"

"Yes."

"And when you thought you lost me?"

"Yes."

"And moving?"

"Yes, Cam. All of that together. You are the most important person to me."

"Like Kendra."

Her name in his young mouth brought the tears raging back to her eyes as if they had never dried up.

"Yes," Sidney choked on the word. "Kendra was very important to me too."

"You don't have to be scared, Mom" Cameron crossed his arms over his chest and stared casually out the window. "I'm just going to go to school and practice. I won't go home with anyone. I will just wait for you with coach like we talked about."

Sidney smiled, and it hurt. "I know," she said softly, acutely aware of how much she did not know, how she could never fool herself into thinking she knew again.

Cameron fell quiet in the seat behind her, seemingly resolved by his assurances to his mother. Sidney's chest only felt heavier. Her heart struggled to beat against the weight. Anxiety tingled in her hands. She tried to wriggle her fingers to displace the sensation.

When she parked beside the curb, Cameron leaned forward and wrapped his arms around her seat to hug her.

"Love you, Mom," he said before jumping from the backseat and slamming the door behind him.

Sidney stared after him until the impatient parent behind her honked. She vacated the drop-off line, waving placations over her shoulder, then pulled over on the street, out of range of the kid drop, and sat staring until all the children had filtered into the building.

She parked in her work parking lot ten minutes late and still lingered in the car. She tugged out her phone, seized by the overwhelming urge to text Kendra. Kendra would have told her to compose herself and get to work. Kendra would have said what she needed to hear.

Adam: Good morning, beautiful.
Sidney: Good morning
Adam: How is it going so far?
Sidney: I think I had a panic attack taking Cameron to school.
Now I'm at work late, hiding in the parking lot.
Adam: Maybe you're not ready. Maybe you should take some more time.

That was not what she needed to hear.

Sidney: I can't afford to.

Sidney clicked Send and forced herself into the store. Though she was late, the store and parking lot were both thankfully vacant. When she opened the front door, the unchanged and stagnant world she had left behind before her life fell apart greeted her. The store looked the same, with dust particles dancing in the morning. Just as it had before Telluride and Adam, the same as it had before Cameron vanished for a few hours, the same as it had before she had discovered Kendra's body, the same as it had before she had had to relocate across town. If she suppressed her thoughts hard enough, she could almost fool herself into thinking she was in one of those 'Before' moments and the rest was a horror-fueled nightmare.

The door clicked shut behind her, encasing her with the stale air. She capitalized on the tasks, drawing focus out of retirement in her brain. Her body felt out of practice as her muscles beckoned for the couch, for her depressive blanket of inactivity. Yet she forced her feet in practiced patterns across the carpet, turning on the demo devices, checking stock of the accessories.

"Goddamn it, Seth," she breathed to herself. "You couldn't stock any of these cases."

The mild irritation at Seth's laziness, him riding his cavalier smile through every shift, brought her mind more to the surface. The agitation focused her in a way only her fear had lately. Their job was not difficult. If she could drag herself into the store now, in the wake of Kendra's death, Seth could have shelved chargers and cases while she was gone. She dreaded to check the status of the inventory.

She should have waited for Seth to arrive. First, to scold him like the mother he clearly still needed but mostly to have the floor covered in case any motivated customers showed up so close to opening time. She checked her phone; he was already over an hour late. He should have been here to open before her shift started.

The door settled softly against its latch as Sidney stepped into the backroom, reminding her to prop it open. She needed to be able to hear the chime if any customers entered. She flicked the switch, igniting the unforgiving fluorescent lights, and snatched a box from the closest shelf to keep the door from closing.

Tall metal shelves carved the small space into aisles. Thin and wide, the shelves allowed Sidney to easily see above the stacks of device boxes and accessory cases. She stepped into the first row and began piling iPhone cases into her arms. Classic black, glittered champagne-colored, thick and rubberized to save the device from its new master.

"Can't even miss a day," she muttered to herself. "Can't expect anyone to do their damn job."

She turned around to face the Android accessories and dropped all the boxes in her arms. They tumbled around her feet in a clumsy avalanche.

The picture was not crisp. It had not been for a long time. Who printed pictures anymore? Who didn't just post them online and have them backed up to some cloud?

Kendra did.

She reached her hand toward the shelf, her fingers trembling violently through the air. They fumbled at the edge of the photograph as she finally snatched it and brought it to her face.

Kendra's face stared up at Sidney from the print, her eyes bright and sparkling instead of vacant and distant. Sidney knew the picture well. The moment itself still consumed in her memory. Sidney's smiling face nuzzled up against Kendra's as they embraced. Their first night as roommates, what would become the first official night of the Divorced Wives Club, with Brady behind the lens to snap the shot.

Sidney stopped breathing and released the picture. It floated down to the boxes at her feet. The print weaved through the air, the grins on Kendra's and her own face shining up to mock her. The floor tilted and spun beneath her. Her hands shot out to grope at the edge of the shelf behind her. She briefly closed her eyes, but Kendra's dead face flashed before her.

Her throat seized. She wanted to vomit. She slammed back against the shelf and heard more boxes tumble to the ground. The room collapsed in on her, forcing down into the pain radiating from the memory at her feet.

The picture had been in Kendra's room, tucked into the frame of her mirror. It had always been there. The only way it could be here is if it was taken from her bedroom.

Sidney's stomach clenched again, harder, knotting itself around her spine. She threw herself from the aisle, ripping her stumbling steps from beneath the boxes heaped around her. She tried to regain herself from her desperate momentum, but she tumbled to the worn carpet. The impact knocked the strangled breath from her throat. It exploded out of her mouth sounding like a sob.

Her cheek rested on the abrasive weave. She could only think of stumbling onto the carpet in front of Kendra's dead body. She felt like she may be trapped in that moment forever. The happy faces in the photograph taunted her from atop the heap of cell phone cases. She flinched away from them and cast her eyes across the floor. Across the room, past the additional rows of shelves, something slumped against the far wall.

Fear and confusion sliced through the haze of Sidney's sadness, sharpened her mind and focused her body back toward survival. She ripped herself out of the past moments—the one in the photograph and the one with Kendra's corpse. She wiped the tears that blurred her eyes and looked again. She was here, in this moment, trying to identify what loomed across the stockroom. A bright green shoelace spilled out from a sneaker, snaking colorfully across the dull carpet. Black denim cleaved to the awkwardly positioned limbs climbing up from the shoes.

Legs. Seth's legs.

Sidney's breathing stuttered through her mouth. She scrambled across the floor to cower against the wall then pressed herself into it and slowly slid herself up.

"Seth?" she whispered, feeling foolish and fearful calling his name. "Seth?" Louder but no less awkwardly.

The lump of legs and shoes did not move. No sound responded. Sidney pinched her eyes shut then forced herself to move past the shelves between them. Her heartbeat rattled through her veins, causing her skin to vibrate in anxious sensation. A disgusting sense of déjà vu clutched her, strangling her stomach into an acidic nausea. The heat gently falling from the vent tickled the sweat prickling below her hairline. The air around her thickened, slowing time and making her fight to move across the room.

"Seth?" she said again, like a dumb character in one of her horror movies about to get slaughtered. Even as that connection batted around the edge of her fear, she could not stop herself.

As her legs wobbled unreliable and weak beneath her, Sidney clutched at the metal shelf. She needed the structure to hold her as the waves of panic crashed against her.

Her eyes crawled around the edge of the last shelf, stretching her sight until she found Seth. His body draped against the wall, propped and positioned to resemble a casual seat. It would have been fitting of his lazy demeanor if he was there to inhabit the pose, if that relentless smile was stretching his lips. His eyes looked just like Kendra's. Petechial hemorrhaging drew terrible maps along the wide orbs, and small, hopeless scratches peppered the skin surrounding the phone charger cord cinched around his neck.

Sidney finally did retch onto the floor before scrambling from the backroom, screaming and crying to the empty store. The display phone and tablet screens flashed at her, mocking as they connected to no one.

27

SIDNEY STAGGERED DOWN the concrete steps, clutching the metal railing. The interior of the police station had become too familiar, haunting her dreams after all these successive visits. It felt like she had never left after Kendra's death, and even as she stumbled out now, part of her lingered back in the drab room where she was questioned.

Her face hurt. Her cheeks stretched taut over the swelling. Her eyelids were puffy, cumbersome when she blinked. Her eyeballs themselves felt raw and exhausted, the same as every cell in her body. Her skeleton was heavy to move, like it would be better placed somewhere dark and final.

Her mind did not form thoughts. It could not. The echoes of the police inquiries orbited around Seth's slumped body in the backroom of the store. The lines of questions reached back and arched into concentric circles, running laps around all the terrible things that had happened. All the events at which she had been the center. Why had she been in the middle? Where had she been? What was she doing? Why her? After so many revolutions, all paths spiraled into her.

She could not think, but she could see Seth, just as

clearly as Kendra haunted her skull. She simply shambled from the station door and onto the sidewalk.

"Sidney?"

The sound of her own name sounded foreign, just like sounds swirling by or another echo in her head. She continued walking, mechanically, her eyes wide but not seeing. She felt hollow, empty and catatonic behind her mindless movements.

"Sid! Sidney!"

The calls finally took shape in her head and drew her awareness back to the world around her. She turned toward the voice.

"Tony?" She could not subdue the dull shock in her voice. "What are you doing here?" she asked, bluntly.

"Hey, Sid." The smile spread wide across Tony's face as he reached out and gathered her into a hug. "Just leaving the courthouse. I got released from jury duty. I wasn't jury material today."

After as many naked nights as she had spent under and on top of Tony, hugging him should have been natural, yet Sidney went rigid. Sex with him seemed so far in her past it could have been in another life. The idea itself felt foreign in what had become her new reality.

She felt the tears starting again and tried to ease away from him. Despite her stiffness, he clung to her, kept her trapped in his embrace. He hushed into her hair until she relented and melted. Lost in the simplicity of him holding her, she succumbed to the second wave of tears.

"Oh Sidney, what's wrong?" he said gently into her ear. The tone sounded mismatched on him.

"Seth is dead," she managed through the sobs.

"That guy from your work? Who had a thing for you?"

Sidney snatched at the edge of her composure and took a step back out of Tony's arms.

"Yes, my coworker," she said, wrapping her arms around herself instead. "He did not have a thing for me. And Kendra is dead."

Kendra's name snagged in her teeth, yet she shoved the cries down, forced the calm into her voice. She dammed up the flood raging from the back of her mind.

"Oh my God, Sidney." Tony paused for a moment, shaken. "Kendra? I'm so sorry. I was wondering where you had been."

"Things have been fucked," Sidney said, plainly.

"It sounds like it. I'm so sorry, Sid," he said.

He stepped forward to hug her again, and the contact had the tears burning back in her eyes. She pulled away, swiping at her tender cheeks. She wished she could hide her ugly, distorted face. She didn't want anyone seeing her in this state.

"I'm sorry," she babbled.

"Sorry for what?" Tony gathered one of her hands into his. "Sidney, I miss you."

Sidney smiled softly but did not look up to meet Tony's eyes. She could not without summoning the tears.

"I can't right now, Tony." Sidney squeezed his hand then released it. "I'm sorry. I just need to go home. I just need to be alone right now."

With the last word, Sidney curled into herself and stepped past Tony, moving back toward her car.

"Sidney," Tony said behind her. "Sid, wait."

He did not pursue her, and she did not turn back. She forced purpose into her steps until his voice disappeared behind her and she seated herself behind the wheel.

***

Sidney opened the door of her empty house and stood for a long moment in the dark silence. Cameron was once again staying with Aiden, far removed from her drama. The quiet without him was terrible, yet it was calming to know he was far from whatever was happening to her.

Her phone quivered in her pocket, as it had the entire day. She had not touched a device since dialing 911 to report Seth's body. Even the thought of a phone brought his bulging eyes back to her mind. She counted all the marks on his neck from clawing at the cord, branding them onto the soft tissue of her brain, carving them into her memory.

She finally turned on a light and shed her purse and keys. She dug her phone from her pocket and collapsed to the couch, reassuring herself that she could still communicate like a normal person. Except with Oliver. Or Jack. Or any of the other "online boyfriends" she had cultivated over the years. She could not handle any more of their attention. The warm glow of esteem it used to cultivate had been perverted and infected by the paranoia that now ruled her emotions. Everyone had become a threat.

She navigated through their profiles, calling up old conversation threads to launch herself there, and blocked them. She then deleted the threads to avoid temptation. Her phone felt lighter without as many strings reaching out into cyberspace. Then she finally glanced through what had survived in her inbox. She looked longingly at her dormant thread with Kendra. She could not bear to remove it from her inbox, to erase what felt like the last trace of her friend. She opened her conversation with Adam.

Adam: I'm sorry, Sid. You know what you need to do.
I'm just trying to look out for you.
Sid, are you there? Are you mad?
Are you OK?
Sidney: No. I am not OK.

That was the most honest thing Sidney had typed in a long time.

Adam: What happened
Sidney: My coworker Seth is dead.
Adam: WHAT??
Sidney: I found him in the backroom today at work.
Adam: OMG! Let me call you.

Sidney shrunk at the idea of having to say these truths aloud, repeating the words that had echoed at the police station. She lacked the strength and the composure. Tony had taken the last of it.

Sidney: Not right now. I just can't.
Adam: Sidney, I'm so sorry.
Sidney: It just keeps happening.
I need to go to bed.
Adam: OK. Try to get some rest.
I wish that I was there.

Sidney did not bother to respond. She didn't know how to. She did not want to be alone, but she did not want him, or anyone, there with her either. There was no comfort for her, no rest, no recovery. She did not even know if she wanted it. She simply switched conversations for distraction, for anything not to be left alone in the wake of the day. To feel close to someone as they were safely far away.

Allison: Hey girl, how are you holding up?
Sidney: Terrible.
   Things got worse.
Allison: What? How?

Sidney took a deep breath. Why was it easier to open up to Allison? Why did it feel safer to confide in a stranger since Adam had walked three dimensionally into her life? Meeting him in real life had altered the freedom of perceived anonymity. The illusion of whispering in the dark flowed so much easier than the calloused reality of confessing to a person who would look into your eyes.

Sidney: I found my coworker dead at work
   today.

It was the first time Sidney had phrased it this way, making it about what happened to her instead of saying Seth died.

Allison: OMG! What happened? Are you OK??

Sidney paused again, ignoring the vibrations of the phone in her hand. The phone quivered to indicate activity outside her conversation with Allison. Yet she hid in the thread, where it felt like just the two of them and safe to tell the truth.

Sidney: I don't think I'll ever be OK again.
    People keep dying around me.
    He was strangled, just like my roommate.

Sidney struggled against a sob and pushed Kendra's face from her mind, the dead eyes that matched Seth's. Red veins of strangulation snaking through her brain.

Allison: Oh my God!

Actually spelled out for emphasis.

Sidney: The police think it's the same killer.
    My home, my work. It has to be about me, right?

Sidney's fingers froze then she typed it anyway.

Sidney: I did this to them.
Allison: Oh no, girl. No, you didn't.

Sidney read Allison's words through welling tears. No matter how many people contradicted her, she knew this was all her fault. She was the root, the common denominator. All roads led to her, and people were dying on the way.

Allison: You can't blame yourself.
Sidney: But I do.

Somehow, typing the truth outside her own mind made it feel more honest.

Allison: What are you doing now?
Sidney: Back at home after the police station.
    Blocking all my online boyfriends.
    My work is closed for now, and my boss is freaking out.
    I don't know if I'll even have a job when they reopen.
Allison: Pretty sure they can't fire you.
    Blocking all your boyfriends?

Sidney smiled in gentle relief at the subject shift.

Allison: How many do you have?
Sidney: More than I ever should have.
Allison: Are you just dumping the online ones?
Sidney: So far?

Sidney had not realized she was considering purging in her real life until she pressed the question mark. Did she mean Adam, or was she thinking about running into Tony on the street?

Allison: Not feeling your new bae?
Sidney: No, he's fine. Everything that's been happening just has me all fucked up.
    I don't know what to think about anything.

Allison: What about the other guy?
Sidney: The toy?
Allison: Yeah.
Sidney: Strangely enough, I bumped into him tonight.
I just can't deal with any of that right now.
He's better off staying away from me anyway. Safer.

Sidney allowed the tears pooling around her eyes to finally streak down her cheeks. She thanked Allison for listening and told her she would message her in the morning. She needed the quiet. She needed to truly be alone, as it now felt like she was meant to be. Maybe her stalker would come find her tonight and put her out of her misery.

For the first time, that thought did not inspire fear. Instead, it conjured a sense of closure—something she found herself inviting as her eyes grew even more weary of weeping.

28

"**DON'T SAY IT,**" Sidney mumbled as she approached Brady.

She could already see the sympathetic, assessing look in his eye as he tipped his thin-rimmed sunglasses. He leaned his yoga mat against the glass windows of the studio and snatched her into a hug. She clutched him tightly for a moment then stepped back.

"Say what?" he asked, innocently.

"That I look like hell."

"Oh honey, you already know." He smiled playfully. "And it doesn't matter. It only matters if you're OK, and I'm glad you came out this morning. Have you left the house since it happened?"

Sidney shook her head. "I haven't been able to. The store is still closed. Cameron is still with Aiden. I'm not really eating. So there hasn't been a reason to."

"Well, you have a reason today." Brady stooped to gather his yoga mat onto his hip. "We are going to breathe through all this bullshit and find your center."

"What if there is nothing good at my center?" Sidney said before catching the words on her tongue.

Brady turned his hips and tipped his sunglasses lower, giving her a naked glare. She knew the look well from any moment her insecurities peeked out during a photoshoot or when she had lamented losing Aiden. She knew what words were coming.

"Girl." He dragged out the word. "You know better."

Sidney huffed and rubbed her face. Her cheeks still felt raw and inflamed. She did not know if her face would ever feel normal again.

"You are going to pull your shit together," Brady continued, eyes locked on her. "You are going to get your ass into this studio and find yourself again. I know it's been awful, but you are stronger than the psycho doing this."

Sidney's breath stuttered as she bit her bottom lip, raw and stitched together with thin scabs. She looked down to watch her fingernails pick at the rolled edge of her yoga mat. He would not be saying this if her stalker picked him next, or if he found Jordan after the stalker was done with him.

Brady gathered Sidney under his arm, gripping her bicep tightly with his fingers, and guided her into the studio. His words echoed in her brain, slowly, becoming a mantra.

Pull your shit together.

Find yourself again.

Stronger than the psycho.

Pull your shit together. Find yourself again. Stronger than this psycho.

With each revolution around the quote, she felt her posture elongate. She felt herself rise. Her strangled breathing deepened to resemble actual respiration. She felt like she could actually feign being yogic. She could be here on the mat. She could pull her shit together. She could find herself again.

Her muscles felt a little lighter as she unrolled her yoga mat along the floor. The squishy plastic slapped the floorboards then slid into place parallel to Brady's. He smiled at her reassuringly. His affection did not thicken her depression, did not enable her woe. He loved her while shoving her forward. Maybe that was what she needed after so many nights alone with her thoughts and the ghosts of Kendra and Seth.

"Welcome to class, everyone," the teacher began. He walked along the thin strips of floor between the mats with his fingers steepled in front of his chest. "Come to a comfortable seat on your mat. Close your eyes and go within."

The receptionist lowered shades over the broad windows lining one wall. The light drew down, and the room closed around them. The dimming made it seem natural for Sidney to close her eyes and creep toward the back of her mind.

"We begin today's class with meditation," the teacher continued, his voice shifting around the darkness behind Sidney's eyelids. She found her eyes chasing his movements even as she turned her awareness inward.

The instructor's voice weaved farther away as Sidney's mind swelled up around the edges, encapsulating her in her own thoughts.

Kendra surfaced first. Kendra always surfaced first. She led with her bulging eyes and ligatured throat. Sidney's pulse quickened in her veins, her throat constricting.

"Keep your breathing deep," the teacher's voice infiltrated her mind, bringing her back in control over her body. "Allow your thoughts to come up then fall away."

Sidney followed the cue, inhaling deeply through her nose until her lungs stretched full. The breath tempered her reflexive panic. She tugged the calm out from her center and draped it over her mind like a blanket.

Pull your shit together. Find yourself again. Stronger than this psycho.

Kendra returned to her mind, though not as a corpse. She drew up the memory of her extending a cup of coffee in the morning, filling a glass of wine in the evening. She saw Kendra's wide smile when she admitted to sleeping with her ex-husband yet again, the way she so clearly still loved him. Sidney grinned gently through her slack cheeks. A stray tear wandered out from her closed eye.

Put on some shit that won't give me nightmares, she heard Kendra say.

Horror. Sidney had brought horror into their home. Every night on their shared television. Every night through their internet router. The stalker had found her through horror and come into their home then come back to kill Kendra. The line of causality seemed alarmingly straight.

Stronger than this psycho.

Sidney realized that if she blamed herself, she thought she was asking for it. That phrase froze in her brain and grew larger.

Asking for it. She was not asking for it. She did not ask for someone to come into her home and her work, to execute her roommate and her coworker. Nothing asked for that. No amount of posting clickbait or flirting with internet strangers solicited what had happened to her. Posting blogs and hosting a website and taking bloody pictures had not invited murder into her life. Sharing generic selfies in internet conversations did not entitle anyone to step into her life and take from her.

The lone tear dried up on her cheek. Her heart pounded in a different rhythm, a solid beat with more purpose. Her rage elevated her out of the mire of sadness.

"Coming forward onto your hands and knees, press back into Downward-Facing Dog," the teacher instructed.

Sidney thrust herself forward, her exhales blowing sharply out against the mat below her. She planted her palms firmly into the pliancy of the mat then pushed her hips upward, until a burning stretch blossomed along the length of her hamstring. The pull on her nerves brought her back to her body for a moment, as she breathed through the intensity, yet the anger still simmered deeper.

Asking for it.

Stronger than this psycho.

Sidney kept an ear to the teacher enough to follow his instructions through the flow. With each movement, her clarity sharpened. With each full exhalation, she found she did feel more like herself. By the time she unfolded herself into Corpse Pose, her mind felt different. The slogging weight of the guilt, depression, and blame had hardened, and her consciousness now walked atop it. Her thoughts had lost the terrible echo that only repeated it was her fault.

Even when she wiggled her fingers and toes to ground herself back into her body and her mind resurfaced from the meditative haze, the change persisted. She sat up to complete the circle of her practice in her starting position yet felt like she was in a new body and a new space.

As the teacher thanked and bowed to the class, Sidney crouched down to roll up her mat and vacate the floorboards for the next yogi. Brady continued to perch on his mat, looking at her expectantly.

"What?" Sidney half-smiled.

"So?" Brady replied, unmoving.

"I think I started to pull my shit together."

"Yes!" Brady lifted his fists in a small celebration then finally moved to gather his mat. "That is a start, honey. What now?"

They ambled out after the practitioners as the next class spliced in between them.

"I get Cameron back," Sidney said as they returned to the street. "Then I get a new job or transfer to a new store."

"Damn, that's a lot for one little yoga class."

"It was a big epiphany." Sidney paused. "I needed it."

"What was the epiphany?" Brady slid on his sunglasses but kept them low enough to continue making eye contact.

"That I wasn't asking for any of this, that nothing I was doing was asking for it, so it's not all my fault."

"Bitch, that is what we have been trying to tell you!" Brady threw up a hand, laughing.

"I know. I just had to get there on my own."

"Well, welcome to the fucking party." Brady nudged her shoulder then reached out to hug her tight.

"Stronger than this psycho," Sidney said softly against him.

IDNEY TOOK A deep breath as she sank into the couch cushion in her basement. The house around her remained unfamiliar and hollow, yet she felt different in it now. Her mind clung to its reinvention, and she finally inhabited her new space. The nervous flinch threatened at the base of her spine, coiling then relenting enough for her to breathe, for her to simply be.

She closed her eyes and took yogic breaths then opened them gently, looking around the room to remind herself how normal it was. The customary popcorn and beer perched on the table between her and the television. Her laptop glowed from the cushion beside her, cursor blinking anticipant of her words. She held the remote as her thumb traced the Play button, watching the sweat trickle down the side of the beer bottle. It all looked the same, but something felt off.

"You're being ridiculous," she said to herself. "It's just a movie. Movies didn't get you into this. It is for the 12 Slays of Christmas; you are watching this movie."

Sidney laughed awkwardly—she was talking to

herself. She squeezed her eyes shut for an instant and depressed the Play button.

The murderous Santa appeared on the screen as the notes of the score wandered a well-worn path through Sidney's memories. Her chest tightened in reflex then expanded in a flood of nostalgia. "12 Slays of Christmas" had been the first holiday gimmick post that she had tried with her site, which she turned into a social media challenge. And she had seen success.

She shoved a handful of popcorn in her mouth, barely tasting it, and washed it down with the beer. Then she drew herself back onto the couch and gathered up her laptop.

She placed her fingertips on the keyboard, worn smooth from such frequent attention. Her hands should have felt at home resting on the machine, yet she hesitated. Where she had once dived headlong into the online world, she found herself lingering in the real—on her empty couch, with her solo horror movie. She occupied her solitude.

Wes: Long distance live tweet
    How you holding up?
Sidney: Can't miss the 12 Slays!
    I'm OK, getting back to normal.

As the familiar festive plot unfolded, she reminded herself to swipe over the trackpad and tweet. If she did not post, was she even really watching?

@FinalGirlScreams: #SilentNightDeadlyNight
    was ahead of its time with killer
    psychology. Even if it portrays #PTSD

horribly. #12SlaysofChristmas #horror #finalgirlscreams
@L1v1ngDead1te: Wouldn't be the holidays without #12SlaysofChristmas with @FinalGirlScreams!
@Romero4eva: @FinalGirlScreams I watch this one every year. For the antlers!
@ZombieonElmSt: @FinalGirlScreams great choice! Xmas classic #christmashorror #12SlaysofChristmas

Sidney smiled to herself and clicked to triage her notifications.

Adam: How are you, beautiful?
Are you OK, Sid?
I can understand if you want your sp . . .

Sidney saw the notifications pop up on the bottom of her screen. She usually answered Adam's messages first yet felt uninspired tonight. Their conversation thread was full of Telluride and Kendra and losing Cameron and moving. If she was going to escape into the virtual world, she could not do it beneath messages capturing the darkest points of her current reality.

He could wait.

When she opened her social media inboxes, scrolling pages of unopened messages greeted her. She rolled through unfamiliar usernames and handles. The conversations had varying counts, but all the message previews said the same.

YOU CANNOT IGNORE ME!

Sidney recoiled from the computer, snatching her fingers away from the keyboard and into her chest. She felt that familiar panic swell over her, seize her chest, and make her small again. Without giving her paranoia the opportunity to take shape in her thoughts, she slammed the laptop shut and tossed it aside, curling her legs into her chest and tugging a blanket over herself.

Her heart tried to knock on her ribcage, but Sidney forced her deep breaths to be louder. She filled her diaphragm the way she practiced on the yoga mat. She stretched her mind away from the repetitive thoughts circling the back of her brain the way she did in meditation. With the distraction of the internet collapsed on the cushion beside her, she felt the moment almost too much. Her mind settled into her flesh as it wrestled down her rising anxiety.

She did not have to answer the messages tonight. Somewhere in the back of her brain, she knew she never had to answer them at all. She could unplug herself from the online world. The online world always felt like a separate world, one she never had to tell anyone about. Yet those ideas seemed ludicrous, tightened the nerves in her chest in a different way. She could not fathom walking away, of only living in the disappointment of her real world.

She wound her fists into the edge of the blanket, depressing the plush fibers in her grip, and plunged her vision into the screen. If she could not flit between conversations and comments like a hummingbird, she could immerse herself in the swelling edge of the notes tickling the soundtrack, in the dark shadows moving across the naughty victims' terrified faces. On the screen, the horror was far away, small enough to fit in the black box.

As her mind walked the worn path of the memorized plot, the echo of the messages faded. The online world receded until she could pretend it was just the couch and the movie. She gathered the bowl and began mowing through the popcorn and chasing it down with the beer. She lounged on the pillows and did not flinch when the antlers made their appearance and the blood splattered. Her breathing did not strangle her as the killer Santa Claus stalked unseen with his axe.

Her horror was still horror, was still the movie she loved. Yet it seemed even more unrealistic now than it had been before her life had descended into her own beloved genre. What she saw on the screen was not what real-life horror was. It was not the constant throbbing on her nerves, the relentless nagging paranoia tearing at the edges of her mind. It was not the empty void in her heart left by Kendra or the days now spent away from her son because she could not function. It was not the steady unraveling of her life that had dropped her onto this couch alone, clinging to the media that once soothed her. Yet it was different now, tainted and changed. It did not deliver the escape and distraction she so desperately needed.

She chomped through another handful of kernels as the music crescendoed from the speakers. Yet under the rhythm of her chewing and the symphony of the false screams, another sound scratched the peripheral of her hearing. Her senses snapped and turned from the movie. She held her teeth still to silence her own chewing, slowed her breathing, and waited.

Her ears pricked, and her brain reached out to listen. She strained to hear so long that she nearly forgot herself. There was nothing.

Her pulse crawled down, and she shook the figment from her mind, pinching her eyes shut. She turned back to the screen with one ear still subtly scanning around her. She finally gathered another handful and dumped the popcorn between her teeth. As she defiantly crushed the kernels between her molars, her ear caught the sound again.

Louder, clearer, closer.

Sidney snatched the remote to pause the movie. Santa Claus raised his axe over the nun. Sidney gathered herself up on the cushion, pulling the blanket into her chest. Her chewing halted again, leaving half-masticated popcorn floating between her teeth. She hesitated, her eyes wide as if she could see the sounds if she concentrated hard enough.

This time, the sound did repeat and take shape. As it collided on the edge of her hearing over and over, it grew closer, louder. She recognized the sound of rocks grating against each other. The cadence of the sound was so familiar, the rhythm made with slow footsteps, approaching. Someone was walking through the landscaping rocks lining the perimeter of her new house, just above the window well that loomed beside her.

Sidney's enforced calm and empowerment abandoned her, replaced by the familiar and pervasive constriction on her nerves. The fear returned, flooding in to saturate every fold and crevasse in her brain, like waters returning to the ground when a levee breaks. She felt small again, contorted and compressed by the strangle in her throat and the pressure on her chest.

"Fuck," she breathed to herself.

She reached out for her phone, igniting the screen and furiously tapping for the phone app. Then she stopped. Her instinct—the instinct she had yelled at the screen of countless moronic horror movie victims—compelled her to summon the police, call for help. Is that not what she always thought they should do? Was that not what she wished she could have done *before* what happened to Kendra and Seth? Yet her thoughts tangled her purpose.

It was just a noise. It could have been anything outside, moving in her rocks. She did not know if it was the murderer, her stalker finally come for her, and the doubts swelled on her brain as she considered having to interact with cops again, having to answer their questions, having them solve and fix nothing. The futility of it was paralytic.

And had she really heard anything? Could her mind even be trusted in this bruised state?

She could not be the victim again. She could not endure that look of pity in everyone's eyes as they asked how she was doing. Not for a noise that may or may not have ever rippled the air.

Yet she did not know what to do now. She could not simply return to her movie, wrapped in her pulsating fear. The scenes would flash against her eyes unregistered. She could not consciously become hypocritical enough to be the dumb girl who investigated the strange noise. She would not sheepishly call "Who's there?" and expect death not to answer. Once again, she found herself suspended in limbo.

A limbo that this stalker, this murderer, had steadily crafted for her.

She might have wished that she owned a weapon, had taken one of the guns in the divorce, had agreed to let Aiden teach her how to use it, and kept it in the house; but such a musing would have been equally pointless as her clearing her own house with a gun at this moment. It was just a noise outside, just footsteps on the rocks. Maybe. If they were even real.

Cold sweat prickling through the roots of Sidney's hair, making it feel like her scalp was crawling. Her phone lingered in her palm. The screen blackened around the unconsummated 911 dial. She sat, undetermined and undecided, waiting for an answer to break across her mind.

The break happened outside her head instead.

She may have been able to classify the footsteps as figments around the edge of her mind, but the shattering of glass was real and present, undeniable. And she was the moronic heroine in a horror movie, about to die.

Her options sliced through her thoughts. She could call 911. She could hide. She could try to get out of the house. She could confront the intruder. The choices presented clearly, but her heart beat too fast for her to formulate a solution from them. The sound of her pulse was too loud for her to hear her own thoughts.

The shattering window upstairs cleared her mind entirely. She gasped deeply before holding her breath tight. Time slowed, and the two seconds between the breaking glass and a body tumbling through the window and landing on the floor above her dragged out. She only floundered in her indecision.

Her mind never surfaced. Instead, her fingers mechanically unlocked her phone and pressed the Call button. She did not entirely register what was happening until she heard the gentle ring from the speaker.

"We are currently experiencing a high volume of calls. Please stay on the line for the next available operator," a robotic voice said from the phone.

All her instinct for nothing. She left the call active in her hand and shot up from the couch, moving to flee.

"Sidney!" the voice bellowed from the top of the stairs.

The voice was entirely foreign, carving new lines along her brain, deep marks heavy with her terror. Who was this man in her house? Who would invest so much time to stalk and torment her?

"Sidney, I know you're here," his tone softened. "I just want to talk to you."

The absurdity of the phrase managed to shock Sidney below her panic. Curiosity blossomed out its wake. Who the hell would break into her house to just talk to her? Who would think she would believe that claim?

She had another flash of every horror movie victim she had ever mocked and tore herself from her anticipant stance. The voice loomed between her and a direct escape up the stairs. She retreated until her back met the wall; then she traced it into the small bathroom. She left the door ajar and the light off as she climbed silently behind the dark shower curtain.

In the cold shower stall, Sidney's breathing seemed deafening. She plastered herself against the tile wall and clapped her hand over her own mouth, as she had seen so many characters do. She was one of them now, waiting for what they always knew was coming.

How had she gotten here? The surreality of the moment was almost enough to derail her focus.

"Sidney, I know you're here," the intruder said.

Why did he have to keep saying her name? Every time she heard it, her stomach ratcheted tighter, her muscles quivering around the tension.

"I wouldn't have come here if I didn't know you were here. I told you, I just want to talk. Why won't you answer me?" he continued, that edge in his tone sharpening.

The measured footsteps moved past the couch where she had been cowering. The architecture of the house channeled him toward her. She heard him trace that same wall she fled along, his fingertips dragging against the texture of the paint. He was going to find her. He was going to be in the bathroom any second.

She could leap out and startle him, shove him aside and dart for the stairs, but she had no idea what she was dealing with. How big was he? How strong? Did he have a gun? Doubtful paralysis found her again, and she merely waited in her fear.

The intruder's shoes met the bathroom tile, and the light suddenly blinded her even as it permeated the deep red curtain. Time stopped with the clear knowledge that she would never see Cameron again splintered her reality. Her heart gave up on pounding and fractured in her chest. Then the rings shrieked against the shower rod, and the curtain was thrust aside.

Sidney flinched then forced herself to open her eyes again. She stared, bewildered, into the intruder's face. A face she recognized.

"Oliver?" Sidney asked, nearly choking on the name.

His smell invaded her air, swelled to fill the room completely with the bitter, acidic bite of disinfectant.

Oliver looked different in three dimensions. The real, unfiltered world was not nearly as kind to him as selfie angles and photo filters. He had sent her countless selfies, as well as pictures of his engorged genitals. Why was he standing in her home with shards of broken glass clinging to the wrinkles in his shirt?

This Oliver could have been the heavier older brother to his online persona. Creases traced the edges of his expression, but not the happy laugh lines. His skin was worn into worry and anger with deep wrinkles digging across his forehead and between his eyebrows. Not looking down at him from a flattering above angle, the soft skin of his neck hung below his chin. His disheveled clothes betrayed how long he had been away from home, wherever that actually was.

Sidney kept calling up his last message in her head, *I know where you live. I'll show you can't do this to me.*

When Oliver lay his small, squinted eyes on her, the tension through his wrinkles softened. His shoulders retreated away from his ears. Sidney watched a clenched fist unfold at his side.

"Sid," he said, pouring himself into the syllable, smiling wide to show his teeth that were not quite white and not quite straight. Something a photo editing app could fix, did fix.

He extended his arms and stepped toward her. Without a thought, Sidney shrunk back tighter against the tile, expecting him to grab her or strike her, preparing for the violence paired with home invasion. Oliver's face changed, falling slack as his eyes drifted toward his boots.

"Don't be scared of me, Sid," he said, quietly. "You know me. It's Oliver!"

"Oliver, we've never met." Sidney vibrated in her fear, and the quiver reverberated into her voice. She tried to flex her muscles tight to still herself.

"I know we've never met in person." He looked up at her again, some of the brightness reigniting in his irises. "Until now. But you *know* me."

Oliver stared at her intently, but Sidney remained plastered to the shower. He shrugged a little, lifting his hands toward her in mock surrender. Then he stepped slowly back out of the bathroom and onto the carpet. When he was at a safer distance, Sidney cautiously stepped out of the shower stall. Her mind whirred inside her skull fast enough to make her eyes twitch, but she did not know what else to do. Horror had only ever taught her what not to do.

"I know the last time we messaged, you were very angry," she said.

Oliver grimaced and looked away again, clasping his hands in front of his waist. He turned his head sharply to one side then the other before relaxing again.

"You're right," he said. "I was very upset. I—I just," he stammered, "I just l-love you so much. I thought you were leading me on. You hurt me, Sidney."

Alarm bells exploded in Sidney's brain. Every cell in her body simultaneously screamed *RUN*, yet she remained rooted to her spot, cowering in the door frame of the small bathroom.

"I didn't mean to hurt you, Oliver," Sidney said, which was true. "I wasn't leading you on. I just had a lot going on here," she said. Like her son being abducted and her roommate and coworker being murdered, like *him* doing all of this to her. Her fear contorted into rage, and she nearly choked on the transition. She forced her posture to remain docile, her voice to remain low and wavering. "You didn't need to come here. You didn't need to put yourself out like that," she continued. "And why didn't you just knock on the door?"

"You stopped answering my messages." Oliver suddenly straightened, grew rigid. His fists wound up at his sides again. "You left me on read. You *blocked* me, Sidney. How could you do that to me, after all we've been through?"

"I didn't mean to hurt you, Oliver," Sidney scrambled. "I've had so much going on lately. So many bad things have happened."

They had been through nothing. They had been through Oliver's aggressive flirting and Sidney's desperate ingestion of his compliments. They had been through doctored selfies and vague personal details. Yet he had put her through everything. Sidney's jaw flexed as she clamped her tongue silent behind her teeth. She forced a slow, invisible breath through her pursed lips and shoved herself forward in a gentle step.

"That's not how it is, Oliver. You should know that," she said, soothingly.

What could she kill him with? How could she hurt him in the room populated by plush furniture and blankets? She forgot the phone hanging in her hand. She could no longer hear if her 911 call had been answered. She fixated on Oliver, stepping closer still.

"If I knew that, I wouldn't be here," Oliver barked.

He arched his back with the words then jerked his

head from side to side. When he realigned himself, he leaned forward and snatched her arm, yanking her across the carpet to him.

"Sit down with me, Sidney." His voice became calm. He stretched a strained smile across his cheeks, but the wrinkles between his eyebrows betrayed him.

Sidney allowed him to pull her to the couch. Her rage turned to poison in her stomach as his touch agitated her skin. She wanted to vomit. She wanted to cry. She wanted to kill him. Every word he said echoed Kendra's name in her skull. Every time his narrow eyes met hers, she saw a flash of Kendra's wide, dead stare. She no longer cared about 911 or the police or help. She only wanted to make Oliver's eyes as lifeless as he had made Kendra and Seth's.

The new emotion infected her. Thoughts of Cameron or Adam or any life outside of this room receded. Her scattered and frantic fear folded in on itself, collapsing and consolidating into a pointed purpose angled directly at Oliver. This stranger in her house who had forced her from her home, who had taken Kendra from her.

He did not know her. Flirtatious messages and pictures of suggestive cleavage were not her. How much real *her* had she given him at all? Maybe she had been leading him on after all, trading a false and filtered version of herself for the hollow interest that she fooled herself into thinking made her feel whole. She was worse than the moronic horror movie heroine. She had done this to herself after all. Just like Aiden and her mother had said, she had invited this into her life.

She vibrated in her fury, her self-loathing, but

wrestled it down until it looked like cowardice. Oliver said he just wanted to talk, but she knew he wanted much more than that. He wanted to punish her, to control her. He wanted to snap and break her down until she fit back into the perfect little online persona he had of her. The one she had crafted herself.

She sat beside him, cowering, waiting. She could feel him feeding off her faux fear. That was what he had come here for. She wondered if he had relished it as he strangled it out of Kendra and Seth too. She thought of Cameron innocently in Oliver's car and nearly lunged out of her composure.

"What do we do now, Oliver?" she finally asked, passive. Her own words nauseated her.

"Aren't you at least happy to see me?" He turned his face to look at her out of the side of his eyes before throwing his glance into his lap.

Sidney's throat squeezed shut as she attempted to squelch the disgust curling on her lips, forcing them into a weak smile instead. The question unnerved her, drew all her writhing emotions up to the surface. She was not happy to see him, but she could be happy to murder him.

"Of course, I am," she coughed out the words. "You just surprised me, coming through my window when I'm all alone watching a horror movie."

"Well, shouldn't you show me that you're happy to see me?" Oliver watched his fingers tangle together in his lap before he turned his eyes up to hers. His body language wilted, and his words wavered with insecurity, yet his eyes glared cold with intention.

She felt her face slacken as her eyes widened. She knew what that look meant. She knew what he wanted her to show him. A blur of his old messages flashed through her mind.

One day I'll come join you in that blood bath.

Makes me want to lick all that blood off of you.

You are hot as fuck naked and bloody. Let me come take a blood bath with you.

Please tell me you're still in bed so I can come join you.

Without the expanse of cyberspace between them, that knowledge railed alarms down her nerves. How had it ever felt safe to read those words from him?

Again, she felt her abdomen fold itself around the sickness cramping through her stomach. The violent reaction to her own stupidity consumed her for a long second, almost completely enough to make her forget Oliver's expectant stare beside her.

"You always told me that you wished we could be together," Oliver continued, his back straightening with his words. His body curved toward her, leaning into the expected intimacy. "Now, we're together. I came here to be with you."

Sidney's thoughts flailed. She knew what was coming, and she scratched at the edges of her consciousness for any way to avoid it.

"But why did you come here now?" Sidney stalled. "We've been talking for a long time. Why now?"

"I told you." Oliver turned his now broader shoulders toward her, his meek persona rippling off him. "You wouldn't answer my messages."

"Then, you came here because you were mad at me. Not to be with me."

Oliver's brows furrowed, turning his wrinkle into a canyon that distorted his face. His entire visage darkened as he pursed his lips. His head jerked on his neck, twitching on its spindle of vertebrae. Then he looked at her with the softer expression he had just shed in front of her.

"And you told me it was a misunderstanding. You said you had a lot going on. Now, I can be here for you, Sid. Like you need me to." Oliver leaned forward, that darkness blossoming in his eyes again.

Every muscle on Sidney's skeleton shrieked for engagement. To run, to fight, to flee. She had to make her mind heavy on her nervous system to force them still. She had to outweigh instinct with intention. She had to play his game better than him.

"But you came to punish me, didn't you, Oliver?" Sidney forced her voice flat.

"That was before." Oliver paused, narrowing his eyes until they were nearly consumed by his stubby lashes. "Unless you are lying. Unless you are leading me on. Unless you're not happy to see me."

Sidney swallowed around the inflating lump in her throat. The sensation of strangulation flirted on the edge of her awareness, drowned out by the other panicked messages. All of her flailed and screamed internally as she held herself resolute on the couch cushion, trying to breathe herself subtly into calm.

She could do this. If he could find her in the real world, break into her house and steal her first gift as a mother, abduct her son, force her to relocate, murder her roommate and coworker, and return to rape her, she could control herself. She could coil around her rage and wait to strike.

"So, are you happy to see me or not?" Oliver pressed, tugging Sidney from her internal struggle.

"You haven't smiled once. You're so much prettier when you smile, Sid."

Sidney ground her teeth hard enough to hear the enamel scrape below her ear. She flexed her self-control and swallowed the vomit welling in her throat, and she gave him the bright fake smile. The false grin she had been conjuring since her marriage collapsed, the meaningless upturn she offered customers. She tugged her facial muscles taunt and pretended to mean it. Her lips pulled tight and rigid as her cheeks struggled to participate.

She produced an empty and terse smile, the shape well-practiced from so many days at work, so many baseball games with those moms, so many times playing nice with Aiden in front of their son.

Oliver's menace dissolved again as he grinned back. His eyebrows changed, undulating from rage to suggestion. The new look was more threatening than the anger and violence she could see beneath his crooked façade. The lust-drunk contortion of his homely face was too ugly in its honesty, in the way it focused through her, as if she was merely an object. She realized that look was what he had felt about her while reading every message and seeing every picture, and that truth managed to shake her the deepest.

"You know, Sidney." He leaned forward and tilted his mouth closer to her. "You're so much prettier without your clothes on, too."

The pungent odor of disinfectant grew nauseating as he leaned into her. She could taste it as her throat contracted against it. His body heat wafting against her only made her stomach tighten more. Her skin teemed.

Rage flashed red over Sidney's vision, blinding her for a long second. The same anger and claustrophobic frustration at every trolling comment on her pictures.

That is so HOT!
Looking hot! I want to lick every drop of that blood off of you!
That chick would be hot if she wasn't on the rag in every picture.
How brave of you to post these pictures! You look amazing.
Don't bother writing. Just post more pictures!
Maybe you should go on a blood diet to lose that extra weight.
I would take a bite right out of that fine ass.

The way it always felt like she was selling herself, the way partial nudity was the only thing that solicited clicks, the disgusting effectiveness of it all.

Then she saw Kendra again. Sadness diffused her anger and brought her back to herself.

"Sidney," Oliver huffed impatiently, his beady eyes now stretched wide.

Sidney swallowed again, tasting something bitter and metallic.

"You're right." The lying smile returned to her face. "I haven't been myself, Oliver." The words bumbled over her teeth and tongue, deformed in their inaccuracy, but she concentrated on keeping the pleasant grin stretched perfectly. "You came a long way for me."

His eyes relaxed, and that lazy, lustful smirk twisted his lips.

"You've done a lot for me, and I appreciate it." Sidney faltered for a second, wavered in the tide drowning her mind, then flitted her eyes up flirtatiously. "I do need to show you."

Sidney forced thoughts from her mind. She shoved them aside the way she vacated her consciousness as she dove into meditation, the way she allowed her body to lead her through a flow with movement. She climbed atop the raging torrent of emotions, using them to rise in herself rather than drown beneath them. She translated their fury into performance.

She detached her consciousness from her body, allowing it to levitate above her like a bobbing balloon. She sent the instructions down the string, commanded her muscles at the length of her nerves, but she observed her body's movements like someone else acting. She watched herself slowly and deliberately slide from the cushion, kneeling in front of him. Her hands crawled around his knees before pressing his legs apart and sliding up his thighs. She saw her eyes spread wide and seductive, knowing how it felt from the times she donned that expression when she wanted, when she was genuinely interested. The motions were practiced muscle memory, heartless.

Oliver's face changed.

The darkness in his narrow eyes deepened and spread until it softened over his entire face. His thin lips upturned in some revolting victory. Sidney smiled back at him, but not in the enticing way he perceived. His gaze grew more hazed and distracted as hers only sharpened.

As she unzipped his pants and reached past the zipper, he moaned softly and dropped his head back.

From her angle, his head disappeared between his shoulders as if he had been prematurely decapitated. She groped around to find him, but his erection barely spanned her palm. Her floating mind wanted to laugh, wanted to make some comment about overcompensating through violence while he throbbed vulnerable in her grip. She also wanted to chop her hand off at the wrist, segment it from herself for touching him and eliciting that sound from his lips.

Finally, she let the sinister smile crack her face. She released the impulse down her arm and squeezed her hand as hard as she could, until her muscles trembled at the exertion. Oliver yelped wildly as his entire body went rigid. His legs kicked out beside her. Her consciousness slammed back into her skull, brought herself back to her body so she could fully experience hurting him. She braced herself against the coffee table and kept her hand clamped tightly, trying to dive her fingers through him and to each other.

She snapped her hand to the side, jerking at an unnatural angle the way Oliver's head had moved when he got flustered. Then she spiraled her forearm, twisting and yanking back as hard as she could. She heard a muffled pop and strangled ripping sound as she felt his flesh wilt under her grip. The skin remained intact, but the traumatized tissue below broke under her clutch.

Oliver's shriek shredded her ears before seizing into gasps. His body bucked hard against her, and she finally released him. She tumbled backward against the table and snatched herself to standing. She wanted to see him writhe.

He crumbled to the floor in front of the cushion

where he had waited for her to show him how happy she was to see him. His body coiled around itself, balling into a meek shape, wrapping around the pain. He whimpered and groaned until the sounds choked around his dry heaves. When his stomach stopped contracting, he sputtered a blur of obscenities she assumed he meant for her.

She stared at him too long as he floundered. When he began to swim his way to seated, time and urgency returned to her senses. He was hurt, but he was not incapacitated enough. He was not dead like he should be.

She needed a weapon. She had seen thousands of scenes with improvised weapons, yet they all abandoned her in this moment of need. She darted from the couch around the room, frantically scanning. She had always scolded Cameron to put away his bat, to not bring it to watch TV. Why did he feel the need to mess with it as he watched cartoons or a game? Why would he even bring it all the way downstairs anyway? Yet there it sat, illegally and illogically propped against the end of the couch. She sprinted to it as all her exacting purpose quivered at the mercy of her panic, at the precipice of what she was about to do.

In all the fictitious murders she had watched, in all the real and fake deaths she had read about, in all the times she had analyzed them, she never imagined herself on this side of the dynamic. She never envisioned herself as a killer, even as she had been desperately fighting off the role of victim. As natural as it all felt to watch Kendra's killer wriggle on her carpet, Sidney's mind registered the deviation with a slight nausea brewing in her belly. She shoved that and all thoughts aside, clutching the bat in both hands. At the abrasive rub of the tape on the handle, she saw Kendra's dead eyes again. The haunting stare removed the tremor from Sidney's grip, her movements resolute again.

Oliver glared up with his beady eyes. She stepped over him, eclipsing the ceiling light. He cowered in her menacing shadow. She locked eyes with him long enough to return the lusty, anticipant look he had given her earlier. Then she brought the bat down on him.

The bat struck him across the ribs. He made a muffled cry, and the blow echoed through his torso. The bat vibrated in her hand. She whipped it back overhead then brought it down on his skull. An audible crack accompanied the blood that splattered her legs. The red droplets sprayed over the move-in fresh clean carpet, landing on the couch and her laptop keyboard.

She hit him again, waywardly precise. Even as the sound of her assault and his protests were drowned out by her front door being kicked in and boots pounding overhead, she kept hitting him. She did not realize that she had begun to scream and cry wildly until the officer seized her arms from behind and dragged her away from Oliver's crumpled body.

30

"WHOLY SHIT, my girl nearly beat her stalker to death!" Brady exclaimed. He bounced excitedly across the pavement, escorting Sidney down the street from the police station.

Sidney chuckled to herself and picked at the clothes that were not hers, a strange folded stack the officer provided when collecting her clothing as evidence. The cloth rubbed against her skin in unfamiliar patterns, draped from her shoulders in foreign angles.

"Brady, stop," Jordan scolded from Sidney's other side. "This is not something to celebrate."

"Fuck you, it's not! Some asshole from the internet stalks our girl, attacks our girl, takes her kid, kills Kendra, then comes for our girl. Then our girl almost kills this fucker!" Brady refused to contain his vibrating blend of glee and pride.

"Almost," Sidney echoed, not sure if she was smiling or grimacing.

"I can't believe you managed to stop yourself, Sid," Brady continued, breathless. "I don't think I could have after Kendra."

"I didn't," Sidney said.

"You didn't?" Jordan asked.

"No, the cops showed up. I had called 911, and they finally showed up."

"Thankfully," Jordan said in a sigh.

Brady rolled his eyes. "Not 'thankfully.' I wish you would have gotten to finish him. How did this even happen, Sid? I know he broke in, but how did you manage to beat the shit out of him? Did you just go crazy or surprise him or what?"

Sidney smiled softly. "I pretended I was going to suck his dick."

"What!" Brady and Jordan shouted in unison, stopping mid-step.

Sidney stepped forward and turned back to face them, enjoying their reactions.

"Yeah," she continued. "Then I broke it."

Both men gasped, their hands instinctively shielding their crotches as they flinched.

"He was pretty incapacitated then," Sidney said. "So I just started hitting him. Until the cops came in and stopped me."

"Holy shit," Jordan breathed, his hand moving up to cover his mouth.

"Clever girl," Brady said, beaming. "Our fucking girl!" Brady strode forward and wrapped Sidney under his arm. "That fucker didn't get half of what he deserves."

"Well, now he can end up in prison for the rest of his life for his crimes," Jordan said, quickening his pace to catch up with them.

"Ugh, square," Brady breathed into Sidney's ear, loud enough for Jordan to hear and roll his eyes in return, a sly smile teasing at the edge of his mouth.

"So, you'll come home and stay with us, Sid?" Brady asked.

"No," Sidney replied.

"What do you mean, no?" Jordan said.

"No," Sidney repeated. "I'm going home. It's over now."

She said the words then felt them resonate through her chest. It was over now.

"Um, sweetie, isn't this the point in the horror movie where the heroine daringly survives and outsmarts the killer only for there to be a final jump scare waiting for her?" Brady turned so she could see his raised eyebrows.

"This isn't a horror movie, Brady. As much as it has felt like one. He's in custody now. What can he do to me now?"

"So, it's over just like that? Just like a switch?"

"No," Sidney laughed, inauthentic and awkward. "I think I'm going to be in endless therapy to get over this. I might need to move again. The aftermath is just starting. But Oliver is gone now. He's over. I can have my life back."

She said it firmly but felt her resolve wobble under her surface. In the depths of her mind, something screamed that her life would never be back to how it was. What if Oliver was released? What if the internet was full of stalkers just like him? What if she could never really put this behind her?

"Cameron," Jordan mumbled.

"Exactly," Sidney said. "I can bring Cameron home now. I can keep him safe now. I have to bring him to talk to the cops tomorrow anyway, identify Oliver from his abduction. We can put all this behind us."

"I don't know, Sid," Jordan said. "I think you should still stay with us. It would make me feel better."

Brady nodded in agreement, his manic excitement dwindling.

Sidney shook her head. "I cannot spend another night on that gorgeous couch in that gorgeous loft. I haven't lived in my house one minute since I moved in. I was too scared. I'm going to start living in it as soon as I can, starting on the couch right next to where I won."

Brady and Jordan exchanged glances.

"But if you two insist on babysitting me," Sidney continued, "you are more than welcome to join me. We just need wine."

"Sold!" Brady exclaimed.

***

The next morning, Sidney rang Aiden's doorbell. The porch beneath her was just a porch, the door in front of her just a door. The painful memories that used to emanate from the structure receded so far into the past that they seemed like echoes from another life. Her fresh trauma eclipsed any pain and torment she had felt from her betrayal and the dismembering of her family. Standing in a new perspective, they now felt so small and distant that her mind no longer registered them.

Aiden opened the screen door wide. Sidney moved to step through, but Aiden stepped forward, pulling the inner door closed behind her. Sidney flinched back, furrowing her brow at him.

"Sidney," Aiden said in a tone so ancient she barely recognized it.

He moved closer to her and wrapped his arms

around her, drawing her into his chest and clutching her there like he once had when he did not hate her. Sidney startled at first before falling into the embrace. She let her hands slide up his back to press him into her.

He finally released her but left a hand lingering on her shoulder as he examined her.

"Are you OK?" he asked, gravely.

Sidney felt the tears threatening to sting her eyes.

"Yeah, Aiden," she reassured. "I'm fine."

"Did he—" Aiden dropped his eyes to the boards on the porch. "Did he—" He shuffled around awkwardly in his words. "Did he hurt you, Sid? Did he do anything to you?"

Aiden finally flicked his eyes back up to evaluate her face. Sidney smiled gently back at him.

"No. I mean, he wanted to. I think he planned to when he broke in, but I got him first."

"Do you want to tell me what happened? I don't think Cameron should know all the details. I don't want to scare him. But can you tell me?"

"Yeah, Aiden." Sidney took a turn looking at their feet. "Can it just not be right now?"

"Of course. Of course, Sid. I mean, you don't have to."

Sidney recognized his stammering and apologetic rhythm, and it made her nostalgic for that past life from ages before—before cheating and divorce and custody battles, before this moment on the porch.

"Aiden, it's fine," she soothed. "I just need a little bit of time, and Cameron and I need to get to the police station now."

"I should go with you," Aiden said, more firmly. "In case seeing this guy scares Cameron."

"Sure. If you want to."

"I want to," Aiden said without looking at her.

He reached behind him and opened the front door, ushering her into the house.

As they drove to the station, Cameron sat uncharacteristically quiet in the backseat. Sidney had not seen him in days, which felt more like months. She wrung the steering wheel with her hands and could not stop staring at him in the rearview mirror. He looked like he had aged two years in the span of their separation, especially with the way his eyebrows knitted together, worry weighing on his smooth forehead.

"Cam, baby," Sidney said, "what's wrong?"

"Am-am-am I in trouble?" Cameron stammered.

"No, buddy," Aiden answered. "What would make you think that?"

"We're going to the police station again," Cameron started.

"Cam, I told you why. You just need to tell us if the guy they caught is the guy that took you from baseball practice," Sidney assured.

"Then why are you and Dad both going? You only both go somewhere if I'm in trouble. Even at my games, you aren't together," Cameron argued.

Sidney glanced over and met Aiden's eyes.

Aiden shrugged slightly and looked out the window before turning to face Cameron in the backseat.

"I'm here for you, buddy," he said. "Even if Mom and I don't live together anymore, we are still a family. I'm always going to keep you safe."

"And Mom too?"

Aiden hesitated then turned back to the dashboard. "Yeah, I'll keep Mom safe too."

Sidney did not react, staring plainly at the road disappearing under her car, but she saw Cameron's posture relax in the backset. His forehead released his eyebrows to float more carelessly above his wide eyes, like normal. Aiden resumed watching the scenery slide by his window.

At the station, the officers escorted the three of them into a small interview room. Cameron sat at the pale and questionably clean table as Sidney and Aiden took a chair on either side of him. Detective Morris sat down across from them, smiling disarmingly at Cameron.

"OK, Cameron," Morris said gently, "I'm going to show you some pictures, and I just want you to tell us if you see the man who took you from the baseball field."

"That's it?" Cameron questioned, wrinkling his nose.

"That's it."

Morris opened the folder in front of him and turned a grid of six photos toward Cameron. He slid it across the table to position it directly in Cameron's eyeline. Sidney reached up and stroked her hand along Cameron's back. She looked over her son at Aiden, but Aiden glared down hard at the pictures, scrutinizing each face.

Sidney turned to glance down at the photo array. Oliver stared back at her from the bottom right, the last picture, just as he was the last she ever suspected. Even though his expression was slack and empty in the picture, she could still see the terrible, lustful curl on his lips. She could still hear him telling her to show him how happy she was to see him. Sidney flinched unconsciously and withdrew her hand from Cameron's back. Aiden's gaze flitted over to check her.

"Do you see anyone you recognize?" Morris asked Cameron, leaning in toward the pictures to mirror Cameron.

Cameron shook his head no, still looking at the photos. Sidney straightened up in her seat, craning over her son to look at the pictures again. Oliver was still right there, staring back at her. She could feel the disbelief on her face when she looked at Aiden. He frowned back at her, confused.

"Are you sure?" Morris asked. "Look again. Look really slow and really close. Do you recognize any of these men?"

Cameron pursed his lips and planted his elbows on either side of the folder. He balled up his fists and rested his face on them, bringing his eyes closer to the warbled light reflected on the images. Sidney watched his eyes march back and forth across the rows of pictures, doubling over and over.

"No," Cameron said. "He's not there. The man is not there. I'm sorry, Mommy." Cameron turned to Sidney, his eyes fattening with tears. "I did it wrong. I don't see him. I'm sorry!"

Cameron's lip wavered. His face welled with disappointment. Aiden reached forward and planted a calming hand on his son's shoulder, as he had for Sidney not long ago. Sidney gathered Cameron into her arms before the sobs could escape.

"No, Cameron, no," she said soothingly. "You did great, baby. You did exactly what you were supposed to do."

She heard Cameron suck in deep breaths against

her chest. His shoulder shuddered slightly against her before lowering back down away from his ears.

"Your mom is right," Morris echoed. "Why don't you have your dad take you down the hall? There's a vending machine with candy down there. I just want to talk to you mom for a second; then you can all head home."

Cameron looked to his father, who nodded in affirmation. Sidney squeezed Cameron one more time, perhaps too hard, before he and Aiden exited the small room. Sidney watched them until the door softly clicked closed behind them then turned her eyes to Morris.

"What does this mean?" Sidney said, the anxiety quickly beginning to unravel below her chest.

"It means Oliver probably didn't take your son," Morris replied, calmly.

"No, it had to be Oliver." Sidney's hands found each other atop the table and started to wind together. "He's the stalker. He attacked me. He killed Kendra and Seth." Her words became more frantic, gaining momentum as they spilled from her lips.

"Ms. Gray, we don't know all of that yet. We do know he broke into your house and tried to attack you. He has admitted to stalking you and breaking in previously to steal small items. But we don't have any evidence that he committed the other crimes yet."

"B-but that had to be when he got the picture, the picture of Kendra that was by . . . " She lost her voice for an instant. "That was by Seth."

"There weren't any prints on the picture besides yours and Kendra's, so we can't prove that yet. So, we don't know right now." Morris paused to allow Sidney to catch her breath, which had run away from her when she stopped speaking. "And from this photo array with Cameron, it doesn't look like he is the one who took your son. Do you think Cameron could be confused?"

Sidney mashed her hands over her face, feeling the makeup smear beneath but unable to care about the state of her appearance.

"No," she said, small and certain. "Cameron would know if it was Oliver. He's very good with faces, has a great memory." Sidney brought her hands near her mouth and resisted the urge to bite her finger, to take out all her frustration on her own flesh. "What now?"

Sidney looked up at Morris. She could feel how wide and desperate her eyes had become, how her bodily composure had disintegrated the second Cameron said no. She felt like a different person again, that person she thought she had left at this police station the previous night, that person she thought she had beaten out of herself as she beat Oliver. Her freedom had been a tease, an aberration. Apparently, this was home.

"You've given us all your online correspondence with Oliver?"

Sidney's face went hot, embarrassment blooming beneath her cheeks. "Yes."

"And you've told us about any other online contacts that might pose a threat or be involved?"

Sidney threw her eyes to the tile floor and wrapped her arms around her stomach, nodding hard.

"Then we continue the investigation. We are still processing evidence from both murders. We will keep going until we can prove it was Oliver." Morris paused again, hesitated. "Or until we find who it was."

Sidney joined her boys in the hallway. The steps that took her to them felt labored and heavy. The misplaced elation that had enlivened her body had been infected by a dark exhaustion, the kind that depression hides beneath. She forced life into her face to smile at Cameron.

"You did so good, buddy," she said, running her hand through his hair and hugging him against her body. "What did you get?"

"Starburst" Cameron nearly spat the words out through a mouthful.

"Good choice." Sidney kept her son against her side and looked at Aiden. He leaned against the vending machine with his arms crossed, another mannerism that conjured less pleasant memories.

"What now?" he said.

"We are free to go," Sidney replied. "The investigation continues."

Aiden frowned and curled into himself for a moment.

"I want to go to Mom's. It's time to go to Mom's, right?" Cameron said between bites.

"I don't know, Cam, I—" Aiden started.

"I want to sleep in my Spider-Man room. I never get to. We moved in, and then I never get to be there." Cameron crossed his arms, the nub of the candy wrapper dangling from his fingers.

"I know, buddy. It's just I'm worried—" Aiden stopped again. "I need to talk to your mom about this."

"Without me," Cameron said.

Aiden nodded.

"Well, can't you talk to her at her house?" Cameron asked, turning his attention back to the candy.

Aiden uncrossed his arms and stood back up from the vending machine, looking at Sidney.

"We can go have dinner at my house, Aiden. Cameron can get to his Spider-Man room. You and I can talk, and you'll know we're—" Sidney started.

"Safe," Aiden finished.

Sidney nodded, and they all returned to the car.

***

As soon as Cameron emptied his plate, he vanished up the stairs and into his Spider-Man room. Sidney cleared the plates from the table and replaced them with beers for Aiden and herself. With Cameron out of sight, she let her posture revert, allowing the pressure she felt in her chest to contort her skeleton. She leaned forward on the table to prop herself up.

"What do you want to talk about first?" Sidney mumbled. "The assault that happened downstairs or the fact that that psycho is not the psycho who took our kid from his baseball practice?"

Aiden scoffed slightly as he took a long drink of his beer.

"With such amazing choices, I don't quite know where to begin."

Sidney laughed gratefully and eased up from her hands.

"And I fucking thought the divorce was the worst life could get." Aiden shook his head then tilted it back to chug again.

Sidney could not have phrased it any better herself.

"Sidney, do you want to tell me what happened last night?" Seriousness returned to Aiden's features.

Sidney sucked in a deep breath and held it as she

390

leaned back in her chair. She blew out the air and brought her beer to her lips.

"I was downstairs watching a horror movie," she started.

"Horror, really?" Aiden's eyes widened. "You could watch horror at a time like this?"

"It's just a movie, Aiden." Sidney felt herself stiffen. She brought her arms around herself. "It was for the *12 Slays of Christmas*. I do it at the beginning of December every year. Anyway. I kept hearing a noise but figured I was hearing things. Then I heard the window break, and I was sure. I called 911, but the line was busy. He was in the house, between me and the door, so I hid in the bathroom. But he found me."

Aiden's lips tightened as she spoke, steadily vanishing into his mouth until his face puckered. Sidney paused to let the story settle, to calm the heartbeat that throbbed under her words. As she spoke, the scene materialized in the back of her mind. Her body caged the echoes of the fear in those moments, still trapped inside her.

"OK," Aiden said gently. "Then what happened?" He swallowed hard. "What did he do?"

"He had me come out and sit on the couch with him. He told me he was mad at me for ignoring him and leading him on."

"Wait, you knew this guy?" Aiden stiffened.

"Not really. We chatted online."

"Jesus Christ, Sidney." Aiden threw himself back. "I fucking told you this is what—" He looked at Sidney and softened. "I'm sorry. What happened next?"

"I told him it was all a misunderstanding. He wanted me to—" Sidney stopped and took a long chug from her beer, feeling the cold liquid undulate down her throat, around the knot swelling there. She shook her head a little. "He wanted me to show him how happy I was to see him. He told me I was much prettier when I smiled, and when I didn't have clothes on."

Sidney did not look at Aiden's face. She did not want to see his reaction. Aiden slid his beer forward on the table then pulled it back close to him. He shifted from one side then the other, suddenly uncomfortable in his skin.

"What did you do, Sid?" he finally said.

"I lied," she replied. "I told him what he wanted to hear. I made him think I was going to do what he wanted to do. Then I hurt him."

"But he didn't hurt you?"

"No."

"Sidney, you can tell me if he did."

"Aiden," Sidney said firmly. "He never got to hurt me."

The story poisoned the air between them then fell dead on the table. Silence seeped in to take its place. They did not look at each other. They did not drink their beers. They sat suspended for long moments, with only the sounds of Cameron's footsteps moving back and forth overhead.

Aiden continued sliding his bottle toward then away from him, rocking in his seat as he did. He stared at his own hand, but his focus burrowed deeper than his flesh. Sidney pursed her lips and quietly watched him. Finally, Aiden pulled his sight back, ceased his gentle rocking, and looked back at her.

"What did Morris say?" he said.

"That there's no proof Oliver killed Kendra and

Seth. That he didn't take Cam." Sidney clipped her words. Something about Aiden's eye contact was too penetrating, made her feel exposed, vulnerable.

"So, they don't think he did any of that?" Aiden pushed back in his chair.

"I don't know what they think." Sidney rubbed her palms over her face. "But I know they can't prove anything."

"Shit, Sid." Aiden hesitated for a moment. His hands jerked about like he was unsure what to do with them. "What do you think?"

"It's him," Sidney replied, and how plainly she meant it startled her.

"No doubt? How do you know?"

"His smell." Sidney's voice shrunk, and she looked down at her lap.

"His what?"

Sidney pressed her lips together hard then met Aiden's eyes. That manic wideness had returned to his expression, the edges tinged with unconsummated anger.

"His smell. He smelled like lemon cleaner. My attacker smelled just like that. It's all I really remembered about him."

"Wait, what?"

Aiden's beer bottle rushed forward across the table and past his fingertips. The rage at the edges of Aiden's face bled in toward his eyes.

Sidney snagged the smile before it could infect her lips. She had forgotten that Aiden did not know. She had forgotten how recently he hated her too much to care what happened to her. But she did relax her features, cuing Aiden to calm down.

"When I went to Telluride for the Horror Show, I got attacked walking back to my room one night," Sidney said, calmly.

"What do you mean attacked?" Aiden's lips had gone so rigid that they seemed to disappear into his mouth.

"I was walking down this path. Someone ran up out of the creek and chased me, tackled me. I fought them off and ran back to the room." Saying the words, Sidney felt the gravel pressing into her back and heard her own panicked breaths as she groped for the bottle in her bag. Now, in the memory, it was Oliver on top of her.

She took a deep breath to keep herself still and her face placid.

"And you never told me."

Sidney shook her head. "It wasn't a big deal. Nothing actually happened."

Aiden stared incredulously at her for a second. "Do the cops think that was him?"

Sidney bit her lip compulsively. "I didn't tell the police," she said quietly. "It didn't seem relevant."

"Jesus, Sidney!" Aiden's hands flew up into the air. "You didn't report it?"

Sidney shook her head again, like a scolded child.

"Did you tell them now?"

Sidney hesitated. With the rapid escalation of crimes, it honestly had never dawned on her to include it in her worthless, fruitless reports. She was not even sure if she had connected it in her mind.

Aiden flexed his jaw, opened his mouth to speak, then withdrew back in his chair. He gathered the beer bottle back into his hand and took a long drink. He began spinning the bottle through his fingers, the glass grating on the tabletop in circles.

"But it's over now," Aiden said, more of a question than a statement. "They got him, so it's over."

"Yes, it's over," Sidney said to Aiden and herself.

After they had drained their beers over the trailing ends of their conversation, Aiden joined Cameron for a boys' sleepover. Aiden insisted just for the night, just until the security company installed the alarm the next day. His gaze lingered on Sidney as he nodded a curt goodnight and disappeared into the Spider-Man room.

Sidney took her phone into her room and collapsed onto the bed. She had heard the phone twitching in her purse consistently since they had arrived home. She had felt the familiar pang of anxious intention to immediately answer yet ignored it. She had chosen to focus on the real life around her and the oddity of her ex-husband sharing a beer with her in her kitchen the night after an attack by her internet stalker.

Adam: I know you have a lot going on. I just
    want to know that you're OK.
Sidney: Hey there
Adam: Hey!
    What happened at the police station?
Sidney: Just more of a waste of time. They can't
    prove anything besides last night.
Adam: But they got him. They'll find the proof.
Sidney: They have to. It's him.
Adam: What are you doing now?
Sidney: Heading to bed.
    My ex is sleeping here.

Adam appeared to hesitate. Sidney saw the typing indication appear and disappear from the thread over and over. Typing and deleting and typing again. He did not know what to say; he did not want to ask what he wanted to know. Sidney just waited, tapping her phone screen to keep it alight.

Adam: With you?
Sidney: With Cameron.
Adam: Are you OK? Do you feel better with him behind bars?
Sidney: I think so. I think I will be.
Adam: I wish I was there for you.
Sidney: You are.
Adam: I mean actually THERE.
Sidney: I know. Me too.

Sidney smiled softly and navigated back to her inbox.

Allison: Girl, that is CRAZY! He broke into your house??
Sidney: The stalker is revealed.
Allison: Finally! And you kicked his ass!

Sidney beamed in the glow of her screen, where no one could see her.

Sidney: It felt good.
Allison: I bet it did! Girl power!
Sidney: Something like that.
Allison: So now what? You start over?
Sidney: I guess so.
Allison: How are you going to do that?

Sidney paused and let the edge of the phone rest on her lip. She stared up at her dark ceiling, trying to draw shapes out of the black. How the hell was she going to do that?

Sidney: I have no idea haha!
    I need to start with a new job. I'm getting transferred to a new store, but I think I need something new.
    I keep thinking about moving farther away, but my son needs to be by my ex too.
Allison: Custody agreements are a bitch!
    But are you OK? Really.

Sidney stared at the question, reading it and rereading it. Was she OK? Could she be OK again?

Sidney: It's bizarre really.
    I feel like a final girl in the horror movie.
    Empowered after the last faceoff.
Allison: Until the sequel.
Sidney: Hahaha

Sidney's words suggested she was laughing, but she did not even smile. She remained tangled in the strangeness of the moment.

Allison: How's the boyfriend?
Sidney: Another thing I need to figure out. Now that this is all over.
Allison: Keep it simple, girl. Maybe you just need some time alone.

Sidney let the conversations flow and wander until her eyes blurred shut.

31

TWO MONTHS LATER, on the other side of the new year, Carla and Amy laughed together from Sidney's freshly-shampooed couch, perched atop her freshly shampooed carpet. Sidney sat in the chair beside them, clutching her wine glass, trying not to see the ghosts of Oliver and herself beside them. Her brain cells were not nearly as clean as the floor and furniture in front of her.

Carla leaned forward, swirling the remaining crimson liquid in the bell of her glass. The red in her glass matched the red on her lips matched the red of her snug and low-cut top. Her giggles lingered in a smile on her lips. She looked to Amy then across to Sidney before raising her glass.

"Last drink of the night, ladies," she said, the wine curling at the end of her words. "And it's to Kendra."

Tears rushed to Sidney's eyes at hearing Kendra's name, at seeing three glasses converge when it should have been four, but she smiled through it as she brought her hand forward.

"To Kendra," Sidney echoed.

"And to that asshole who killed her getting the needle," Amy added.

"They got him," Carla said. "Only a matter of time now."

The glasses clinked together in a song, and the three swallowed the last of the wine in unison. Amy's phone buzzed against the coffee table, and she snatched it up.

"Perfect timing," she said, licking her lips. "Uber is here."

They gathered up their glasses and ascended the stairs. Carla and Amy continued to chatter and laugh softly as they walked, yet Sidney felt trapped in the echo of Kendra's name and her absence, in the mention of Oliver. Like a fly caught in a jar. The haze of the alcohol on her brain made the jar seem smaller.

Carla and Amy gathered their purses and took turns hugging Sidney before they pulled the front door open and stepped out into the night. Sidney eased out onto the porch behind them. She could make out the headlights of the idling car at the curb. Both girls turned to smile and wave at her again before disappearing into the dark of the driveway.

"Oh hey, Tony," Sidney heard Carla say.

"Hi Tony, what are you doing here?" Amy said.

"Ladies," Tony's voice came from the night, "looking lovely as always. I just wanted to check on Sid."

Carla and Amy retreated back into the halo of Sidney's porch light and turned their eyes back to her.

"Hey Sid," Carla called, smiling slyly. "Tony's here to see you."

Carla's affinity for Tony lingered in the edge of her words and the curve of her grin.

Tony stepped forward into the light and flashed his

signature smile at Sidney. She felt her pupils dilate and chest contract simultaneously.

"Hey Tony," she said, half her voice abandoning her.

"Can I talk to you for a little bit?" Tony asked, glancing at Carla and Amy for approval.

Sidney also looked to the girls then shrugged automatically. "Sure. Come on in."

"We'll leave you two to it then," Carla said, stepping toward the Uber.

"Have a good night," Amy echoed as she followed Carla.

The two women giggled softly as they linked arms and disappeared into their car. Tony looked down and licked his lips, slipping his hands into his pockets as he walked closer. The familiar flutter shivered down Sidney's skin, a muscle memory reaction, a trained cellular response to Tony.

She did not want him to come closer. She did not want to talk. She wanted to close and lock her door, arm the security system, and finally get a full night's sleep in this house. She wanted to step forward, but everything with Tony was backward. She could feel the regression seething beneath her surface, and she hated how easy it permeated her mind.

Sidney leaned against the door frame. Tony stepped up to her and cocked his head. Sidney felt herself smile instinctively, and even though she still wanted to shut the door, she held it ajar for him. He slowed his pace as he passed her, gliding himself through her personal space so she could feel his body heat. Her nerves crackled somewhere between excitement and irritation. The contradiction muddled

Sidney's thoughts. She shook her head to clear them as she closed the door.

Tony walked in commandingly, taking long circular steps as he surveyed the room.

"I like the new place," he said, finally. "It's different."

"What do you mean?" Sidney asked.

"It's just you," he said. "Well, you and Cameron."

Sidney wrinkled her brow, looking at him blankly. There were reasons they never did much talking. She had not missed his unimpressive wit and seemingly pointless words.

Tony finally circled his way to Sidney's kitchen table and pulled out a chair, helping himself to a seat. Sidney rolled her eyes and stifled a sigh before sitting across from him.

"Sid, how are you?" he asked.

Tony leaned forward, propping himself on his elbows. He slid his hands across the table closer to her. Sidney knew he was asking for her hands. She simply looked down at his hands then back up and stayed still.

"I'm fine, Tony."

"But I haven't seen you in months, Sid." Tony leaned back in his chair, drawing his hands back across the table. "I ran into you in public, and you all but ignored me. You never answer my messages."

"So, you're here because you think I'm ghosting you?" Sidney's spine went rigid. Her body language solidified to communicate anger, but her mind immediately cowered, feeling the same fear as when Oliver rattled off her list of offenses. She crossed her arms tightly over her chest, digging her fingers into her biceps.

"No, no, that's not what I'm saying. I'm trying to say I'm worried about you. I know you lost Kendra and that guy you worked with."

The stiff chair dug into her legs. Itching sensations crawled up her back. Tony's words abraded her brain. His eye contact sent tension from her chest down her limbs. Each time she looked at him, she could feel herself flush, and no longer in the pleasant way. To avoid shifting in her seat, she stood and moved into the kitchen.

"Do you want—uh—a beer or something?" she asked, not looking back.

"Sure."

Tony waited while Sidney retrieved the beer from the fridge. Her hands trembled as she reached forward, but it was not fear that quivered on her nerves. The anxiety felt different, bubbled below her skin in a new sensation. She pushed her arms through it and snatched the bottles from the shelf.

"You still look good though, Sid," Tony said as she returned to him.

She felt his eyes move down then back up her body in a familiar pattern. She knew that tilt of his head, that subtle sideways recline. Her body knew she was supposed to smile and feign a flattered blush, tug at her lip a little with her top teeth, yet she did not. The actions faded, untaken, in her brain. She planted the bottle in front of him and faced her body away from him as she returned to the chair.

He kept that lazy gaze on her. She drummed her fingers along the glass of her beer. She looked to him but did not want to reflect that lust on his face, so she glanced away, awkward, waiting.

"Come on, Sid," he finally said. "Talk to me. I'm here for you. I want to be here for you."

Sidney stifled the grimace from contorting her face. She fought the confusion out of her eyebrows. What did he think he was doing? This had never been them. His place was in her bed then out the front door, not at her kitchen table, not being *there* for her.

"I appreciate that, Tony. I really do." Sidney paused and spun her bottle in her hands. "But I don't need to talk anymore. Honestly, I'm sick of talking about it."

"I get that." Tony's intense gaze wavered. "We don't have to talk," he said.

Tony eased back in his chair, swigging from his beer. Sidney watched him get more comfortable in her chair. His presence grated her nerves. He felt like a splinter in her brain with an angry infection blossoming around it.

"So, uh, what have you been up to?" Sidney finally violated the silence.

"Nothing much. Nothing like you. Just working, you know, keeping busy." He looked down at the table then flicked his eyes back up to her. "I've missed you."

Sidney knew she was supposed to say she had missed him too and lean in to kiss him. The steps in the choreography were deeply treaded in her mind, yet that felt like another life, another person. Tony did not belong in this new house or this new life of hers.

"Look, Tony, it's really good to see you, but I think I should call it a night."

Tony's eyes lit up.

"Alone," she clarified.

The light faded.

"I need to just go to bed. After all that's happened, I need to be by myself for a while."

Tony pursed his lips. A darkness passed over his features for an instant as he reclined; then he regained his smile.

"That's OK. I understand," he said. "Just let me finish my beer, and I'll take off."

"Thanks, Tony." Sidney smiled gently, riding a blip of affection for him.

Tony sat still for a long minute, staring at his immobile beer bottle before bringing it to his lips. His face remained changed, weighted. His dumb, wide eyes narrowed slightly. His smooth, young brow betrayed him with tiny furrows. Sidney once would have felt guilty at disappointing him but now only looked forward to locking the door behind him. It felt good to tell the truth, to tell him no.

"So, how's your new boyfriend?" Tony smacked his lips along his teeth.

"What? What are you talking about?"

Tony slowly sat up straight and looked into her face. "Your new boyfriend," he repeated. "The one you met online, the one who came to Telluride, the one who helped you move after Kendra."

Sidney's fingers abandoned her bottle as she drew her hands into her chest. Her spine flexed until she leaned back in the chair.

"What the fuck, Tony?" she breathed. "What are you talking about?"

A wicked little smile snaked across his lips. Sidney's crawling anxiety solidified, squeezed around her tightly.

"What? You don't know? But you're so much

smarter than me, Sid. I'm just young and dumb and safe. I'm just the toy."

Sidney's brain shattered into a million panicked thoughts. A blanket of confusion heaped on top of them, trapping them like animals under a net. From within the flurry, she stood slowly and stepped behind her chair.

"Tony, I—I—" Sidney could not find the words.

Tony's eyes narrowed, arching into grave slits, yet they smoldered in a dark excitement. His features thinned and stretched as his eyebrows pointed higher up his forehead. His cruel grin only widened until his face became unrecognizable, until he looked like Oliver, and the face she imagined in the dark of the Telluride night. He looked nothing like the dumb boy she had summoned to her bed then dismissed from her mind immediately after. His wide eyes with their thick, simple stare had become so calculating. There was so much behind his eyes now.

"You what, Sidney? You never said that—that I'm a toy? You didn't mean it?"

Sidney's lips continued to wag in the air yet could not assemble the right syllables.

"How?" she finally managed.

Tony slammed his hands down on the table, rattling the beer bottles, and released a guttural laugh. He hopped to his feet and pranced in a circle beside the table as he giggled. Sidney flinched at first until the startle dissolved into plain bewilderment.

"Oh, you dumb bitch," he chuckled. "You told me. You fucking told me yourself."

Sidney frowned, shook her head to dislodge the expression, then succumbed to the perplexment again.

Her alarm steadily thickened and grew with her impatience. She was sick of playing games. She was exhausted with people worming their way into her life to try and toy with her, make her what they wanted for themselves. She felt that rage again, the defiant anger that had flared over her before bashing Oliver's head.

"Tony, what the *fuck* are you talking about?"

Tony slapped his hands down again, leaving them planted on the tabletop and staring at Sidney with wider eyes. He released another shaking laugh as he looked into her eyes. Then his face softened into something more playful again, the look she remembered when he would reach for her the next morning. On the rare occasions she had allowed him to stay that long.

"You sure are chatty online, Sidney. You'll just post about or tell anyone just about anything. Anyone who will listen to you, anyone who will pretend to care. Tell a girl online that she's beautiful and special, and she'll just keep responding. She'll tell you just about anything."

Tony crossed his arms over his chest and planted a finger on his pursed lips, eyes still grinning. The realization cascaded over Sidney's brain, consolidating her thoughts back into a singular consciousness. All the wayward voices collapsed into one shouting the answer against the walls of her skull.

"Which one were you?" Sidney's voice fell low and angry.

Tony beamed in a way Sidney had never seen. Not the look of victory when she pulled him into her bed, not the lazy smile after she had had sex with him for hours—some perverted sort of pride. The condescending face and the way he was relishing her struggle made his face entirely foreign.

"What's the matter? Don't you know?" He toyed again. "Do you tell that many people all your business?"

"Fuck you, Tony!" Sidney pushed her chair against the table and stepped back further.

"Aww, come on, Sid. Not bad for a toy, huh? Not so much smarter than me now." Tony moved forward around the table, and Sidney bristled.

"Max?"

"Yeah, but you didn't like him very much, did you? He wasn't even toy material."

"Jack?"

"Right again. He wasn't your favorite either."

"Who else?"

"So many you ignored." He looked down briefly. When his gaze returned, it was not inflated with lust. It was hungry in a different way, ravenous the way Oliver's squinted eyes were. "You can tell me. Safe space."

Sidney's jaw dropped softly and silently as her eyes widened. She walked backward, along the table, as Tony continued to round the other side. She stared directly into his pleased eyes as she soundlessly snagged her beer bottle and held it beside her hip.

"Allison," she breathed, the word tickling nausea as it slid across her tongue. "*You* are Allison?"

A rapid scroll of her conversation thread with Allison whirled through her mind. Every confession she had made, every tidbit and detail she had volunteered so happily. She felt a flash of how safe it had felt to confide in Allison, and picturing Tony typing back to her seized her throat. She could not have felt more exposed if Tony had ripped the clothes from her body.

"Turns out the way to win your heart is to pretend to have a vagina," Tony said, slyly. "Is there something you want to tell me, Sid? Would you love me if I had a pussy?"

"Fuck you, Tony!" Sidney shouted louder.

"That's all I'm good for, right? That's all you wanted me for, right? Until you found someone better online to replace me. No, fuck you." Tony's smile nearly cracked his face.

Sidney took the moment he was enjoying to snatch the chair in front of her and drag it out as Tony lunged forward. Tony tangled in the chair before throwing it aside. Sidney fled around the table, running around the entire edge. She flung her arms out in front of her, clawing at the air as she raced for the front door.

Tony stomped around the table and seized her at the waist. He spun her around to face him, her arms spiraling out from her sides, and slammed her back into the wall. He grabbed at her wrists as she flailed her arms, pinning her with his hips. The pressure of his pelvic bones disgusted her. She struggled to buck against him.

"You didn't think I just came for the big reveal, did you? I came to have some fun. After all, I'm only good for one thing," Tony grunted against her.

"You knew exactly what we were, Tony. I don't owe you shit. I don't have to be with you just because we had mediocre sex a few times."

"Mediocre?" Tony's voice dropped. He leaned back to reveal the shock on his face. "It was way more than a couple times. You kept coming back. And you definitely came; I know it."

Sidney glared at him as she arched her back to shove him farther back on his heels. She brought her foot stomping down onto his. A small bellow escaped his lips. Instinctively, he rounded down to draw the wounded foot toward his hands. Still clutching the bottle, Sidney slammed it hard against the wall. It shattered, the vibration humming against her palm as shards of glass rained to the carpet below. She swung her arm hard until the jagged edge of the glass dragged across Tony's cheek.

Tony's yowl ascended into a deep shriek. His hand shot up to cradle his face as the blood trickled from the cut. Sidney kicked hard at him, aiming for his groin, wanting to channel all her rage to damaging that one point in his anatomy. Yet her foot missed its target, landing instead along his thigh, toppling him to the floor in front of the door.

Sidney whirled around and ran back, deeper into the house. Like a horror movie final girl clutching her improvised weapon. Even in her panic and her flight, the parallel was not lost on Sidney. But she would not run up the stairs. She heard Tony continue to whine as he struggled to his feet and she sprinted past the table.

She snatched the doorknob on the back door as Tony barreled after her.

"You don't get to leave! I'm not done with you," Tony yelled.

Sidney looked over her shoulder at the sound of his voice. His eyes bulged from their sockets and looked terrifyingly distorted in the shadows. She ripped the door open and plunged herself into the night.

She stumbled off the unfamiliar stoop and careened onto the dead grass. She had never been in the backyard since moving into the house. She was in foreign territory at the edge of her own new home. Sidney scrambled to her feet as Tony tumbled after her, equally unprepared for the terrain. He landed near her feet and scrambled after her. She kicked hard at his face, connecting with something solid, as she leaped over him and ran toward the gate.

The rough wood scratched her palms as her fingers read the texture of the boards until they discovered the smooth metal of the latch. Her grip fumbled in the surging waves of her adrenaline. Half of her mind was fixated behind her, straining to hear Tony to approximate his position. She loosed the latch, and the hinges screeched. She resisted the urge to look back again and hurried around her house.

She ran past her own car, lamenting her keys tucked in her purse on the counter. Her bare feet slapped the pavement, past where the Uber had spirited Carla and Amy away. She sprinted down the road the way she entered and exited her street, but she had not learned the neighborhood. The other avenues, the neighbors in all the houses around her remained completely foreign. She did not know where to go. Could she pound on a stranger's door for help? That never went well in the horror movies.

She kept running in the dark.

Her footsteps on the pavement became rhythmic, punctuated by her heavy breaths. The sounds of the night and the cars in the distance faded below the symphony of her flight. The repeat and monotone of it all nearly sedated her until a different sound rippled on the edge of the darkness. Sidney's heart raced as her mind reeled to identify the noise. It grew closer, louder, but her brain could not classify it.

When her hearing finally translated the sound into something recognizable, Tony's racing footsteps were already bringing him into focus out of the black around her. She whipped her head around to see his shape in the dim glow of the streetlights. His arms pumped as he ran at full speed toward her. The blood streaming down his face mangled his features more than the twisting shadows.

Sidney spun on her feet, feeling the asphalt grind into the pads of her toes. Before she could launch herself in the opposite direction, Tony was on her. He collided with her back, propelling her forward. The pavement flew up to meet her face, and the smack of her head silenced her thoughts.

***

The world swayed in a strange, bobbing rhythm as Sidney resurfaced. She came into her head first, throbbing slow and heavy. Then, as her awareness spread down her body, she felt something pressing hard into her abdomen, smashing her organs. Her neck whined in a stretch, and she realized her head was dangling and rocking side to side. Her fingertips tingled as they hung long and lifeless past her hanging hair. When she finally managed to open her eyes, she made out the blurred shapes of Tony's shoes walking beneath her.

She twitched to animate her limbs, reminding her digits they were attached, the same way she did when she was coming out of the final *savasana* in yoga. Corpse pose. Blood and sensation prickled along her skin with a wave of fresh adrenaline. She felt the swell surge through her—and started flailing. She kicked her legs hard and reckless, teetering on Tony's shoulder. Tony's steps halted, and he wrapped his hands tightly around the back of her thighs. She arched her back against his restraint, slamming her fists into his back.

"Sidney, stop it!" Tony hissed, groping to maintain control of her.

"Let me go! Get the fuck off of me!"

Sidney shoved hard at Tony's neck, feeling his footing falter beneath them. She capitalized on his wobble, bucking her body away from him. His legs lurched beneath them and moved them in a clumsy and awkward dance in the shadows from the far streetlights. She felt his hands clawing over her, desperate to keep his grip. Then she felt nothing but the air as she tumbled from his shoulder.

Her smooth careen stuttered as the harsh pavement greeted her. Her body thudded against the asphalt and absorbed the impact through her soft tissue. All the air whooshed from her lips, spitting out the dirt still on them from when he had tackled her. She coughed with her empty lungs and curled onto her side into the pain. She wrapped around the ache for a thick moment, whimpering against the road. When she finally groaned and flopped onto her back, she sputtered breath up into the dark night above her. Her hips rolled, and Tony's legs tangled in hers. The contact made her seize, and she kicked violently to propel herself away from him. She scuttled backward, pebbles embedding into her palms, until she was out of reach.

Tony crumbled around the curb, his face turned

down away from her. His arms folded up protectively, cradling his head, his back arched and shoulders rounded. Blood pooled below his face, puddling black on the poorly lit concrete beneath him.

"You bitch. You fucking bitch," he spat, gathering his hands beneath him.

Sidney moved to stand, snatching her feet under her, but her leg seized in pain. The hip that had taken her fall locked around the sensation, refused to fold and bear weight. She gasped and flinched at her body's betrayal then continued crawling backward on her hands. Tony dragged himself up, unfolding slowly to stand with more blood poured from his lips. He spit toward his feet as he stared at her sideways. Then he lunged for her again, snagging her ankle with his hand.

"Enough, Tony," Sidney cried. "Get the fuck off me! I've had enough!"

"It's enough when I say it's enough," he growled.

He joined her back on the ground, seizing handfuls of her clothes and crawling up her body. She shrieked when he pressed down on her injured hip. The pain sent a spire up her nerves. Her arched back only pressed him down on her harder. She hated the sensation of his body weight, how close he was to her. She hated that she could not shrink away from him; that the more she fought, the closer he seemed to get. Her skin crawled at the feeling, and her muscles itched anxiously to dig her way out from under him.

Tony wormed his way up her until his face hovered above hers, dripping blood onto her cheeks. His hot breath plumed in Sidney's face. The pressure of his weight on top of her, the way his chest and hips pressed down into her tugged cords of familiarity through the fresh panic and rage coursing through her. He felt like a stranger on top of her, even though her body should have known every contour of his form. That contradiction only enraged her more. She grit her teeth so hard she heard them scrape against each other, loud in her ears.

She hated that she knew the feel of him. She was disgusted by the fact that she had had him inside her. Yet, more than anything, the heat flaring through her was fueled and accelerated by how stupid and oblivious she felt. She was deafened by a symphony of all the things she had willingly told him when she thought he was other people.

"Come on," he said. "We're going back to your house. Stop fighting!"

His voice carved burning tracks into her mind. Her muscles throbbed, constricted beneath him as she thrashed and pushed futilely. She hated that she could not fight him off, that he now physically controlled her just as he had been manipulating her for so long.

Tony pinned Sidney beneath his weight and his strength, squelching her resistance. He kept her down as he brought himself up and straddled her, snatching for her wrists. His pelvis crushed her ribcage, restricting her breathing and sending panic throbbing in her brain. She desperately evaded his hands and drew her arms tightly into her chest, ripping them away from him.

He continued to grope at her. His movements became more jagged, frustrated. His face contorted tighter, squeezing more blood onto her. He looked less and less like the safe, dumb guy she used to use and more like the person he was, the person she should have seen all along.

He finally ensnarled one of her flailing wrists, instantly forming a vice around her arm. His face lit up in victory, momentarily flashing young and innocent again. His expression perverted back to anger and purpose, and he yanked her up with his full strength and scrambled to pull them both to their feet. Sidney tugged against his grip, tried to make herself heavy, yet could not resist the momentum. Her bare feet skidded along the asphalt. She wrenched her wounded leg straight, pain unfolding along the limb. She howled as it blazed over her nerves, climbing up from the hip to wrap around her torso. Tony doubled over, flinching but maintaining his grip on her. He tightened his fingers until he cut off her circulation and hauled her closer, dragging her where he wanted.

Sidney turned to face him and stopped pulling away, gave up on resisting. She looked through the blood covering his face and into his eyes, sharp with the hatred between them. The forced eye contact caught him off guard, caused him to hesitate.

In that breath, Sidney launched off her battered feet and wounded leg and drove her body into his. Tony's eyes managed to go wide from confusion to shock before their bodies collided. She threw herself into him with abandon, unleashing all her rage, sloppy and reckless. Her shoulder collided with his chest then skidded up to the bottom of his chin. She heard his jaw rattle and teeth knock together above her head. His head snapped back, and in that brief instant mixed in surprise and pain, his hand released her.

Time slowed down for a moment in her liberation. Tony spiraled away from her in what felt like slow motion, as if she could step back and watch it happen.

An inflating sense of victory and excitement rushed over her as she snatched at her balance and stumbled onto her footing. Tony's body continued to careen back, a bewildered look softening his features. He managed to snag an instant of eye contact before his face spun away from her.

The world whirled back into real time as Tony's face planted into the curb. His arms flailed through his fall yet never managed to soften his landing. His head slammed hard on the unforgiving corner with a sickening thud, a thick sound laced with a sharp crack, making Sidney cringe. The crunch in the impact enticed her. It made him sound so vulnerable. She stepped forward gingerly, leaning and arching to see around Tony's head.

Tony's skull remained seated on the curb. The mass of hair was still, but Sidney knew he was alive from the rise and fall of his shoulders and the low sputtering she could make out against the concrete. She stood for a long second, looking down at Tony, wounded and incapacitated, flashing through at all the things he had planned to do to her when he got her back to her house. She let her head fall lazily to one side as she squinted down at him.

Finally, she nudged his thigh with her toe, and the wet breathing thickened into a groan. Tony's hands reanimated and flailed along the street, searching for orientation. Not unlike her own when she regained consciousness over his shoulder. He rocked on his damaged face. Life found its way farther back up his arms, and he began fumbling back at her. Sidney almost flinched and shrank back, yet she steeled herself.

As Tony's fingertips clawed around her ankle, Sidney yelled loud and raised her other foot. With him unwittingly holding her steady, she stomped hard on the back of his head until she heard another undeniable crack.

32

Nine Months Later

"**WHEY MOM**, you know what I decided?" Cameron said, walking into the kitchen.

"What's that, buddy?" Sidney replied, digging popcorn out of the pantry.

"Next time, I want a Black Panther room."

"Didn't you just get a Spider-Man room? Don't you still love Spider-Man?" Sidney planted a hand on her hip as she turned to him.

"Black Panther is pretty awesome," Adam said, following Cameron into the kitchen. "But it is hard to choose between him and Spider-Man. If you did an Avengers room, you could augment the Spider-Man you already have with Black Panther. And Captain America. And the Hulk."

"Yeah!" Cameron jumped.

"Don't encourage him," Sidney laughed. "You're new here. You don't get a say."

"He's here until Sunday," Cameron countered. "I think he can have a say."

"Only because he's saying what you want."

"Can we watch a horror movie tonight, Mom?"

Sidney hesitated for a moment. Her hand hovering

with the folded popcorn bag between her fingertips. Adam looked at her gently and waited.

"Yeah, buddy. Let's watch a horror movie," Sidney said, smiling.

"Really?" Cameron's voice grew higher in his excitement. "Like a real one?" He paused and lowered his voice. "A rated R one?"

"Maybe."

"What about *Jaws*?" Adam offered.

"Oh, good one. That might work," Sidney replied.

"Oh, I get a say now?" Adam grinned.

"Maybe. I need to work on my article while we watch though," Sidney said.

"That's fine." Cameron jumped in his spot again. "Let's go! Let's watch it!"

Sidney placed the bowl of popcorn on the coffee table then sat on the couch with Adam and Cameron. She gathered the remotes and navigated to the movie. Cameron practically vibrated on the cushion as she pressed Play. Sidney smiled to herself, drawing her laptop onto her knees. As the opening credits reflected in Cameron's wide eyes, she brought her fingertips to the keys.

The Horror of Real Life

Life is like standing on a frozen steam. It may seem solid, but there is always something flowing and threatening underneath. Horror is that current under it all.

Most of you know that horror came into my real life this year. I found myself in scenes I have watched countless times in various horror movies, and it was nothing like I expected. Horror in real life is not like horror on the screen or on the page, but real life is never like the movies.

When I have written about horror before, I always talked about it being a safe place to explore fear. Now, however, the recent events in my life have taught me that horror is who we are. Horror is in all of us in real life. We pretend it's not there. We tell ourselves it's only in the movies, but it is out there at all times, waiting and stalking us. It is that cold current under our surface.

I could react to this realization by running away, by sticking my head in the sand and avoiding all things bloody, violent, and scary. But would that make it go away? Would that make it not the world?

Instead, I'm choosing to stay. I'm pressing play on a horror movie right now. I am not letting two psychopaths take my genre from me or scare me away from posting pictures or interacting with people on the internet. I am not letting them poison the world for me. I am staying in horror because horror is as much me as it was them.

Sidney included her favorite photograph from all her collaborations with Brady. She included the image of her bare, blood splattered body splayed against the bottom of the dry bathtub. She remembered how the dried fake blood had ripped at her skin. She recalled how the discomfort of the position burned. Yet, Brady had been right; it looked better this way.

As Sidney quickly proofed the article, her phone vibrated beside her. She glanced down at the notification flashing on her screen.

Richard: Hey beautiful! I saw your . . .

Sidney ignored the message notification, swiping it away unread. She posted her article out on the wide internet for the eyes of countless strangers. Then she closed her laptop and set it aside.

ACKNOWLEDGEMENTS

The internet can be a dangerous place, and I appreciate all the kind and supportive people I have met in the virtual world. Thank you to anyone who spares a moment to support me on their phone or screen.

As always, my writing is only possible with the support of my family and friends. They hold me together and enable me to create, especially my lighthouse. A special thank you to all my beta readers for this book who invested the time to offer their feedback and improve the story.

Thank you to Joe Mynhardt and Crystal Lake Publishing for polishing this book and bringing it into the world. An enthusiastic and relieved thank you to Karen Runge for prying the adjectives from my trembling fingers and giving my story the edit it needed. Thank you to Lisa Vasquez for designing an unnerving skin to cover my words.

And thank you for reading.

THE END?

Not if you want to dive into more of Crystal Lake Publishing's Tales from the Darkest Depths!

Check out our amazing website and online store.
https://www.crystallakepub.com

We always have great new projects and content on the website to dive into, as well as a newsletter, behind the scenes options, social media platforms, and our own dark fiction shared-world series and our very own store. If you use the IGotMyCLPBook! coupon code in the store (at the checkout), you'll get a one-time-only 50% discount on your first eBook purchase!

Our webstore even has categories specifically for KU books, non-fiction, anthologies, and of course more novels and novellas.

ABOUT THE AUTHOR

Christina Bergling is a Colorado-bred author who knew she wanted to publish books in elementary school. Limitless Publishing released her novel, *The Rest Will Come*. HellBound Books Publishing published her two novellas, *Savages* and *The Waning*. She is also featured in over 18 horror anthologies, including *Collected Christmas Horror Shorts*, *Graveyard Girls*, *Carnival of Nightmares*, and *Demonic Wildlife*. Her latest novel, *Followers*, was released by Crystal Lake Publishing. She spends her non-writing time with her family or hiking, dancing, taking pictures, traveling, and sucking all the marrow out of life.

Readers . . .

It makes our day to know you reached the end of our book. Thank you so much. This is why we do what we do every single day.

Whether you found the book good or great, we'd love to hear what you thought. Please take a moment to leave a short review on Amazon, Goodreads, etc. No need to write an in-depth discussion. Even a single sentence will be greatly appreciated. Reviews go a long way to helping a book sell, and is great for an author's career. It'll also help us to continue publishing quality books. You can also share a photo of yourself holding this book with the hashtag #IGotMyCLPBook!

Thank you again for taking the time to journey with Crystal Lake Publishing.

Visit our Linktree page for a list of our social media platforms. https://linktr.ee/CrystalLakePublishing

Our Mission Statement:

Since its founding in August 2012, Crystal Lake Publishing has quickly become one of the world's leading publishers of Dark Fiction and Horror books in print, eBook, and audio formats.

While we strive to present only the highest quality fiction and entertainment, we also endeavour to support authors along their writing journey. We offer our time and experience in non-fiction projects, as well as author mentoring and services, at competitive prices.

With several Bram Stoker Award wins and many

other wins and nominations (including the HWA's Specialty Press Award), Crystal Lake Publishing puts integrity, honor, and respect at the forefront of our publishing operations.

We strive for each book and outreach program we spearhead to not only entertain and touch or comment on issues that affect our readers, but also to strengthen and support the Dark Fiction field and its authors.

Not only do we find and publish authors we believe are destined for greatness, but we strive to work with men and woman who endeavour to be decent human beings who care more for others than themselves, while still being hard working, driven, and passionate artists and storytellers.

Crystal Lake Publishing is and will always be a beacon of what passion and dedication, combined with overwhelming teamwork and respect, can accomplish. We endeavour to know each and every one of our readers, while building personal relationships with our authors, reviewers, bloggers, podcasters, bookstores, and libraries.

We will be as trustworthy, forthright, and transparent as any business can be, while also keeping most of the headaches away from our authors, since it's our job to solve the problems so they can stay in a creative mind. Which of course also means paying our authors.

We do not just publish books, we present to you worlds within your world, doors within your mind, from talented authors who sacrifice so much for a moment of your time.

There are some amazing small presses out there, and through collaboration and open forums we will continue to support other presses in the goal of helping authors and showing the world what quality small presses are capable of accomplishing. No one wins when a small press goes down, so we will always be there to support hardworking, legitimate presses and their authors. We don't see Crystal Lake as the best press out there, but we will always strive to be the best, strive to be the most interactive and grateful, and even blessed press around. No matter what happens over time, we will also take our mission very seriously while appreciating where we are and enjoying the journey.

What do we offer our authors that they can't do for themselves through self-publishing?

We are big supporters of self-publishing (especially hybrid publishing), if done with care, patience, and planning. However, not every author has the time or inclination to do market research, advertise, and set up book launch strategies. Although a lot of authors are successful in doing it all, strong small presses will always be there for the authors who just want to do what they do best: write.

What we offer is experience, industry knowledge, contacts and trust built up over years. And due to our strong brand and trusting fanbase, every Crystal Lake Publishing book comes with weight of respect. In time our fans begin to trust our judgment and will try a new author purely based on our support of said author.

With each launch we strive to fine-tune our approach, learn from our mistakes, and increase our reach. We continue to assure our authors that we're here for them and that we'll carry the weight of the launch and dealing with third parties while they focus on their strengths—be it writing, interviews, blogs, signings, etc.

We also offer several mentoring packages to authors that include knowledge and skills they can use in both traditional and self-publishing endeavours.

We look forward to launching many new careers. This is what we believe in. What we stand for. This will be our legacy.

Welcome to Crystal Lake Publishing— Tales from the Darkest Depths.

www.ingramcontent.com/pod-product-compliance
Lightning Source LLC
Chambersburg PA
CBHW072036190726
48294CB00005B/1289